THE NIHILISTIC NEVERENDING NIGHTMARE

ACKNOWLEDGEMENTS

I want to personally thank my Grandparents for without their support and guidance, I never would have made it quite that far, and of course all the friends I've made along the way with their guidance with wisdom, which includes 2 small business owners.

DEDICATION

This is dedicated to those fighting for their liberty and their right for a free country. Ukraine. If anyone deserves freedom from Tyranny, it's you.

PROLOGUE THIS
WORLD IS TRULY A HELL

Two years since the initial assault on our US borders on both the east and west coasts from Russian and Chinese forces, engineering specialists provided by Black Eagle have continued to rebuild. Debris removed and replaced with high-rises allowed the continuing of jobs to return back to their offices, stabilizing the economy. Today, Americans from around the region remember what was lost, and the sacrifices made, and many are paying homage to the relatives and friends that were lost.

Samantha Harris prepared scrambled eggs for her husband. Cracked them flawlessly, poured the milk in, and whisked, careful not to spill any out of her glass bowl. Her frying pan heated with butter slowly melted all over the surface. Just the finest butter for her husband, and only the finest eggs. The bacon sizzled on another pan. Brown and wavy, on its way to crispy, smelling savory on this fine morning. The sun was just rising through the windows, white curtains pulled back.

"Well, that smells heavenly." Michael walked right through the door, closing it behind him with his beaming smile, she loved his smile. The most beautiful thing about it wasn't his perfect teeth, or that carefully trimmed beard, but that it was genuine. He was genuinely happy to smell the food, regardless of who was cooking it, but she knew, above all else, her husband was pleased to see her. And as usual, even with all the horrible things in the world, that was something that made her feel warm and fuzzy inside, like little birds were flapping around inside her chest.

He turned on the coffee pot to prepare a few cups of pour-over coffee—none of that industrialized nonsense. Coffee these days was almost impossible to find, especially in the supermarkets. The war with Russia and China made things very difficult for shipping coffee internationally, however, in their little community, there were a few greenhouses with coffee plants, and produced no small amount. However, still due to basic economics, the price for coffee in these greenhouses were higher than the supermarkets when they were stocked. This was often the last resort for most people to make a decent cup of coffee. All things considered; she was happy they had that much.

Samantha swirled the now fully melted butter this way and that inside the scorching iron bowl; it ran down the edges like waves on the shore, simmering and spitting.

A vibrant squealing tire sounded from across the street, scratching at the innards of her ears, and it was all too familiar.

A large Humvee was right in front of her. A whistle in the air. A sonic boom pushed her to the ground. Warm blood trickled down her palms; glass shards sliced into her. Another sonic boom brushed her hair with warm air. The jagged metal that was part of the Humvee's door crashed around her, and crimson water dripping down her face.

"Get down!" Canine cried out, pushing her into a ditch, laying atop her. Canine, in that fair face, turned her head briefly, her muscles tensing up, ready to move. "Get up! It's do or die!"

Canine pulled Sam up from the ground. Sam heard gunfire roaring overhead, and the screeching tires chasing them, and watched as the vehicles nearly flipped themselves over the rubble of what used to be Massachusetts. But the rubble, broken glass, and shattered wood made it all but recognizable.

"Sergeant! RPG!"

"GET DOWN!"

Her grasp slipped, and she flipped the frying pan over the stove, eggs sputtering all over the sizzling bacon, and the rest of the counter.

Her body froze, her eyes rattling inside her head, and her body gave, caving onto the floor, screaming. Her legs pushed her away from the stove hastily underneath cover, and yet, still dirt debris splashed all over her face.

The flames cackled, roaring, and sputtering underneath the rage of blown up vehicles, piping hot metal, and shattered glass, carving at her face. Her own blood painted her face, and the crimson water was boiling hot.

A noise, muffled.

"Get it away from me!" she cried, bringing her hands over her ears, looking straight forward. "Get it away!"

"SAM!" she turned, and looking into her face, was that red head, that beautiful redhead with freckles.

"Erin! Get me out of here! Get me out! I'm scared!"

A hand firmly grabbed her shoulder.

"SAM!" A firm tone called her name. Her hands jolted right in front of her, feeling warm tears down her face, and she was looking right at Michael, not in a flaming rubble, but here she was, holding herself firmly in the fetal position, underneath the table. Cover. It's safe. It's safe here, under the table. Nothing can hurt here.

Except on that night when it all happened, the kitchen table was the first to go, shattered. It wasn't the only thing that shattered that night.

"SAM!" Michael's soft hand caressed hers, grasping it firmly, yet with a soft embrace. Real and warm, it was. Not hot. Not like that night when even the touch of snowflakes was boiling. He gently grabbed her wrist, pulling her out from the table.

The strength of her legs returned, now standing, she stumbled into him; his arms wrapping around her shoulders, hugging her tightly, firmly, and yet, in the way that only he could, softly. His breath matched hers, unable to see anything but the flames, but she felt the warm, stiff brush of his rustic beard, scratching her neck. "It's a flashback. It's a flashback. It isn't real. Breathe with me."

The warmth of the kitchen surrounded her, penetrating flames, slowly dying out, but the exploding debris continued, the dirt, iron hot on her bare legs. She inhaled. And the scent of the bacon reached her nose. She exhaled. Again. And again. And again!

"Tell me what you see," tenderly he spoke.

Her head moved back and forth, looking at her kitchen, and the sun shining from outside. She saw the stove, the pans on the ground, bacon, and uncooked eggs over the floor. The stove was off. No flames rising from it, no smoke. "I see, I see the stove. It's off. The pans and breakfast are on the floor. "Oh, Michael, I'm so sorry!"

"Don't be sorry," he said. "I don't care about the brunch. I care about you."

She took several deeper breaths before turning her gaze to the paper towels. "I have to clean that up." Now she understood, why Ted Anderson worked so much. Keeps the mind busy. *Must stay busy.*

She broke from his embrace and clumsily walked over to grab the paper towels. Michael's hand touched her wrist gingerly, and without any sudden movements. She looked back to him. "Let go, Michael, I have to clean this up. I'll make a new breakfast."

"Are you okay?" he asked.

"Yes, I'm fine," she answered, turning back to the towel, and pulled some of the soft fabric off the sanded brown roll.

"Are you okay?" He repeated.

"Yes, I said I'm fine," she said, and knelt to pull the pans off the floor, walking them carefully to the sink. She turned around with the paper towels, and Michael was right in front of her, frowning. His eyes were glazed over; he was crying. *Why are you crying? Is brunch really that important to you? I said I was going to make more.*

"Are you okay?" he repeated himself a third time.

A third time. Why does he keep asking? She didn't know, but she knew one thing. She felt a large hole in the center of her chest. She looked down, seeing that there was no such hole in her chest, but her hand touched it to ensure her brain wasn't fooling her. And then it hit her, the hole grew heavier. She felt a lump growing inside, and she looked to him again, eyes laser focused into his, daring and discerning gaze. Again, she found it hard to breathe, the windpipes in her throat tightening up.

"No, I'm not," she answered, and she felt warm tears falling down her face. "I'm not okay, Michael, I'm not!" He slowly approached her. "These flashbacks always come. They're there when I'm awake. They're there when I'm asleep. They're there when you're away. I keep seeing things, and the one thing that haunts me the most, is the trigger I pulled."

"Sam, you didn't kill anyone," he replied, hugging her tightly. "You saved someone. You saved me."

"But was it the right thing to do? I see his face as clear and vivid as I see yours, and there are times when I'm looking at you, and I see his face, and whenever I see his face, I feel the urge to clean my blood-soaked arms when there's nothing to clean!"

She wept into him, dropping her paper towels on the floor.

"I know. I know," he said.

"Do you think, what I'm seeing, what I'm going through was what Ted was going through?"

"I'm afraid he's no longer with us to answer that, Sam. You know that," he answered. "But he gave us a chance at life now, and he'd want us to live the best lives we can."

Ted. Even after all this time, you and I are seeing the very same thing. I can see it now. Truly, this world is the Hell we've made. We made this Hell, we chose it willingly, and after we've chosen it, there's no hope to fix it.

Contents

CHAPTER 1

TOUCHDOWN

Anonymous reports suggest the Russian Navy is removing its shipyards. We don't know why Russia is moving toward the west, but the Eastern Front seems a likely vantage point for them if hostilities grow. The ships appear to be mostly carriers, with some destroyers. Among these carriers, there are a number of super carriers, the likes of which dwarf our USS Carl Vinson. At this time, we don't know what kind of equipment is on these vessels, Secretary of Defense Brown reports.

Ted Anderson, the man with an unknown past best left buried. Jennifer knew this as she watched him, finger hastily tapping on her arm as she waited for him to finish making himself at least somewhat presentable. After much fuss, he was finally—himself, if that was the appropriate word for such a man. He at last had his jacket and some pressed khakis and donned his gloves. Typical. She knew much more of him after speaking to him over the last several months.

To bring up the past only brings pain to him. She knew that all too well, but she didn't even need to bring it up. His nightmares did that, and he came running to her, calling to her when they do. She's the first person he speaks to. The only person really. He had to be treated with the care he never knew, to overbalance the amount of instability that was forced into his past, instability he didn't ask for nor wanted.

But the reason Ted was in her Seaport apartment today, was because Michael's brother was coming into town. Flying in from deployment from overseas, or so that's what Michael told her. They would be picking them up by Michael and Samantha shortly, to go greet his brother at the airport. She previously arranged for Ted to be here for that very purpose. But of course, whenever it would be a bad day for Ted, it would be a good day for Jennifer. And like so, she noted especially, she was having a particularly good day.

Ted carefully put a hat on his head, while Jennifer tied up her hair wrapping it in a black scrunchy. She looked at him closely, still trying to piece together all his little intricacies. After all, he was a very complex person with multiple layers that she knew even he wasn't aware of. She noticed his hand trembled as he hastily retracted it into his pocket.

"Tedward," she walked over to him briskly, clasped his trembling hand with hers and pulled it out of his pocket. She gazed down at him as he tilted his head up. No smile upon his face, for which she was exceedingly thankful, for this meant he did not feel the need to lie to her. She was grateful for that. Truly. That alone was progress. "What's wrong?"

"What is—what is the name of the man we're picking up?" he asked.

"Jeff Clemens, I think," she said. "He's Michael's older brother. By a lot, I hear. Nearly fifteen years or so."

"That name sounds too familiar," he said. "What does he do?"

"Army. Like you," she said. "Tedward, I understand if you don't want to come. You can just hang out in my apartment until I get back. Would you like that?"

Tedward appeared to be deep in thought, his eyes watering ever so slightly as he blankly stared at her blue fall dress. She knew enough not to interrupt him during these moments. Whenever he did this, he was considering all possibilities which laid before him. Carefully thinking. Taking into account all possible consequences of his actions to come. What would happen if he came? How many different scenarios could he piece together? To him, maybe it seemed safer for him to not do anything. But what about the possibilities down the road? A week from now, a month, and so on. Of course, Jennifer only speculated this.

Jennifer squeezed his hand tighter, waiting for him to finish. He exhaled heavily before returning his attention to her. He wiped the tears away with his fists. "I think, it is best that I come."

"Okay." She nodded.

Her phone rang. *It must be Sam. Outside already, but we've just decided Ted would come. Dear Tedward, my sweet Tedward, why do I feel filled with a certain kind of dread?* "Hello."

"I'm outside. Is Ted coming?" Sam replied on the other end.

"Yes," she answered. "We'll be right out."

Jennifer led Ted by the hand. She covered her eyes as the sun shone into them but noticed that Ted bothered not to shield himself from the harmful rays.

She found Michael's SUV was in the parking lot.

Sam rolled down her window, "Hey, you two, come on, we don't want to be late. Michael already has lunch reservations!"

Jennifer sighed, sighing with Ted following behind her, trying to prepare herself for whatever manner of dread was to follow. "Hi!" she said, drawing out her friendly greeting; she glanced back over to Ted, she saw his hands shaking to adjust his seatbelt before it finally clicked locked. *Just another layer to unravel, dear Tedward. I have my reservations about this. Is this, okay?*

"Hey, man, how's it going?" Michael turned to his seat to offer a hand to him.

Ted's lips stretched into a fake smile, even if they all knew it wasn't real. "I'm doing well, Michael, and yourself?"

"Great! I'm excited to see my brother for the first time in a while. Military type. I'm sure you understand."

Ted chuckled, "that I do."

Careful Michael. Be careful of the words you say, we don't want to start all over again, Jennifer thought.

Jeff Clemens looked out the window as the plane landed. Restlessly, his eyes scanned the ground level of all the personnel, the equipment, and of course, the open doors. There were many open doors. *TSA will have fit over that.* He sighed, waiting for the plane to dock. The lights flickered on, and he stood to remove his carry-on from the overhead bin.

The hallway out into the airport was gray, boring, and unsurprising, the way he preferred it; honestly, didn't want any surprises. Exiting the terminal, and into the airport, he checked his corners, looking swiftly to the left and to the right. Carefully watching people and all their activities as he walked down the escalators, and into the baggage claim. Military personnel stood upright by the baggage carousel: heads jerked left and right as they checked each corner they passed, just like his does. Every corner must be checked, and every stone turned. Never know when a suicide bomber might come in and blow everything to shit. Especially with those open doors.

He stood out by pickup, his luggage on the ground. He held a piece of paper as he read the address of the hotel he would be staying at for a few weeks before he redeployed written upon it. Folding the piece of paper, he forced it to retreat into his wallet. He peered to the overhead pass, hearing the number of vehicles honking their horns. It was nice and chilly here, made up for the balm and sweat on the cursed plane with other military corps returning to their loved ones. *Those troops really know how to perspire on a plane.*

Bored, he cracked his fingers with his thumbs on each hand, feeling the strain on his fingers. It reminded him of the single-most irrefutable fact—he is getting too old for this shit, in his late thirties. He was already beginning to feel it, but that didn't mean he wasn't in great physical condition. After all, he had to be to continue fighting for Black Eagle.

Much plagued his mind, thinking ahead of himself, the news, which was never good these days. Hell, it was never great to begin with, everyone lying by omission, no one knew what fact or fiction was anymore. He stopped listening because it was the same day after day, just a different player on the field as global lines crossed from between nations, and last minute alliances were made. Although he stopped listening to the news, he could never escape it. His colleagues always made a point to remind him by sending him unwanted emails. War loomed over his notifications everywhere, reminding him he wanted to get out, but of course, getting out with a pension was ideal. Only three years left. And he was done. Forever, and hopefully to escape forever the chains that bound him, the orders he followed which led everyone he fought with to a certain Hell. His hands weren't clean either. His hands weren't clean. They never will be. He knew this, accepted it as part of his history, should the world find out about everything he's done, the general populace will march right on beacon hill, calling for him to be hanged.

His vision barreled down his.50 cal, aimed down the desert plains. Soldiers around the vicinity of Area 51 pushed themselves further into the collapsed building, tripping over dead carcasses of other soldiers, trying to finalize the execution of Task Force Seven for their collaboration with Germany to overthrow the US government. A single man, swiftly dispatching soldier's left and right, sweat beading down his face, and dripping on his blood-stained uniform. The man he recognized as Ghost, arguably the most dangerous person who ever walked this earth.

Ghost, lit up by blue veins, struck, shot, and stabbed, until even the vehicles were nothing more than skeletons of their former selves. Ghost entered his sights, and finally stopped moving. Jeff took a deep breath, exhaled, and squeezed the trigger. The recoil pushed against his shoulder as the bullet left the barrel, bearing down on its target. The bullet struck Ghost in the chest, pushing him back a step, and blood sprayed out his back still drooling out of him like molasses from a strainer. The blue veins all over Ghost's body faded, but the body still stood defiant.

Ghost, of course, had the audacity to place his hand over his chest as he glared directly at him. He saw those words form on those accursed lips; that traitorous bastard recited the Pledge of Allegiance.

The bomb's dropped, and the corpses were scattered. Smoke encapsulated the top of Area 51, and flames rose from the ground. When the dust settled, before he could confirm if Ghost was truly dead, his radio coughed: "Exit the vicinity now," Malcolm called. "Area 51 is about to go nuclear, evacuate now!"

Shit!

Jeff turned his back on the carnage, running away from the devil, and the bodies left behind. It wasn't long until he was picked up and transported safely away by another Humvee before an even larger explosion shook the ground, gas pumping out of the earth like an erupting volcano and casting nuclear ash across the skies. It poisoned the air, and anyone within ten kilometers had their life cut drastically short.

And to think, we've managed only two years after achieving world peace. Funny how fragile it can be.

Jeff bit his lip, gazing over to the many people getting picked up by other passenger vehicles, and others jumping into larger shuttles, driving off to go rent a car. He patiently waited for his brother Michael to pick him up. Considering the exorbitant costs involved with achieving peace, it was a worthy price tag. That transaction, the lives spent, the funerals, it was all worth the cost. *And there shouldn't be anything stopping us from doing it again.*

A seven-passenger car drove by and parked in front of him. It honked obnoxiously, and the window rolled down. A beautiful blond-haired woman with a ponytail smiled at him, waving, Michael was on the other side pressing a button releasing the trunk door. The windows were tinted, but there were outlines of two more people in the back. The doors opened, and a woman pushed herself inward to make room for him, and another man, head downcast crawled out of the vehicle.

"Jeff," Michael called out from the driver's seat. "Hurry up and get your bags in the trunk. Ted will help you."

"Thanks. Late as usual, Mike." Jeff shrugged, turning his attention to the overpass, cars honking like tuba players.

"Yeah, well, especially now, come on, we don't have much more time before we lose the reservation!" Michael shot him a smile.

Jeff turned to grab his bags and didn't notice the other man climbing out of the SUV, until he stood right in front of him. He saw scars on his face and slight burns on his arms. He knew this man, and this man was supposed to be dead. His heart rate shot up immensely. Exhaling thickly through his nose. The man smiled at him with a gleam in his eyes. Jeff, finding himself trapped with nowhere to run, traded a smile.

Ghost!

"Sergeant Jeffrey Clemens, I remember you. How the hell are you?" said the other man enthusiastically.

"Fine, forgive me." *How the hell are you still alive? I blew a hole through your damned chest. A bomb landed on you. There's no way in Hell you outran a nuclear meltdown.* "I can't seem to remember your name." *Play dumb. He doesn't know you know yet.*

"Sorry. Ted Anderson. 75th Ranger Regiment," he replied, stretching out his hand for a firm handshake. "Now, you remember?"

You know he's dead right? You're not fooling me. "Ah, yes, now I remember. I seem to remember you falling off the grid after the little, *accident,*" Jeff shook his hand firmly, and he felt the hand, a firm shake with inhuman bone cracking strength. *He's gonna fucking kill me.* "How have you been?" *Shit!*

"Fine as I can be, after you know what happened. I would like to chat about that some time, whenever you have a minute. It would be nice to catch up with an old war buddy," Ghost had a smile on his face, ear to ear it was.

Why'd you take his name of all people? He was the real hero in all that mess, as unbearable of an ass he was. "Sure, but not right now. Not the best place around it, and besides, you ought to know much of what happened was classified."

"Not talking about the operation, itself. Shall I?" he flashed a grin, but this was no normal grin. Jeff knew it. He's seen this grin far too many times to not know better. This was his little way of saying, 'I know you're not buying my little act, and I know you're acting yourself.'

"Please," he yawned, covering his mouth. "It was a very long and irritable flight."

"I don't need specifics," said the man masquerading around as Ted Anderson. He reached around him to grab his last duffle bag and moved it around to the back.

I'm going to die! I guess I can't put this off any longer now.

Jeff walked around to the other end of the SUV, and he sat in the back. The trunk door shut. Ted stepped into the SUV, closing the door, and secured his seatbelt. He carefully scanned Ted for any kind of weapon. *Who am I kidding? It's Ghost. He doesn't need one.*

Jeff's heart was pounding inside his chest, his heartbeat pumping behind his ears. *Michael, how do you know him? Do you know how dangerous your position is right now? And now that I'm here, it only makes the situation that much worse.*

Jeff retracted his hand into his pocket, trembling profusely.

"What time is the reservation?" The woman in the front asked before interrupting herself with a raised finger pointed to the roof of the car. "Hold that thought," she turned to look him in the eyes with a warm smile. "Sorry. I'm Samantha. Nice to meet you, Jeff. I've heard so much about you."

Jeff chuckled. "Probably nothing worth noting, I'm sure. I'm barely around." He smiled to her before focusing his gaze back to Ted, who without a doubt, already knew he was being watched.

"We're going to the Grendel's pub. We are just on time to be late," Michael smirked through the rearview mirror at his brother, and they drove off.

Jeff bit his lip at that one. Late to pick him up. Late to lunch. *Will you be late to my funeral too?*

Ted and Jennifer spoke, while Jeff pretended to doze off in the back, keeping a close eye on anything Ted might do. After all, *he* was the dangerous one here.

The SUV stopped at a parking garage. *Great.* He yawned again, hoping to force Ted to let his guard down, because that was the only way to beat a man like him. He did it once. He can do it again. However, something tugged at him. There wasn't anything remarkable about Ghost this time, nor did he do anything suspicious. He merely spoke and laughed with Jennifer, almost like they'd been dating for years, and he might pop the question at any moment. But Ghost was a liar of all liars, and none of those feelings were true. How could they be when he didn't give her his real name? *But you don't have a name. Do you?*

The trees were bare, planted along the sidewalks, and people walked about, careless and happy with one another. Meanwhile, Jeffrey checked every corner of every building they walked by. *Can't be too careful—overseas or back here.*

"Ted," he didn't force a yawn this time. "How did you come to meet Michael?"

"Well, you better talk to Samantha about that one, really," Michael interjected, turning his head to him. "After all, he is really only a part of our—"

"Dysfunctional little family," Jennifer finished, turning her head back to face him, grinning politely.

"Right, our dysfunctional little family here because of her," Michael continued. "But more on that later. We are almost too late for it to be fashionable anymore."

"You need to get better with time, Michael," Jeff said, turning his head back to Ted, who offered a generic ass smile. *Go to Hell, you lying sack of shit. Malcolm would know what to do.*

"Hey. I'm early for business, not personal or family matters. I thought you'd have known this by now." Michael led the way down the slanted pavement into the warm array of sunlight, beaming down on them. "Come on before we lose our reservation."

Jeff shook his head. They crossed the walkway and descended the brick stairs into the dark lit place.

"Reservation for five," Michael announced to the smiling hostess at the wooden stand.

"Good of you to show up. I was about to give away your table."

"I like to be fashionable." Michael jeered, elbowing Sam in the side. "Isn't that right."

"Can you be normal for once?" Sam rolled her eyes.

"Right this way."

The hostess led them to a table in the back of the room. A dangling chandelier overhead cast an orange light over the space. Jeff sat on a cushioned seat, followed by the others. A server placed five glasses of water in front of them. On either side of Jeff was Jennifer and Michael. He scanned the room, careful to watch for anything, looking for an out to call Malcolm. He would want to know about Ghost being alive, after all this time.

"So, Sam, do you care to explain?" Michael asked.

"Hmm?" she sipped some water. "Oh, right. How do we know Ted? Several months ago, I saw him in the Boston Public Garden during one of our little picnics, and at the time I thought nothing of it. Something weird was going on with the weather."

"It *is* New England," Jeff replied.

"You see!" Jennifer said, pointing across the table. "That's exactly what I said."

"Well, anyway, it wasn't until the following Tuesday that I formally introduced myself to him as we all happened to be at the same bar at the same time. I started talking to him about that strange weather occurrence, and the rest of us, Jenn, Michael, and Erin, huddled around him. The rest was rather," Samantha's voice trailed off.

"It was rather turbulent," Jennifer finished. "Really, I don't think we need to say any more than that."

"Only a few months huh?" Jeff turned to Ted. *Well, you always were the convincing liar, but what are you planning here? Sabotage the Federal Bank? No.* "So, Ted, how long have you been in the area then."

"What Sam said was the long and short of it. I haven't been in Boston for very long." *Or so you tell everyone.*

The waitress came by, refilled their water glasses, dropped off two pitchers of water, took all their orders and scurried off to give the orders to the kitchen.

The bathroom. Perfect.

"So, how long are you going to be around?" Ted asked from across the table, giving him an amiable yet fake smile.

Bullshitter. You and I both know you aren't happy to see me. "I'm only going to be around for about a week before I get deployed again." *Of course, the fact that you're here complicates matters exponentially.*

"Well, you two seem to know one another quite well," Sam commented as she brought her glass to her lips. "Same regiment?"

"Not exactly," Jeff swiftly replied, scanning everyone around the table. *Ghost, how will you reply?*

"I suppose one could say we were," Ghost answered.

Shit! Jeff tilted his head and forced his lips to raise in a smile. "Often times we found ourselves on the same battlefield. But never within the same unit." *Still as sharp as ever.*

"Jeff, have you heard anything from Mom at all?" Michael asked.

Jeff turned his attention to his brother. He didn't want to take his attention off from Ghost, who sat too close for comfort, yet he knew in maintaining such attention, eyebrows would be raised; he didn't need that. He sucked in the air through his teeth. "Unfortunately, no. I've been way too busy with planning for—future efforts."

"Are you referring to the Collapse?" Michael asked.

"Is that what they're calling it?" Jeff thought his brother was referring to almost all of Europe, Africa, and Asia being engulfed in flames of war. He didn't even know why this was all happening. It hasn't reached the Western Hemisphere though. *Yet. It's coming far sooner than anyone thinks.*

"Yeah."

"Well, yes," he waved his hand palm up. "Classified."

"Yeah, too bad we weren't able to repeat what we did last time for that, wouldn't you agree?" said Ghost.

What do you want me to say? "Well, whatever it was, the price was worth it, and we should do it all over again. It was deemed necessary. The price wasn't too high."

"Really?" Michael asked incredulously. "I'm certain that's classified too."

"Yup," Ghost and Jeff replied simultaneously.

Not a moment too soon, and the waitress came by, and asked them if they needed anything. *Perfect.*

"Where's the bathroom?" he asked. She directed him down the hall and to the left at the brick sign.

"Thank you."

"I have to go too actually. Great idea!" Ghost said, putting his napkin on the table to stand up.

Damn it! That isn't something men do. Is he—going to kill me in the bathroom? A convenient enough place. Perhaps feign that I slipped, struck my head hard against the sink to break my neck in half. But I—but I shouldn't be surprised. He is The Ghost after all, always seventeen steps ahead of everyone, minus that one little incident. He's like a virus, and a very adaptable one at that.

"Great, I wouldn't want to get myself lost along the way. You've always had a better sense of direction than I ever had," Jeff said.

Jennifer removed herself from the booth to allow Jeff up. He followed Ted, scowling the entire time; he carefully monitored Ted's hands, both of which were in his pockets. *He has a pocket-knife tucked in there doesn't he? Just my luck.*

The door into the bathroom was a swinging-door on hinges, swung both ways. The two entered the bathroom together, and much to Jeff's dismay, it was empty.

"Good to know you haven't lost your edge, you dirty little bastard." Ghost said to him, and he wasn't smiling. This manikin of a man frowned, and his eyebrows tilted upward. *There's the Ghost I know.*

Any hope of reporting this to Malcolm was destroyed with Ghost looming over him. *Probably thinking I'd do exactly that.* He sighed. "What do you want me to say, Ghost? What's done is done, and we can't take back what happened."

"You have no idea what you did to us, do you?" Ghost asked. "Do you know what was in my mind these last several years?"

"I don't care to know. You were never a soldier, not a brother in arms to me."

"What were we to you except monsters? The fact is, you being here is a bit of a problem for me."

"And you being alive is a problem for everyone. I'm not going to ask how you survived all that. You wouldn't tell me anyway." Jeff scowled and walked to the urinal. "You're right. You're a monster. A dog like one who lost control, you deserved to be put down, and yet here you are." *You all were.*

"Well, the truth is partially out. Some of it, anyway. Tell me, why?" Ghost stood to the adjacent urinal. "Why were we executed? All these years, I still can't figure out why. All the codes of conduct, I obeyed them all to the letter."

"Classified," Jeff said.

"So, that's how it is then. You won't tell me why, so I guess I'll go on returning back to my nightmares."

"Nightmares? What are you talking about?" Jeff flushed the urinal.

"I supposed a cold-hearted son of a bitch like yourself wouldn't experience it. Never mind. Forget I said it," Ghost replied.

Jeff turned the faucet on, put soap on his hands as he washed them underneath the hot water, and he saw Ghost looking at him through the mirror. "What now?"

"One more thing. If you so much as think of doing something that is going to force me to start over, I will rip your fucking limbs off." Ghost scowled at him through the mirror.

Those eyes. Those fucking eyes! I've seen those before, but they weren't in your heard. Butcher's, was it? She went on a killing spree last I saw those eyes in her. You really expect me not to do anything? Forget it.

He looked down, and his hands, both trembled erratically as they bathed in the faucet's waterfall. Knowing entirely who Ghost was, only added many questions, some he already asked, others, well, they'd be bubbled up to the surface soon enough. Death was certain, almost like taxes, but here, death was more important taxes, and his poor little brother now attached to the moral quagmire. Michael had no business in this. It was for the better really.

He finally heard the door creaking behind him, and then he was alone. But he couldn't stop shaking. His heartbeat raced. *Michael, you're in the middle of this.*

CHAPTER 2

BROTHERS

Russian trade reports state that the commodity tariffs are unjust, leading to a hike in transportation costs for the following imports to the US: mineral fuels, metal, stone, steel, iron, fertilizers, and inorganic chemicals. Press Secretary Jenna Walters reports: The tariffs are in place to bring in revenue to move the country in a more stable direction for the economy and combat climate change effectively. These tariffs will reduce the supply and demand for such commodities, and we will resort to more home-grown materials to further employ Americans.

Jeffrey sat on his couch. The one person he didn't want to get any closer to, was the one person he needed to always stay within earshot. The consequences of someone loose in Task Force Seven was a calamity waiting to happen. Even still, for a monster, a killer, he seemed to be fitting in quite nicely.

This reminded him ostensibly of the common witticism for getting someone out for Halloween who didn't want to dress up, or who hated it; 'Just go as a serial killer, they look like everyone else.' And Ghost fit the bill perfectly, behaving like everyone else.

Meanwhile, alliances were crumbling to dust all over the world, and the world was nowhere near safer. What did ten years of relative peace mean when it crumbled apart so easily? The lives lost. The tragedy meaningless, and of course, the needless blackmail from that bitch, Nakamura.

J. Nakamura.

Of course, Jeff knew Ghost had no clean slate. He wasn't a good boy, as she would often refer to him. 'Good little boy,' she would say, and for what? Blowing up an orphanage? Though, if he was being honest, Ghost only ever did those things because the creepy bastard only watched him do it. Blackmailed by the bitch of course. Jeff would go down in history as a murderer and a baby killer. Hell, even a rapist if the world knew the truth, all because of that dreadful bitch. *Hell is too good a place for you, but you better be burning there all the same!*

She's dead though, strangled in her office. No one really knew who did it, but no one bothered to send word to the authorities. Perhaps they should have, because it wasn't much longer until her husband was found, chopped up in pieces, no doubt in a fit of rage. Likely by the same person, whoever that was. They did suspect Sergeant Ted Anderson to be the culprit, but after they went searching for him for answers, they only found him hanging from a noose, strategically swinging on creaking rope over a kicked over chair. The trail went cold after that. The military was filled with murderers these days, all with something important to lose, and would do anything, even stage a coup, to hide the truth.

Jeffrey was no exception to that. He knew. His crimes swept underneath the rug, and it needed to stay that way. His parents and *especially* Michael would never forgive him for all he did in Area 51, or over in Bagdad. Sure, the great of the cause, but what of the cost to others? His family valued certain things above their own freedom. They would never truly understand what was at stake here, or why he did the things he did. It was all in the name of America's freedom, and if that freedom cost the lives of some reluctant animals, so be it. In this case, it was a traitor, anyway.

But onto more necessary and urgent matters. The fact was that if Ghost was still alive, there was a possibility, no, a certainty that the truth would come out. And Jeff had to protect it, no matter what cost, even at the cost of his brother.

A simple call should suffice. That's all he needed. Questions he needed answered before anything else. How long has Michael known this fake Ted Anderson, how does he know him, and what other connections does he have? He must push for this information to even think about being in the same room with him, which now seemed all but inevitable.

He took his phone out of his pocket, exhaling and dialed Michael. *By your phone always. How convenient.*

"Hey, Jeff, what's up?" Michael's voice sounded hurried.

"It seems I got you at a bad time,"

"No, you didn't wake me. I'm just on my way to drop Samantha off. What's up?"

"I have a few questions about some things as they are alarming to me." He spoke coldly. "I hope you have a moment to answer them."

"Rather unusual timing, but sure,"

"How did you come to know Ted Anderson?"

"Sam already told—"

"I need to hear it from you," he pushed.

"Fine. Sam was experiencing some hot flashes when she started noticing him, and as it happened, we just happened to be at the same place at the same time," Michael answered.

I don't know why he would go out of his way to find you—not when he wouldn't have known our relation. Maybe I'm just paranoid.

"Anyway, he had just moved here a few weeks ago at that point, so it's been several months now."

"Uh huh," Jeff replied. *Two questions answered in one.* "Does he meet up with anyone, like from his army days? Anything like that?"

"Jeff, what's this about?"

"Nothing at all, just curious,"

"Well, if you really want anything more specific than what I told you, you're gonna wanna talk to Jennifer. He's closest to her. Not that we aren't friends, but there are things he only tells her, so even if he was meeting someone other than her, I wouldn't know."

So, I must step in the Lion's Den, eh? Shit. "Okay, thanks Michael."

"No problem," he replied. "Anything else?"

Yeah. "Oh, and one more thing. Do know you someone renting an apartment?"

CHAPTER 3

NEW ORDERS

Opinion: Janica Williams of the Houston Press. President Samuel Snells is a joke of a president. Repeating mistakes that the nation made years ago during the first and second world wars, remaining at ease, and not stepping in to help allies overseas during the struggles. With tensions around the world at an all-time high, it remains likely that President Snells, true to form, will sit back until one of the hostiles reaches our borders here in the USA, effectively, bringing a conflict directly to us: War.

It's a tale as old as time, and this time, the USA is not a world power anymore. Russia and China have grown their influence within global markets and military prowess over the last ten years with research, development, and innovation. Our conservative president will not change for the sake of balancing the budget as his highest priority.

The American people don't need a balanced budget right now. They need services, and action. The likes of which our president refuses to give us.

Jeff peered outside the transparent glass of his hotel room, gazing downward into the empty 2:00 a.m. streets. The raindrops on his window blurred images of puddles and parked cars under the streetlights. He drew the curtains closed.

He went over to his bedroom door and listened. No footsteps. No breathing. *Good. He didn't follow me here.* But then, Ghost sat close to him the entire time; he could have planted a bug on him.

Jeffrey checked his coat pockets, pants pockets, took them off, shook them until all the lint poured out, and no bug. No wires, no other electrical devices. On to his briefcase. Jeffrey took to his luggage, poured everything out of it, checking all the pockets, the surface area, combing it with his hands to look for anything out of place. Grabbing hold of all his clothes, shaking each one of them. Same thing. Nothing. He checked his keys, and wallet, opened them out, inspected each card and crevice before taking to his phone. Same thing: nothing.

Wow. I'm honestly disappointed.

He took his phone into his room, the furthest place from the door on the off chance, and presumably unlikelihood, of Ghost listening in to the other side of the door. *Don't be hasty. Be thoughtful and stay ten steps ahead. That's you Ghost, always telling me those things, and yet here you are dropping the steps like they're flies. Even the best makes mistakes, eh?*

For good measure, he got on all fours, looking at the carpet floor, ensuring there were no tears. Nothing to indicate this room was tampered with. Of course, how would Ghost know which room he was staying in? *But it's Ghost. He knows everything.* Seeing nothing of note, he sighed, sat on his bed, and took out his phone to finally dial Malcolm.

It rang a few times.

"Come on, pick up! Pick up!" he tapped his shoulder repeatedly with his index fingers, one of his many nervous habits.

"Clemens, you have any idea what time it is?" said Malcolm.

"Yes, but you're going to want to hear this,"

"Spit it out!"

"Ghost is alive,"

There was silence on the other line.

"You don't mean, Task Force Seven Ghost, do you?" he said.

"Yes," he answered. "He's living as Ted Anderson. *The* Ted Anderson."

"How is that even possible? That Ted Anderson is dead. He hanged himself."

"I don't know. But he is. And I saw him today. I'm sure the grimy little bastard had to stop himself from killing me out in the open."

"Shit. How positive are you?"

"One hundred percent."

"He's like a cockroach," he hissed. "New orders. You don't have vacation. Stay there, talk to me if you need funds for procurement of any supplies. Big players afoot, and we're getting real friendly with Russia, but we can't have Ghost on the loose. Stay close but stay reasonable. Don't provoke him. Periodically, check in with me, and no one else. Nakamura better be burning in Hell for this."

CHAPTER 4

SENSELESS INSANITY

Suicide rates have spiked more than 200 percent in the last year, says expert magazine, Psychology Analysts. Among those within the population, teens suicide rate spiked, as did the following demographics: Veteran, Black, and Hispanic American. Meanwhile, the Caucasian suicide rate dipped by 3 percent.

Mental health professionals are in need of help. They are over booked, and the US may see a decline when it comes to the mental health of psychological professionals as they are over worked. Additional experts argue that the rise in the suicide rates is related to the lack of government assistance related to health care, pulling funding from Medicare and Medicaid services across the US to reduce the amount of coverage to professionals, and related to higher co-pays for individuals, again, spiking up since 2023. These issues extrapolate the effects of undiagnosed mental illness among Americans.

After saying goodbye to Jennifer this evening, Ted closed the door behind him so she could rest. She was doing lots of resting these days. He didn't know much about the treatment for leukemia, but whatever it was, whatever chemical she was being induced with was taking a toll on her. She was bursting with energy before, but now, while still having sprints of that energy, by the end of any given day, she was left exhausted utterly.

His feet took him down the hall, and he pressed the elevator button. He exhaled as the doors opened, and he stepped into the threshold of this metal box, this prison, before selecting the main lobby button. Leaning back, his hands retreated into his pockets. His anxiety escalated, body shaking amid the stress Jeffrey now put him under.

His eyes narrowed and he gritted his teeth, scowling at nothing in particular.

He wanted to kill him. No. That's putting it lightly. He wanted to break every bone in his body. Make him squeal and bleed out black blood and watch him suffer till the lights in his eyes fade. See how he likes it, the son of a bitch. He deserves nothing better, and yet he'll be buried, family will miss him. Better than he deserves.

I could kill Michael and make Jeff watch him bleed out. No, Sam would never forgive me. Just calm down. It won't solve anything.

The doors for that claustrophobia-inducing container opened its doors and he passed through the threshold, and left the building, running to the parking lot to his car yet again, pushing past the street, and avoiding oncoming traffic, as only he could, nearly getting side swiped by the car as he inhaled a mixture of *essence*. That alien form of matter coursed through his veins, black veins forming as the part of the car that *would* have hit him but instead just passed right through him. He was a *Ghost* after all. Nothing about him made him inherently human.

Finally, he arrived at his car. He jumped inside, fastened his seatbelt, and revved the engine a few times. Funny, he knew how machines worked, just as he himself was nothing more than a machine, a tool created for the sole purpose of taking lives, but he didn't understand people as well as he wanted to. Sure, he could masquerade as one to play the part of one's identity for a day, but that was the limit.

He pressed the gas pedal, edging forward and onto the street. Driving through the oncoming traffic of Boston before taking a number of different turns through various streetlights, tunnels, and one-way streets which made Boston, as a general rule, one of the worst places to drive in the world. As they say here, if you can drive in Boston, you can drive anywhere. Boston drivers were an aggressive bunch, able to drive through the worst of calamities. Pothole? No problem. Detour? Yeah right. One-way? Drivers only ever drove one-way.

One day to masquerade as a person. That was his limit. But here he was, completely lost in the identity he chose to make his own; polite, patient, and calm. Of course, inside, he was none of those things. Patient, maybe. Not calm—his nervous anxiety told him that. He was not polite, not with the expletives that roam around his mind, especially not since earlier today; he threated to rip someone's fucking arms off.

No matter. He'll continue to play this part. It's the part that Jennifer knew, rather, she was aware of the façade all too well, and Sam, too.

They knew him to not be the polite person, but the crude individual who had a questionable past on which he could speak nothing of. Not because of the confidentiality of it, but for their own safety. If President Sam Snells knew he was still alive, he would send the entire military down on his head, which, undoubtedly, would put Jennifer and Samantha in harm's way. Those were the two he truly cared about. They went out of their way to save him from his own darkness, and because of that, they were worth protecting. No matter what the cost.

He arrived at the relative safety of his place of residence. He pushed the door shut, and one by one, locked each lock to the door, including the chain lock, the bolt, and the knob.

No one's getting through that.

He knew that was a lie. All it would take was a damn battering ram to shatter the wooden door, finely painted white. He leaned against the back of it, hands trembling. He exhaled, stepping forward into the room toward the display case that held Ticker's spear and Slither's bow. Unharmed.

"You had your chance!" A voice cried out from the corner.

He jolted, turning toward it. *Roach.* She was in her BDUs, of course, still whole, no loss of limbs—not yet anyway. She scowled, teeth gritting, and her fists trembled at her side.

"You had your chance. Why didn't you take it?" She shouted. "He was right there." She pointed an angry finger at him, tears glazing over her eyes. "After everything he did to us, all of us, why did you let him live? You should have ripped his fucking arms off."

He sighed and walked into the kitchen. *The nightmares again.*

"Don't you ignore me!"

Steps hastened behind him. Her arm grabbed him, pulling him firmly to the ground. The wrench was like an old burn. "Don't walk away from this. You need to kill him. Kill. Him."

He looked into her eyes; the hair that was once tied back now framed her face. His hand grew cold, trembling in her grip, her firm grip. Tears glazed over, streaming down her face as she was crying. "You have to do this. Who else can?"

"No," he replied, feeling a weight of regret on his chest. *She's right. Only I can do this, but—*

"Ghost, we can't rest right. No one knows who we are. Who we were," she pleaded. Her free arm fell off, bleeding on the floor. A gash in her chest opened, her snake-like intestines pouring out, staining his shoes. "No one knows what we did for them. Our badges of honor, the ones we earned, wrongfully given to others who dared not lift a finger. What became of the lives we gave? Buried? No. We were burned and not a physical trace of our existence remains. Just you. *You* have to do this. Who else can? Who else is capable?"

"She's right, Ghost," another voice in the corner.

He gasped, turning his head. Another girl, red hair tied back, and that familiar hilt at her side, a rifle strapped to her back, and her unforgettable side arm. She tilted her head to him; a disappointed face staring down at him. *Butcher.*

"No. You're wrong," he shook his head, closed his eyes tightly. *Go away. Go away! Get out of my head.*

The cool air warmed in the room, caressing his skin. He looked forward and the walls faded. The sand coursed the earth, stained crimson underneath the scorching sun, and whirling winds pelted against his face. The sound of a gun firing a large caliber entered his ears. He fell backward, the hot sand shredded his clothes. The bullet soared and struck Butcher in the face, blood spraying out the back of her head.

He panted heavily, with warm tears glazing over his eyes. Looking down at his arms, they shook, rapidly. His heart raced with each breath he took. The shakes tore through his body, rattling his bones and boiling his sanguine fluids.

Butcher looked at him, eyeless, and crimson, thick liquid pouring down the side of her cheek.

"Do you see it now?" Butcher asked.

Roach was next to her, bowing down, vomiting with her intestines on the floor.

"Get out of here." He cried. "Get out. Leave me alone."

"Do you want this to happen again? To someone else? Is that it?" Butcher asked, her hand firmly resting on his shoulders. Her gloves were torn with red water poured out her hands, glistening.

"No!" His hands reached over his head. He covered his ears, and his warm tears streamed down his face. "I can't. I can't do it. I have something here, and if I do that, I'll be forced to leave it all behind. I don't want to lose—"

"So what?" Roach turned her head. One leg separated at her knee, and more blood leaked out over the sand. She hopped forward. "We don't mean anything to you anymore. Is that it?"

"No. That's not it at all." He closed his ears, but that didn't stop them from talking to him, and it didn't stop him from hearing this nightmare.

"All of a sudden, Ghost has a house again. A roof over his head. A job, a life, like the good little civie you are," she said, condescendingly. "You have friends, a family even. Just because you have those, we don't mean anything. You hear this Butcher? You listening to this?"

"Yeah." Butcher leaned back again; arms crossed over her chest. "Fine," she breathed lightly. "Ghost, or Ted, whichever lie you want to believe, just let the children die again. Snells did it before, he'll do it again unless you do something. You're just a tool. I mean, look at you. You can't even function right now, crying in this little dipshit of a corner. I guess we never meant anything to you. And you were the closest thing we ever had to a father, a proper father, not one with uniforms raping us to see how many times until we finally snap."

"That's not—" he dropped his hands into the blazing hot sand.

"The only thing we ever had was each other. The closest thing to siblings and a family was us. And you're happy to throw it all away!" Roach cried. "Does none of that mean anything anymore? Were we a joke to you? Or were we just tools?"

"Ghost," Butcher closed her one eye. "If there's part of you alive in there, and you truly care about us, you'll kill them all. Every last one of them."

He breathed heavily as his flashback faded, returning him to his home, crying like he imagined a baby would after seeing these things. He pulled his knees to his chest, back against the wall as he rested his chin on his kneecaps, rocking back and forth.

CHAPTER 5

FAVORS

Several high-profile military personnel reported missing in the DC Metropolitan area as their service has ties to the 75th Ranger Regiment.

Detective Hernandez claims they're "doing everything [they] can to locate the suspect." Detective Hernandez rejected further questioning.

John Spadero stood outside the night street; raindrops rippled in the puddles of the empty street. A black unmarked van with tinted windows drove in front of him. The driver's side rolled down the window, and a tanned woman with raven hair and blood red eyes glared at him. "Your bargaining chip is in the back."

"Thanks." He replied grimly with sunken eyes. He walked to the back of the van; his trench coat swayed in the wind. His pocket vibrated, drawing the phone out of it, checking the caller ID: Sander. His hand swiped the phone to his ear, "Spadero here."

"Do you have an update for me? I need additional information on the target. I don't need to tell you how urgent it is," Sander said in a rushed tone.

John sighed as he leaned against the van, implanting his handprint onto the tinted glass. "Not yet. Some of these soldiers, former or not are tough as nails. Though, I have one in hand, and I just got my bargaining chip. I'll break this one."

"Report to me with an update."

"What is this about?" John asked, his eyes focused on the ripples in the puddles. "You'll tell me that much, won't you?"

"Possibly a rogue. We have one for sure, being Sarah McCurdy. This other one is an unidentified individual. This person doesn't cover his mana trail," Sander replied. "After all, things will get suspicious should they pick up on trails and heightened levels of mana, which they think is radiation. Excellent cover, really. Get to it and get back to me."

"On it," John hung up the phone and placed it back in his pocket. He swung the two doors open, revealing a woman in her late thirties, clutching onto a little sleeping child. The woman trembled as her eyes stretched open and stared into John's eyes. He felt like he was looking at a trapped animal in a cage, trying to forestall its execution. *Fitting.*

"Out."

He stepped away, keeping a trained eye on the two of them. The boy stirred, rubbing his little eyes with fisted hands.

"Momma, where are we?" The boy sleepily turned his gaze to John.

I gotta dirty my hands again, just to learn the truth, and only with the truth can the world become a little cleaner. Such a shame this is even necessary. You should have spoken; else I wouldn't have to resort to this.

"I don't know sweetheart." The woman tried to sooth the boy and feign a mask of confidence, but her sweat and quivering body told a different tale. Her hand brushed the boy's hair. "I'm just going to answer some questions. Then we'll be free to go home."

"Precisely right." John placed his boot on the edge of the van's threshold; this time John faked a smile. "Just a few questions and we're done. Then you can go back home." *Six feet under, that is.*

"Don't you dare touch him." She snapped as John approached.

John scowled at her, "Madam, get out of the van. The sooner we finish here, the sooner we can leave."

The woman had a snarl which softened as she pulled the boy down next to her. She started to climb out of the van. John immedi-

40

ately snapped his fingers at her. "I can't hold the van. He comes too." He pointed his finger at him.

"Gerald, come on, dear." She reached her hand back into the van. The boy took it, and she pulled him out, easing him on the wet street.

John led them to the building. The high-rise was near empty, and the windows were boarded up. Glass from shattered windows littered the ground, crunching as they stepped on the shards. John opened the door and guided the two down the iron grooved stairs, further into the dark. Gerald clutched his mother's arms as she walked down the metallic steps. John closed the final door behind them, and they were in a large room filled with yellow flickering lamps, some swayed with the sudden movement in the room.

"Jack. I brought something for you." John called out, sneering as he held the boy and his mother close to him.

"I'll never talk, you monster." The man called from the other room.

"We'll see just how far your resolve is. How long will you let the truth lay silent? I am determined to get the truth out somehow, and you are my last stop." John called back. "You wanted this. I gave you an out."

John kicked the wooden door down into the other room, and there was Jack exactly how he left him; beat up, bloodied, tied in numerous ropes and duct tape. There were photos sitting on the table in front of him. The man tilted his head up toward them. His swollen eyes couldn't open, but John imagined they would be wide indeed.

"Jack! Jack! What happened to you?" The woman cried out, running out to the man. She embraced him and looked in his eyes as John shut and locked the door with its numerous tumblers.

John walked to the corner of the room, hoisted a metal chair, and slammed it on the ground at the table. He pulled the woman away from Jack. She shrieked. He pushed her to the chair. The boy leaned against the locked door, arms quivering, retracted to his chin, staring at the table with gaping eyes.

"Jack," said John. "Talk. I want answers, and I want them now."

"No."

John abruptly grabbed the woman's arm and slammed her wrist on the table. He pulled out a knife and stabbed the table with it. "I've been patient enough with you. Speak. This can be easy, or difficult. Take your pick."

"Babe, what is he talking about? Just give him what he wants!" she sobbed.

"Dadda! What—"

"Silence, boy." John snapped, turning to him briefly and scowled. "The adults are talking."

The boy gasped, pushing himself against the locked door. His teeth grinded together, hands down, clutching at the door.

"Nothing," said Jack.

John assumed Jack was scowling behind the blood and swelling.

"Fuck it,"

John pulled the knife out of the table. He firmly held her hand in place and kept her pinky nail firmly pinned down. He squeezed her nail until the color began to fade. He placed the blade of the knife just underneath the manicured nail.

"Just don't hurt my son," she pleaded.

"That all depends on Jack," John explained. "What's it gonna be?"

"What are you doing?" Jack's chair budged as he struggled against the restraints. "Leave her alone. She has nothing to do with this. I don't—I don't even know what this is."

"Bullshit. Give me something better than that." Jack pushed the blade into the nailbed and pried off the nail. She wailed. Blood dripped off to the sides, the tender skin exposed. *Don't you dare make me pry off toenails.*

The screech scratched John's ears. He grimaced as he pinned down the next finger on the table. She squirmed, trying to rip herself away to no avail.

"MOMMA." The small child's strangled scream came from be-hind him.

"Just tell me what I want, and this stops," John scowled to Jack.

"MAKE IT STOP." The woman shrieked.

Her wrist tensed, and with her free palm, she slapped John across the face. He turned, and with his hand grabbed the other wrist, breathing in the mana from the air, blue veins climbing on his fingers, and with a reinforced thumb, sprained her wrist, and slammed it again on the table. She sucked in air through her teeth, closing her eyes tight.

"Time's wasting." John didn't give Jack a moment to reply. He stabbed the nailbed of the next finger and pried the nail off. The blood started to drip onto the table, her shriek scratched his ears. The floor squealed as the iron legs scrapped across it as her futile attempt to pull herself away, failed. "Now, talk."

"Fine. I'll talk." Jack's chair stopped moving as he bowed his head down. "Just stop."

"Who is Ghost?" John asked. He pinned her middle finger on the table.

"Ghost," Jack gazed up at the ceiling, presumably to jog his memory. "Why do you care about a dead man?"

"Wrong answer!" John slipped the blade of the knife underneath another nailbed, prying the third fingernail off. He pinned her index finger on the table as she screamed, trying to get out of his grasp. John breathed in the mana from the air, and bright blue veins were risen on his skin, his hands. "Answer the damn question."

"I told you. He's dead." Jack cried. "Stop it."

"I have been asking you this question all day, with the same damn answer." Jack stabbed the other nailbed and pried off her fingernail. He pinned her thumb on the table. "I don't care if he is dead or not. I want to know who he is. Who is he, Jack?"

"He's dead and meaningless, what possible thing do you have to gain in me telling—"

"DAMNIT." John swore and stabbed his knife through her thumb. The thumb severed and was pushed off the table, blood splattered on it. The woman screamed, her eyes tearing. "You should know this, I would not be asking about Ghost if he was dead, now, would I?"

Jack finally went silent. He looked up to John with a grim face, a face even darker than when Jack cut his wife's thumb off. "That's impossible."

"Now, we're getting somewhere. Why is it impossible?" John moved to the other side of Jack's wife and pinned her other hand on the table, ready to start over. He shot a scowl over to the boy in the corner. *If I can get that answered at least, I deduce something else from this.*

"He's dead. KIA in Area 51. Training exercise," Jack replied.

"Was there a body?"

"No."

"Then how do you know he's dead?" John asked, "And don't tempt me. I have five more fingernails. And ten more toenails. Don't make me add your son to this."

"He was last confirmed at the base of Area 51. The base itself was blown to shreds, never mind the nuclear reactor that blew up. Where he was, is now filled with radioactive waste. No one would dare touch his body even if there was one to recover."

"So, the military falsely claimed him as KIA, and not MIA?" John inquired.

"So, it would seem."

"And he was last seen on Area 51, which was blown to bits, and then was the epicenter for a nuclear meltdown. Correct?"

"Correct."

"How did Area 51 blow up?" John asked, knowing full well what radiation really was. Enough of it would cause cellular damage to normies, and might blow up persons' mana veins, which, if Ghost was a Caster, it would have still killed him.

"The same way they all do. There wasn't enough water in the reactors at that moment in time, and the failsafe systems in place didn't work," Jack replied.

"That's a highly classified base. You mean to tell me they were sufficiently primed for failure?" John asked.

"What do you want me to say? I wasn't stationed at Area 51. I was leading the 75th Ranger Regiment."

"What the hell was an entire calvary doing at a training exercise at Area 51?" John didn't believe that Ghost was KIA. Not like this.

Jack didn't answer.

"No matter, we'll come back to this, and I expect an answer," said John. "Now, who is Ghost?"

"Ghost was the captain of Task Force Seven," he answered. His wife quietened down, her screams now a whimper.

"Who is Task Force Seven?"

"An elite division on the Army. They were well hidden and trained alongside with the special forces."

"What did they do?" John cataloged this information in his head. He would write it down later and report this to Sander, and of course, the four Casters assigned to this manhunt in Boston. So many pieces adding up, none of them made sense without the common missing link.

"They infiltrated high valued military bases from across the world. They led counter strikes, and often held execute authority, including overriding commands from the colonels, and answered to General Snells alone. They assassinated high level targets, forcing our enemies in a constant state of disarray."

"They gave a captain rank equal to that of a general and answered to only one person in the US Army?" Spadero raised his eyebrow, staring into the muddled eyes of the man sitting across from him, blood dripping out of his nose into neat puddles.

"Sounds surreal, but it's true. Even my rank by the time I retired, I would answer to Ghost if he and I shared the same battlefield," Jack spoke solemnly.

John recapped. "Is that the long and short of it?"

"Yes."

John sighed heavily. His finger tapped against the iron table, warm blood sputtering underneath, dripping on the floor. He heard the dripping of thick coagulating fluid on the floor as the room felt eerily quiet. He even stopped hearing the whimpering of the brat in the corner.

"Good. What does the official record say about that incident at Area 51?" John pressed further.

"I can't give you the full report. Reports were collected and submitted to Lieutenant Nakamura, and then finalized underneath General Snells. Lieutenant Nakamura is deceased, killed in her office in Georgia, and you know General Snells, the president."

"What happened to the rest of Task Force Seven?"

"Falsely documented as KIA in the training accident at Area 51."

"Who else was in Task Force Seven?"

"I only dealt with Ghost. The last reported dead were Slithers, Ticker, and Butcher, and Ghost was the final one."

What the hell is all this mess? None of this makes sense, and if all of this was true, it would be impossible to cover it up as well as it's been covered. And still, nobody knows anything.

"Now, I did my own digging, and like I said, you're my last stop," said John. "Do you care to explain to me exactly why there are no records of Task Force Seven? All I found was a few faces and code-names." He noticed a drop of blood on his slacks. *Shit.*

"I couldn't tell you. Like I said, all our reports concerning Task Force Seven were submitted to Lieutenant Nakamura. Presumably, she submitted all the reports to Snells, who drafted the final report."

"So, people were aware of them, but there was no official record proving their existence. Is that correct?" John asked.

"Yes."

John let go of Jack's wife's hand, and his blue veins retreated underneath his skin. *A dangerous force, as it were. No official records of them existing, minus this little conversation, and that is the only thing I have on this Ghost. I'm not done yet. I have two names, one of which is impossible to get, but perhaps...* "You said Nakamura was dead. How did she die?"

Jack surrendered the information. "I don't have all the details, but the reports say she was found dead, strangled by someone on a Georgia base."

"Suspect?" Jack asked. *This is a lead!*

"There were a few, but only one was ever a serious suspect. His name was Sergeant Ted Anderson," Jack replied.

"Where is he now? To the best of your recollection." *Ted Anderson. The missing link. You know something.*

"Memory serves right," Jack hesitated. "Ted Anderson was in the 75th Ranger Regiment. He was heavily involved with the secret projects with the CIA, of which Snells and Nakamura were deeply invested in for some reason. He's reported dead."

John leaned over the table, and covered his forehead with his hand, rubbing his temples. *Damnit.* "Killed in action?"

"Negative," Jack replied like a soldier. "He was hanged."

"He was executed?" John looked back at the swollen face.

"I don't know."

"Yeah, why would you," John replied. *No loose ends were left untied. Snells. Ted Anderson. I suppose I'll need to make another trip.* John smiled. "No further questions, your honor."

John took himself away from the table and shifted his body to the door. The woman rushed over to her husband. Watching the boy scramble and embracing his father, John reached out of his back pocket, and retrieved a Glock nine-millimeter pistol and aimed it at the grouping. "No witnesses." Jack and his family screamed as John pulled the trigger in rapid succession. The muffled nozzle produced bright lights as each round was evacuated from its chamber striking each target in the head. He returned the Glock to his holster.

A look, he took, one final look. The man was useless, he had no respect for the likes of him. Utterly useless. His swollen head had a hole in it, one eye lightly opened, and his head bowed down as if to pray. His wife, now on the floor, blood pooling out of her head, and who could forget the boy whose sensitive cranium shattered. *Jack. Why did you make this necessary?*

He let out a deep sigh, pulling out his knife again, and he drew runes in the air. The purple veins were pulled from his body and concentrated into the sigils. The shapes were pushed out and placed themselves carefully on the bodies. The bodies slowly turned to ash, burning away. He felt their bodies becoming mana, and he imbibed them through the runes. The runes faded away; the veins fleeting into his body.

Sander picked up the phone immediately as if he expected the call. *I'll never get used to that.*

"What information did you gleam?"

"Almost nothing to go off of," John started before he went into the details of the interrogation, line by line, almost verbatim. John was twiddling his thumb with his other hand. "The loose ends over here have been tied."

"Good," Sander replied. "Spadero, you seem to be hiding something from me."

"I wouldn't say hiding," he chuckled nervously. "More like, I have an idea that has not been able to formulate a complete thought yet."

"Shoot it at me. I'll make sense of it."

"Ghost, whoever that is, is alive, so, he somehow survived being at the epicenter of a nuclear meltdown. What if, it was not Ted Anderson who killed Lieutenant Nakamura, but Ghost masquerading as Ted Anderson?" John reasoned. "This is the only conclusion I can come up with, and mind you, all speculation. No solid proof. Evidence is completely circumstantial."

"Are you suggesting that Ghost, who happens to be in Boston, is not using his own name? Perhaps using the papers and effects of Ted Anderson as an alias?"

"Affirmative," said John. "The only other lead I have is President Snells. All other ends are tied. And I can't get close enough to Snells without causing a scene. You know how dangerous that is."

"We'll assume this Ghost is Ted Anderson then."

John hung up the phone.

Sarah McCurdy walked into the office, Administrator Colton stared at her with wide eyes, heavy bags underneath them. He folded his hands and propped up his elbows. She closed the door behind her and waited for it to click shut.

"Well, where is it?" He spoke coldly.

"Here," she walked forward with her bag.

She carefully placed the bag on the floor, opened it up, and pulled out the Grail, placing it firmly on his desk. The golden Grail had numerous ancient Anglo-Saxon engravings, elegantly embedded into the outer rim of the cup. Other runes were carved down to the bottom, layers upon layers of them shifting around in circular motions. The bottom of the Grail was fused into the bottom of the Box, which was dark purple and made of an unknown metallic alloy, not of the same material of the Grail. The runes over the Box and the Grail were illegibly overlapped with intricate polygons.

Additionally, she at least didn't know the original language the engravings from the Box depicted. The crimson liquid inside the Grail rippled constantly, and dark black smoke emitted from the Box.

"It was encumbering to get it here unnoticed," Sarah continued. "But what was the point of all that? What are we to do with it?"

"You don't need to know that. All you need to know is the head Administrator has been withholding information from everyone as of late, and can't be trusted with such an important artifact," he said coldly. "I don't have use for you right at this moment so you may leave."

"Where?" she snapped. "There isn't anywhere for me to go. Casters are still looking for me."

"I don't have the time to deal with—"

The phone rang.

"Hold on," he picked up the phone. "Colton."

Sarah watched the numerous contorted facial expressions of Colton on the phone.

"Okay. I'll ask around to get you information. I'll get you something within seventy-two hours. Colton out." He hung up the phone. "Hang on. I need to make a call. I may have somewhere to send you after all."

Sarah nodded, feeling uneasy with the Administrator as he dialed a set of numbers.

He looked up as he brought the handset to his ear. "Go wait outside. I'll call you in, in a minute."

Samuel Snells looked out the window of the Oval Office at green lawn lit up by spotlights. The sky was starless. He let out a sigh, and pulled his hands behind him, his left hand massaging his wrist.

Making those promises to the people, doing all the things he did was to ensure world peace. Not for himself, or any promotion, rather, desiring it for his children's sake. But the report he just read told him that all was meaningless; it was only a matter of time. Russia and China would be on their doorstep, and those were both forces he was not fond of.

He about-faced and walked back to his chair. A file lay on his desk, and on that file was the "Black Eagle" emblem. Something he started, and something and someones he didn't want to resort to as frequently as he did. The military isn't what it used to be, that was certain. *But what went wrong?*

The phone rang, disturbing his thoughts.

He exhaled deeply, not knowing who it was. A call at 1:00 a.m. was never a good sign.

"Snells' office," he swiftly pulled the phone off the received and brought it to his ears.

"Snells. It's Colton."

His heart skipped a beat, and his hand trembled with the phone in his ear. This was the only thing worse than the threat of global war reaching his shores. "Colton. To what do I owe the—"

"Enough with the fucking niceties! You were supposed to do something. You remember what it was?"

"I need a little more information than that."

"The deal we made that landed you in the White House. Do you remember what it was?"

"That I am supposed to erase all involvement with your Administration. And furthermore, I am a dog to you, and will obey your orders."

"That was the memo, wasn't it? Now, what didn't you do?"

"I don't have any active ties with your organization," Snells replied, perplexed.

"I told you how to do it. Why didn't you erase everything and everyone related to Task Force Seven, like you were supposed to?"

His eyes blinked. Another skeleton in his closet. A project that required the creation of Black Eagle Company. If a loose end remained, and word got out, all Hell would break loose. A World War would pale in comparison. "What are you talking about?"

"Don't play the village idiot with me." Snells pulled the receiver away from his ear so the yelling wouldn't pierce his ears so much. "One of them still lives."

"That's impossible," Snells interjected.

"Is it? Is it? How many bodies were accounted for?"

Snells no longer had the record. The record was supposed to have been deleted along with everything else, especially with Nakamura's sudden murder, a few months after Task Force Seven was exterminated. "I don't have access to that report anymore. It's gone since it was part of the arrangement."

"Fucking damnit. You do it just to piss me off don't you?" The voice on the other end of the phone was filled with ire. He never again wanted to see this man in person. He only ever met him in person once, and that was one too many times. "Get all information and reports you have and send them all to me. I don't care how you do it, I don't care how long it takes, get it to me within two days."

"Those reports are all gone," Snells said roughly, hand firmly clasping on the phone.

"That's not all true, now, is it? You will do this; I don't care who or what you must do to get it done. If you don't do it, I'll kill you and replace you with someone who will!"

The call dropped.

He covered his face in his hands as he leaned over the desk, his dark thinning hair now messy. *All I wanted was a world without war, and in creating that peace, I have only made it worse. Well, I am a soldier, and orders are orders.*

Colton put his phone down and stared at the wall. His face cringed thinking of all the wasted effort. Of course, Snells would do what he asked, but he had much on his plate. Not that Colton particularly cared. It needed to be done.

Colton bit his lip, exhaling heavily, pondering just the problem that lied before him. Sander was getting close to this Ghost. Should Sander get Ghost, so many questions will be asked, and many of them ultimately lead straight to himself.

You've got Culain and his team there searching for him, without a doubt to take him to Camelot. Use that to somehow find McCurdy, or even link me to the Holy Grail. I thought I had everything figured out. And Congressman Spadero, here, also, he's one of your players too, isn't he? Loyal as he ever was to Camelot, the blind fool! He tapped his fingers violently on his wooden desk. *Now, I can't just assign someone to look for Ghost: that would be too obvious, and we don't know what kind of guise this man is wearing.* And of course, using McCurdy will create a whole slew of problems and connections he didn't want created. *He's in Boston. Perhaps if he was killed by the tensions we've been seeing lately. But the battlefield is messy, there's not a guarantee it will work out the way I want it to.*

"It's the best worst option right now," he exhaled deeply as he picked up the phone again and dialed another number. It rang in his ears.

"Good morning, Colton," answered the man on the other end.

"Oh, piss off. It's 1:00 a.m., Mikhail," Colton said. "I need a favor."

"You Americans always are so polite first thing in the morning. I haven't had my cup of coffee. You have a hostile way of asking for favors," Mikhail replied with a thick Russian accent.

"I have a big problem." Colton sighed.

"What is it the great Colton cannot do himself?"

"I need a war."

There was a pause. "Why?" Mikhail was no longer playful.

"Nothing fancy. What is it going to take to shut you up about it?" He ignored the concerned question.

"No! Your tricks will not work on me, not like last time," Mikhail replied. "Why do you need a war? And with who specifically?"

"The Cold War will suffice," Colton continued. "But if you must know, there are complications, and I need someone killed. And I can't just do it; in fact, someone in the Administration cannot be directly involved in this individual's death."

"Who is it?"

"You see, this is why you don't ask questions. I don't have a name yet, I just know a relative location, and I would hope a war with Russia might resolve that problem."

"No. I'm not giving you a war, my friend," he replied.

"Mikhail, you owe me one, and I've never gotten payment for that favor I did for you. Are we not friends?"

Mikhail chuckled on the other line. "What friend tells his friend to fuck off at one in the morning?"

"Look, if you don't want to do it for me, then fine," Colton replied. "Do it for Mother Russia. Russia has been wanting to punch Uncle Sam in the face for quite some time, has she not?"

"That's a lot of people you are asking me to kill. Does this serve our Administration's purpose? This person's death I mean."

"Look, I'm trying to stop another World War here. We all know what happened with Hitler, right? I'm trying to prevent that from being necessary," he lied.

Mikhail was silent for a moment. "Are you being serious?"

"Yes," he answered.

"And Sander, does he know?" Mikhail returned a serious tone.

"Yes," he answered. "So, can I get that war then?"

"Yes, for the Administration."

"For the Administration, may whatever God holds dominion over our lives forgive us," Colton said.

He hung up the phone.

Gwen is becoming a problem.

"McCurdy! Get your ass back in here!" he called.

McCurdy walked back to her seat as he shuffled some documents into his file below his desk.

"It turns out, I do have a job for you. I can only trust you with this. Gwen is aware of our little arrangement. You will be safer there. I need you to monitor her. Do whatever she asks, and report back to me. I want to know what she knows, and what she's researching. *Especially* what she's researching."

"Why not just ask?" Sarah held her hand out to the side. "She reports to you, doesn't she?"

"Don't get smart with me." He snapped. "Just do what I ask. Don't get on her bad side, and for god's sake, don't get caught."

She rolled her eyes as she hastily walked to exit the room.

Gwen Swan. What exactly are you keeping from me?

CHAPTER 6

LOOSE ENDS

The thoughts of one with a conscience: I was awarded the congressional Medal of Honor today. Me, along with Lieutenant Nakamura, for being so instrumental in the brokering of world peace. It sickens me. The ends justify the means they say. Do they though? I'm not so sure. Not after everything we've done. Especially this medal. It doesn't belong to me. It belongs to them. It belongs to those that earned it. This medal is trash. How can anyone accept this with a straight face? It's disgustingly sick. Our forefathers would be ashamed. The world would be sick, and we declared public enemy number one if anyone found the truth.

S nells sat down in his chair after the call with Colton, hands folded with interlaced fingers, leaning over his desk at the Oval Office, still reeling from his call with Colton. The threat was plain and simple, and he knew Colton was good on threats. He had crossed Snells before to prove a point, which was loud and clear as a whistle. Who'd ever think, the most powerful man in the world was nothing more than a lap dog for some shady organization he didn't understand. And yet, here he was. Shaking like a scared puppy.

And yet, there was something else at stake here. Creating Task Force Seven was no small feat, and red tape was ripped apart to make that happen. Nothing about Task Force Seven, their creation, their operations, or even their trainings were legal or ethical.

All of them were supposed to be dead. Sure, some bodies weren't recovered, but those that were unrecoverable were right at the epicenter of the meltdown almost nine years ago. No possible way anyone could survive that. Colton told him that one of them survived. That isn't possible. Just can't be.

But say it was. And there was a person born who could survive a nuclear meltdown, fat chance of that for certain, and if someone survived, why would they stay silent after all this time? Was there a purpose?

The carcasses stunk as the flames died down, ashes rising in the early morning desert sun. Thirteen bodies, black, charred, unrecognizable. Malcolm stood there with that disgusted scowl upon his lips. He shot Snells a hardened snarl, the likes of which was seen only among the worst of people. But Snells always liked his results.

Task Force Seven colluded with Germany to stage a coup. That was the lie he cooked up to tell their comrades. Evidence planted on Ghost's computer system to prove that. Malcolm planted it underneath Nakamura's directive, which ultimately came from him.

Of course, there was a reason to that madness.

This was all necessary. An end to justify the means. Leading to what nations would call the greatest brokering of world peace the world had ever seen. All it took was to create a common enemy fiercer than anything. Banded together, the world took it upon themselves to stop fighting one another: provided Task Force Seven was eliminated.

All sixteen of them became devils. And this was to be their end. No one would know the truth. But the truth is, he came in like a thief in the night, ripping children away from their parents, telling no one, stifling the cries of the media for thirty-two children who went missing.

The truth is, the reason he chose to have them all killed at the end of it was not because the world required them to be disbanded, but he knew these children would never be able to integrate into normal lives, especially without any family support. It was inevitable that they were end up behind bars, and of course no prison could hold any one of them.

Snells retracted his hands to grab the receiver of his phone. His hands trembled with the weight of the falsehood he had chosen to believe. He killed them. Their blood was on *his* hands. Their slavery was on *his* hands. The childless parents were on *his* hands. It was all *his* doing.

But suppose Colton was right, and one of them managed to survive, living among them all. And that person had plenty of time to stage a coup and rip apart the world that created what they were. It meant they *chose* not to. Whoever it was *chose* not to lash out with vengeance. Whoever it was *chose* not to seek justice. And that meant, Snells was wrong, all those years ago. And there was a chance for them to integrate out into the world. And he murdered them for no reason.

He turned to a portrait of his family. His little girl, Jacqueline, her dress swayed in the wind outside their family home in North Dakota. "If I was anyone else. It could have been you out there, burning."

And yet, all that to say, the truth could come out, and if it did. He's finished. The peace he built will come crumbling down as a sham, regardless that the world was burning in flames, and he had nothing to do with it. But he will still shoulder the blame, and all those with Black Eagle. They trusted him when he led them, and to think of their lives being chained underneath the oppressive weight of guilt, and blackmail.

He shook his head. His guilt doesn't matter anymore. What does, is getting those files and records off to Colton, or else, who knows what Colton will do to him. There was no telling with him. And there was this Administration, this grand syndicate which seemed untouchable. God, he felt like he was playing around with the mafia, and since he's played, he has no choice but to continue to play, trapped. *Payback's a bitch, ain't it.*

He removed his hand from the receiver. He secured the line before dialing.

"Snells, do you have any idea what time it is?" Malcolm said on the other line.

"I have a favor to ask," Snells replied. "You remember Task Force Seven, don't you?"

No response.

"Malcolm?"

"Yes, I remember. What of it?"

"I need all files and records sent to me immediately, it is vitally important."

"Okay. I'll send it discreetly. Expect it tomorrow."

Snells hung up the phone. *Receive it. Send it to Colton. Wipe my hands clean of it. Call it a day.*

"Who was that at this hour?" Malcolm's wife Alexandra asked.

He yawned as he rested his head back on his pillow. The heavy comforter laying upon his body. The bed shifted and squeaked as she turned to him, wiping the sleep from her eyes. She was a light sleeper. Surprised him most of the time. He couldn't even rollover without her noticing.

"Snells." He turned his body to hers, brushing her sleek hair, gazing into those eyes, moonlight shimmering.

"Are you deploying yourself again?" she asked, caressing his cheek. Her touch was like a warm pillow. It was too comforting for a world shrouded in darkness.

"Well, not related to this. No. Unlikely," he pecked her on the lips. "I just have a busier day tomorrow."

Suspicious. A call from the President regarding Task Force Seven. Shortly after a similar call from Master Sergeant Clemens. Ghost. What we did to you was inexcusable. But what have you been doing all this time? Revenge would be understandable, but if you wanted revenge, you would have fought back by now.

Thinking back on the coincidences: *Snells. What the hell did you get us into?*

CHAPTER 7

BITTERSWEETNESS

Removal of funding from the behavioral health coverage from Medicare and Medicaid services has led to an exponential increase to the suicide of Americans and resulted in a number of undocumented and undiagnosed mental illness.

Press Secretary Jenna Walters had this to say about these reports, "it wasn't a priority when funding the rapid expenditure funds into the health care system. People with mental health needs can still work and contribute to society in a healthy way and are in no way at risk. Concerning the rise in the suicide rate, who are we to tell them what not to do? It's their choice. No one decided to do that for them. They chose that. Their bodies. Their choice. Who are we to take that from them?"

"Ted?" Jennifer asked as they were walking through the Boston Public Gardens; this place was special to her. To her, he confided his trust in, and admitting for once that she was his friend, and that he trusted her. She knew that. The sun set behind the dark clouds, and her stomach started to growl. That, and the added pain to her bones made this much more unbearable. She'd elected to wait and have it looked at later. "I'm hungry. Do you need to eat something?"

His hand rubbed his stomach, rubbing it like a pregnant woman does with a baby growing inside her, "I think it might be time to fill it."

Of course, that was about as much of a straight answer he would give. Jennifer was relieved that this wasn't completely life threatening, so she shrugged it off, and took his hand and jerked it downward. "Good. I'm in the mood for something specific."

She turned her head around, carefully looking for anyone who she might think Ted would find to be suspicious. The snow glistened in the moonlight on the ground, lightly coating the sidewalks, the streets, even the cars. Men, women, and children clad in their thick winter coats, pants, and gloves walked in and out of the subway station, talking away. Nothing out of the ordinary, no one was standing idly by. No one was watching. It was safe here, if safe was the appropriate word for such an evening. "I'll let you decide if you want to eat it here or come back to my place. I have work in the morning."

"I don't—I don't think I can manage dining right now," he stammered.

She felt his hand tremble in her own, and his hand was cold. A natural cold, not influenced by his *special* veins. But her own scientific curiosity caused her to question what it was, even if she would never be able to study it in depth.

"I understand. Then we'll go, order, and leave. Simple," she answered and shot him that foxlike smile of hers. "We'll take it back to my place."

She guided him down the streets. The winter coat clad people walked to and fro, darting through the busy Boston traffic which navigated the many-laned one-way streets. They scurried like rats, kicking up snow as they avoided being run down by industrialized horses. Of course, the drivers of these horses didn't find it funny, nearly weaving into poles, honking their horn to play the urban symphony.

There were so many things she wanted to ask him, but she knew better than anyone else not to really ask those questions, or rather, to push for an answer. He was the type of person that wouldn't say anything, and just merely disappear, avoiding all human contact until he took up another name, and went to another play, bought another house, and lived in solitude till the end of his days. She knew he wanted to do that last time they pushed him, and they had pushed hard.

But there was one question, as it involved Jeff Clemens' sudden arrival. Not the arrival itself, but it stirred something inside Ted—she knew it. It was apparent in his demeanor, and Ted even went out of his way to guide the man to the bathroom just a few months ago, which she had to admit, was well out of character for him, regardless of the persona he chose to adopt at that moment in time. The other thing remained: Jeff never left Boston like she was led to believe. But of course, leaves get extended sometimes, but there was not firm answer from Jeff as the reason why his leave was extended, and until further notice. And of course, all these things changed when Jeff met Ted like war buddies, but she was certain they were anything but. Jeff seemed to know Ted, and while she didn't know the whole story, she knew much more than any of her friends. But why would he pretend to know who he was? And then there was the reality that Ted wasn't Ted's real name. She knew that and accepted it, and that he couldn't share his real identity for something he didn't commit. Previously, he alluded to the fact he was framed for something that he didn't do and was still paying the price for. That was reason enough to hide. That was all the reason she needed. But was it possible Jeff knew Ted wasn't who he said he was? If so, why did he play along? Or was he merely stupid. Yes, that's it. Jeffrey knows something's awry. This would more than explain Tedward's recent behavior, and his anxiety soaring. She learned to catch those things, primarily in the shaking of his hands, and if they weren't visible, he hid them.

She took her other arm and hooked it around his, pulling herself closely to him, sharing the body heat during the cold late November nights. The heavy dark clouds oppressed the moon from the other side. They walked further away from the Government Center MBTA station, down the stairs, and crossed the four-lane highway to the Quincy Market. It was very quiet. Some people strode around the various shops, but not to where Jennifer and Ted were going. Making their way over the cobbled pathways, they entered the back building, where the walls were glass, and further in, taking a right turn into the shop. There was a man standing behind a podium, operating the phone and he greeted them.

"Table for two?" He said as he finished with the phone.

"Take-out actually." She smiled at the man, pulling one of the paper menus from the desk, and handed it to Ted.

Ted scanned the menu. She preferred he didn't pick something at random. He still didn't taste anything, after all. *Is this okay? Ted, I can't read your mind, so it's okay, you can tell me that much can't you?*

"Chicken ramen," he said.

That was fast. "I'll take the same, but I want the spicy one," she replied, and took out her card, presenting it to the host. "It's under Jennifer."

"You didn't have to pay for it. I could have done it," Ted said.

"Hush, my Tedward. I will not hear it." She pushed her fingers to his lips. He smiled a fake smile, and while at one time those smiles would have been old and unforgiving, this one she didn't mind. At least she thought it was feigned. He gave her a lot of deceptive smiles, and barely one that wasn't deceiving. *He's still wearing a mask, but it isn't for me. It's for himself, at least, I think.* "It's a gift. If you want to give me something, make me something. Put some of your soul into it."

"I understand."

She took his hand and led him to the light brown, polished bench for guests to sit at while waiting for their food.

Surprisingly, the food didn't take very long. She was presented with one large bag with two carefully wrapped bowls, and some wooden chop sticks.

"Time to go." She assured.

Jennifer's living room was brightly lit with Christmas Decor. There was even a nice Christmas Tree decorated with all the cute little bulbs, tinsel, and red and green lights, all of which, Ted helped put together. Ted brought the takeout to the little island and took the bowls out, placing the chili ramen in front of her place, and his regular ramen right next to it. Jennifer danced around, grabbed some matches, and lit her pine-scented candle and brought it carefully to the island.

She smiled at him and reached for his hand from across the island. He frowned as he reached for hers. "Are you okay with this?" she asked.

He nodded, looking cautiously into those eyes. His eyes were slightly glazed over with chronic anxiety of course, fear of the great unknown that was undoubtedly coming. "Yes," closing his eyes as she showed him to do in prayer many times.

"Father, thank you for this meal, and the hands that prepared it. Please use it to nourish our bodies. Thank you for this opportunity to share in this together and thank you Father for our provision. While others may go without, we have plenty, and we have You. Please forgive us when we go astray, and please be with all those that need you, and be with those who live in the dark. Amen," she prayed.

She opened her eyes and released his palm. She noticed him studying her hands. She took the pair of wooden chop sticks and broke them apart. Her clumsy fingers took the top one, held it like a pen, while rested her ring finger below the other one and stirred her ramen, before wrapping some of the noodles with the chicken and rings of red chili. She took a bite.

The taste was spicy and had a slight ginger and lime taste to it, along with its unique spice. It wasn't too spicy, nor was it mild. "Thank you for the meal!"

"I didn't buy it," he said, copying her movements perfectly and without deviance to eat from his own bowl.

"Sh!" She slurped the noodles into her mouth, chewing and gulping. "Don't ruin this for me. Let me pretend. Have you used chopsticks before?"

"No," he said.

So, even with no direction you can learn something and master it almost instantly. Tedward, you must a very high IQ. Such a shame that your mind went to waste, and your true personality was burned away.

The broth dripped from his noodles. He never broke eye contact with her. He waited patiently as he took the noodles to his lips and slurped the noodles down. His mouth closed and he chewed slowly.

His fingers trembled uncontrollably, dropping the chopsticks which rattled on the island's surface.

"Tedward?" Deeply concerned, she looked at his hands and moved her gaze to his face. His face contorted. His hand retracted to his mouth, as if stifling some kind of cry. He didn't answer.

She hopped down from her chair, and stood by his side, wrapping her arm around him, and resting her chin upon his shoulder. "Tedward?" She asked again, and she feeling his chest taking stagnant gasps for breath.

"I can—I can taste it," his voice muffled into his hands.

"Are you going to be okay, Tedward?" she asked, petting his arm.

"I'll be—I'll be fine." He stammered.

Eight years is a long time to go without any taste.

"Why don't you take another bite?" she offered. *Is this really the right thing to do?*

His hands reached for the chopsticks once again, poked the ramen, pulling the noodles up from the broth and brought them back to his lips; inhaling, sucking the noodles down swiftly into his mouth, the hot ramen spitting on her face.

She closed her eyes, wiping the broth from her face with a napkin, and when she opened her eyes, she noticed the most peculiar thing. People who didn't know him wouldn't have taken notice of such a thing, but his brown eyes glimmered in the light for what seemed to be the first time, and his lips curved upward naturally. Even some color returned to his cheeks. Lips were pulled back revealing his teeth. She never was too close to notice his teeth though; he had white, healthy teeth. Even his eyes closed ever so slightly, revealing a smiling face.

Not the nasty, deceitful smiles that lie to the beholder. This was a genuine smile. Tears streamed down his face, but of course; he was just reacquainted with an old friend. *Happiness, or some equivalent, however brief it would be.*

He chuckled. Another feature that he overused frequently, but it was fake then. Not this time. It sounded so much different, and not something that was rehearsed a thousand times.

She felt a burden lifted from her chest, and her lips naturally curved into a bright smile. "Well, how is it?"

"It's—" he stammered. "What's the word for it?"

It was a genuine question.

"Delicious if you like it. Disgusting if you hate it." She guided him to an answer.

"Delicious," he replied.

"Well, if you like it so much, we can have more tasty food. Just promise me you'll enjoy it." She smiled, returning to her seat so she could look into the eyes of a very happy Tedward, who enjoyed the meal for once.

"As long as I can still taste something, I'll enjoy it. I promise. Disgusting or otherwise," he answered.

"Well, don't enjoy the disgusting food." She pointed one of her chopsticks at him, winking. "That's not how you enjoy food."

CHAPTER 8

IDENTIFICATION

Leading economics researchers state the tariffs are leading to the rise of a trade war within China. What effect will this have on America? These tariffs are both placed on building materials and gasses, and agricultural supplies and food, such as tea, rice, spices, fruits, and vegetables, of which, previously 50 percent of American imports are from China.

That import dropped 13.4 percent from last year, and researchers say the imports from China are only going to drop down lower.

An anonymous tip from China said the government is actively seeking to change their supply chain to exclude American business and grocers, and trade more directly with neighboring nations, to reduce the need to supply chain to the Americas.

Culain sat at the end of the bar inside Teri Nation. His long fingers constantly tapped the blank piece of paper in front of him. The bar tender served him his glass of red wine. Looking down, he rolled it circularly so the dark liquid inside sloshed around. He sniffed the glass, just like those pompous pricks do at those fancy shmancy balls. Honestly, he never understood why they smelled the wine. Something to do with flavor he guessed, or quality? He sniffed his beverages for a more practical reason, to see if someone would be dumb enough to try to poison him.

"Lighten up. You're so damn serious all the time."

Culain sneered as he tilted his head back. Ilya glared at him, her hands on her hips, tapping. "You took your sweet ass time gettin' here."

"Yeah, well no one bothered to pick me up from the airport." She scuffled around him, sitting at the stool next to him, smiling at Scott as he hurried over. She planted her buttocks on the stool. "Besides, I had some family business I needed to tie up first. I had to fly over to Moscow to take care of that before returning here."

"What will it be tonight?" Scott asked.

"I'll take your house brandy, please!" She hid her accent well.

"Right away." Scott moved behind the bar to pour her drink before handing it to her.

She took it from him. "Thank you, dearest."

"Careful, or I might take her from you," Scott joked while casting a glance at Culain.

"Go ahead, take the bitch. I don't care. More trouble than what she's worth," he shot back. Culain scowled as Scott moved over to the other end of the bar to start taking care of a large group of people that just came in. It was almost always like this on Tuesday, for some reason he didn't quite understand, but he didn't care. He just hoped it wasn't important. Of course, Scott was accustomed to Culain's rash behavior by now.

"So, where's Alex and Blanka?" Ilya sipped from her glass, scanning her red-rimmed eyes over the countertop.

"I gave them the day off. The congressman finally came back, so he'll be helping us a little more directly moving forward." He sipped his drink as he turned to her, elbow propping his chin off the bar top.

"Spadero?" she asked.

"Yeah. So, Sander has his hands tied. What did he report regarding our little, 'Ghost'?"

"I don't know any more than you do." She sipped her drink again, wrapping her left arm around his torso. "Well, would it be the worst thing?"

"Uh, yeah, it would." He brought his voice low.

"Yeah, you're probably—" she nearly brought her glass to the bar top as her fingers trembled around it, ice clattering inside. She smiled as she turned her head mechanically to the right side of the bar as if she sensed something... *off.*

Culain looked behind her, trying to figure out what had her in such alarm. The only thing he noticed was a couple of people. Nothing out of the ordinary there, but what would really have Ilya in such ire? And then, he noticed a man. This man was shorter than those around him and had a very sturdy body in his suit. There were scars on his face. Culain looked closer, and he saw a striking resemblance to the kid that showed up in his email.

"Ilya," his hand reached to her collar and pulled her close, whispering softly in her ear. She turned to him. "Is that him?" *Please don't be him, because this just became damn near impossible if it is.*

"Yes," she whispered back, her teeth clenched as she scowled. "You son of a bitch. You burned the bridge we need to cross, you Irish cunt."

He sighed, covering his face with one hand as he brushed his hair with his fingers. "What?"

"You need to be nicer, you piece of potato cabbage! The people he's with. You threatened with that shitty limerick!"

She jabbed his chest with her finger. The tip of her finger was warm, and his eyes glanced down to see the numerous shapes of mana veins at the tip. The temperature in the room dropped. He swiftly grabbed her finger, squeezing it tightly. "Not here," he shook his head. His eyes scanned the bar and he rose his hand in the air. "Check, please!"

Scott brought the check over. Culain pulled out some cash and slipped it into with the checkbook.

"Come on, we need to head back." He stood from the stool and walked, briskly passing by the group who seemed to be having a joyous time. He glanced over, catching a glimpse of the man they were looking for, and for a moment, things seemed to slow down as he sensed Ilya scurrying behind him.

He collected all the information he received from this *Ghost*. The man's eyes filled with a look that was all too recognizable. A man filled with guilt, regret, and a cancerous despair. And those bags underneath those eyes were familiar.

Damnit. So close, but yet, so far away.

He turned the corner and they moved and evaded numerous people and their drinks.

"This complicates things," Ilya said from behind him as they exited Teri Nation. The snow fell softly on the pavement, and the two walked several blocks before arriving at their hotel.

They took their keys and moved up to the elevator to the upper floors. The elevator was full, and Culain and Ilya stood shoulder to shoulder, silently staring at nothing in particular as the elevator emptied, and then ascended to the top floor. Culain scratched his chin as the door opened and they departed the box, moving down the hall several doors and rapped resoundingly on door number 76.

Footsteps shuffled from behind it. The door creaked open, and a bright light shined in his face. He pushed his way through the doorway and went into the living room.

"If it isn't one thing, it's something else. What happened?" Alexander brushed off Culain's rash behavior. He was used to it by now.

Blanka yawned, covering her mouth, drinking a cup of hot chocolate, leaning against the window. "Break over?"

"Well, Culain done fucked up. Shame on you." Ilya slapped the back of his head.

"How were we to know?" he snapped back at her, flicking her forehead.

She winced, rubbing the spot he flicked with her palm. "Tell them."

"We found him," he answered.

Alexander let out a deep sigh, crossing his arms and looked at the ground. "And what stopped you from calling us so we can put an end to this manhunt?"

"There were people there." Culain glanced over to Blanka who looked down, tilting her cup at the ground. It was empty.

She stood, glaring at the ground. She winded up and threw the empty mug. Culain sucked in the mana from the air through his mana veins in his hands, and the room lit up blue. The temperature dropped; his hand swung and struck the mug, shattering it to dust, and particles of glass spread through the room.

"What is the real reason? Surely, that wouldn't have stopped you of all people," Alexander continued to push him for an answer.

"Really?" Culain snapped, pointing a trembling finger as he scowled at her. "I'm not about to k—"

"Culain!" Ilya snapped her fingers repeatedly in his ears.

He hated that, and he turned back and slapped her hand out of his face.

"Keep it down!"

He closed his eyes, exhaled deeply as his mana veins receded back into his flesh.

"Culain, what happened?" Alexander asked softly, rubbing the sleep from his eyes.

"This was at our own usual spot. Remember those people that tried to speak to us several months ago?"

"You mean the ones you threatened?" Blanka asked. "What about them?"

"He's all buddy buddy with them," Culain answered.

"We had one job." Alexander kicked the coffee table. It flipped over sending the coasters flying to the ground. One shattered underneath the couch. "How do you manage to screw it up *before* we get the assignment?"

"We need to get someone from Boston involved in this," Ilya suggested. "Now, we can't do it, because the couple that Culain threatened to murder will start asking questions they don't need to know the answers to."

"Do you have someone in mind?" Alexander asked.

"Spadero has been trying to get more information on him, but he still comes up empty," Culain softened his tone.

"I want to go home." Blanka stamped her foot on the ground. Her eyebrows pointing downward with creases over her face.

Ilya tilted her head, her silver hair dropping over one side of her shoulders. She walked briskly to her, wrapping her arms around her. "I do too." She scowled at Culain. "Get Spadero on the phone and fix this."

Culain shook his head as he shifted to the other room to call Spadero.

"What is it, Culain?" Spadero voiced coldly.

"Do you happen to have any additional information on our Ghost?" he asked, keeping it abrupt.

"Not really. I'm still sifting through this bullshit report Snells gave Colton. It's a bunch of nonsense, and nothing we can reasonably use. The only thing that really puts anything to use, is the fact that Ghost seemed at one point friendly with a Sergeant Ted Anderson, deceased. I just got this the other day. We still have no information."

"I think we've identified him. Still no name though," Culain replied.

"How inconvenient."

"But I think we've established some kind of pattern. He is real close with some people who frequent a local bar on Tuesdays," Culain continued. "It would appear we may continue to see him, but we can't get close enough."

"Why?" he drew out the question.

"I may have threatened his friends' lives before I know who they were." His finger tapped the back of his phone.

"God fucking damnit! What bar?" the voice was so loud Culain had to pull it away from his ear.

"Teri Nation," he replied.

"What time on Tuesdays?"

"They get there between 9:45 and 10:00 p.m."

"Don't you, or anyone else in there go there! I'll handle it. I'll feed you intel as I find it."

CHAPTER 9

ON THE MEND

Oil spills in Saudi Arabia leads to an estimated fifteen tons of crude oil lost from the supply chain. Saudi Arabia has reported this year, they will be reducing their crude oil shipments to other nations by 15 percent.

According to a report by the largest logistics brokerage, Perfect Transportation Solutions, diesel is to go up by more than 15 percent to match the change in the supply of fuel. Skyrocketing those solutions, according to one broker, will make transporting goods from the ports to the warehouses and stores even further. This broker said she pays for one load, $850.00 from Upper Marlboro, MD to Delaware, OH for 40,000 pounds of dry groceries, and up to $950.00 for refrigerated goods for the same lane. She expects once the market catches up to the change in fuel prices, she is expecting to add nearly $200.00 to both of those lanes.

Erin was in the waiting room, in line at the reception desk of the Memorial Hospital in Worcester. *Was it Wooster? Worchester? Woostah? Worchestah? Woosteshire?* One of the towns it was in, the unpronounceable town because the locals made it so with their numerous dialects. She shook her head at the name, stepping forward. The receptionist was a young man, perhaps just out of high school, and on his way to college. He wasn't a teenager; she knew that much. He had a bit of a scruff.

"Appointment?" He looked up to her.

"Yes, I'm here for visiting hours, actually." She smiled down to him. "Emily Gutenberg," she wrote down her mother's DOB, and slid it into the boy's hand, who took it down, typed it into the computer to look for her appointment. She turned her head up to the ceiling.

"Here you are," he said, pulling out a visitors' pass and handed it to her.

"Thank you." She took the pass in her hand, pulled it over her neck as she followed his instructions down the hall, walking over the tiled floors, squinting at the bright lights emitting from the ceiling, and the white coat doctor's and the various nurses in their scrubs helping patients attached to life-maintaining devices.

This was a very versatile hospital, she found out. Not many like it. At least, not any from Bridgeton, Maine. That's why her mother was here in the first place, to get the best possible care she could. But it was expensive. Even the insurance couldn't pay for everything. The medical out of pocket expenses had skyrocketed over the years as the insurance providers were willing to pay more and more, effectually inflating the cost of medical care.

She hissed at the cost of the medical care. She was not poor by any means, and neither was her family, and yet, even now, the cost of the medicine to deal with the cancer treatment was eating a hole through even her wallet. She was better off than the rest of the family, she had to care for her mother in any way she could, and this was the best way, though, not ideal.

She knocked on the door to her mother's room. Her mother, laying down on the hospital bed resting, had sensors attached to her skin to measure her vitals. They showed she was still healthy enough, but still in need of the various treatments and medicine to help manage the tumor before an appropriate procedure could be scheduled to have the tumor removed, or most of it anyway.

"Yes, Erin, come in," her mother, in her thinning hair, turned, smiling her bright smile, and the sun shone in all the clearer. "Be a dear and shut the door behind you, will you?"

"Yes," she said, crossing the threshold, gently shutting the door behind her. And she pulled up a stool next to her mother, and placed both her hands on her Emily's hands, gently squeezing them. "How are you feeling?"

"I'm well, now that you're here," she replied, her hand squeezing Erin's fingers. The strength in her hand still had not faded.

"I'm glad, but what if I wasn't here?" She asked, leaning closer.

"Well, the pain would be a little less bearable," she answered.

"How's the treatment going?"

"It's going well. Not ideal, but no one ever wants to be here. Erin, don't get cancer. It's not fun," she replied.

"If that was something you could avoid, you wouldn't have it," she answered.

"True." Her face turned, facing the ceiling. "The tumor is receding though, according to my doctor."

"That's great news."

"Now, now, I'm not out of the woods yet," she said. "I still have it, and I'm sure it could swell up any minute if it isn't taken care of properly."

Erin nodded. She knew they wouldn't schedule the removal of the tumor until they've been paid in full. Getting the finances for something like that wasn't easy. Scheduling it was difficult with the health care insurance provider still saying it wasn't 'Medically Necessary.' Since they consider it not essential, regardless of how far the tumor went without the proper treatment, the plan won't cover a cent of it. The hospital was requiring over $50,000 dollars out of pocket to schedule it, and because the surgery would not have been approved, the insurance wouldn't pay for any of the other services she needs to recover from that. More unknown out of pocket expenses. God only knows how much any of that would cost.

She leaned forward, tears glazing over her eyes. "Do you think they'll accept a payment plan?"

"I don't know. I never asked," she said. "But, I think Erin, it's safe to say that without that surgery, what I'm resting on is my deathbed."

"I'm sorry." She exhaled.

"Don't be sorry." Her mother's other hand reached over the side, placing it firmly on both of Erin's. "It isn't your fault, and it may very well be my time."

"But—"

"Erin," she interrupted. "If the Lord calls me, I'm ready to go. It's the world we live in really, I may get placed on a waiting list even if the hospital has what they want, or what they need to perform the procedure. There isn't anything I can do about that.

"You know, I see people here, and I hear them. Scared out of their minds. Because for them, this life is all they know, and it's the only thing keeping them going, a false hope that they will be healed, and that the last chance of their hope is a life changing procedure that they're fortunate enough to meet all the *requirements* to have their services covered in full. They're terrified, and they hinge on the fact that they need to live life as long as they can. Do you know why they're scared, Erin?"

"No." She spoke softly, looking carefully at her mother's weak, but smiling face; her mother's eyes glazed over.

"Because for them, they've accepted that there is nothing beyond this world. For someone like me, and perhaps even the Catholic priest in the other room," she continued. "We accept that there is a life beyond the one we know, and that we'll go to whatever it is. I want you to know, that if tonight, the Lord calls me, I don't want you to be sad, because I'll be happy. And I'll be sure to keep watch over you."

"Thanks, Mom." She bit her lip, squeezing her mother's hands tighter.

There was a brief moment of silence as they stared into one another's eyes, and Emily's fingers caressed her daughter's knuckles.

"There's something else that's bothering you," she said. "I can tell. What's wrong?"

Erin pursed her lips. "Mom," not knowing where to start with her own convictions. *But I made a promise not to say anything about it. I don't even know what it was I saw, or if I'm crazy.* "Something happened a number of months ago, and I can't say what it was because I promised I wouldn't talk about who or what to anyone. But what I saw, and what I experienced that day made me question God. I'm having a problem reconciling what I saw, and the God I thought I knew, but now, I don't even know anymore."

"Erin," she said. "We're not meant to understand everything. I've told you this a thousand times. The Bible isn't a textbook. A very vague roadmap at times, sure, but that's it. Don't turn it into a textbook. It won't make sense logically. Those who do end up being confused use the contradictions inside to disprove anything of the supernatural, but the supernatural exists."

Supernatural. Yeah, that's what I saw.

"As you know, the country is hopelessly divided right now, and our brothers and sisters in Christ are partially to blame for that," Emily wiped her forehead as if there was sweat on it. "And the reason, because they think God to be above reprieve, and therefore, should never be questioned. I disagree with that wholeheartedly, and you should always question. You may not like the answer, but that's okay. But always question."

Erin let out a sigh of relief. Still unsure of what to make of Ted's colored veins over his body that one night still bothered her, since it wasn't part of the natural human anatomy. But with that, she chose to chalk that up as the supernatural, which in turn, was not outside the realm of possibilities, that she was aware of, and could accept it as such.

"Thanks, Mom."

Knock.

"Who's that?" she asked.

"I'm not sure," Emily said, frowning. "Come in!"

The door creaked open, and her care manager came in.

"Mrs. Okofa," Emily said. "Whatever you have to say, you can say it with my daughter in the room."

"Sure." She smiled as he closed the door. She sat down and looked both of them in the eye. "So, when are we scheduling this procedure?"

Erin jerked her head. "Mrs. Okofa, we haven't paid for it yet. We can't schedule it."

Mrs. Okofa looked down in her chart, frowning in confusion. "Well, someone authorized the procedure. So, when are we scheduling it?"

What?

"What do you mean someone authorized it?"

"There is nothing in the way from scheduling it," she replied. "Someone authorized the procedure, and I would not be in this room right now otherwise."

"When was this authorized for?"

"Fifteen minutes ago."

"Well," *who paid for it?* "Mom, you want to schedule it?"

"Do we know who paid it?" Emily asked. "I'd like to thank them; this was no small thing."

"If that was what prevented us from scheduling it before, I can't really tell you. I don't know that information." Mrs. Okofa replied. "Just give me a few dates and I'll work on scheduling it for you with the administrative staff."

Ah, yes. Mr. Anderson. Was this you? If it was, thank you.

CHAPTER 10

SUMMIT

Critical commodities dwindle from the supply chain as demand is on the rise. Imports to the US suffer. President Snells is still holding onto the tariffs despite Congress and the Senate's plea to remove them. There is complete bipartisan support behind this.

Senate majority leader Tran of TX stated: These imports are reducing efficiency in dealing with world leaders around the country. Much of what is affecting us right now has to deal with the lack of insight coming from the President. These imports are increasing productivity of supplies that frankly, we don't even use. I half suspect we'll be building cars out of vinyl within the next year if we keep using our own supplies. I don't think I need to explain why that's a bad idea.

Adam was in the archive, one of the main rooms to be precise, where there was a green screen. The room filled to the brim with wide mahogany bookcases, with dusted off red spines on a variety of different books, written by many different authors throughout the history of Camelot. Of course, there was a great fire long ago, 300 years after the death of King Arthur, and someone re-transcribed all these texts and reprinted them. It was an arduous task that was done by hand. Of course, they take better care of their buildings now to avoid this from happening again, and a mass digitization project was underway.

Adam pulled out a book carefully; this one had a green spine with a blue and red stripe down the middle. This was by far the oldest account, and it detailed the account of the reign of King Arthur when he took everything and made the Administration to protect all of creation from unraveling itself. He read it a thousand times, but this time, he placed it on the table and opened to the end of it. Just to see if there was something, something he missed.

For years, he toiled, scanning pages, new and old, much like the pages of the book he had in front of him. Searching for an answer to the question, a solution rather to defuse the curse his kind was plagued with. He was sick of it. He knew all those under him was sick of it. Needlessly killing normies and the like for being innocent spectators, controlling the very world they inhabited. And all he had for a lead was this book detailing some obscure prophecy that didn't make sense because there was something about it that just felt incomplete. Not just that the ending was missing, and of course the ending was in fact missing, but also the middle seemed to be gone. This was a short section detailing the return of King Arthur and how salvation for Casters might be achieved, but of course, it was missing vital information: How? When? Where? All he could gather is that when King Arthur would return, he might be flying on the back or wings, or even talons of some metal bird. Whatever that meant.

The prophecy was vague. The details were vague, and the solution was still out of his reach. The piece of the one puzzle he wanted an answer to, above all else. This answer, to him, was monumentally more important, in his eyes, than the missing Holy Grail and Pandora's Box. There were two unknowns. Two strangers. Both seemed nearly impossible to track down, though one might be easier than the other. Not by much.

He slowly closed the book shut and sat back, folding his hands on his chest. "Fifteen hundred years since your proposed solution to all this mess, and it only leads us down a rabbit hole none of us want any part of. Fate. God. Death. It's all the same," he leaned back in his chair, waiting for his screen to light up with faces; the summit had begun. "Your solution is not wrong, but there has to be a better way than killing the innocent. How much longer can we continue like this? It's only a matter of time before one of us embraces nihilism, and who would blame them?"

His eyes shot to the door. It creaked open and Bridgette stood behind it.

"What is your report?" he asked.

"We still haven't a word from Culain on this Ghost, nor have any new leads come about as to the whereabouts of Sarah McCurdy or the Grail," Bridgette sighed. "I thought you might like to know that."

"Any other unwarranted Portal Storms? As the traitor she is, I still think there's some merit as to that individual on Dyatlov's Pass, and something tells me they may be connected in some way."

"No."

He leaned forward, propping his chin up as he bent over the table. "Three vital pieces of information. Three unknown motivations. Three individuals. Almost all of which we know absolutely nothing about, and I fear they may be connected somehow. If I can get my hands on one of them, that may be the key I need. But I need someone who can pull something out of a hat just to get one of them." He exhaled heavily as the first face popped up on the screen, followed by another, until ten faces were on the screen. "Stick around, Bridgette. I need to bounce a few ideas off you after this."

When he turned his attention to the screen all the usual faces were there, ready and waiting. There was only one woman among them, Claire from France. They all reported in promptly, all revealing their faces, some smiling, others jaded. All of which, different walks of life, different demeanors, and of course, differing objectives. He couldn't discount the possibility of someone being a traitor, as minimal that reality might be, it is still a possibility.

Well, time to get started.

"You all know why I called for this summit," Sander said, addressing them on the screen, tapping his finger on the table with his left hand. A pad of paper was in front of him, and he turned a clicking pen in his right hand. "Now, this has been an issue for several months, and we are nowhere closer to solving any of the problems.

Obviously, one of them can wait. Secondly, we have a rogue somewhere in the Boston area of the United States," he looked specifically to Colton, "He's not cleaning up any mana residue, which is a problem for reasons I don't need to dwell on. The other, is the biggest problem of all. The Holy Grail is still missing, and we are nowhere closer to finding it. Stolen by Sarah McCurdy, who is also nowhere to be found."

"I don't have any new information on either of those two," Colton began. "I have been actively working with Spadero, who is in communication with Culain to try to find this Ghost. I don't have a reason to suspect he is a Caster, nor have I heard from McCurdy."

"Could be a possessed normie," Hector offered, the Caster who was assigned the territory south of the Rio Grande.

Shit. That won't do. That won't do at all. He shifted uncomfortably in his chair, looking carefully at Colton, who was the first to speak. The first to speak usually hides something. But not always.

"That is a little too optimistic, Hector," Claire puffed out smoke. "Especially for someone about whom so little is known. Honestly, it is far more likely that he is this *Devil's Pass* character that was reported. Ukraine, was it?"

"Why do you assume this Ghost was under my domain? We don't know that," Mikhail said.

"We don't know anything." Elias exclaimed. "We need concrete information, not speculation."

"But without an idea of where to start, we are hopelessly speculating," Claire continued. "We have a goal, but no foreseeable way to achieve that goal here. The report McCurdy gave us on the individual was lacking in detail."

"But can we trust that report? After all, that report came from a traitor," Wang interjected. "Quite frankly, what if we cannot trust Colton."

"Enough of that." Sander spoke sternly, glaring at the Chinese Administrator. "We don't have time for any of that. You all know, just like all of you, I appointed him in his role. He can be trusted." *Though I cannot completely disregard that possibility.*

"I think we're asking all the wrong questions here, Sander Bucho," Daiki said. "I think we need to know just how urgent this is. What are the stakes involved?"

"Excuse me?" Sander replied.

"Well, the Holy Grail, which is fused with Pandora's Box, has been greatly unused since it's fusion, thanks to King Arthur," Daiki continued.

"That was a horrible idea," Hector spoke sternly. "Look at where it got us. A history of murders on our conscience. But do continue."

"If we knew why someone would want the Grail to begin with, perhaps that can give us more of a firm foundation as to where to locate it. That is the pressing issue," Daiki finished.

There was silence in the room. The faces turned their heads up as if to think heavily on the subject. Most of the faces told Sander they were thinking earnestly on the subject, getting all the cogs turning, as it were. But so much time has passed, how much more time before whatever leads they have run cold.

"Sander, Arjun speaking," said the Indian. "What function did the Holy Grail serve prior to King Arthur fusing it as a lid to Pandora's Box?"

"Nobody knows. I've scoured documents and history books prior to King Arthur's reign, and there is nothing to signify that it's ever been used as anything but this lid. Clearly, if someone removed the Grail from the Box, a direct link to Pandora and Earth would be formed. Which is why it's the lid. No one's been able to study it since," Sander answered.

"So perhaps this person wants to remove the Grail from the Box to find out what it does. So they separate the Box from the Grail—"

"That is no small feat. The fusion is paired with magical weaves no one understands," Sander interrupted Mikhail. "It is beyond anything I've seen or studied, and I'll dare not touch those weaves."

"And if the fusion was bypassed by force, what do you suppose would happen?" Colton asked.

"I'd assume the force needed to make that happen would rip the Box open and shatter the Grail. And with it, the Threads of Creation would come undone," Sander answered.

"You assume, so, you don't know?" Claire asked, tapping her cigarette to an ashtray.

Before Adam could answer, Obi said, "Why would someone want to do that? That is a fool's errand. Unless there is some kind of benefit to doing that, there would be no real motivation to even have the Grail or the Box."

"Yes, but that would just be too evil of a problem for one of the Casters of our ranks to do, not to mention trying to clean that up would lead to—" Oliver trailed off.

He might be on to something then. But what are you thinking precisely. You certainly don't have anything to hide here, and no connection to any of the mysteries we're unfolding.

There was some silence in the room as Oliver gathered his thoughts.

"Yes?" Mikhail urged him. "Don't keep me and the motherland waiting in suspense. What's going on in that head of yours?"

"The problem is we don't know exactly how the Box was fused to the Grail, so even entertaining that idea would be pointless," Oliver dropped his head to his computer screen as he casually yawned. "Forget I said anything."

"No, I think you might be on to something. Go on," Claire replied.

"Fusions are like locks. Mana veins intricately woven in between objects and left there. We don't know what those patters are like as they are invisible after some time, and we ourselves can't sense the intricate patterns. My assumption is that the pattern used was so incredibly complex we don't use it anymore, and if someone was to attempt to undo that pattern, they may not only sever the Grail from the Box, but in so doing, might break the Grail. There is no easy solution for anyone to try to sever the connection from both artifacts."

Daiki tapped his finger on his desk, and it was loud enough for everyone to hear it. "Sander Bucho, what might happen if someone attempted this, and the Grail was destroyed?"

"The Holy Grail is what holds creation together. We Casters, our souls essentially started there, or something like it. If that was destroyed, we, and all life, all creation would cease to be. If someone broke the Grail, and it is impossible, they would do the impossible and destroy everything: Hells, Heavens, and Earths," Sander answered. *The worst possible outcome.* He already felt his heart rate skip a beat just thinking of the idea.

"So, in short, it would not benefit anyone for even trying," Claire replied.

"Unless they were a true nihilist," Mikhail commented.

"Or believed they had sufficient enough power to destroy the Box once it was removed from the Grail," Colton said.

"We all know it's impossible," Wang said.

"That won't stop someone from trying," Obi said. "And if it happens, they might weaken the connection between the Box and the Grail, and the dark spirits from the other side will start inhabiting this side of creation."

"We've seen this before," Adam replied gravely. He knew where the history books repeated something like this. It was nearly a hundred years ago with the rise of Hitler. Well, that is how they told the stories to normies. He was placed there. The Administration put him up to it.

"No." Elias spoke sternly as if to read his mind. "None of this. I will not do it. We solve this before it gets to that."

"We need to start making preparations if we need to repeat it again," Mikhail sighed.

"But if we accept that we're going to do this, again, and kill millions, if not *billions* of people, *again*, we won't solve the problem. And when it gets out of control, we won't be equipped to deal with any of these mysteries that have now fallen on our laps." Elias said, his face rejuvenated, and his voice filled with passion. Of course, Adam knew the German was none too proud of his nation's history. Why would he be? They have two world wars under their belt, and to think to add another one, but on who's soil would this start?

"Colton, Hector, work together to track down and find McCurdy immediately. I will have Culain and Spadero continue their investigation of the Ghost. He, whoever he is, likely poses the least possible threat. Mikhail, I need you to pair up with Claire to find out what happened over at Devil's Pass. Get me something. Anything. I want to find out who this person is, and I think that whoever it is, has his hands in more than one of our administrations. This person needs to be ousted. Meeting adjourned."

Sander pulled himself out of the conference call. Exhaling heavily, he turned to Bridgette, who looked at him disapprovingly.

"Really? Another World War? Are you serious? Look, maybe one of the Casters is sick and tired of all this unnecessary killing and wants to destroy the Grail. Maybe they think a universe that doesn't exist is better than the universe we live in. Damnit, Adam."

He knew she was spouting off nonsense. She didn't truly believe that, or at least he didn't think so, but there was something there. "We created these circumstances, have continued to these last fifteen hundred years. We've been cultivating a world where nihilism may be the best alternative, and our worst nightmare. Dear god! Bridgette, you're a genius."

He pulled up his email and started typing away.

"Why?" She looked at him, confused.

"You may have offered us the very information we needed to find a motive," he replied. "Yet a problem remains. Where is it?"

No doubt Hector will call me within the next few days to arrange a meeting to locate McCurdy. Fool. I already know where she is, and I'm not telling him.

Colton shut his monitor off. He glanced over to his safe, locked with gray mana veins protecting it from damage from the inside. The safe itself rested above an arcane circle he drew to keep the mana and the curses inside, preventing spilling. No one except he and Sarah knew where the Grail was, and he intended to keep it that way, at least until further study could be made to remove the Grail from this Box and rid this conflict once and for all.

He turned forward, looking at all his recent files, pulling one up, with a younger woman, late 20s with silver hair and red pupils. *Gwen Swan*, the file read. It was easily a hundred pages long, containing every accolade the woman had under her belt. He knew she was hiding something, but the question was what?

She couldn't be trusted, but she was far too valuable to attempt to discard, assuming that was even possible.

He scratched his head, evaluating the world map for all possible scenarios.

"I have the Grail. Sarah is in Alaska with Swan. Gwen is hiding something. Hector will likely call me tomorrow to start looking for Sarah. I must think of something for that little scenario. Mikhail will be sending troops to the East Coast to get rid of this Ghost. I need to kill Snells. Still waiting on the other file." He kicked his desk. "Some pompous bastard was out and about, supposedly with some Georgian accent in Devil's Pass. I doubt that's related to any of this."

"But Gwen is dangerous." He tapped his fingers firmly against the wooden desk, weighing his options and all the intricacies of all his plotting.

Three unknowns he counted. The first, was this Ghost character. Still no good information was sent his way pertaining to his precise location or identity. The man should be dead. Of course, if he was a normal man, he certainly would be. He may have been one of the few who belonged to a Caster's family, perhaps the Old Blood. This unknown man over by Devil's Pass. Why was he looking for the Grail there? It made no sense, unless to purposely throw everyone off. And Gwen. A dangerous manipulator if ever there was one. Of course, she had her uses, and wasn't someone he could easily dispose of. She made that abundantly clear. The main problem with her was she would never do anything without knowing the reason why, and she also knew she was the only Caster willing to do any of those things, leveraging that fact to her advantage with negotiations. He couldn't lie to her, or else risk her wrath. Gwen was a problem. She knew too much. And if he attempted to dispose of her, it must be all or nothing, because after a failed attempt, who would she tell other than Sander?

CHAPTER 11

BOSTON DUCK TOUR

Hostilities continue to rise across the sea. While Russia is underneath acquisition of bordering nations, the tensions appear to be reaching their arms overseas with Russian and Chinese fleets sailing from across the seas.

Chief Commanding Officer Malcolm is not concerned with the military forces overseas. He stated he has divisions in space monitoring would be enemies of the state, and would harp on them quickly should, "[They] so much as think about firing a missile."

Jeff sat on his couch in his little studio apartment he arranged with Malcolm, his direct Superior Officer with Black Eagle. After all, he was to remain there to keep an eye on this *Ted Anderson*. Of course, Jeff knew who it was. Stood and walked to the window, opening it to allow the gentle air to fill the small space. The cool breeze moved by him and brought a chill when it pressed his damp shirt. He scanned the surrounding streets.

Gazing toward each trash can down Summer Ave right in Dorchester, he wiped the sweat from his brow before he returned to the couch, flicking through the channels until he found the news station.

Tensions are rising with the US and Russia. According to sources inside the White House. Russia has halted all trading to the US President Snells declined to speak further on the matter, but did tell us that he is, 'working on speaking with the Russian President to open up trading again.'

"We saw that coming. Damnit," he said to himself. "Steel, fuel, and iron." He turned off the TV. "Those are imports we desperately need. I suppose Snells could strong arm him, but is he trying to avoid conflict?"

Jeff couldn't help but consider the idea that Snells grew too soft. Of course, peace often did that. *What was the saying again? Great men make great times; great times produce weak men, and weak men create bad times.* It doesn't solve anything—it just makes things a little more tolerable.

His phone rang.

"Michael, what is it?" he answered it.

"Hey, we're going on the Boston Duck Tours this afternoon. Wanna come with?" Michael replied.

His hand trembled, remembering precisely why he was kept here instead of redeploying. Not that it made any of this any easier. *Mr. Anderson. Ghost. What or whoever you are. You aren't bombing shit on my watch.*

"Is Ted going to be there?" he asked.

"No, I invited him, but he declined. Said he was busy, and all that." His tone dropped ever so slightly.

Jeff knew Michael well enough to understand that there was sympathy in his voice. As if this little errand Ted went on was something passionate or filled with tragedy. Ted Anderson or Ghost was the source of so much tragedy. *What did he have to be sorry about?*

"Sure. I'll come over. Where are you meeting?"

"At the Prudential Center on Huntington Ave. You remember, it's right off the Green Line."

"I'll be there."

Jeff stood outside the Prudential Center. His eyes scanned the streets, the trash cans, anything that might have something hidden inside it. One can't be too careful. He waited for Michael as he eyed numerous pedestrians jolting by, some in the hurry to get somewhere. Hands briskly wiping their pants hastily back and forth, slipping into the snow. Other were much less worrisome, loitering around, their hands in their pockets to shield them from the winds, icy winds they were. Though the clouds appeared ready to drop some snow, it was a clear day.

The sound of patterned speeches and footsteps clapped behind him. Jolting, he turned, eyes gaped open as he saw people coming out of the Prudential Center, many chatting away with little silent jeers, eager for this Duck Tour.

"Jeff!" a hand waved higher than the rest.

It was a small hand, a soft one. He settled down, feeling his heart rate rise underneath all the stress of sudden noise. One can't be too careful. *Especially when someone like Ghost could be around.*

"Michael," he said, reaching for his wallet. "I'm about ready."

Michael squirmed his way through the crowd of people pushing their way to the ticket booth for the Duck Tour. His other hand held Samantha's. She wore a winter jacket over some jeans. Behind her was a man, much taller than Michael, and he pushed himself forward adjusting his glasses. He followed closely behind Jennifer.

This man shook his hand firmly when he got close, introduced himself bluntly as Tim. He should have known. Any man who introduces himself in such away is always named Tim. Almost like all the Tims in the world have their own little convention on how to introduce themselves to strangers. *Fucking Tims!* Maybe that's why he didn't remember seeing him before. Now that he thinks of it, he remembered Tim at the bar, though, barely made an effort to talk to him, as Ghost was always nearby. Always watching.

Jennifer had a soft demeanor, a gentle voice, and yet, with all those fluffy traits, he could tell when he looked at her, and the sharp glare she gave him, despite that smile. She told him without saying anything, that there was one thought that connected her to him: Hatred.

What do you know, Jennifer? What did he tell you?

Of course, he knew he would never get an answer to either of those questions, but perhaps he could get some clues. He was certain she didn't know he knew she lied to him, or that he saw right through her ruse. Despite the fact he caught on this little sharp gaze, like a fish on a hook. Forcing himself to breathe, ignoring the fact that his throat tightened with anxiety, he found this to be a precarious situation to be in. After all, Jennifer might be the bait, and he the fish, and Ghost could very well just string him along. Jennifer might not realize this, but Ghost was using her.

Ghost, always scheming, getting civies caught up in your web of lies. What are you plotting? If you aren't blowing up orphanages, you're always planning some coup. Who are you trying to overrun?

Jennifer moved past them, and they eased up toward the Duck Tour.

The five of them purchased their tickets, and moved onto the amphibious boat, the wheels on the ground, ready to start driving, and the tour of Boston to commence. He didn't care for Boston all that much. Too much noise. Too many people, and of course, the stench of regrets as he saw a man, with the BDU jacket, smoking a joint around the corner. There was a patch on that BDU: Airborne. Homeless. Of course. The same fate that they all shared. It was inevitable. At least, so he thought. It wasn't a fate he wanted to share. *That doesn't suit me at all.*

He took a seat next to Michael, and Tim on his other side. And then, his duty tugged at him, and he turned to Jennifer. "So, no Ted today?"

She turned a grin toward him. *She's good at faking a smile.* "No. He had some things to take care of."

"What things would those be?"

"Oh," Jeffrey felt Michael's arm around his shoulders. "You don't know. He's in stocks."

"On a Saturday?" he raised his eyebrow, turning abruptly to him.

"Yeah, well, he's somewhat of a workaholic now," Sam chuckled. "He was working 120 hours a week I think, that's what he said, right Jennifer?"

"Just about. Fortunately, he takes time out of his busy schedule for me," she said, twiddling her braid with her fingers. Jeffrey saw her smile, gleaming toward Samantha as if to trade a few silent words he wasn't a part of. Without context, he knew he'd never be able to listen in on *that* conversation.

"Yeah, tough one to crack, that one," Tim replied. "Sam, I want to say, you did the right thing. Skipping out on brunch that day."

Is this the context I'm missing? Jeff thought to himself as he resolved to merely listen, and almost entirely remove his mouth from the equation.

"Yeah," her curved lips flattened. "Well, sometimes I'm not so sure, but I think we have Jennifer to thank."

"Perhaps," Jennifer said, her voice dropped low. He noticed she stared daggers into his eyes. "It is best not to talk about him right now, after all, the tour is about to begin!"

The boat drove into the water, splashing on both sides. It reminded him of the many people at sea, lost. Memories and dreams became useless once drowned out at sea. No one would ever notice them gone. Not the dreams anyway. His own dream vanished; just like theirs. Just like the many he killed, stealing, and murdering their dreams. After all, one's dreams stop at their deaths.

They say Russians die in war just to die, and the French once died for love, while the English die for honor, and Americans die for freedom. Yes, he willingly gave up his freedom to give it to others, but now, he found the poison inside his mind pulling the nerves in his brain apart, his guilt for stealing the freedom of others. Yes, that's precisely what he did. And now, he was enslaved to the reminder that was his curse. He deserved to die, but even he can never admit to all the crimes he committed. How could he when all he wished was for the guilt to numb?

"Hello! Are you listening?"

He shook his head, turned to Michael, who was trying to get his attention. "What?" His brother showed some concern, and even a warm squeeze on the shoulder. His shoulder tensed up.

"Are you okay?"

"Yeah, I'm fine," he ignored the lady speaking about the tour.

"Okay, so, I was trying to figure out how long you've known Ted. He doesn't seem to try to get out with us nearly as much since you ended up staying." Michael said.

"I'm quite fond of an answer myself," Sam added. "I'd love to know why you aren't out there. I mean, war is picking back up. Not that I'm not happy you're safe, but I feel like the government isn't taking the overseas conflict seriously."

"The government hasn't had need to take anything seriously in over a decade," Jeff answered. "I still have some leave time here, and my CO decided it was time for me to take a little break, get some R&R. The functionality of our military doesn't rest solely on me." *Damn civies. Never understand anything beyond the only world they've known. Toss them in fire, and they'll sing a completely different tune.*

"But what about your relationship to Ted? He seems to want to distance himself from you. Even I've noticed that," Tim said. "I was under the impression that bonds of military brothers and arms were unbreakable."

They're supposed to be. But considering Ghost, that makes it impossible. Considering who I am, and what I'm forced to be, that camaraderie is forever out of our reach. This dynamic forced Jeff's heart to race, insulted, irate, and of course, humiliated that people such as these, who know nothing of the Hell he's seen, forcing him to think back as to why he can't enjoy a moment's rest. Maybe they meant well. Or maybe, using him as a tool to further understand their 'Ted'. A tool. A disgusting truth.

"Ted and I had a complicated relationship. We ran into one another a few times, both in the briefing environment, and in the grit of the battlefield. To say we were in constant disagreement on solutions was an understatement. I swear," he chuckled, "sometimes we were close to just throwing fists at one another." *That's true enough.*

"Siblings often throw punches at one another. It's what we do," Jennifer smiled. "But my Tedward isn't the confrontational type."

Liar.

"Of course," Jennifer said, as if to answer his sudden thought. "He can be abrasive at times, but more so to himself than anyone else. It was almost as if someone close to him hurt him."

What did he tell you?

He wanted to scowl. No. He wanted to punch her in the face. Just for knowing. Whatever it was Ghost told her could get him shot. *Ghost, I hope you know that by not being here, you can't defend yourself.*

"He's very abrasive to others, from what I remembered. Wasn't always the ethical soldier, after all. But the higherups always did like his results," he responded. *Jennifer, I can play this game too.*

"How do you mean?" Tim asked, pushing his glasses up closer to his face.

Wait. How old do they think he is?

"I can't get into any specifics, but he did many questionable things, as no one at war is ever presented with a moral choice," Jeff answered.

With closed eyes, Jennifer shook her head. She turned to Sam, "So, sad of me to ask this, me being the romantic one, but I do want him to come out more with us. I can't be the only one to help him."

"Still no therapist, right?" Samantha asked, picking up on what he guessed were Jennifer's subtleties.

"Hush." Jennifer snapped.

"Perhaps," Tim interjected, leaning back into the seat, looking at the rippling waters at the side. "It would be good to get him to do something. Like these tours, or perhaps something else. Help ease his mind into something a little more public, make him feel like a real human being for once. Yeah?"

"He doesn't do anything." Jennifer scolded him. *Oh, he's doing something all right. I don't know what, but that shit's gotta stop!* "It's like pulling teeth just to get him out, but I must admit he's been more open. After all, I managed to get him to order out with me for once."

"Didn't you do that when you were, uh, you know?" Sam asked, as if hiding something just because Jeff was right there. *I need context!*

"No, that was take-out. We went to this noodle shop and ordered some ramen. Like, he ordered it. I didn't do it for him," she smiled, seemingly forgetting Jeffrey was there. "Sam, I forgot to tell you. He said it was delicious."

Sam blinked. "He did? Like, you didn't beat it out of him, did you?"

Michael. Why did you invite me here? At least present me with a situation I can actually use. I can't use this. I'm like the spare wheel here on a bus. Let's hope one of those tires don't pop.

"No. And that was the best part." She was vibrant; her personality was shining all the clearer, like someone who knew some despair, but above all, someone filled with a certain type of joy found in so little people. A joy that, regardless of circumstances, nothing could take that away.

I could. I can do it so easily. But why the attention on taste?

"I don't get it. Explain it to me," Jeff requested.

"He can't taste anything. Or at least, he couldn't. Not until just now," Sam replied.

"Sam, I saw him smile," Jennifer continued.

"He's always smil—"

"No, Michael dearest," she waved her finger at him. "Not like that. I could tell. It was plain that this smile was more than just a mask. He cried over noodles."

"Jennifer, I'm going to invite Ted to come get some coffee with me downtown next week." Michael shifted in his seat, pulled out two slips of paper, and reached over to Jennifer, who extended her arm to meet his. "I'll give you the details when and where, but why don't you come by, crash our little coffee bromance, as it were," the two of them chuckled, as if they both knew of some joke shared only between the two of them. "I got these from work. Take him to it."

"The Boston Symphony Orchestra. It's been some time since I've been to a show there. Do you know what's playing?" She pursed them, not bothering to look at them.

"You could read the tickets you know," Michael snickered.

"Michael," Tim interjected. "If you know Jennifer, you *would* know she never reads anything. Other than Jane Austen."

"Hey," she poked him in the chest. "I read!"

"What was the last thing you read?" Tim asked.

"'Sense and Sensibility.'"

Jeff took a mental note of the information being discussed here. The love of literature, a romance novelist in particular seemed odd. Not in the context of them talking about it, but rather associating this with a dangerous man, Ghost, who by all accounts of who knew him, would say there wasn't a single romantic thing about the man, nor amiable. He bit his lip, contemplating the different personality this Ghost showed them, his brother of all included. He continued to listen as the bystander, knowing who *this* Ghost was.

"Point made. Ha!" Tim pulled his arms behind his head.

"So, anyway. It's some anime soundtracks by a string quartet, a choir, and I think there's a brass section. I don't watch anime, so I'm not all that interested in going. I got these from work. I don't know why they chose this of all things to give us, but hey, it's free."

You all, Ghost has you all wrapped around his finger. Doing whatever he wants you to do, telling you whatever sob story he can come up with. If you knew the damn truth, you'd know the monster he is. Blowing up orphanages in Bagdad. I still can't fathom why he'd do that, of all things.

A loud alarm.

Clemens bolted upright, the red lights shining brightly. Swiftly pulling himself out of his barracks bed, he darted toward his gear. The rest of his platoon followed as they rapidly marched down the hallways, with their equipment fastened to their bodies, side arms, long-ranged hunting rifles, grenades, and flashbangs. Overkill for a base like this, considering no one knew where they were.

"Prisoner escape. Task Force members: Seven, Nine, Eleven, Thirteen, Twenty-seven, and Thirty-one, are on the run. Send out the hounds now." Nakamura's voice, stern as ever.

The howling of the canines echoed down the halls. Footsteps clamoring. Rifles engaged, safeties off, and the dark night was none too favorable against these people. But of course Seven would know that, the creepy little bastard.

Pushing through the door, his eyes scanned some scrappy work for hiding tracks, "Eleven o'clock."

His platoon pushed past the dirt, scouring the tracks. His company found themselves in a desert storm, hiding just north of Area 51. Any tracks were now erased in the storm, almost like Seven would know that a storm was coming, predicting the impossible. He was filled with surprises.

The dust obscured his vision, pelting him, hot and scorching. It crawled their way into his BDUs, searing and marking his skin underneath. The uncomfortable sensation was irritable. He grimaced as the sand scratched his face.

What are the other little shits doing?

Surely, they'd all be missing, yet the rest of them are just hiding in their bunks or sleeping. Not even a peep. They found nothing.

Little shit. Of course, what the hell was I thinking. Seven ain't an idiot. He'd thrown us off into a different direction. Damnit.

"Target sighted. Target picked up, returning to base," Sergeant Ted Anderson.

Of course, Ted would've known that we went the other direction, took a gamble in any other direction and happened to find them.

"You find all of them?" Nakamura's voice choked in.

"Affirmative."

"Everyone, return to base."

Seven, you son of a bitch!

The missing members of Task Force Seven were thrown out of a Humvee, operated by Ted Anderson, who gave him a mirthless smile. The sneer was one of contempt, but oddly, not one at Clemens. It was just easier to justify against someone like Clemens. After all, he himself knew he was unlikeable. By anyone really.

Clemens averted his gaze to scowl at the little devils on the ground, their hands zip tied, kneeling on the dirt. Nakamura, in her exhausted agony came walking out of the facility, her hands behind her back, her black hair tied firmly into a bun as she frowned. It was never good when she frowned. No. Not like last time.

And his worst nightmare. She scowled at him. *She's going to chew me out.*

"Clemens. Where were you?"

"The locks were fastened before I was relieved from my post, Lieutenant," he answered. It was the truth.

"So, you didn't kill, Smith?"

"No, ma'am."

She shook her head, clearly disapproving his answer. It was the truth, but here, at Area 51, truth didn't matter. Just orders. Nothing else. Fall in line just like everyone else or be hammered down. Or find oneself hanging from the tree the next morning. It wouldn't be the first time.

He remembered what happened to the last soldier who refused to fall in line, asked one too many questions. Ted Anderson asked questions too, riding that small, thin line, but never more than what was necessary. Clemens never asked questions. Not his business. Just follow orders, or be just like Gunnery Sergeant Ramirez, hanging for all to see. Set as an example by Nakamura, and no one questioned anything since. Don't cross her. A lesson he learned early with this new reforming company: Black Eagle.

Her hands came to her sides as she looked at the demons, all with bruised and bleeding faces. *Ted Anderson wasn't kind to them.*

Seven's eyes were swollen; one was left open. She knelt in front of him, her hand caressing his swollen cheek. He hissed, jerking his neck back. "D—don't touch me!"

"Aww," she said. "My sweet little boy. Don't be like that. I'm trying to protect you. Why'd you run?"

He didn't answer. She pulled out a handkerchief, and spat into it, wiping the boy's face like he was her child.

But you're not a child. You're a murderer.

She turned, whistling, "Anderson, have Seven tied up behind a post."

"Ma'am," he scowled, pulling Seven up from the ground.

"No! No! No!" Seven squirmed, but to no avail; the zip ties did their job. Anderson dropped the monster on the ground, took the rifle off his back, and struck him in the head with the butt of it. He was knocked out, blood staining the sand covered floor.

The rest of the shits remained silent; those little arms clung close to their chests. The girls had their hair covering part of their faces, turning their head in sudden movements, terrified as their bodies quivered.

Nakamura turned to Clemens with a devilish smile. And when she smiled like that, one must be prepared for the worst, and no amount of preparation was ever sufficient.

"Clemens, get in my office while I tidy things up, I've got a favor to ask."

Favors. More like death threats.

"Yes, ma'am."

Clemens sat in a chair in Nakamura's office. The room was brightly lit, and it had a wooden desk, and of course, pictures on the wall which showed a part of who she was outside the uniform. A family woman, married to the Colonel—a prick just like her. The door creaked behind her.

He jolted.

"Oh." The door slammed shut. "Don't even bother standing up."

Her voice, cold when she was in here, at least to him. Seriously, one might think she didn't like him.

"Now, clearly, Smith is dead. I need to write a report on what happened, and he was to relieve you." She sat at her desk, a clipboard in hand. "Tell me what happened."

"zero hundred hours, he came, relieved me as per protocol. And I left to my barracks. He was alive when I left," he answered. His hands were in front of him, and his thumbs were shaking.

"Now, he was murdered. His head twisted back like a Russian doll," she replied. "Are you telling me you didn't do it?"

"No, I didn't."

"It would be best if you didn't lie to me," she snapped. Her eyes narrowed, staring into his.

"That's a lie. I didn't do it. There are cameras you can look at to confirm who did it." *She's trying to frame me.*

"Honestly, I could check. But I'm not going to." She jerked her head to the side and sneered. "Why can't you be more like Sergeant Anderson? He plays the game we play just as well, follows the rules."

"You can't get away with that. There has to be an investigat—"

"Clemens. Do you see any military police?" She was right. None here in Area 51. "I arranged that. Go ahead and try to test my patience again. Seven is tied to a post out in the back."

"And?"

"You're going to beat him to a pulp."

"No."

She frowned. "Let me remind you. You're expendable. They aren't. When I decide to hang you, you're not going to stop me from slandering your name to your family." She leaned over the desk, her chin over her folded hands. "I told you I'd keep quiet after your little incident, but if you don't play along, I'll hang you for the jeers."

His heart sank, and it became painful to even breathe; jaw dropped open. The one terrible thing he did, causing him to grow cold with all the horrible things he would continue to do. But this was something even the Devil would be ashamed of, for devils don't do this. Only humans do, and they are far worse. But then again, orders are orders. His entire palms shook, sweat dripping down in angst.

"You ordered me to do it," he attempted to stare her down.

She tilted her head to the other side. "Now, that's not true, is it?" She sneered.

He sucked in the air through his teeth.

"Do we understand one another?"

"If you want him beaten up, why don't you do it?"

"Because I don't hit quite as hard as you," she answered, pointing out the window. "Now, he's out there. If I find he can walk tomorrow, you'll be hanged."

Clemens nodded.

"Dismissed, and make sure not to disappoint,"

"Yes, ma'am." He frowned, clenching his teeth and his fists at his side.

"Good doggie."

He dashed out of the room, slamming the door behind him as he made his way, furious, stamping his feet with every step, scowling with a cringing face. *Ted Anderson. You son of a bitch. Seven, if it wouldn't get me killed, I'd fucking kill you.*

He rushed out of the facility, marching past the chain-linked gates.

There he was, dark hair over his swollen face, blood dripping on his side, chained behind a wooden post. The little demon coughed, his legs sprawled right in front of him. The boy's face averted his gaze from the ground, staring wide eyed, tears glimmering in the moonlight. *What did he have to be sad about? Nothing.*

Clemens grimaced as he bolted toward the boy.

"NO," he cried.

Clemens grabbed him by the hair, lifting his body from the ground, legs dangling down.

"NO! NO! NO!" the boy's cries were akin to that of a baby, high pitched screaming.

Clemens squinted; ears pierced. His hand formed a fist at his side, thrashing at the demon, tied, defenseless against the post. His fist made contact, striking it hard in the face.

"MOMMA! HELP!" it cried.

"You have no Momma!" Clemens thrust forward, his knee striking Seven in the chest. Ribs cracked. He pulled Seven's hair back, punching again. And again. And again. Until the screams stopped, and just raspy breathing sounded. Seven hung by its wrists, face swollen, blood drooling from its mouth.

Clemens grimaced, kicking it hard in the stomach until Seven spat out shattered molars.

Seven coughed, tears dripping off his cheeks into the sand.

Clemens took his fists again, striking Seven in the face, blood lining his eye lids, dripping down. He pulled his feet up, kicking its shins.

"Momma," the devil cried.

Faker.

"Help me. Please. I'll be a good boy."

He kicked its shins again.

Crack.

"MOMMA! Help me, please. I'll do whatever you want. Please!"

He kicked the unbroken shin.

"Ah! Momma!" it cried, taking a back hand across the face. More blood drooled to the ground.

Clemens pulled its hair, shoving it to the post.

Thud.

"Momma, please."

Clemens tightened his fist again, punching it in the jaw.

Cough. Again. *Cough.* Again. *Crack.*

It breathed. Whatever this thing was, it breathed. It can't scream anymore, blood drooling out of its open mouth, unable to close. Broken jaw. Broken shins. Fractured ribs. This ought to be enough.

Good riddance.

"Good job."

Clemens turned around to Nakamura holding a cam recorder, undoubtedly recording the entire incident. She was escorted by Ted Anderson, and two other armed guards. "I'll save this for later. At ease."

She walked toward Seven and knelt in front of him. The devil panted, unable to speak, but turned its ugly head toward her.

"How's my little boy?"

Clemens looked down, uncomfortable as he stood at attention. In that moment, he wanted nothing more than to strangle her, but he would be shot before he got his hands around her filthy neck. She looked, bringing her hand near its puffy cheek. It jerked its head away from the hand, touched carefully by her other hand.

"There, there. Did he hurt you?"

Again, it didn't say anything, just drooled, but its head nodded. Her head reached forward, touching its bloody, swollen head.

"Ahl. Ahl," it said.

"Are you going to run again?" she asked.

"Nol. Nol." It coughed.

She patted her hand on his cheek. "Good boy. Don't do it again, okay?"

It nodded.

CHAPTER 12

COFFEE

As exports drastically slow down, along with the hostile interactions coming from overseas by way of the east and the west, and asked about the disruptions in the supply chain for supplies, Chief Commanding Officer Malcolm had this to say:

I'm not worried. I get my supplies direct. Our acquisition team gets holds of their due of the supplies before Uncle Sam does, so our operations remain undisrupted. It gets harder, sure, but for us, business is as usual. Now, that doesn't mean it doesn't affect us, so we have research and development on a couple of projects, and with them, we've been able to produce some significant tech. Currently, foreseeing some issues rising with the supply chain disruption, we are slowly working our way back to steam powered and electric technology. Currently, we have a tank in development that is strictly electric. We expect once it's done, it can fully operate for three weeks without a full recharge.

Ted Anderson stood over the edge of a roof staring down at a large apartment complex, with curved windows where he knew Jeff Clemens was assigned. This bothered him. Not that he could trust Clemens. He didn't. He could throw him far but trusted him no further than where his eyes could see him.

He peered down, eyes scanning past the particles of falling snow-flakes, shining brightly in the streetlights as they coated the ground, chilling his bones. He rubbed his hands together, exhaling into them to bring them warmth. Physically, it didn't bother him, but he knew that should he force himself to violence, he would want to be as nimble as a fox. And he couldn't do that when his bones were rattling, now, could he?

What bothered him the most was the fact that Jeff knew his identity. Or, rather whatever identity was known to anyone inside of Task Force Seven and Black Eagle. The fact he was still here and had not returned to duty was cause for concern too.

Who owns it now? The damned group of mercenaries with execute authority, and arguably better discipline than the rest. You told them, didn't you.

His lips curled into a scowl.

I told you, didn't I? I told you if you forced me to leave the life I've built, I'd rip your arms off. But he couldn't prove anything. No evidence, just a history of very lucky guesses, but that wouldn't be just. It wouldn't be right. But why did he care for right or wrong? Nothing has ever gone right for him. Except *Jennifer.* He could at least try for her. He could try to do the right thing and hear Clemens out.

Jennifer's face flashed across his mind. Her hair, her smile, not toiled or corrupted like his were. The smile, and gleam she shared with him time and time again was just enough to make him forget, however briefly, his chronic torment. She made him feel like something. Like part of him rekindled, not work down as he constantly was. Her patience with him fueled the husk he once was and turned it into something a little more human. Ted Anderson now had something to lose.

Is this really that much to ask? Maybe you could at least tell me why you tried to kill us. You owe me that much.

His phone rang. Michael Clemens.

What does he want at this hour? Unfortunate timing, I was about to pay your brother a visit. He answered it. The wind whistled behind him. "It's Ted."

"Hey, Tedward!"

Ted stifled a chuckle. He found the pet-name funny, coming from Michael, who knew just enough about him, more or less, and understood what was fundamentally true: Ted's mental state not being healthy. And it was a name specifically usually Jennifer called him.

"Michael, what can I do you for today, at such a late hour," he asked.

"It can't be too late if the wind is whistling in the back. You're wearing winter gear, right?" He chuckled in the background.

Ted imagined Michael grinning on the other end of the phone.

"Well, anyway, back to why I called. I wanted to get some coffee with you tomorrow if that would be okay. I hear you like chess?"

He sighed. "I've played it. I don't particularly like anything. But you know that."

"That's not what I heard," he cackled on the other end of the phone, audibly too loud, that Ted pulled the phone from his ear. "I heard you like ramen."

Jennifer.

"Well, joking aside, everyone likes something. The trouble is, finding out what that something is, and having the passion and energy to enjoy it. So, I wanted to do something with you. Just you. Just me. Now, normally I'd ask if there's something you want to do, but well, you know. You claim to not like anything, so we'll do something I want to do. I'll play chess with you. Let's grab a sandwich or breakfast or whatever, and some coffee. How's that sound?"

"And you think I'd enjoy that?" Ted laughed in near hysteria.

"Glad I got a laugh out of you. I'll assume that was real," he chuckled back. "But to answer your question, who knows. You don't know if you like anything or not, so at least one of us will be happy. So, how about it? You know what? I'll pull a Sam. You don't have a choice. I won't take no for an answer. I know someone who knows where you live, and so help me, I'll get Jennifer to get you to come out with me."

"That is something Sam would do?"

"She rubs off on me. How about the café shop on Washington Street. Right by Lafayette Ave?"

"You mean the Gremlin Café?"

"Ah, you know the one?"

"Yes,"

"10:00 a.m. tomorrow. I'll meet you there!"

Hanging up the phone, he shook his head as he gazed down on the time. *2:00 a.m. Shit.*

He exhaled white air from his lips as he turned back into the building. *Another day, Jeff. You better be thankful; I still have half a mind to murder you.*

Ted walked off the subway car early the next morning. Not early for a man who only sleeps for half an hour, and every single nap was an existential crisis waiting to happen. He really should seek therapy, he knew that. He knew he needs *something* to keep his nightmares under some control. After all, these nightmares had a nasty habit of seeping into his reality, and he couldn't fully comprehend what was real, what was a memory, or what was a nightmare. He didn't have problems with his dreams. He didn't have any. Only nightmares.

Ted walked up the escalators into the street, filled with an abundance of trash pouring out of the trashcans strategically placed on the sidewalks. He heard the squeaking wheels of a skeletal cart to his left. He knew what it was. Just another thing casually discarded with a pulse as something less than human.

He turned his feet, shifting away from one end of Washington Street leading down toward the old Town Hall, and averted his gaze down the street leading to Chinatown. The pedestrian-only street was lined in carefully placed gray bricks. This street wasn't designed for vehicles. As he took his first step in this direction, people rushed past him in their winter garbs, some simple, others more extravagant as if others were dressing to impress someone. Men and women alike, careless, not a care in the world, none at all. Sure. It wasn't like war was on their doorstep. But then again, most of these people have no memory of war. Not like him. Implanted in his brain, never to forget it, only death would grant him that luxury. *All because of the sacrifice we made. All because of the weight of those sacrifices was thrust upon our shoulders.*

The wind picked up as he emerged from the building's overhead. The crunch of the snow on the ground underneath his boot filled his ears. The snow was compact, perfect for, what was the word—

A little child ran in front of him, as the large menacing tree with green and red lights loomed over him atop the store on the opposite side of the street. The little boy in his hat, his clothes, grabbed some snow in his hand, clumping it together, firmly molding it into a grenade, and took it, handling it as if it was one, before hurling it across the street, striking another child in the shoulder. The cluster of snow dispersed into dust, brushing into the face of the other child, who cried out, laughing with an open mouth, and two missing teeth, one on the maxillary, the other on the mandibular jaws. The smile was cute, authentic even, filled with a joy that Ted could never have. Something that was stolen from him. No matter what money could bring him, no matter what glee Jennifer brought to him, and any hope that is neither here nor there. Nothing could ever return childhood, and no number of apologies could ever return friends, that ought to have been buried in the ground, not shot up to pieces like a witch during the Danvers' Witch Trials.

He walked on, taking a left on Washington Street. His laptop was resting at his side, holding his portfolio and all his notes. The streets were still fairly empty at this time. The cool breeze kept bringing him chills. Not typical. After spending some time in the northern parts of Russia, he didn't think he'd feel chills again, and yet here he was, walking through the bristling weather, chafing his cheek.

He found the café, the sign hanging out of it, just inside a hotel of which he didn't care to find the name of. The sidewalk was lightly trampled on as he walked by the snow-covered trashcan, a black steel canister turned pale with flakes white. He exhaled, stepping forward as the white breath churned. He took another step, and suddenly, just like many times before, the temperature dropped yet again. Bones rattling inside. Exhaling heavily, he rubbed his arms, clinging to the friction for a piece of warmth.

He realized something: he wasn't breathing in that cursed *essence*. Whatever it was, it wasn't him doing it. Turning behind him, eyes scanning past the people flooding outside the subway tunnels, and turning corners up on Lafayette Ave, he couldn't shake the feeling he was being watched. Something he was good at picking up, but he couldn't quite gather the intent of such a person sneaking about on a late Saturday morning.

He hissed as the air warmed up slightly, and brushing the snowflakes off his hair, he turned inside the glass door, pushing it open. The smell of freshly baked bread assaulted his nostrils. There was something about it, something familiar...

"Ghost! Ghost!"

He awoke abruptly, eyes forward, scanning the darkened room. A sweet aroma filled it as he rubbed his eyes. He turned, pulling his legs over his cot, standing up. Door creaking open, and shutting silently, a girl coming closer, with a roll running to him, the steam coming up from it.

"Ghost! Look!" Slithers said, smiling at it as she held it in both hands to his face, gazing hungrily, and as if she was looking at salvation in her hands. Her hands were coated in patters of white lines for the innumerous scars she had, from debris, glass, rusting iron and bullets. He reached for her arms, seeing similar scars on his arms.

"Slithers," he stammered, hands trembling uncontrollably. "You shouldn't have taken this. If they find out—"

"So, what if they do. I want them to find out. I don't—I don't care anymore. We're animals. We should behave like animals! Trapped in cages are we." She ripped it in half and brought it to him. "Listen. You don't care either."

"How did you get this?" He shook his head. "You couldn't have made it to the pantry on your own," he said, reluctantly grabbing his half, and bringing it to his nose. He squeezed it gently, it was so soft, softer than his pillow.

"Ted Anderson gave it to me."

"Ted Anderson," he repeated, taking bite out of the bread. Tasting sour and tangy, chewing softly. "Ted Anderson."

"Ted Anderson," they repeated together.

The walls closed in around them, fading everything to black, suffocating him as the air grew heavier, and the temperature, standing on ends was worse than Northern Russia. His eyes closed, and opened, consumed the horror of the flames filling the room, rattling of metal shells dropping down the cold hard metal grates above.

And there, Slithers lay in a pool of her own blood on the ground. Knife protruding out of her chest, limbs scattered on it. Black blood. Black blood. Black blood.

He turned, and the vest on his chest weighed heavily as his vision faded, blood pouring out of the walls, and covering him completely.

He looked around himself, feeling a fog sweep over him. Light-headed, almost non-existence fueling his angst. He felt his heart beating faster and faster. Lost. He swept his hands in front of him, trying to find something that was physically real. Something he could touch. Something he could use to pull himself out. But all that was there was nothingness.

He exhaled heavily, white breath coming out of his mouth, pouring into the café. He opened his palms, his eyes opened wide staring blankly at the sign in front of him. Unable to process the words he was reading, he clenched his fists, and unfolded them repeatedly.

"Hey, man!" a firm hand clenched his shoulder.

Exhaling heavily, palms sweating at his side. Heart racing as the panic poisoned his veins. He turned abruptly, arms raised, and his teeth grinded.

"Whoa!" Michael put his hands up nonchalantly, a slight smirk on his face. "It's just me."

Damnit.

He sucked in a deep breath through his teeth and let out a brief sigh of relief and returned that dreadfully fake smile. "Michael, don't do that again."

"You got it." Michael's smile brightened. "Hey, why don't you grab a spot. I'll get us something. What do you want?"

"Coffee," he answered, looking back into the café, scanning for a place to sit.

"And to eat?"

"I smell fresh bread. Whatever just came out of the oven,"

"That's it?"

"Yes," he sighed, taking himself away from Michael. He walked briskly to a seat next to a window. It was cozy, and this table in particular was near a fireplace, crackling wood, burning coals. This place was filled with familiar scents, some pleasant, and others horrible. Never before did he come to a place both beautiful and terrifying simultaneously. He chose to tough it out, but how long could his mind take it?

The leather seat was rich and comforting. He never sat in one of these before. Even in his day jobs, he only ever had the office chairs. Nothing like this brown, cushy, leather chair. It squeaked under his weight, and he looked at the table in front of him: wooden, lightly sanded on the edges, polished dark. He wiped some crumbs off the table and onto the floor, feeling it's smooth, flawless texture under his rough, defective hands.

He snarled out the window as the snowflakes fell again, dancing carelessly in the wind, just like everyone else: careless. He felt the unwavering suspicion of someone watching him. Just him. Why would he have drawn attention, but because he did have that little episode at the entry way. No. Everyone was watching him, sitting by himself in the corner.

They bit down on their food. Sandwiches, eggs, sausage, all those aromas hurled toward his nose, and unwanted attentions presented themselves, looking at him not as a person. He knew better. It was the same stare he received from other soldiers, marines, and sailors when they found out who he was with, or what he was. A monster.

Oh. Yes. They'd run if they knew the truth, and the police would be here in ballistic gear followed by the National Guard to put me down. Especially if they knew I was still alive. Black Eagle would not be far behind, but why aren't you moving? You definitely know. Why haven't you done anything or moved on me unless—

That's it. You have a spy here. Don't you? But who is at the top this time? It isn't Snells.

"Here we are," Michael interrupted his insanity as he set a bowl of fresh rolls, steam rising from them. Michael placed some butter and jam to the side and a butter knife clattered on the table. *Dangerous thing here.*

Michael placed his cup of black coffee on the table in front of him, swirling restless ripples inside the cup, just itching to pour over.

Michael sat down, his breakfast sandwich was resting peacefully alone on a plate, steaming in front of him. Bacon, eggs, and a toasted English muffin, with undoubtedly melted butter.

Ted gazed back over to his bowl of rolls and pulled one out, squeezing the soft roll in his hands. He brought it to his mouth, biting onto it, inhaling the delicious yeasty aroma, tasting the soft, sweet roll onto his tongue. Another thing he remembered, another thing he forgot. Something he was forced to forget, as his memory of Slithers passed through his mind, warm tears streamed down his cheeks, taking small savory bites. He finished the first roll and reached for another, eyes glancing to Michael who's eyes were closed and lips were moving but no words came out. Michael's hand stopped moving.

"Don't stop eating on account of me," Michael chuckled as he placed his coffee back down and took a large bite of his breakfast sandwich. "Ah, eggs. Can't beat those first thing in the morning!"

"What were you doing?" Ted asked, curious as to why the man wouldn't just take a bite first. "Just now. What were you doing?"

"I'm surprised Jennifer didn't tell you." An eyebrow raised. "Praying. I always pray for my meal. I'm always thankful."

"You did that silently though," he questioned further. His hands retracted from the table, folding over themselves underneath the table, clenching firmly.

"Yes, I don't have to speak loudly. He hears me. I know He hears me. He grants me my requests just as easily as He denies them."

"And what did you pray for just now?" Anxiety filled Ted's hands, shaking underneath the table. His heel lifted and struck the ground repeatedly. He almost forgot someone else was tracking him. Just as he was reminded, a cold draft pushed through the café; the door opened and a singular woman walked through the room, shot a smiling glance at him, with the same tired look inscribed in her face as he knew he shared with her. He didn't know her. Didn't care to know her, as elegantly as she walked through the line to order her own cup of coffee.

He almost forgot Jeff, but he found himself growing fond of Michael, and this relationship they were developing. But it was complicated with Jeff in the picture. Far too complicated for his liking, and it would have been better if Ted left in the summer, just like he planned. It would have been better.

Yet, here we are.

"I thanked Him for my food," Michael answered plainly. He looked Ted in the eye, the curve on his lips straightened, and his eyelid dropped halfway down both eyes, much like Jennifer's very playful gaze. But for Michael, it was something entirely different. "And I prayed for you. Your health and wellbeing." He sipped on his coffee cup as Ted gasped softly from across the table.

Why?

Michael tapped his cup with his finger as he rested it on the table. "Look, I know I haven't exactly been around you much. So, I suppose you might say you don't know me, and what I know about you I get from either Jennifer or Sam. And I know you aren't well. And please," he said as Ted shifted uncomfortably in his chair, "do not blame Jennifer. What you don't want the rest of us to know is still with Jennifer. What Samantha, specifically, knows, I know. That's it. I know you can't seek conventional help. I don't know why, but that's all I really need to know. In fact, I don't need to know any more than that until you're ready to talk."

"What did she—"

"What she said doesn't matter," Michael interrupted. "You know, I don't know if Sam ever told you this, but she thought you to be heading off the deep end, like a-blade-becoming-a-little-too-friendly-with-your-wrist deep end." His voice dropped down low so only Ted could hear him. "When she first thought of it, I read something in the news. It was interestingly horrifying enough, but who would ever think that America would finally beat Japan with the world's highest suicide rate? One thing we don't need to be beating them in. But I guess, what brought me to that was my acknowledgment that we aren't doing enough for others. Of course, it doesn't help that when you needed it most, the government stopped funding suicide prevention services. And police aren't going to get involved in something like that, for God only knows what reason."

Ted listened carefully, not breaking eye contact, maintaining his composure, but on the inside, he was screaming. He brought the coffee to his lips; the bitter taste brought some satisfaction to him. He wasn't sure why, but he didn't like it too much. But he drank it to seem like he needed it to stay awake during the global stock markets. Which he didn't. The nightmares made sure he was awake.

"But here I am, talking to you, someone who needs help, and someone that the government thinks is better off dead, just like everyone else. And I want you to know, that despite it all, we are going to be here with you. But, I think the real tragedy here, is that war has a habit of killing the living. And not just literally. Personalities are burned away. And it saddens me we will never know who Ted Anderson was meant to be. Just who he's become, a man diverged from the path he was originally designed to follow.

"Ted. Whatever you need, Sam and I, and of course Jennifer are only a phone call away. Call us at 3:00 a.m. I don't care. Neither do they. I mean, Sam might. You don't want to get in the way of her beauty sleep," he laughed, finishing his sandwich. "She'll rip you a new one."

The words stung deep, a lump was crawling up his throat like he was going to vomit. The heart sank, growing heavier with every breath. Placing the cup down, he raised another roll to his lips. Warm tears still. The memories. Few good ones remained, and he was confident there would be a day where he would forget the good ones and forget what his friends looked like. After all, he didn't have much to remember them by. Just the spear, the bow, and a fading picture. That's it. Nothing more. He felt Michael's eyes looking at him. Not down on him, but at him, trying to figure out how to help, but he chose not to say anything.

Michael made it known, he was there. And he wasn't going anywhere. While Ted couldn't trust him entirely, Michael trusted him enough to offer him help, even if it was just another person to call.

"Ted, if you don't believe me," he offered again, sipping down the rest of his coffee. "If you find yourself in Alaska, for whatever reason, and you need someone to be there. Call us. And we're on the next plane out there. I don't care. Just call us."

Ted's eyes gaped open, bringing another roll to his lips, blindly eating it. The lump growing inside his chest seem to lessen, slowly wiggling itself down into the abyss of his stomach. *But Jeff is going to make this relationship of ours exceedingly difficult. Michael, how can you say any of this when I* "Thank you," *want nothing more than to bury your brother in the ground?*

"No problem, man," Michael replied, pulling out a little box, which slid open to a checkered board. He opened two small brown boxes underneath the board and started pegging all but two pieces in it. He placed the two pieces into his hands, and behind his back.

Ted's heart raced.

Michael pulled his hands out, closed, palmed facing the ground. "Pick one."

Ted gazed carefully at each hand, wondering which hand held which piece. Chess was a game of strategy, of which, no one knew battle strategy than he did. He could play distracted, and it wouldn't make a difference.

"This isn't the stock market, Tedward, it's okay. Money isn't on the line," Michael chuckled.

He shook his head and pointed at the left one. Michael flipped his hand over, opened his fist to reveal the black pawn. *I suppose you need to get every break you can get. Or maybe you're the lucky one.*

"Hey, maybe you'll get your bad luck after all," Michael joked.

Of course, when they first met, they had a conversation about luck, and the farce of luck was that good luck wasn't all that lucky, and it was better to have bad luck, since at the very least, you could be better prepared should things take a turn for the worst. Consistent good luck leads to complacency, risking being easily fooled. *I don't want to hear that right now. Not when everything else is coming down to the ground around me. Your brother is a wild nuisance.*

"Shall we begin, Tedward?"

Ted flipped the board, so he was black, and pegged his piece in. "Yes. Let's."

"May the best man win."

They played a few rounds across the table as Ted ate his sourdough rolls. Of course, he wasn't going to let those sweet memories get out of place. Michael wasn't a bad player, not at all.

"You're very good at this," Ted remarked.

"Chess President of my college's chess club!" Michael moved a pawn forward, replacing it with a knight, and puffed his chest out with great pride.

Bold move. But that won't save you.

Ted moved his queen right in front of the King. The queen sat with the King locked in place. The only move for the King was to take the queen, however, what queen remains unprotected by her loyal knight. Michael didn't see this coming, clearly, as the pawns were arranged in such a way that allowed his larger pieces to advance down the center. This bold strategy would work much like Blitzkrieg, with one fatal flaw: should something with enough sense go behind the front lines into enemy territory, well, that always invited disaster.

"Checkmate," Ted declared himself victorious, however bittersweet it was.

"Again?" Michael wiped his brow. "Never have I had a chess game end like this before, least of all, not on me. You, Tedward, I announce my defeat and my undying support to your throne."

Ted blinked as he looked down on the chess set. He glanced upward, unsure if this was meant to be a joke. He couldn't quite tell, and Michael was hard to read sometimes. Sometimes he could figure out his motives, but not today, he seemed a little more off than usual.

Ted's phone rang in his pocket.

And who might this be?

"Excuse me." Ted said politely as he took out his phone. Erin. *What does she want?* "Gutenberg Press?"

"Funny Ted, funny," she replied over the phone. "Seriously though, I have a question for you, that you I can trust will answer me honestly."

"Whatever it is, sell it," he answered.

"Wait, what? You don't even know what I was asking about it,"

"I guessed you were going to ask me some stock related question, weren't you?"

"Clever as ever, Mr. Anderson," she cackled over the other end of the phone. "But who would want this? It's Gernazation USA."

"Definitely sell that. That's worthless," he replied.

"Okay, thanks. I was planning on it,"

"Out of curiosity, why did you even buy it?"

"It looked good. Now that that's out of the way, I wanted to thank you," she said over the phone. *Thank me?* "I don't know how I'll ever pay you back."

"For what exactly?" He asked. "Forgive me, Gutenberg Press, I don't remember what I did for you."

"You saved me from a terrible trade for one," she answered rather sarcastically. "But onto the actual reason for my call today: someone paid that hospital bill for chemo. Who else could it be? Someone who has lots of money, and not a want for it. You may never acknowledge you did this, but I know. And I won't tell anyone else. But I wanted you to know I'm thankful for it."

"You're welcome," he replied.

"Well, I'm sure you're busy, I'll let you go. Talk to you soon!"

"Bye,"

Ted hung up the phone and withdrew it to his pocket.

"Well, that sounded like an obviously boring conversation. Michael, what did I tell you about bromancing?"

"Dear God. Why now?" Michael chuckled, turning his head around.

Jennifer walked with her own coffee cup, wrapping her arm around Ted's shoulders. Ted noticed she wiped her nose with a napkin, blowing it hard before swiftly discarding it to the trash. He didn't see the color dilation from the napkin.

Ted's heart felt uplifted, rising from the pit of despair that was caused by the smell of freshly baked bread. But Jennifer was here, whole, and unspoiled by the traumas of war, though she did have her own experience with people who saw war. Those in her family who, like Michael said, had their personalities burned away. But Jennifer reminded him of what he was. The good and the bad would continue to plague his mind, but now with her, it was at least somehow bearable.

"So, tell me." Bringing a spare chair, Jennifer brought her face close to his, cheeks rubbing together, invasive in her own Jennifer-like brand as she was. She was excitable, her hand squeezing his shoulder. "You didn't beat him too bad, did you Michael?"

"I'm afraid I couldn't beat him at chess if he was blindfolded," he chuckled.

"Tedward," she turned her face toward him, gazing into his eyes.

"Hey, hey, hey." Michael exclaimed. "I can't bromance him, but you're practically romancing him. Why can't I have a bromance?"

"Because," she averted her gaze back to Michael. "You're not *bromantic*. Where's the candle lights?"

"I've got a fireplace behind me. What do I need candles for?" He retorted.

Ted chuckled lightly, his gut reacting in rhythmic vibrations.

"This is why you deserve no bromances, amateur." She threw her hair back and laughed. "Anyway, Tedward, I've got some tickets for tomorrow to go to the Boston Symphony Orchestra. I like music."

"What's playing?" he asked, as a polite nicety. He didn't truly understand music at all. He knew there was a military band, but it was all white noise to him. It didn't really mean anything. The only thing he could say he enjoyed was reading, and even then, that reminded him of the numerous different briefings he'd had and orders he'd read when he was deployed. Nothing was ever for enjoyment. Though, he could say he found this engagement today was fruitful.

"Looks like some local orchestra for some miscellaneous soundtracks from various anime."

Ted blinked, "What's anime?"

"Oh, it's some Japanese medium for movies or shows. It's densely animated, some heavily rely on absurdism. I'm not a fan, but great music though." Michael snapped both his fingers and stood up. "I've gotta get going, I'll leave you two alone together."

Jennifer sneered at him. "Yes, Michael, I really, really want this."

"You can have him." He turned away, walking briskly out of the café, waving on his way out.

"So," She held his cheeks firmly her warm and soft hands. Warmth spread through him, his breath caught in his throat. At that moment, it was the only thing he could think about. "How about it? You get to come out, it's just you and me, and of course a hall filled with people you don't know, most likely."

"Sure, I'll come along. What time?"

CHAPTER 13

BREAKING DOWN

Snells initiated a peaceful draft that is expected to inflate armed forces by 30 percent from draftees alone.

This is the first Peaceful Draft since 1940 when FDR first signed the Peaceful Draft during WWII. The draft still excludes woman from registering for selective service, and men between the ages of 18-23 are being called up from the local recruiter's office to sign, imposing them to service.

Press Secretary Jenna Walters claims, "It is up to us to decide the fate of our world. We cannot trust the allies from overseas to help us in this conflict. Russia and China have declared war on us. It is the position of the government than everyone must do their part to ensure the survival of this democratic republic."

Ted looked up at the black night sky, snowflakes drifting down endlessly from the heavens, a place he was forbidden from entering when he died. The beauty of the snowflakes was unfettered; they fell different shapes, different sizes, coalescing onto the ground where he stood. It covered his shoes and soaked his pants and coat as he waited outside the Boston Symphony Orchestra Hall. The lights outside shone brightly, both the streetlights loomed over him, and the golden yellow lights shone from inside the hall.

Snow dusted the ground, being kicked through the scattered and disorganized steps of those around him. He turned around, scanning those coming out of the Green Line station. He didn't remember the name of the stop; the Green Line was still confusing with its number of different routes to all different parts of Downtown Boston.

Then, at last, she came up the stairs, walking in her blue dress, the top tucked away in a winter coat, a hat, and some earmuffs. He carefully looked at her nose, still skeptical. That napkin, he had a hard time forgetting about it. Up the nostril, as he stole a quick glance as to not be rude, was not bleeding. She approached him, and clumsily, with her leather gloves, she pulled out the tickets. "Dear Tedward, art thou ready?"

He raised an eyebrow. "As ready as I'll ever be, William Shakespeare."

She cackled as she took his hand in hers, the soft flesh sent warmth to his palms. Never really had cause to hold someone's hands before. Not even Slithers. This hand, smooth all around, curved, and a faint pulse he felt beating into his. There was nothing of note on the hand, like a blank canvas with nothing but the future to mark it. She led him up the stairs as he marveled at the building itself. The marble rimmed pillars welcomed them into an exquisite red backdrop, filled with carved frames and windows. He sighed as they walked into the vestibule to the ticket window, and through the halls.

Jennifer led him inside the main hall where the instrumentalists were preparing their tools for the main event, the golden statues and other various decorum lined up on what looked like mini balconies for spirits atop them, looming over, watching them as they walked through the crowd to get a spot.

Another thing that was flung into his attention was the dress. Jennifer dressed the part, sure. He didn't. He had a collared shirt, and some slacks, with no tie to go with it. The belt was passable at least. He was hopelessly underdressed and that was an understatement. How did a man like him end up coming to a place like this, and a woman like her? He was so unrefined.

As he sat down next to her, something else came to his mind: why did he care about how he was dressed? He wasn't in the military anymore. He didn't need to play a part, but he felt like he needed to, now everyone was going to be watching him. And not paying attention to the orchestra, not that this was his concern, but he didn't want to be the center of attention. Not here.

His heart beat faster as more people showed up, taking their seats, glancing over him. Why wouldn't they? He stuck out like a sore thumb. There was no lie here. No need for it. He just needed to calm down. He took measured breaths.

A cool gentle touch caressed the top of his hand. Startled, he opened his palms. The touch remained, but firmly pressed his hand to the arm of the seat. Turning his head, Jennifer was there, finally sat down, and her hand rested atop his, and her fingers, gentle, delicate, saw fit, it seemed by their own accord, to interweave themselves into his fingers like a basket, damned to fall apart. Slowly, his heart rate slowed down, and his fingers relaxed again on the arm of the chair.

He leaned into her, mouth breathing into her ears, "Thank you."

"You're welcome, Tedward," she whispered back.

The lights dimmed as the instrumentalists took their places, picking up a variety of stringed instruments, drums of various kinds, and trombones, and trumpets, and tubas, and other various brass instruments he didn't recognize. *This was much more than a quartet.*

The chatter dulled down as the choir came out. They took their spot and the lights fell upon them.

And then, the music began to play. It was soft at first, soothing with the backdrop of the choir singing different parts of differing tones, and slightly altered tempos, this much he could tell, but why was the choir so disorganized? The violinists started to strum their strings with carefully precise movements of the bow, moving back and forth, scratching his ears as the high pitches started to scream. And the brass. Nothing was worse. The brass was horrible. Sounded like the horn of a ship sending out an SOS.

He wasn't sure what it was like to feel enjoyment, but he was certain this wasn't it. But he continued to listen, until the music stopped

again, coming abruptly. Started again. Stopped with the violins ringing in their last note, like the last gasp of breath before a corpse's soul
was released to either Heaven or to Hell. *Shit.* His other hand started
to tremble as visions of flashing gunfire and grenades coursed over
his mind, clearly paving the way for room for more nightmares, and
this was something he didn't need.

Just tough it out. It's not real. It's not real.

He exhaled rhythmically again, heavily as the air in his lungs felt
compressed and restrained, pushing the air out of his air sacks. He
wanted to throw up. He took his other hand as he covered his mouth.
Tears slid down his face.

*Ticker's arm flung right in front of him. Warm blood coalesced on his face,
dripping down as he felt a foot kicking hard in his side, a rib cracking.*

Ticker. Ticker. Ticker.

His hand reached out for something, and the room was clapping
for the intercession. He felt Jennifer's hand squeezing him tightly.
The lights came back, lighting everything in the room, and everyone
stood up, chatting again as others made their way out to the bathroom.

"Ted," she whispered, her hands framing his face. "Are you okay?"

He ignored everyone else around him. The only thing that mattered was the warm hands on his face, and the person they were
attached to. His hands reached up, holding onto her wrists gently,
almost like a dead fish. He didn't want to break her. He didn't want to
scar her. He didn't want to fill her with the same poison that plagued
his brain. She was, precious to him.

Exhaling into her face, she frowned as he slowly, mechanically
shook his head. "Can we—can we go? *Please.*"

"Yeah. Let's go. Why don't we come back to my place first?"

Ted was seething, teeth sputtering, clashing against one another like
halved coconuts. The door opened. She ushered him forward, his
body shaking, but not because of the cold, but because of something

else. "Ted. Sit down. Couch." She said, slowly closing the creaking door, hearing the latch lock behind it. She secured the deadbolt just in case Ted felt unsafe without all the bonds latched.

Ted took a seat, shaking, hands trembling in front of him as he exhaled heavily, hyperventilating uncontrollably. His eyes focused forward, looking at her TV stand. He leaned forward and his shoulders rolled. She walked over to the kitchen, turned the tea pot on.

Feeling some moisture swell up in her nose, she took a napkin, and wiped it. Blood stained the napkin red. *Not now. Please.* She discarded the napkin into the trash, washing her hands waiting for the water.

When the kettle whistled, she pulled out two mugs, placing teabags inside, poured hot water into the cup, and steeped. She the removed the teabags, removed them to the trash, and poured the milk in. She brought the tea over to the coffee table where Ted was having an episode.

It won't be long now, and the lights are going to start going haywire again.

"Tedward, take off your coat," she said, sitting next to him. He didn't respond, still breathing heavily, eyes still locked on her TV stand. She looked to the stand, and his eyes seemed focused on a collection of Blu-ray sets. Nothing of any real importance. Her hands reached out to his, separating them, and then to his coat zipper, pulling it down. Her hands reached into his jacket to pull the sleeves off. Still no reaction. Nothingness.

She sighed as she took a sip of her tea. *Well, it's coming. Just. When?*

There it is.

She felt her bones chill. Her hands shivered as it reached for the cup, and its temperature was dropping. The lights in the living room dimmed and shut off, but the room was lit with another light, rainbow-colored veins on Ted, dear Tedward, lighting up the room, and shutting nearly every electrical appliance off in her apartment. It was almost colder in here, than it was out there.

It wasn't long before the temperature returned to homeostasis, and the steam from the tea floated from the cup. She stretched out her hand as the light faded, grabbing the ceramic handle. It was warm to the touch. *Odd.* She brought it to her lips, sipping cautiously. *Also hot. As it should be?* She turned to Ted, her arm around him as she leaned into his shoulder.

"Tedward, if you can hear me, please grab that tea," she pleaded. "It's right in front of you. None of this is real."

His breathing steadied as he leaned forward, his hand fumbling around in the dark, grabbed hold of a cup clattering atop the table before bringing it to his lips, pushing it forward until the liquid poured into his mouth.

"Ted, do you want to talk about it?" she asked.

His head turned slowly to face her; eyes gaped open. Fear in his eyes, like a little puppy, awaiting punishment from its master, or that of a little baby boy, gentle spirit, and a want of nothing but safety, but all he ever got was abuse. Yes. Those were the eyes she saw. She couldn't see much of anything else. The only light now in the room was the shimmering moonlight, reflecting through the snow-filled clouds.

"No," he said, turning his head back to the table. "And yes."

She placed her head on his shoulder. "I'm right here. I'll listen when you're ready to talk, but right now, just drink."

Ted took another sip and placed the cup, clamoring as it struck the table. He took a large gulp of air, and choked on it, drawing in another breath, and did the same, choking on it. She felt his body shake, not just with the sudden movements of the breath, but his shoulders were trembling as he stared at another living nightmare.

Another tragic symptom of his condition she didn't understand how to deal with. But over the last several months now, she knew when he was experiencing a nightmare in the real world, where he can't tell the past from the present. The nightmares were so vivid, no one could tell the difference, and perhaps only someone who dealt with something similar to he, would be able to pull him up from this living Hell.

Of course, it didn't help that he didn't sleep more than half an hour a night. That alone can't be healthy and was most likely only making it worse. She saw his shirt breathing in and out, as he coughed. She held herself away from him to see that his hands covered his face. *Tears.* He was crying.

"Hush," she spoke softly. She wrapped her arm around him, pulling his body into hers, his head resting on her shoulder. His moist tears wet her dress. "There, there. Tell me what's on your mind when you're ready to." Her hand brushed through his hair as he continued to sob.

"It's hopeless," he whimpered. "It's hopeless."

"What's hopeless?" she asked.

"Everything was pointless," he sobbed.

"What's pointless?" she asked.

"War is coming. It's inevitable," he sobbed. "I don't—" he choked. "I don't want to fight again."

"No one's forcing you to fight, Tedward. I won't ask that of you," she spoke softly. "You've done enough for us already. You don't need to fight anymore."

"But what if—but what if—" he couldn't bring himself to finish the question.

"If it comes here, it will come here," she replied. "Such is the nature of the world we live in. We can buy peace for a time. And war will return once that season of peace is over. There is no cure for war. It will come when it's time. It's inevitable."

Ted gasped for air, silently holding her tightly. "Then does that mean—" his voice trailed off again.

"What are you thinking Ted?" She knew he was going to start asking tough questions. Questions she had only a cursory knowledge of how to deal with.

"There was a man once," he began. "He gave me something. Something dear, and something I long to forget was ever a gift, and here I am, throwing that gift aside."

"What did he give you?" she asked of him. A probing question, and a question that needed some elaboration. Over this past year, he spoke of horrors, of his friends now lost, but never before was there a mention of a man, and on so vague. Another layer, another mask, another façade to his personality slowly coming undone. It's a shame really, that this was even necessary. Sadness. Bitterness. Isolation. Hopelessness.

It reminded her of a short story, one that held merit, for one born into a world of Hell. Filled with so much violence and grit:

The soldier stood at the gate of heaven, and his head was downcast at the gate. Said he to the Lord, "Sir, do you have room enough for me? I don't need much. Just a space. I understand if your house is full, but I thought I'd ask all the same."

The gate didn't open.

"Sir," he spoke again unto the Lord. "There isn't much food elsewhere. Nor shelter. Nor good company. If there isn't enough in your house, would you just say so. I'd hate to keep bothering you like this."

The soldier's head remained downcast. Unable to bring himself to face whatever should open that gate. He was not worthy. He was not good. He was not good company. He was not even worth mentioning. He knew this. But he thought to ask all the same. What harm was that? But the fact remained, that there wasn't one good thing about this soldier.

Knowing all the dead he left in his wake. Knowing all the crimes, and pillaging he'd done to accomplish the mission, and to make it home, who would dare open their home to him. The history would follow him, to the end of his days.

He was tormented by grief. One might even suggest that he was in a living Hell. The war was no longer on the field, and his weapon wasn't a gun. The war was now within the confines of his own mind, and this time, he had nothing to defend himself with.

"Sir. I will leave you now, and never return. I'm so sorry to bother you."

The soldier never looked up, only did what soldier's do, about-faced, and turned. Walking slowly, defeated as the man was not fond Hell's gates, and whatever guarded those gates would gladly receive him, regardless of what his past had done.

And the gate opened behind him. He dared not turn, dared not look. Only bad things would happen should he even think about looking upon the face of the Lord.

The gate slammed shut behind him, and footsteps drew near, and said, "Turn and look upon my face."

The soldier turned, and slowly, reluctantly dared to look upon the face of the Lord. "Sorry to bother you," the solder said.

And the Lord replied, "Come here, will you, there is plenty enough to eat inside, plenty of room. You've already paid your due to Hell."

"I don't know what it was he gave me, all those years ago, after the fires, and after he—" he trailed off, weeping harder into her shoulder. "After he died."

His body slid forward onto her lap, crying like a little child. Her hand rubbed his back as he wept. "There, there. Tell me what you want to tell me, and here it will stay. It will not leave my lips. Whatever you say will stay in this room. Ted, do you trust me?"

"You're the only one, the only one living I trust," he answered.

"Then tell me, what happened to those you did trust?"

He turned, she could feel his body reluctantly turning to face her, and her hand rested on his belly as he stared coldly at the ceiling. His arm swayed on the ground, and the other now covered his eyes, hiding tears, but there was no hiding it from her. She already knew.

"It was supposed to be a training exercise. Nothing more," he breathed heavily. "They were my friends. I learned everything from them. Everything was supposed to be a dud, blanks, nothing that would kill anybody, but I knew when one of my friends stepped on a claymore, which was supposed to have a laser to sensor failure, but no. They didn't care at all. They set off real claymores." She saw his fingernails scratching his forehead, drawing blood. "They hunted us like dogs, sending us scattering in all directions. At the end of it, I still remember my squad hanging in there with me to the end. And she, she told me to find the light. She told me to live.

"But is this really living? I barely sleep. Still, I can't sleep. Still, I have nightmares pushing in through my senses, triggering these flashbacks that I can't tell are real or—" he trailed back into weeping yet again. "Yesterday, at the café, it happened again. I saw her face, one last time with a smile, one of the few smiles we ever shared, before we realized we were born in Hell, and our parents were demons and devils. And demons and devils can only spawn devils and devils worse than they were."

Jennifer's hand stretched over his as he continued, softly resting. She felt it; empathy, the absolute despair he was born in. She remembered what he said: *I didn't have a choice*, and the only choice she knew now that he ever had, was *who* to kill.

"And again, at the orchestra, I saw his arm, severed right in front of me. Saved me. And he's gone. Dead. Their remains are gone, nothing left of them, not even the records. I know. I've looked. There isn't a trace of where we came from, who our real parents were. Just tools of war.

"And what pisses me off the most is that we sacrificed everything, not by our own choice. Everything. We fought for peace, and they held on to it for what? Ten years? They couldn't even manage ten years without pissing on it." His hand on the ground tensed as did his body on her lap. "And Jeff Clemens is here, alive, and doing well, reminding me of the piece of shit he is!"

Her other hand rested on his skin, and his shirt lifted, allowing her to touch his belly. She didn't know exactly why she wanted to touch it, but out of the sake of old curiosity; this part of him was never exposed to her, and yet, her fingers touched wounds, hardened scars underneath the surface. Scars like gashes, malformed healing underneath with previously broken bones which were forced to mend incorrectly. Dots of scars, which she imagined were bullet holes. To think he survived even that, was astonishing.

"He shot her, and him, and me," he rambled on. His sobs subsided, and he continued to rest on her lap.

"Does he know who you are?" She breathed heavily, hoping against hope that Jeffrey didn't recognize him, for at this point, she was certain she was looking at someone who believed himself to be better off dead. He had no family, and she knew isolation, he was like an orphan, lost and alone.

But you're with me now. I won't leave you. I'm sorry.

"Yes."

And that was that. Nothing could truly be done about it now.

"And he recognizes that you are—you?"

"Yes," he spoke softly. "And it terrifies me. More than the night-mares because I know Hell isn't far behind. I don't know when, and I can't predict it. I am going insane. I want to—I want to—"

"As I said, nothing leaves this room." She already knew how hor-rifying the truth was, and that whatever Uncle Sam did was unfor-giveable. She remembered a quote from her uncle, 'Patriotism is sup-porting your country when it deserves it,' *and I am certain it never did.*

"I want to kill him so much. He took them from me. He took their futures. We were promised we'd go home."

"Tedward," she leaned forward, removing his hand from his bleeding forehead, and sat him up. "Stay here," he held her hand as she rose from the couch. She walked over to the kitchen; his hand didn't let go.

"Don't leave me. *Please,*" he pleaded. She could tell he desperately tried to hang on to something; something worth holding on to.

"I'm not leaving you," she promised, smiling back at him. "Trust me."

His hand slipped out of her hands as she walked away, turning into her kitchen, and pulled out a washcloth, soaking it in hot water. She wringed it over the sink, walking back to him. *He needs something much more than reality, he needs God. But how can a man like this accept a God like mine? Or perhaps, did You curse him? Or is he like the blind man, and You made him live this way so that all may know?*

Extending her hand over to him, she wiped the blood off his fore-head. She leaned forward, taking her hand behind his head, nudging him to bend down, and she planted a soft kiss upon his forehead. "Tedward. You're mine. Do you hear me? Don't forget that. And I am yours. Don't forget that, for I won't. Whatever you see coming for you, I'll bear it with you. I'll be right by your side. Do you hear me? Where you go, my heart will be also. Do you hear me?"

"And when you die?" he asked, and she felt his arms around her, holding her close as he breathed heavily.

"Did I misspeak? Where you are, my heart will be also. Even if my body dies, my heart lives on, and it will be with you. Just as God is with me, so too am I with you."

He became flustered like a child. Averting his eyes away from her. She imagined Ted felt much like that soldier did when faced with the prospect facing the divine, or the accursed.

"Now, do you understand?"

His body trembled into her, whimpering, crying, more tears he had to cry, and with recent developments, his angst must be through the roof.

He barely managed, "I do."

TWO FRONT WAR

It's been a month now. Since my last fight, that is. As I pen this, I still hear their screams scratching like nails on the chalkboard. They refuse to stop screeching in my ears in the night. I take my meds. I go to therapy, but even that isn't quite enough, now, is it? I can't even look my wife in the face anymore. It's times like these I feel completely, utterly alone. My body is a disgrace and is better off floating upriver somewhere. If my wife found out all the things I did, she'd leave me. And who could blame her? I'm a terribly rotten person. I'm defective. Always have been. And the messed-up part about it, is I let them take the blame.

Sam Snells walked into the briefing room, escorted by his Press Secretary. The dark room was filled with chatter at the Pentagon. Secretary of Defense Johnson, and the General of the Armies, Admiral of the Navy, as well as many intelligence officers of both branches stood at attention at the table.

"At ease," he said, glancing at the files on the table.

Everyone sat down promptly as he walked over to his seat.

"Johnson, give me the situation straight," he demanded, tapping his pen on the table. The secretary stood behind him.

"Admiral Smith?"

"Russian fleets have stalled three-thousand knots east of our borders. Carriers, including mega carriers in the rear, destroyers up front.

No submarines detected," Smith stood up. He could hardly be seen with his dark skin. "Chinese fleets are still advancing. Similar makeup to the Russians. Again, no submarines."

The admiral adjusted the ships on the map, indicating where the fleets were.

"Flight capacity?" Snells replied.

Not one to show his feelings, but the truth was, he was terrified. Russia or China was not someone to be trifled with. But to add both together was to invite catastrophe. There wasn't going to be much opportunity for defense if they're working together. China, he understood. He didn't negotiate well with China. That was on him. But Russia? Why were they converging on him?

"Intelligence suggests they have lots of fuel to run a long war. Each carrier is sufficiently supplied with Chengdu-j20s and Su-57s," Smith explained. "Intelligence suggests China will attack the West Coast first. It also suggests that Russia will wait for an opportunity."

"What kind of opportunity?" Snells asked.

"For us to abandon the East Coast," General Gernardt answered.

"What options do we have at our disposal?"

"Well, we can't just assault Russia, despite knowing their intentions," Johnson said. "And just an outright air bombing over waters to halt China's fleets is problematic without advancing our own fleets."

"We could advance with our own fleets and marines, fighter pilots on standby for refueling with strategically anchored carriers," Gernardt suggested.

"Submarines," Snells adjusted his tie. "Why aren't there submarines?"

"Neither radar nor sonar detected any," Smith answered.

"I don't like this," Snells stared at the map of ships circling around the United States.

It was possible to mask the existence of submarines especially hiding underneath fleets that size. But there was someone researching technology that would make submarines impossible to detect, regardless of how close they were. Radar and sonar wouldn't be able to pick that up, even without interference with other vessels. And now that research developer was MIA. MIA and location narrowed down to Boston where he could be doing God knows what. That research developer was Ghost. *And if China and Russia both had it, it could mean only one thing. Ghost was behind all of this.* He sighed. *So, you're not as innocent as it would seem.*

"Did your intelligence officers ask why there were no submarines?"

"Negative," Smith replied.

Shit. I was too thorough, and discipline of our troops shot out the window.

"We have to assume they have submarines," he leaned back in his chair. "I didn't want to have to do this again, but we may need to call on Black Eagle."

"I would advise against that," Johnson said. "Not a good look to be using mercenaries to do our bidding, fight our wars on our territory. Mr. President, you have the election coming up to think about. Using Black Eagle is going to come across as weak, and your opposing party will use that against you."

Why is that the thing you zeroed in on? Ah. Because if I don't win, he risks losing his job.

"Then what do you suggest?" Snells asked.

"Reinforce the borders, call upon the reserves. Push training for the new recruits and get them out in the field stat," he answered. "Prepare the defenses and swing back with a counter strike with stealth bombers once they reach the border."

"You're suggesting we leave the door open?"

"What can I say, I have an open-door policy,"

Snells frowned, tapping his finger on the table.

A phone rang. The secretary stepped outside as Snells was considering his options.

"Either option is not good for publicity," Snells replied. "But that's not what's important."

Gernardt frowned at him, shaking his head. Smith did much the same. "Either way, it can't be good, and there is no good option here. For if we advance, and we make good on their bluff, there's a chance those submarines are hidden well, and God only knows what kind of arms they have. We might as well be walking into a—"

"Mr. President," the secretary said from the door. Snells turned his head to her. "The First Lady is here to speak with you."

He sighed, putting his hands on his thighs to stand. "Five mikes."

He stepped into the brightly lit hall and his wife stood giddily with her clipboard. "How does the planning go?"

"Fine," he shook his head. "What is it? I don't have time for whatever this is."

Andrea looked around the halls, ensuring no one else was within earshot. "Now dear, that's no way to talk to me, now, is it?" She frowned. Grabbing him firmly by the collar, pulling him down. Her warm breath caressed his ear. "Now, you are going to do precisely as Johnson says. Or else Colton comes knocking down our bedroom door tonight. You understand what that means don't you?"

What?

He looked her in the eye. Not knowing the purpose for such an intrusion was bothersome, and now, here she was telling him how to do the job he was elected for. *How does she know who Colton is?*

"Oh, don't give me that!" She berated him. "Go in there, be a good little boy."

His heart raced. Here he was, forced to think on the fly. Colton. He was a rabid dog that bit onto his arm, and refused to let go, and called all the other dogs to roost, biting and twisting his arm until he chose the play catch. But now, the ball was in his hand, and he didn't throw it, he may end up like Jezebel, feasted on dogs right below the window of the White House. It was generally assumed the president of the United States of America was the most powerful man on the planet, and now, Snells was certain that couldn't be farther from the truth.

"So that means—"

"Yes. Johnson is one of us, so Colton will know. It is part of his plan. Now, do as you're told, or you won't live to see tomorrow." She smiled as if she didn't just threaten him. "Now, you're a busy man. I won't hold you up anymore my dearest."

A couple of officers walked past them, talking among one another in hushed tones. Andrea walked down the other end of the hall.

It was this moment he realized he was nothing but a puppet. And there was no room for personal agency. He simply had to do what he was told. When he was told.

CHAPTER 15

MOMMY

Outraged parents show up in droves at the CA State Court House after Sandra Mills (38), was accused of alleged sexual assault of her child, Mark Mills (13) after she gave birth to another child. Picket signs requesting justice, shouting obscenities as Sandra Mills was seen entering the courthouse. After several months of deliberations, the Grand Jury is reportingly giving the verdict.

Several months passed into the early summer winds, and Ted found himself walking again through the park of his town, Waltham. The trees shaded him from the oppressive heat, wavy heat waves wiggling up from the stone slabs in the ground. His sneakers kicked forward as his hands were resting in his pockets, defying the rule they told him all those years ago. There were couples coming out, holding hands, and he paid special attention to the children at their sides, all joyous smiles, closed eyes, and bright teeth, despite the deformities of missing teeth.

Remembering the day Clemens knocked all his molars out, and they weren't ready to come out. *What did I ever do to him?*

He strode off the path, taking off his shoes, and folding his socks into them, holding them carefully as he attempted to settle down. Finding a trunk, he leaned down against it, back against the rough exterior. There were couples, families, children, dogs barking—oh, that gave him a new kind of thrill. *Damn dogs.*

His hand rested on the moist blades of grass underneath him, furling his hands through them like Jennifer did to his hair during his last emotional break down. *Been a few months. Nothing's triggered it. Not yet. It's bound to happen soon. Should I be here?* Thoughts rattled his fatigued mind, eyelids drooping down, slowly over his eyes as he faded out of consciousness...

The night was dark. The moon was out, crickets, roaches scurrying across the floor, rats clawing at the dreaded walls. He bent his back forward.

A pain jolted in his wrist. Metal restraints. "I see. I can feel pain here. This must be the time before they stuck me in that damned electric chair!"

"Now, now," said a calm, familiar, and caring voice. If anything at all could be said about that woman, Nakamura, those definitely weren't it. He still couldn't see anything, couldn't feel anything except the steel cuff around his wrist, and his—his ankles. "A good little boy doesn't use foul language like that."

He gasped, heart pounding. "I can't—I can't breathe." He exhaled heavily, rattling the chains tied to the cuff around his wrist, and the bedframe. He kicked up, the muscles tensed, cracking the bone in his ankle. "No! No! No! Get away!"

The mattress beneath him squealed as added weight pressed down on it. A firm weight. Next to him. He can't tell what it is. A monster. Yes. A fitting word for one such as her.

"But why would I do that, baby boy?" She asked.

More pressure weighed in on his other side, and tentacles for hair framed his face, black, horrid things, scratching and cutting the sides of him. His body tensed up, blood cooling down rapidly, restricting his movement. Rapid breaths, exhaling and puffing his chest. Sweat covered his wrists, and it felt like the air left the room, none to breathe in, and suffocate. With wide open eyes, he saw nothing. Total darkness. Absolute emptiness. He felt tears streaming down his face, gritting them as her warm breath, came to him, breathing that horrid stench of rotten air, like a monster trapped in their own cave, unable to come out.

Clenching his teeth. Gasping for breath. Muscles frozen in place like petrified wood. No. It would be no mistake to say, in this moment, his body finally gave way to the horror inside his mind, and he too was empty. But why did any of this happen?

Slithers' familiar, tormented scream echoed in his ears, the nails scratching inside him, like nails on a chalkboard.

"Shut up! Shut up! Shut up, Demon Bitch!" came another familiar voice, a voice he hated, almost more than he hated the woman breathing down his neck, drooling over him. Clemens.

"Hush little baby, don't you cry," Nakamura sang.

"No! Stop it! Get away!" the damned nursery rhyme was supposed to bring calmness to them, but it only presented sheer terror for what followed.

The monster's ice-cold hands touched his belly, lifting his shirt as she continued to sing.

"Please. Don't touch me!"

He heard Slither's howling in agonizing pain. "Don't touch me. No. No. No!" It was like nails on a chalkboard.

Another voice. But not the voice he recognized resting above him. Clemens. "Shut. Up."

He heard a slap in the corner. And Slithers was silent. Another monster. An evil person. A wretched being beyond saving.

"Shush," she coddled him, and he felt the weight of her body on his. He couldn't move, not with her on him, not with the cuffs around his wrists and ankles. Even if his muscles were allowed to move, the terror freezing everything in place as he felt her cold hand touching his cheek, turning his frozen neck, and he gazed into this monster's eyes, cold dead eyes, almond shaped. "I'll make you feel good, baby boy."

No.

The drool coated him, coalescing around him as a barbed tongue scratched his lips.

He jolted up right, head sweating, arms forward to protect himself. He gazed forward, and the rest of the people enjoying their day like they should, like good little boys and girls. He folded his hands together, and pulled his knees to his chest, looking down at the space between his legs. So long had it been since that night. That horrible, wretched night. He felt chills running up his spine as if he was there, in that moment. But the dream, it hadn't been as vivid as the rest. It faded, almost.

He noticed the marching footsteps of runs. He turned his head to the left of the common, and a large group, say two-scores of people, men and women in ROTC shirts running in between groups of people, marines, it looked like, with that boring beige hat, rimming in a perfect circle as if everything was all fine, and it was an honor to serve one's country. He studied each individual.

You're all gonna die. And what good will it do anyone really?

They were of different body shapes, sizes, ethnic groups, all running in with one another, but there was one woman who was above the rest, it seemed. Very fit for her age, and quite frankly, it would seem, faster than everyone else. She was an Asian woman, paler than the rest by a margin, and those—

"So," an unfamiliar, but calm voice behind his tree interrupted his thoughts. He turned abruptly, and he saw that same woman at the café in the winter. "I've seen you before." *Yes, I know.* "What brings you to this neck of the woods?"

He looked up to the woman, suspicious of her. This would be the second time he's seen this woman, and the second time both people seemed aware of one another's existence. The only difference last time, was he was no out in the open. Alone. He could run, for whatever he suspected this person wanted of him, but that would only raise questions that had no answer.

"Good enough spot just to sit. Does one have to have a reason to sit in one particular place, or must he have a reason for every little thing that he does?"

"A sharp mind, just like mine, do you care if I have a seat?" she asked, flipping her black braid behind her. She had an accent. It wasn't one he was around recently, so he couldn't quite remember where he heard it from.

"Don't let me stop you, I was just leaving anyway. You can have it," he said, unrolling his socks over his feet.

"Now, I didn't mean to pull you up from your spot. You seemed so peaceful,"

Ha! No, I wasn't.

"It's quite all right. As I said, I was just leaving."

The constant questions and polite nagging of this woman was bothersome. She didn't at all appear to be someone worth mentioning, but here she is, clearly very important, but to what degree, and to whom. Who was she to take such interest in the likes of him?

"Come on, have a chat with me."

"Why? I don't know you, nor you me." *What is your purpose here? This is no chance meeting.* He smiled softly.

"Why, how do you get to know someone without chatting with them? If you want to know someone, you introduce yourself, and you talk to them. Find out what makes them click, and if amiable, offer the same in return." She smiled back, offering a handshake, almost like a business transaction. "I'm Blanka, nice to meet you. And you are?"

"Ted." He reluctantly shook her hand.

A dangerous place to be, out in the public. Trouble is, you simply just can't run, especially when someone has your attention like this.

"Ted, pleasure is all mine, I'm sure."

You have no idea how right you are. Now, what do you want?

"I have a few questions for you," *there it is.* "You see, there was an incident out in the edge of the financial District in Downtown Boston about a year ago. A number of people died, and a car was totaled."

He vaguely remembered. They tried to mug him. Wrong person to try to do that with.

"Do you know anything about that?"

Shit. It's the police. But why are they asking me?

"I know nothing about the incident, Blanka," he lied.

"Oh, but surely you would have seen it on the news,"

You are a god-awful interrogator. If it was anyone else, the trail is cold. No one would remember the exact details. Let alone a news story from over a year ago. Damn you. "No offense, detective,"

"Oh, I'm not a detective."

You lying sack of shit.

"Well, the news is dated if anything else, but I have no memory of it. Fairly, the news is saturated with doomsday conspirators and world leaders pissing on everyone."

"Sadly, you are correct. And what pray tell, are your thoughts on that?" She finally sat down.

Good. You're making me nervous. "Everyone's gonna die. We all do someday, right? Better sooner than later, I'd wager."

"I take it you're a betting man?"

"I'm not betting on anything right now, but curiosity has gotten the better of me, dear," he turned to her eyes, gazing into them, looking for a hint of deception, but he couldn't find any. Either, she is an exceptionally good liar, or not one at all, which means, she might not be the police. "Why ask a stranger about a criminal act of which occurred over a year ago that anyone not involved would have no memory of?"

"You never know what someone might say about something so obscurely meaningless, wouldn't you agree?" She chuckled, sharing the trunk. "You seem terribly formal, or is this just the way you hold yourself, *Ted?*"

The way she said his name sent a shiver up his spine.

"Very formal indeed, I'd not be a shrewd businessman if I was anything but formal," he replied. "But I doubt that is the real answer behind your motive for asking me such a, as you put, meaningless scenario."

"Perhaps you are right, and yet, perhaps you are a horrible gambler," she smiled, tapping on the tree behind them. "You see, I'm a bit of a betting gal myself. I bet a lot of things, sometimes I wager money, other times I wager people and their independent relationships with one another. Children especially." *You're one of those people.*

"But then again, lives are affected by the games I play, and perhaps in the same game of business you play, enriching some and pissing on others."

I'm glad I'm not the only one who is not entirely formal.

"And what is your point in all this? Come on, you're leaving me in suspense." *Why are you coming to me specifically with these inquiries?*

"I suppose you'll have your answer at the proper time," she removed herself from the tree, standing up tall. He put his shoes back on before standing up, looking up at her chin. *You are standing far too close to me.*

"And how will you present to me my answer to your inane inquiries?"

"I'll present to them at such a time fitting for the occasion. Until then, farewell, Ted," she said before turning away.

"And if you have no way of finding me, what then?" he asked.

"Let's just say a little birdie told me our paths will cross again, real soon. Much sooner than you'd like, and it will be, how do you say it here, *tragic*."

Damn you.

He watched her walk away, her skirt swaying in the wind like feathers, and head back to the path. Her pace was brisk, faster than he walked, even. And he was not a slow walker.

Who are you? You don't remind me of someone I'd met at Black Eagle all those years ago? Is it you I sensed watching me?

144

CHAPTER 16

SUSPICIONS

Numerous power outages have been reported throughout the community of Boston. Engineers have been working on the issue, and stated, "The breakers are short circuiting." Still, there is no reported reasons as to why the circuit breakers are short circuiting, and this has the engineers perplexed. The engineers have replaced the circuits with each instance, but no long-term solution has been proposed. These shortages leave Boston in the dark at night.

Crime rates have not been affected by the shortages; however, Detective Henny with the Boston Police Department stated there is a correlation between the short circuit breaking and missing person reports. Since the problem remains unidentifiable and there are no suspects, Detective Henny advised to travel in the dark in groups, supervised.

Spadero gazed at the sky, his suit and shirt tucked tightly, pants firmly pressed, wrinkle free. *Fucking congressmen!* Allow some of them to be elected, they said, it'll be fun they said.

Yeah, right. Making the nights longer just to hear themselves speak. What might they say, if I told them their opinions don't actually mean anything, and we just let them talk to make themselves feel like they have any sway? Yeah, even Sander wouldn't let that slide. As laid back as he is.

The night sky was brimming with excitement, for once. Someone finally paid the electricians to do their damned jobs and fix the power circuits that keep getting shorted out. Generators were still running, so that's a good sign, but times are tough in the empire, and still, he had this little rat to deal with, and he hadn't been able to find time to get to it.

It's almost like these damn Threckets know he's a piece of the puzzle. I really should just let Culain deal with it so I can get on with this manhunt and put it to rest. And finally, the mystery can go die for all I care. Where was that bar again? When did they frequent it?

He remembered Tuesdays, but he didn't remember the name of the bar. Foolish of him for not writing it down.

He walked down the streets, into the hotel lobby, yawning of course, got to make it look good. Briskly walking up the vestibule, pressing the button to open the elevator, as his other hand remained in his pocket. He needed to plan further details with them, now that, supposedly, he had more time to capture this damn rat.

Stepping inside the elevator, he leaned back as he watched the doors shut. No one entered on the way up. *Good. Let's keep it this way. Don't want to accidently make a corpse in here, now do I?*

The elevator took him all the way to the top in silence. Just what he needed after that fraud of a congressman.

He walked down the hall after being released from the horizontally challenged canister, to Culain's door, knocking on it firmly with his fist.

The door opened to an irate Culain. *Good. Keep him angry. Keep him waiting.*

"Come in," he snarled.

He didn't need to be asked. Spadero pushed past him, and took a spot on the couch, resting his arms nonchalantly around it.

"I can't really wait any longer for this, Ilya," he said to the white-haired Russian. "I really need you to pay attention to those alarms and warn Culain promptly. I need you four to—" he scanned the room. Alexander was opening a beer, Ilya was staring out the window for a long-lost answer to a question she didn't realize she had, and Culain was shutting the door. "Where's Blanka?"

"She'll be running in shortly. Heaven knows from where," Alexander burped.

"So unrefined," Ilya replied to the question designed specifically for her. "Yes, I got it, but we can't be everywhere at once."

"You all are going to owe me after this," Spadero shook his head. "Do you have any idea how difficult it is taking orders form two heads of Administration? Do you? In my case, it's actually three, and I must manage everything and everyone else, and I'm about to blow a gasket."

Culain shook his head as if he didn't understand. "Pissant. Don't you think we're doing everything we can to give you the time to get to our target? And what do you mean, multiple heads of Administration? This should only be coming from Sander."

"I have my orders from both Admin Colton Cancer, and orders from Adam Sander, and of course the Head of the House," he scoffed. "What else would I be talking about, you potato munchin' bastard?"

"At least the insult was original," Culain shook his head. "You Americans always want something. You will get what the Administration says is due, nothing more. We serve the Administration of Camelot. You are no different." He scowled, tapping his arm with an impatient index finger.

"My point is, I'm going out of my way to help you with this missing piece of the puzzle, which isn't my problem," he snapped.

"The Holy Grail is missing along with Pandora's Box. It is everyone's problem," Ilya scolded. "I will do what I can on my end, just make sure you do your damned job."

"Who are you to give me orders? You're in my territory." He tilted his head back and faced her.

"We are of the British branch; you are of the American. We outrank you, anyway. The fact that you're taking orders from Sander is a sign that he trusts you of all Americans to get the job done, and report to him, and to us alone." She turned and walked to him. The room grew cold, ice-like veins protruded from her arms and face, poking him in the chest with her icy finger.

Few can play with elements. Flexing much, Ilya?

"The only reason we now trust you is because Culain ballsed it up, and," she pointed her finger at him, "fuck you, too!" She returned her finger to Spadero's chest. "And we have no choice, but we all serve the same cause, or are you likened to a traitor?"

He didn't need to hold on to it for long, but this was a stressful situation when the threads of the world could come undone. What did the world ever do for him? Just force him to work twenty-hour days, and he really only needed one job. And he was forced to work two jobs to put up a front for the Administration, and make sure the appropriate bills were passed and shut down to keep the normies in their place. Oh, the things the normies would go off about if they knew what really happened behind these closed doors.

The door bolted open. Blanka was giddy, smiling from ear to ear. She was the only one of the four that smiled. She closed the door behind her and took off her jacket, kicking off her shoes, bolting to the refrigerator, pulled out a can of beer. She cracked it open, taking a sip. "Ah, much, much better."

"And where were you coming from?" Culain snapped, locking the door.

"Off in a little charming place north of here, actually. Waltham. Ever hear of it?" She leaned against the counter, her beer off to the side as she placed one leg over the other.

"What were you doing there?" Spadero asked, turning his attention away from Ilya and her icy finger.

"Piss off, peasant!" Culain snapped, grabbing a cup off the table and walking it to the sink.

"Oh, Spadero, when did you get here?" Blanka chugged the can of beer, crushed it with her fingers and tossed it to the waste basket. She opened the door to grab another.

"I've been here." His eyes narrowed as he leaned forward, hands folded atop each other.

"I see, well, I didn't see you when I came in, so, might as well have just surprised me," she replied.

"So, it would seem," he said, rather rudely.

"Hey! Mind your own business!"

"No, Culain, I wasn't done scolding him for his blatant disregard for the importance of this mission," Ilya replied softly. *There's a codeswitch if ever there was one.*

Blanka chuckled, one arm resting over her belly as she flipped her hair behind her, the open can, the beer sloshing around inside.

"What's so funny?" Spadero asked.

"Never mind that. Blanka, what were you doing?" Culain asked.

"Spadero, you are so easy to poke fun at. Forgive our little clan here." She swayed back and forth, sipping. "Ah. That is some good beer, if I do say so myself. So, anyway, what was I doing? Oh," she snapped her finger before slamming the can on the counter. "Culain, fuck you very much, by the way,"

"Oh, piss off!" He retorted, cleaning the cup.

"I swear, Culain, how do you manage to piss everyone off within a matter of minutes," Alexander shook his head, leaning against one of the bedroom doors.

"How was I supposed to know?" He threw a fork at Alexander, who caught it in one hand.

"Can we get back on topic please?" Spadero shook his hand, slamming a fist on his knee. "You animals."

"The only animal here, is you. Surely, even our little rat out there has a little more humanity than you," Blanka stated. "Our rat, one little rat hunted by five large cats for reasons we ought not know, but do cats have any other reason for playing around with their yarn at all? Not this cat. I find not the joy. But, since I can't go home, I'll find some enjoyment out of it."

"What are you babbling on about?" Culain interjected.

"I was in a rather bumbling city today, lots of ROTC guys showing up, running their rounds, no doubt. Mother Russia will have their fun with them. Isn't that right, Ilya?" Blanka sneered.

It wasn't a question, and clearly it was in reference to the events unfolding overseas, lots of which wasn't public knowledge, or rather, wasn't supposed to be. Spadero was thinking about the scope of the prospect of WWIII. Something so large involving so many pieces to fall in line could only be the work of the Caster's Administration, and yet, no one thought to tell him. A simple oversight like this was bound to go unnoticed, unless there was a faint possibility, someone else was pulling strings *outside* the Administration.

"Waltham it was, and from what I remembered, a man with some scars on his face, and resting back against a tree trunk, resting before bolting upright like someone was going to attack him, and yet, there I was minding my own business when I invited myself to sit next to him."

"What?" Alexander breathed out.

"I'm sorry, I don't understand babble," Culain said, turning to Alex. "Get that beer away from her."

"No." She turned to hide her beer. She chugged it again, crushed it, and gave Alexander the empty can. "Get your own beer." *Two?* "I want another."

"Finish your story in English, and then you can get blackout drunk," said Culain.

"Our little Ghost. A handsome man. Ilya, why didn't you say he was handsome?" she burped.

"She's drunk. And now useless. Get her to bed," Spadero exclaimed.

"Hey. Hey. Hey," Ilya scolded him yet again with the icy finger. "Shut yer American trap mouth!" She turned to Culain. "Take her to bed. And don't be...Irish."

"I don't wanna go to bed." She burped again. "I'm fine."

"What is that supposed to mean?" he grabbed Blanka before she stumbled back into the refrigerator for another beer. "Seriously, you're such a light weight. It was only two beers. What did you have before you came here?"

"She's drunk off something else, clearly," Alexander snorted.

"Clearly if she took all this time to get here," Ilya sighed as she sat. "We need her sobered," she turned a glaring eye to Spadero as Culain walked the drunk into her room. *Don't be Irish? What does that even mean?* "What did you come here for anyway?"

"Things may have changed since Blanka ran into the Ghost, but I was coming here with a plan on how to reach him and get him alone. Too bad Blanka ran into him first because it might complicate things a little bit," he replied.

"We know that," she said, condescendingly. "That's why we asked for your help, to uncomplicate it, but right now, that seems like it's a little out of your wheelhouse. Look, what we need is more information about where he's coming from, and possibly, at nighttime, get him alone. That is what we need. We don't need to involve his friends if we can help it. What they don't know won't kill them."

Shaking his head, he stood. "Well, this was a waste of time. Tell me what she says when she's sober will you? I might need that information. I need to know exactly what she said, and what he said, so I can come up with a good ruse to get him alone or invite him over for drinks."

He briskly strode his long legs out to the door, unlocking it to depart.

"We will feed you information but be kind when you talk with her again. I'll have her call you," Alexander said.

"Sure thing." Spadero slammed the door behind him.

CHAPTER 17

SAKURA RILEY

China is taking a page out of Russia's book and acquiring other countries along their borders, expanding to include Vietnam, Cambodia, and Thailand. Sources remain unclear as to why these nations were allowed to be purchased through Chinese influence and alter their state lines.

When asked, Press Secretary Jenna Walters said: It is concerning that these acquisitions are happening as supplies dwindle within our country. We assure the American people, we are being prepared to the highest degree to ensure our nation's survival, and to reopen trade with Russia and China.

It was a nice hot summer day, a day to be outside, and muggy, yes, that is what she was used to down in the southern ramparts of Atlanta, but here she was, inside, in the cold room, with her roommate for whom she didn't really much care for, having the AC on full blast, chilling the room. Not nice at all.

Inside, she sat at this desk, looking out the window, left one slightly ajar, despite Keisha's protests, who was very loud. She had a squeaky voice that one. Unfortunately for Sakura, she also had a loathing for high pitched noises. After constant nagging, she reluctantly shut the window, allowing the last warmth of the sun to scatter. *Really, the nerve of these liberal northerners.*

Her English textbook was placed meaningfully atop her desk. She was reading it in preparation for class the following morning, but something was eating at her. She wasn't quite sure what it was. Her raven hair wasn't properly pulled back, as a respectable future officer should, just like her mother, her birth mother, that is, not like her adopted mother. Of course, she didn't complain about the Rileys; she was truly thankful for them taking her in and allowing her to follow in her birth mother's footsteps. Truly.

Sakura loved her mother and her father, what little memory she had of them. They departed from this world at least a decade ago. Shortly in their projects from securing some semblance of world peace that she had the opportunity to enjoy, but now, it was not the time to be comfortable, but to secure it. It had to be defended at all costs, whatever cost it was.

Whatever was paid to secure peace last time, she would be proud to pay such a thing again. Whatever it took, so her children and their children could prosper, just like the USA had the opportunity to do for these last ten years.

Her dreaded roommate turned on the news. Again. She was now subject to a non-update update. Always the same with the same old news story repeating over and over again. These days, everyone harping on the Russians for wanting to expand their borders, but the reality was, when didn't Russia want to expand their borders. One country sets sanctions, while others refuse, no matter how loud the populace cried. It was all more of the same.

"How can you listen to this? Do you really think anything new could be gleaned from this?" Sakura turned, her arm resting on the back end of her chair, frowning.

"Sakura." Keisha shook her head. "Of course, I know. How can I not know? But as a citizen, I need to know as much information as I can, when it comes available. That's how you avoid ignorance."

"It's the same thing, and it's everywhere."

"And you think that to be any less of a threat to us now?" Keisha challenged. "Anyway, I have to get to class."

Sakura's hands clenched at her side as she watched Keisha leave the room, shutting the door behind her. Keisha was infuriating. Sakura had to turn the tv off, getting rid of the pessimistic, nihilistic news coming her way. It reinforced the thought that she should do something, but while she was here, she could do nothing but study, especially with the sun setting.

World peace. It almost seemed like a distant memory now. Peace was a sort of calm before and after storms, but even the unsettling of the news source, and the content of said news in a world where news was biased. No matter who you listened to, someone was lying right to your face, and laughing as you chose to believe them, or someone else. Who cares who gets hurt? No one died from a lie, right? Not like those harm anyone.

But she remembered something, something from long ago, something her mother said to her, prior to her departure from this world:

"My cutie. Stay young, will you? Peace, it is such a wonderful thing really. Once obtained, it is so precious, and it must be safeguarded, whatever the cost. You can't make an omelet without breaking a few eggs, isn't that what they say? Whatever gets broken gets broken, but you can fix that, should you choose to. When the time comes, you will be expected break a lot of eggs to preserve peace. Can you do that?"

"Yes, Mom. I'll break all the eggs. As many as it takes," Sakura said to herself.

She yawned, putting her textbook back in her backpack for tomorrow. Peering out to the sunset, she decided now was as good a time as ever to go for a nice long run through Boston before the university's curfew.

She peered outside the window, hoping it was a little less muggy outside for her run. Feeling the cool breeze, she hurried outside with her wallet, water, and her phone, just in case. Hurrying down the stairs of the university, she strode off the grounds and into the cross walks, running through the heart of Boston. Her body dashed toward the center really, where many interesting things happened, well, interesting to her at least. For someone living in Boston all of this may very well just be the mundane things for the day to day. After all, she admitted, while interesting to her, these things were of a regular occurrence here.

She ran with long strides, feeling the sweat cake her shirt to her chest, as she came up to the grand church building, she saw a lot of people milling about. She'd never been to a church before. Not where she's from, and the Riley's weren't the religious type, no, not at all. Seemed like interesting things were happening, but she thought it was something or somewhere you went to in the mornings, specifically, very specifically on Sundays. Why Tuesday? Why at night?

She stopped, panting, drinking her water, carefully taking each step as it came, the lactic acid building up in her legs, stiffening them up. *Perhaps now would be a good time to come in, rest. I can leave soon, right? Not like one of those cults.*

"Hello," said a bright man, a little heavy set situated behind a table.

In front of him was a little banner, reading: *Café*. It was decorated with elegant letters, and on the table, markers, and name tags.

"First time?"

"You could say that," she said.

"Oh, you sound just like that other fellow,"

She tilted her head curiously. "Other fellow?"

"Someone who's been coming here. When I first met the guy, Ted's his name, he always said that. 'You could say that,' I mean, it doesn't mean anything really. I just noticed."

The man motioned for her to take a name tag, and so she did, writing her name, *Sakura*, in large letters, large enough to be read, and placed it carefully on her sweat covered shirt. "How did you hear about café?"

She glanced over to the crowd of people heading into a side room, a large open area filled with people intermingling with one another.

"I didn't," she said, gulping down another mouthful of water. "I was just running, and this looked interesting, caught my eye. What is this exactly?"

"It's a Young Adult ministry with Park Street Church, catering to the 20s and 30s. We get a lot of new people around here," he said, pointing inside. "You actually came on a good day. There's refreshments in the fellowship hall, where everyone else is."

"Thanks, I guess I'll let myself in,"

Just as she said that a firm hand grabbed her shoulder from behind.

"Hi, Brian," said the man behind the table.

She turned abruptly, twisting her hand body around and stepped away.

"Whoa," said the man with black hair and a rustic beard, whom she assumed was Brian, as he took and wrote his name down on his nametag. "Easy, we're all friends here. Newbie?"

"You could say that," she repeated.

As part of some cruel joke she was on the outside of, and wanted desperately to find out, Brian threw his head back in laughter. "You sound just like Ted. What's your name?"

"Sa—Sakura," she pointed at her nametag, barely hiding her stammer. "Just what it says here."

"Where are you from?" he asked, stepping toward her, but not touching. She was allowed to turn on her own as she walked side by side with him into this *fellowship hall*. Nervous, her breathing became shallower as she crossed the threshold.

"I'm from Georgia." She tried to ensure her southern accent was not apparent, especially up here; however, the movies never really got those right.

"What brings you to Boston?" he guided her to the coffee table, and the plastic coffee containers for instant coffee. *Disgusting*. He poured himself a cup, and walked over to the long table, grabbed a plate in his free hand and filled it up with cheese and crackers.

Delicious.

Grabbing a plate herself, and a napkin. *Mustn't appear to be a slob after all.* "I just started at BU, and I am getting ready for an entrance exam. I'm considering ROTC."

"Oh," he said, a smile beaming on his face. Several people walked in, and it wasn't long before some additional chatter came about, assaulting her ears with a few different vocal frequencies. "You may actually want to talk to Ted. He was in the Army himself."

Brian turned his head this way and that, as if looking for someone. No. He definitely was looking for someone. His eyes narrowed, homing in on something. She glanced that direction, and a man, shorter than the woman standing next to him.

"Hey, Ted!" Brian called over the crowd of people.

Both the man and woman turned to them, but the man seemed to take special interest in her, making it a point to make eye contact, and he frowned. Such eye contact, fierce, and unreasonably intense. He looked like she expected she looked while staring at Keisha, irate. Now that she got a look at his face, eyes sunken in as if with no sleep. She didn't see that often, but she did know enough to understand insomnia. There were scars on his face, some parting where his eyebrows were. This was a man who had seen some shit.

The woman had a concerned look on her face, not nearly with the amount of ire the man had, for whatever reason was still a mystery. Sakura could only assume that she would find out, but hopefully when she does, it won't end up a tragedy. She couldn't envision what kind of tragedy he was imagining, but it couldn't be enviable. Such a shame if it ended like that, really.

"Come on, let me introduce you," Brian said rather enthusiastically.

She followed him through the crowd of people, and the closer they got to them, the more anxious it made her. She felt no motivation or desire to be in conversation with this woman, she wasn't the important one; she didn't have any answers to questions she had, but this *Ted* fellow would have interesting answers to some questions, being in the thick of it all at one point or another. Each step was heavier than the last with the weight of anxiety, or lactic acid. She couldn't right tell which.

"Ted, this is Sakura. I thought you two should meet," Brian said.

The woman sighed and shook her head rather disapprovingly, like they knew the content of questions for which, none of them had any reason to suspect. But these people, whoever they were, had keen eyes and minds, keener perhaps than her own.

"And what, pray tell Brian, would be the reason to bring Sakura to me, rather than anyone else of this entirely fine event you have scheduled and brought me to?" Ted said. He had a way with words of telling someone rather verbosely, 'Why would I want to talk to this person?' Verbose and formal. "Well, rather, you have this lady to thank for making sure I'm here every week, and not in some ditch elsewhere. One might be fearful that I might be infested with rats eating on my insides. Terribly tasting meal I'm afraid."

Sakura coughed up some water, bowing her head, covering her mouth.

"Well, you speak from the heart, it seems like, good grief," Brian exclaimed, patting Sakura on the back.

"Funny, I thought I was speaking from my lips, but regrettably, that shows you I know nothing about the human anatomy," Sakura looked up to see a sneer across his lips.

"Hi Sakura, please forgive my Tedward, he has a certain habit of words. One might say he often quotes Jane Austen, or even the great Shakespeare." The woman reached down to shake her hand. She clasped both her hands around her free hand, which, now had spit all over it. "I'm Jennifer. Pleased to meet you. So, what business have you with my Tedward?"

"Oh, I should mention, she's up here for school for ROTC. I thought Ted would be a good person to talk to about that, no?"

Silence.

Jennifer's eyes drooped down low, shaking her head, obviously disappointed. "Brian, text me next time you want to introduce someone to Tedward. He's very sensitive."

She pointed a finger at Brian. Clearly, she was overprotective of Ted. If he didn't look so war beaten, he would be so cute standing next to a woman so tall. Of course, not in the romantic way but more like a mother protecting her teenaged son from the horrors of the world. But regrettably, coddling someone was far worse than allowing them to make the mistakes themselves.

Jennifer turned her gaze back to Sakura. "Mind what you say." She then turned to the man called Ted, and her mouth approached his ear, whispering something specifically for him to hear. *More coddling.* Jennifer turned over to Brian again. "Come, knave! Let me explain to you why you don't just introduce people to Ted."

She took Brian's hand with force, pulling him away from the conversation, leaving Ted and Sakura alone. Ted's sneer on his lips never faded, watching as Jennifer as she disappeared with Brian into the crowd. If bones could rattle, they'd be rattling inside her.

"So, as you rightly guessed, I am Ted. You, are Sakura, presumably, unless Brian is playing his games again and I need to play twenty-questions to figure out the answer."

"Yes, no games here, no lies here," she said.

"If I had a dollar for every time someone told me that, and lied to my face, I'd be rich." He chuckled, as if it were true.

"Well, I guess, I do have one question. I'm heading into ROTC, and the Army officer training after that. I already have good referrals, but what does being a patriot mean to you? I want to follow in my parent's footsteps as patriots, and they passed before they could tell me what that means."

"A patriot?" he asked, standing up straight, ignoring the fact she mentioned both her parents were dead.

"My mother once told me," She watched his lips curved into a scowl. *Struck a nerve, did I? Sorry?* "That it is my duty to serve as a *patriot,* and I guess there are certain things I can't reconcile with what's going on."

"How do you mean? I know the world is falling apart, and that itself is a cruel joke," he replied.

"Well, can a country fight for freedom without being patriots, or is the mere act of serving one's country an act of patriotism itself?" she asked.

"Well, that's ambiguous, and I personally think that anyone who wears the charging flag on their shoulder is nothing short of a traitor."

She crinkled her nose. *Shameful to even say something like that.*

"When I was in," Ted continued, "you didn't question the orders you took, the lives you took. You didn't ask what became of the people who fell in your place. You'd get your comfort knowing that all the horrible things you did were for the *greater good,* or so they told you anyway. Sometimes, it becomes a, 'I'm going home, so the others can't' and trying to reconcile that is impossible. I'd be lying if I said it was easy. I'd be lying if I told you it ever got better.

"The truth is, patriotism is a flawed concept, and shouldn't even be in your vocabulary. Because in the end, patriotism is hinged on the fact that you are right, and everything else is wrong. And free thought is plagued, both in the civilian world, and the military. There is no exception to this rule. The military is big on 'orders, are orders,' and you follow that rule to the letter on which it is stated and written. No questions. Don't question your superiors and you'll be fine. You'll fall in line with the rest of them. They don't want innovation, just obedience. Mindless drones."

He stepped forward, finger pointing at her chest. She didn't know why, but she felt insecure with this man, as if he knew something she didn't.

"The other facet of this formulaic relationship that you'll form is the illusion that you are a person. You are not. You are nothing more than a number, a statistic, with a set amount of uses, carefully cataloged somewhere by your superiors who assign you a specific value, which, just like the stocks, adjust over time. Your use will deteriorate as your body deteriorates, and you will be useless, and like so many before you, they will find the most efficient way to dispose of trash. Discharge? Is it beneficial or cost effective? Or is an accident much more effective? So many ways to go." He spoke with the demeanor of a villain of sorts, one of those ones with a lot of experience manipulating people, almost like he planned to push her away from either him, or the military. But she couldn't disappoint her mother.

"You didn't answer my question," she pouted, crossing her arms, looking down to him.

"But I did, and you simply weren't paying attention," he chided, retracting his hand into his pocket. "So, what else is on the docket for today?"

"Why don't you tell me about the events unfolding. What are your thoughts on—"

"An inevitable tragedy," he answered, completing her thought for her. "What's the point of it all, really? You fight, you die, repeat, over and over again. There was peace for ten years."

Because of my mother.

"And here we are, World War Three is on our doorstep, and it was all but unavoidable. What became of the hearts of those who died for the peace? It was pointless. So, what if we offer up monuments? Doesn't mean anything when they're knocked down, shattered by way of a nuclear bomb. The question you need to ask yourself, is what is the price you're willing to pay? What is the price you will accept from others? Or will you be like my CO and be a rat, and not pay anything for the cost involved, but lay that cost on others to pay? And in the end, with it all being worthless because when you die, regardless of you succeeding or not, will you find satisfaction knowing that in a generation yet to come, this world will be scattered, shattered, and covered in ash? If the answer is yes to that last question, by all means, waste your life."

She exhaled through her pursed lips, looking down on a bitter old man. Her fist clenched her bottled water. *Be kind. Be respectful. Hard to do that with someone by the likes of him.*

She turned her frown upside down, making eye contact. It's only respectful after all. *You don't like him or anything. How could you?* "Thank you so much for taking the time to talk to me, and your intriguing input."

"Glad I could help," he smiled, teeth shining in that creepy way a villain does in a movie.

About-faced, she walked to get some more cheese and crackers. *Free for the taking, right?* She pops a cracker in her mouth, and a woman walked right by her.

"Oh, didn't see you there," the woman reached over to grab a plate.

"No problem," Sakura smiled brightly, fighting those negative emotions of extreme ire toward someone who clearly hates his country, and his countrymen. The blatant disregard of sacrifice, and lack of willingness to move on, to do what needs to be done. *We don't need men like him.*

She made eye contact with her, the blond-haired woman with bangs hanging to frame her face, and the rest neatly tied back.

"New here? I don't think we've met," she stretched out a hand.

Sakura took it in hers. It's only polite after all.

"Samantha Harris."

"Sakura," she answered.

"Oh." Samantha exclaimed, "feel free to just call me Sam, everyone does. Forgive me if this is too personal, but are you a second generation or third generation? Just, your name, isn't typical for an American, and you speak perfect English. So, I'm just assuming, I don't mean any offense if you are actually from Japan."

"What?" she chuckled. "No, none at all. Our family's been here since the concentration camps, unfortunately." *Always with the concentration camps. I get why that was done, but still. It pushed my family into generations of service, whether we wanted to or not.* And so, she silently thought to herself if she was continuing on that path or wanting to striver for it for her own reasons. Was the future hers? Or had it already been decided?

"I'm sorry to hear that," Samantha said, taking a bite of some cheese.

"It's okay. We've been in the military since then, serving in what way we could. It was our way of saying, 'we forgive what happened.'"

"That's very big of you, and your family, and you still share those ideals, so it's nice the fast-paced American culture hasn't changed that in your family history," Sam continued. "But what brings you here? Sorry, I know you've probably been asked that already, but I'm interested in you."

"What?" Sakura was taken aback, heart racing as she shot a glare.

"No." Sam said, waving her hands nonchalantly. "Not in a romantic way, I have a boyfriend, if that's what you were thinking. No, as a person. So, what brings you here?"

"Er. Well," her glare softened. "I was just passing by. I was on a run, taking a break from my studies."

"Oh, what are you studying?"

"I'm going to school for ROTC, but I actually just finished talking with Ted, the—"

"Were you kind to him?" She asked.

"As kind as a Sakura Tree," Sakura said, chewing on another piece of cheese.

Samantha let out a sigh of relief. "Good,"

Good? Why is everyone coddling him? What makes him so special. "He's special," as if to answer the unasked question. "It was hard for him, for more ways than one. It's kind of hard to come back from all that."

"From what?"

"Trauma," she said. "But, we'll not talk about that. That would be for him to tell. Honestly, even I don't know everything, but the one other person who would know close to everything would be Jennifer."

"I see." It was all beginning to make sense. Jennifer and Ted had some kind of relationship, and she said something specifically to him, what was it?

"Anyway, are you going to stick around for the study?"

"Study?"

"This is a Bible Study, every Tuesday night."

Sakura gazed outside, watching the streetlights turn on. "I suppose I have time to spare, I'm all caught up. But, it shames me to say I've never opened a Bible."

"For many people, it's their first time. Sometimes it's also their last, but sometimes they continue to read it," she smiled.

Another man came tumbling in, tripping over his feet, wearing BDUs. He tumbled in; his eyes glazed over as he saw the cheese.

Cheese. Everyone here likes cheese for some reason. I like it too, but not enough to go goo-goo over.

"Hey, you made it back." Sam called him over, waving her hand.

"That I did. Didn't want to forget."

Samantha eyed his BDUs. "You know, you really should think about civie attire."

"I still think it's funny you know that's what I call you," he chuckled, filling his plate.

"I have Ted to thank for that," she laughed.

Sakura noticed him rolling his eyes. "That man needs some serious down time," he turned to Sakura. "Who's this?"

"Oh, she's joining us this evening. Sakura, this is Lamar." Samantha introduced.

He stretched out his hand to shake hers. "Pleasure."

"We don't use BDUs anymore," Sakura commented.

He threw his head back, chuckling as some crumbs escaped his dental prison, and onto his beard. "Nope. Not in the service anymore, discharged." He wiped his face clean. "But you're right, everyone uses the ACUs now. I don't have those. No reason to."

"So, Sakura is going to school for ROTC,"

"Is that right?" he asked. "Well, we better start calling you ma'am."

Samantha laughed at that.

"What? No." she said, turning away. She knew her cheeks were turning red.

"Lieutenant Sakura, uh," Lamar chuckled.

"Riley,"

"Lieutenant Sakura Riley." He smiled, nodded, and turned to Sam. "That has a nice ring to it actually. Well, any man or woman would be proud to serve under someone like you, I'm sure."

The people around them started walking into streams, heading back out the door. Sakura shook her head this way and that, peering through the people, seeing Jennifer and Ted holding hands, and he didn't waste a moment to shoot a glare at Sakura as they passed by.

"Time to go. Come on," Samantha said. "Sakura, follow me and Lamar, we're going to a small group. There will be some fun after. There always is."

Sakura followed behind Lamar and Samantha, growing ever conscious on how she smelled, not that anyone said anything with her BO perforating the room. She followed, blending in with the crowd into the lobby, heading up a few stairs before exiting the lobby, following down another set of stairs, very small, as if to bypass some rubble in between buildings, and in another room. She followed into some chairs, pushed into some long gray tables, and around this room, which had windows overlooking the side of the street, were bookcases filled with books, and books above them, which could only be accessed through other rooms above them, much like balconies.

She sat next to Samantha, and Lamar was on Sam's other side. Another man came in and sat next to Sakura.

"Sam, you didn't save me a seat?" he asked.

"Michael, you didn't meet Sakura."

The man snickered as if he didn't mean the sarcastic remark toward her. "Michael, nice to meet you. Newcomer?"

"Yes," she said, dumbfounded that she's answered this question effectually an inexhaustible number of times, and she didn't want to answer the question again. "Sakura. Riley."

"Michael Clemens."

"Now, like usual, we have a number of new faces here, and we don't know you," said a man in the corner.

She noticed Ted out of the corner of her eye, and he shot another glare at her. *What's his problem?*

"So, we'll go around, state your name, where you're from, what brings you to Boston, and the icebreaker, hmm, if you could be remembered for one thing before you die, what would it be?"

She took note of all the monotonous answers, and the general overview of the demographics of people in the room; several different ethnicities, many local to the United States, and of course from around the world. Many of these people didn't fail to mention their concern with the tensions rising everywhere toward everyone, and no hope in sight. Despite that blatant concern, none of them wanted to be do bodies, no action, none of them wanted to be remembered for doing anything remotely worth mentioning. Clearly, none of them had the state of the country at the forefronts of their minds. *Why?*

"I'm Michael, I came here for work, and never left really, I'm from Vermont. Remembered? I want to be remembered as the last one laughing!"

The room was fueled with awkward laughter, but none from Ted, who leaned back in his chair, hands folded over his chest as he scanned the room.

"I'm Sakura. I'm from Atlanta," she began, nervous about exposing her roots. "I study at BU for the ROTC program, and to be remembered, I want to follow my parents' footsteps and keep serving, so I want to be remembered as someone with unwavering commitment in service to my country."

"How very patriotic of you," Sam said.

Ted would clearly disagree with you. Ted's the real traitor, isn't he?

"I'm Sam, and I'm also from Vermont, came here for work, and mostly to follow and stalk Michael." More laughter. Even Jennifer lightened up, cackling with her hair hanging over the back of her seat at the other end of the room. "Remembered for anything, I don't want to make it in the history books. Something always unpleasant pops up, but if anything, perhaps that I could do one good deed worth remembering for the little guy."

"I'm Lamar," he said. "I'm still adjusting to civie life, came here for a job after the marines, and I guess I'm from all over, ha! I can't think of something to be remembered by, but there is someone who's memory I'd like to remember."

Sakura turned her head, and Ted, also out the corner of her eye, glared at Lamar. *You hate him too, huh?*

"There was a man once, never wore a patch or anything like that, but he saved my life a number of times, but ten years ago, he just vanished. I'd honestly like to thank him for saving my life. He taught me the value of it. Don't remember his name or anything."

Interesting.

She listened to everyone, one by one they shared their answers, and who they were. Then her blood boiled, and her left hand retracted into a gentle fist, and released pressure. The man she grew to hate in such a short time: Ted.

"Ted Anderson, I've been in Boston, for about a year now. Came here for work, and someone decided I should stay here, so I stayed here." He let out a sigh, placing his hands behind his head, averting his gaze to the ceiling. "What do I want to be remembered for?"

There was a silence in the room, all waiting for an answer from Ted, as if he was going to say something absolutely profound and that it was worth listening to. "I don't."

That's it? She frowned. *That's seriously it?*

Shaking her head. She didn't care if he saw her disapproving answer. Simple enough really, but all that to say, she got no useful information from him at all, and that he's just an unbearable ass.

The study of the Bible commenced, but truth be told, Sakura was too fuming to understand any of it, and all of it went over her head. Not that she considered herself dumb by any means, but rather, Ted managed to piss her off by setting these expectations, and failing all of them, much like wrapping a noose around someone's neck, taking him out to a cliff, and attaching the other end of the noose to a number of cinderblocks, and tossing them out to sea, watching their souls depart from this world in a last effort of defiance. Soldiers were supposed to be patriots. It was who they were. Who she understood them to be, disciplined and self-sacrificing, proud to have served. All of these, he failed to meet.

But regarding anything she read that night, she couldn't tell someone what she read. In fact, she couldn't recall any of it, not even the name of the individual book.

Despite everything with Ted, she was glad to have stumbled onto an event tonight. It was good for her to take an extended break but, damn that man. The man should just go and jump off a damn cliff with all his nihilistic tendencies. The experience was good, but Ted pissed her off so much she couldn't enjoy all the good things about it.

Lamar touched her shoulder as she grabbed hold of the parking sign. "So, did you enjoy yourself here?"

"Yes, I'd say it was enjoyable."

"Sakura, do you want to hang out with us tonight?" Sam walked over with Michael; hands interlaced.

Sam swiftly turned to Jennifer. "Jennifer, Teri's?"

"Not tonight." Jennifer called back, guiding Ted off into the street toward the subway station. *Good.*

"Next time, then." Sam turned back to her. "How about it? You don't actually have to drink or even order anything. We just go there to hang out."

"Since Ted's not going," she was not going to be subtle about her distaste toward him, "Sure."

Sam frowned.

"Well, considering his history," Lamar began, "I still don't fully understand him myself. I figured I of all people here would."

"What do you mean?" Sakura asked.

"How do I explain this?" He tapped his chin. "Ah, if I were to go to the store, and wait in line at check out, and there's another person behind me, who also served, but I've never met them before. All it takes is one word, and we're talking like we've known each other all our lives, because no one understands a veteran like another. It's a brotherly bond that can't be broken. Ted is the exception. Someone in his unit, or his past, or multiple people must have screwed him over real good to make him not trust anybody."

CHAPTER 18

UNCERTAINTY

World report: The US fleets remain ocean bound at our harbors, fully manned and gunned, both on the East and West Coast. Destroyers, Cruisers, and Carriers were recommissioned.

Russian fleets sail further in, closing in across the Atlantic Ocean. Submarines were reported scouting. The Russian Atlantic fleet is on standby. Chinese fleets sailing in from the west, carriers, destroyers, and Cruisers recommissioned with heavy artillery rounds. The Chinese Pacific Fleet is on standby.

Passenger flights have not been canceled from overseas.

Bridgette sat down in the main hall, her legs hovering over the carpet with her knees bent. In her left hand, she held a cup, steaming hot tea. The way it should be, steeped nice and proper. Not like horrible people make a habit of ruining a perfect cup of tea. Americans. They don't know how to make tea, or enjoy them, truly awful people. Like McCurdy, the blond-haired wanker.

Bridgette exhaled deeply, sipping her tea before placing it back down on the table, set very finely with green embroidery. Ancient Anglo-Saxon symbols woven into the old world to this one, intertwined relations, corrupting the Threads of Creation in an irreparable way. It was only a matter of time before creation undid itself.

And yet, she thought, one hand dangling over the side of her arm rest, the idea that one of them would be so fatalistic to make the choice for everyone else, that life was meaningless; moral and religious principles were null and void and held no value. Of course, one who truly believed that didn't hate the world, they just hated the people in it. Earth, so tragically beautiful, filled with love, but the despair was ever growing, ripping hearts to shreds before their time was up.

It was all over the news. Oddly enough, Camelot wasn't responsible for these wars, for once. Humans managed to wage war and focus on killing one another all themselves at a mass scale. Shouldn't be a surprise, really, for humans were only good at breaking things. Even most of their creations were shams, not worth mentioning, and the things worth mentioning were horrible. Casters didn't build weapons of mass destruction. They didn't need to. With enough planning, humans managed to do that all on their own.

"You okay there, Bridgette?"

She looked up, and Adam briefly smiled, but that same tired expression on his face remained. She knew why, another sleepless night. He took a seat across from her, steam rising from his cup.

"As fine as I'll ever be." She frowned, tapping her toe on the ground, her hand warming up to the cup of tea.

She closed her eyes, breathing in mana from the air, and the chair on which she sat, weaving them inside her mana veins like little cyclones of storms inside her body. Red veins protruded on her palms, heating the cup. *Gotta keep it hot after all.*

"You know, sometimes I wonder if these gifts of ours were designed for war, like we so often use them," said Adam, pulled out his palm and absorbed mana from multiple sources, showing his mastery of castery, and snobbery. Temperature changed to a draft, cooling down just a little, but not enough inside Camelot's lobby to draw attention. Truly, a master at snobbery. A little black western jackdaw chirped in his hand, fluttering its wings for the first time, and dove from his hands, fluttering as it flew up, and out the nearest window on this fine occasion.

"Was there a point to that? Don't keep me in suspense." Bridgette frowned.

"No." He forced a laugh. "I found something—"

"ADAM." She cried. "What in God's name is going on? I'm in the dark. I want to know what's going on, and these goose chases are taking us nowhere."

There was silence in the lobby, and many Casters inside, male and female of equal ratio trained their eyes on her, clicking their tongues as they ignored the outburst. Adam's lips curled downward into a disapproving frown.

"I'm sorry," she said, picking up her tea again.

"It's fine." He replied.

Ha, no, it isn't.

"I've told you everything I know. I have you in meetings with me, discussing these matters. Because you speak your mind, and without restraint do I trust you, and that you are no stranger to tough decisions. We own the whole world, and yet, here we are, clueless about any of this, which implies someone on the inside wants something, but what? There's no way anyone, no matter how hopeless would go through with the desecration of creation."

"But it isn't outside the realm of possibilities," she said, calming her nerves. "That's what scares me most. You know, some days, I go about, getting some tea, reading a book to get me out of this Hell I've been thrust into. And the people of creation, the ones we share no faith in—the ones who can't know what we are, or what goes on in the grim darkness of the night—who say the world is better off dead, and the people in it. That is what terrifies me. The darkness of humanity mixed in with our own darkness, is far worse than dealing with these Threckets, demons, and devils. Humans are far worse."

"I know." Adam pursed his lips, leaned back, and brushed a hand through his hair. "And we're nowhere near finding a solution. I've tried everything, and everything I haven't tried has been tried by someone else. I'm beginning to think there isn't a solution to this curse."

"Maybe this was a curse without the possibility for atonement," she said. "Why would there be? What grace is there for someone who fused Pandora's Box to the Holy Grail? God banned us from those gates. We live in a Hell, and what makes it worse is we still serve Him; knowing that we'll only ever see Hell, and at best, nothingness. And just end up in a hole in the ground, six feet under, forgotten."

He nodded. "Indeed, there are days I wake up where I think death might have been easier, except that little promise of prophecy."

"What prophecy?" she jerked her head, scowling. "The one where King Arthur will rise from the dead again, and guide us all to Avalon? That prophecy? A land we thought was promised to us, only to end up being a mirage."

"It's a hope, a possibility," he replied.

"Adam, it's a false hope, with nothing to back it up." She took her palm into her mouth, biting it firmly. "The moment that we, whatever we are, are born, we are born into the throes of death, and only through the sense of duty to protect a world, a creation we don't have any stake in."

She felt tears coming down her cheeks, and Adam leaned forward, eyes locked in with hers, listening intently. "What's the point? If King Arthur comes, what about those who came and died before? Those who were lucky enough to just have the worms eating their corpse? And those not good enough for that? We live in this nightmare everlasting, for what?"

"Bridgette," he spoke softly.

"You said it yourself, 'Death might have been easier.' Then let us be done with it." She waited for a response from him, to allow him the faintest notion of a chance. There was nothing out of Adam's lips.

"Is it really our fault that we were cursed so? And thus, submitted to a life of torment without any hope of it getting better. What hope is there? *Tell me.*"

Her hands firmly gripped the table. The rest of the Administration inside the lobby looked at her, and Adam, eagerly waiting for his response. This told her: they were thinking the very same thing. They were suffering the same thing. They were living the same thing. What was the point of all this?

"Bridgette," he began, softly as only Adam could, "The only thing that is certain, is uncertainty, and with that uncertainty, we can be certain that not everything is lost, and that there's a chance, no matter how infinitely small, that this Hell can be undone, and we can go home. I am banking my last guess, my last chance at this unknown and the mystery of both men, the Ghost, and whoever was at Devil's Pass. Maybe then, they can provide some certainty, and make things a little less uncertain."

"Administrator Sander," came a shy petite voice scurrying around like a detestable rat. A woman held a manilla folder with loose documents, her auburn hair not quite tied down, swaying back and forth as she approached them.

"For God's sake, just Adam." He turned away, breaking away this dramatic discussion, and what better way to make her forget her cynical tendencies and thoughts than a disruption like this? But, it must be important—"

"Out with it, Rebecca," he snarled.

"Sorry," she bowed her head. "I was doing the research you asked me to correlate it to Devil's Pass, and all I really found was, well, missing pages."

"What?" he asked.

Missing people. Missing Holy Grails. Missing Pandora's Box. Missing answers. Missing pages. What else will go missing? Sooner or later our minds will be mush, and thus, missing also. Great. Sarah McCurdy. Fuck you. We will find you. We will take back this Grail. I will fucking kill you and feed your carcass to the rats! You cunt!

"Pages in the archives. They're missing,"

"Yes, I heard you the first time."

"Out with it!" Bridgette threw her teacup across the room, shattering it on the wall.

"Like did someone rip out the pages or...?" Adam surmised in that mocking tone that told her enough. He was through with a bunch of other crap no one wanted to deal with.

"No, like, when the monks of old rewrote everything, pages weren't documented,"

Adam bit his lip, probably trying to keep his composure, and clearly failing, though, Bridgette knew it prevented him from swearing most of the time. "Get me a detailed report. I want the name of the book, the volume, where the page, or pages are missing, and if it is the same typographical error throughout like volumes. I want the history of those books also in that report. Work on it with haste. I want it tomorrow. Get as many hands on it as possible." He turned to Bridgette. "I'm going to bed. I must deal with this tomorrow. I suggest you do the same."

She watched Adam walk off, moving down the corridors into the Administrator's room. She lived here with the Casters, well, the Casters inside this facility designed as an emergency response unit to combat Threckets at a moment's notice. Rest was often in short supply, but yes, rest sounded nice. Hell, who knows. Maybe she could finally get a full four hours.

CHAPTER 19

FIRING RANGE

It is clear now more than ever that the Russian and Chinese fleets are working with each other to assault the US borders, with fleets on both sides. The US fleets remain harbored, and there is no word from Press Secretary or the Secretary of Defense. We'll take you now to Chief Commanding Officer of Black Eagle Company was available for questioning, and had this to say:

It's a crying shame is what it is. I have my fleets. I have my soldiers and my technology. We're ready to fight, I just need a funding source. I have solicited Snells himself for funding, yet he seems to be avoiding my calls. It might be time for him to retire, assuming there's an America left to retire in. We're a company, not affiliated with the government. We don't risk our lives for free.

Sakura laid in her bed, still had her pajamas on, the camo style that she loved. For whatever reason, she liked the idea of various shades of green and brown molding together in various shapes. When she found out the military transitioned to pixelated gear, though, for good reason, she was none too impressed. She would keep these until they started fading out, color, threads, and all. The Saturday morning sun was beaming down on her face, and she covered her eyes, yawning as the sun irritated her nose, forcing her to a violent sneeze.

Her roommate, someone tolerable at least when she was sleeping, snoring far louder than any alarm clock. She imagined the military alarms when horrible things were happening were exponentially louder than everything and everyone else, drowning out even these obnoxious snores.

Her phone rang.

Who could that be at this hour? The sun was just rising. Her roommate stirred, and she took her phone. *Lamar. God why did I give him my phone number?* It was polite to give something someone asked for. That's why. She took off to the outside hall, closing the door to avoid Lamar hearing the obnoxious woman in her dorm.

"Sakura," she said, leaning back against the wall, one leg crossing over the other.

"How'd you sleep?"

"Fine."

"Hey, question. Do you like guns?" Lamar asked on the other end of the phone.

Why, of course I do. I shot them all the time, until that is, I came here, where the guns I shoot aren't allowed.

"Yes, why do you ask?"

"I've been dying to go shooting with someone, and no one around wants to, I know a place in Dorchester. You interested?"

She spent months up here already, rarely went home down in Georgia, and she had to assume her touch with the trigger finger was getting rusty. Not many places to go around shooting here, and not like she could hunt here either.

"Sure, why not. Where?"

He gave her the location of where the closest T-stop was. *These people really need to learn to drive.* Upon giving her the detailed instructions on how to get there, she walked back into her room, pulled up her laptop and grabbed the driving instructions online, and dressed in her jeans, and grabbed a plain t-shirt before driving out.

She drove out with her truck onto I-90, heading eastward toward the ocean, before traversing through the tunnel. It would be crowded, and dangerous if one doesn't pay attention to the signs. Impromptu drivers cutting you off for no apparent reason except to dangerously merge across three lanes into oncoming traffic to turn into a tunnel just too sharp for their turn. She thought she should hear screeching or crunching metal coming from the other end of the tunnel. *These Boston Drivers are insane!*

Continuing driving and avoiding all manner of calamity, (which was the minefield of caffeine, sleep depravity, and the recklessness and probably suicidal drivers inside this city, filled with nothing but disdain for their own existence). Upon arriving, she parked safely at the driving range, and there Lamar was, in civie attire, standing outside the range, which was inside a large and tall building.

She shuddered.

Not her favorite. A controlled environment for which anyone could feign to be an expert in marksmanship because they don't have to account for longer distances, velocity of the round and the type of rifle used, the lack of moving targets, wind resistance, and the temperature outside causing rounds to go haywire off course if too hot or cold. Firing guns wasn't a science, it was an art that few truly understood. Of course, an art that no one in Boston would understand, since they only allowed certain types of firearms in the hands of civilians, herself included. Hell, she couldn't even bring her AR15 here.

"You drove?" He asked.

"Yeah," she replied, slamming the door shut, locking it with her key. "All right, let's go."

"Eager?" He smiled as he turned to head into the door.

She smiled back. "Well, I can't exactly go out in the backyard and start shooting, now, can I? Someone will call the police and have me arrested. I can't have that."

"No, especially if your aim is to be a commissioned officer. You need to have a clean record, but here," he led her to some shelves. The instructor was inside the shooting range, observing one round of individuals, eyes and ears covered. "You can go crazy. What type of rifle do you prefer shooting with?"

"Bolt-action," she replied. "I prefer a Forthington."

"It's all they got here for bolt-action, actually," he replied, picking out a box of rounds specific to the Forthington design. There was no worse way to blow out a barrel and have one's face blown up with shrapnel than to fire any gun with the wrong kind of ammunition.

"Did you say you served in the marines?"

"Yes," he said as he pulled out his wallet. He brought the rounds to the cashier, "Two lanes, please."

"Sure thing." The cashier took the card, ran the transaction through, and Lamar left with the boxes of ammunition. "When was the last time you shot anything?"

"Six months ago. I was out huntin' with my AR15," She gasped, letting her accent slip.

"The good old AR," he said stiffly walking, one legged staggered over the other toward the firing range.

"War wound?" she asked.

"Hmm?" He said as he pushed the door open into the firing range. It was much more secluded than the other one, with a separate instructor handing them the goggles and earmuffs.

"Your leg?" She spoke louder.

"Oh, that." He shouted, going onto his lane. "Yeah, remember the other day I talked about someone who saved my life?"

"Yeah,"

"Well, the truck I was in exploded, and a large part of it landed on my leg. I had to take an extended leave of absence to heal it back up. The man who saved me secured the position before pulling the entire front end of the burning truck off me," he replied. "Truth is, just being in the truck when it blew should have killed me. Luck was on my side that day."

She tried to envision what this looked like as the instructor was going over safety protocol and measures. Nothing she hasn't already heard over a thousand times. The instructor cleared the floor to start firing. Her target was a small dot, resting far down range, on the backboard as it connected to some concrete behind it.

Holding and pressing the stock to her shoulder, loading the rifle's cartridges, and her trigger finger just above the trigger, she breathed steadily, lining up the sights with the target, dead center. Exhaling, she squeezed the trigger. *Bang!* The rifle kicked back into her shoulder, pushing her back half a step. The bullet traversed, spinning through the air, striking what she thought was the target, as the paper rippled. She fell into a rhythm. Pulling the bolt-action lever. Reloading the round from the cartridge back into the chamber. Aiming down the sight.

"All right, that's enough!"

She didn't realize she shot that much already; the box was completely empty. She sighed with disappointment.

She wheeled her target up to her, and when it reached her, she pulled it off the stables and looked at her results. *Dead center. Same as always.* Indoor ranges never gave her the variety she craved in a shooting range, one of the many reasons she preferred hunting over shooting cans.

"How'd you do?" Lamar peered over his corner.

"Take a look for yourself!" She said excitedly, waving her results right in front of him.

"Dead center. You're a good shot, much better than I am." He pulled out his sheet, and she noticed one hit dead center, but the other ones were much more focused around the edges toward the white. Clearly, he was out of practice.

She followed Lamar back out of to the parking lot while many people came in and out of the firing range. "I wanted to ask, since I couldn't get any information out of Ted. It's been bothering me, since I don't have a clear way on how to answer it..."

"Yeah, you're not going to get much out of Ted, like I said."

"You wouldn't be talking about Ted Anderson, would you?" Said a man, largely built, and a serious face. "Sorry to interrupt, I know the guy, how's he been?"

"Honestly, I don't know," Lamar answered, scanning the man up and down. "Did you serve?"

"Yeah," he said. "Still do. 75th Ranger Regiment back in the day, with Sergeant Ted Anderson."

"My man. Bring it here." Lamar and the man hugged each other. Clearly, they didn't know each other as they talked almost like old war buddies, almost as if to catch up on their lives. This was the brotherhood Lamar mentioned. 75th Ranger Regiment was no joke, and yet Ted seemed to be of a different cloth altogether, rejecting this same brotherhood which she was witnessing now.

"Sorry to interrupt your reunion, but my question," she said to them.

Lamar turned to her. She got the other man's name out of the small talk: Jeffrey Clemens.

"Sorry, Sakura, what was the question again?" Lamar asked.

"How would you define patriotism?" She asked. "Like I said, Ted wasn't helpful."

"He always was a nihilist," Jeff explained.

"Supporting your country. Giving life and liberty to a higher goal, protecting the Constitution we serve, the democratic republic we serve, and the people who reside here," Lamar said. "Well, that's what it means to me."

Lamar bit his lip. "Hey, Jeff, whatever happened to your unit after the wars?"

"Our unit was ultimately disbanded. Not the 75th, but our unit was merged into Black Eagle."

"I didn't realize that was your unit," Lamar said.

"Black Eagle?" Sakura had heard of them before. She didn't know who they were or their purpose, but it seemed evidently odd to her that the Ranger Regiment would rename themselves to Black Eagle.

Unless even now, she didn't fully understand the entirety of the scenario.

"Never heard of them?" Jeff asked.

"No," she replied.

Jeff raised an eyebrow as if he didn't believe her. "Really?"

She was silent.

"It's mostly out in the open now. I'm surprised. Black Eagle was inducted twenty-five years ago under the directive of General Snells at the time," he answered. "It ultimately turned out to be a mercenary group, which didn't hire themselves out to the highest bidder, but only to the US There are things we do and can get away with, that Lamar could never. It grew exponentially, especially after these last few years as they took applications from other servicemen from around the world. It is effectively one large governmental branch, with its own funds and resources. Currently, it's about as large as the US military, all six branches, and a much better research and development division. Think of it like the French Foreign Legion."

"That sounds like a colossally bad idea," she said. *Hiring out mercenaries? Rules of Engagement? Lack thereof? What couldn't go wrong?*

"Very efficient actually," he answered. "Without restraints, it is very easy to take out key personnel when needed. It takes a specific type of person to be in Black Eagle."

"And someone with lots of mud on their boots," Lamar agreed.

"Welcome to a moral quagmire. That's what you get with war."

"Sounds like something that Ted said," she said.

"Well, say nothing at all for Ted Anderson. He was the best at his job. No one could ever take that away from him, but he was always a prick," Jeff said. "Well, see you around. I've got places to be."

CHAPTER 20

REASSIGNMENT

Long Beach Washington was struck with cannon fire from a nearby destroyer. Chinese fighter jets are soaring over Seattle, dropping bombs on civilian targets. Cruiser ships pulled in, deploying amphibious vehicles, dropping off and securing the coastal state of Washington, allowing envoys to deploy infantry on the shorelines.

No response from the Military personnel led to drastic preparations by Chinese forces, deploying heavy calvary units.

Chief Commanding Officer Malcolm in a report: It's a tragedy. There is literally no reason that had to happen. I can't do anything. My hands are tied by the bureaucracy.

Sarah leaned forward, sniffling as she gazed into the mirror of the brightly lit bathroom of the airport; gazing deep into her green eyes, watering, and her red hair shriveled, combed, and tied back. Her button up shirt wrinkled, a loose button at the top, and her black slacks pressed. The only thing neat on her person, or it would have been if someone didn't vomit their lunch on her shoes, still polished, shiny enough for her to see her reflection, not that she ever wanted to, unless to find herself deep in thought.

Deep in thought. Such a state she often found herself in, not bothering to negotiate or talk with other people.

Her glazed eyes reminded her of the curse she'd been born with, just to live in this world, along with everyone else with this damned Caster's Administration, and who could forget the crimes, historically they committed to cover up the truth. Where do these lies end? Where does the truth start? She was certain even now, the head of this organization didn't even know what was going on. Falling in line, just like everyone else.

The truth was lost somewhere; she was certain of it. If she wasn't, she wouldn't have even gone through the hassle of listening to Colton in the first place, and conducting a heist to steal the Holy Grail, golden rim. For something half cursed, fused with Pandora's Box, it was pretty. Other than that, it was the painful reminder that she necessarily killed humans she got close with. Humans—*normies*, people who can't use the radiation through their veins, because it would kill them. Of course, that wasn't the only thing that separated them from the normies.

What else but that curse come down from God that they would never enter the Kingdom of Heaven in their own deaths, but at best, just merely die, with their souls brushed away like a vapor of the wind. Nothing. Emptiness. In the end, no one would truly miss them for attaining such a high standard of living, of killing, and of protecting the truth everyone wanted hidden, even from them. The grand prize of this life was just that—death, and it almost unattainable, and those that failed, which was almost everyone, was certainly cast into the number of different Hells based on how many innocent lives they let die. Never mind the amount of innocent lives they killed, of which, Sarah could number herself in the hundreds.

Of course, killing people was necessary. It came with the territory. She expected no less, but she never chose to do any of it, just born, cast running, provided she knew exactly who her birth parents were. She didn't. Just tossed to an aunt and uncle who was accused of some shady dealings before their lives were ultimately snuffed out and consumed. Fed to the Threckets in their last deal, sent to their graves, and early deaths, if you will, fed to beasts by none other than Adam Sander, the English Swine. But could she fault him for that? He was just doing his job after all.

That's what she kept telling herself anyway. She kept repeating it to herself in the hopes that one day she might believe it. It would be a lie to say even if she accepted it, that, it would get easier.

This obscure reference to things and texts and events that none of them truly understood led them down a dark path of nothing but horrible deeds, tragedies, and murder. Yes. Murderers are fitting of a murderer's death, and she was one of them. Deserving of it from the moment they were born, and they should accept that. They were not of this world; they should stop pretending like they belonged to it, fitting in as one of them as if they didn't have their own jobs to do, working to put on a show, working to hide the truth, the moral quagmire of the world they lived in. This world filled with political machinations, all of which were controlled by the British Empire. Sure, the world thinks it was dead, and gone, but the truth was, the British Empire was alive and well by way of the Caster's Administration, who had their hands in every treasury in the world, and a mole in every politician's house, pulling every single string.

She brushed her hair back one last time, straightening it out, walking briskly into the overcrowded airport terminals, taking her luggage with her, her one duffle bag with some clothes: just a few sets of clothes before she would be reimbursed with some unimaginably thick down coats. Until such time, onward to the next task, the next person to royally screw over, and murder. No shortage of murders on her hands these days. What's a few more to add to that damned list?

She sat down in one of the seats, watching the clouds in the night sky roam by, other aerial crafts outside, and of course, paying close attention to every face. One of them might recognize her. Thanks to this, the whole world was after her, a manhunt, to scour every single stone to look for her. Fortunately, she was in Colton's territory, and he planned the whole thing. She would be lying if she said she wasn't curious about the Grail, or Colton's intentions with it.

She exhaled heavily as she leaned forward, hands folded over one another, patiently waiting for her terminal to be called forward. Eager to be done with it. Eager to get to the next step. Eager to do God knows what.

Her terminal was finally called, and she stood, bag in hand. She walked with everyone else, blending in like the habitual liar she was. Standing up front, she walked onto the crowded plane, shoving her duffle bag into the upper shelving units and sat in her spot, next to the window, where she could watch the darkness swallow up the plane. Swallow the light and snuffing out their lives like little flickering candles representing what little hope their arrogance held over them. Fools. That is what they were. They all were, given so much, and yet, with a blink of an eye, they can die, and who would be to blame but themselves?

Truth be told about humans, they're conniving dastardly creatures who aren't worth saving, really. They're stupid. They're smelly. They're cruel. Anything to be said about the sake of human ingenuity or innovation, cultivation was not produced by the hands of man, but by the help of the Caster's Administration, but they'd never admit to something as good hearted as all that. Let them think they own the world, and you'll have them believe they have the power, and therefore, with untrained minds, they'll make foolish decisions that will lead them down the path of death. And here she was, along for the ride, to watch them die.

Sighing, she pulled out the manilla folder Colton gave her. She couldn't have electronics on her person: too trackable.

She slipped it open with her light on as the plane took flight. She opened it, and on it was her target. No specific instructions on eliminating her, just to observe, as if Colton didn't trust her to do the job right, or was there something else hidden from her? Even Colton, just like the rest of them, was known to be a liar.

Gwen Swan was a woman, tall with silver hair, it would seem, and quite a résumé even as Casters were concerned. Holding the governor's office. *Hard to do a lot of activities while in that position.* She was the head Administrator for the Alaskan district. *No small feat there, either.* Sarah skimmed the line that brought some light upon her accolades, which again, was impressive.

She was younger than Sarah was, but not by much. Even so, she studied underneath the wing of Sander, and, by the looks of it, must

186

have had a death wish. She had slayed nearly four hundred Threckets herself and had an affinity for elemental magic of various kinds.

As much as Bridgette would insist, elemental casting was not forbidden like necromancy was, but it was strongly discouraged. It required an impressive amount of control from the various sources of mana coming in from certain objects, and not only that—it required a specific amount. Trying to cast a specific kind of spell, pulling mana from an inappropriate source was a great way to get oneself killed. And adding in the scientific requirements of elemental magic, well, it should be almost impossible, since no one has been able to develop any system where mana usage could be measured.

This reason alone made Gwen extremely volatile and supremely dangerous.

Moving around her wasn't going to be easy, and quite frankly, any and all support for her task was unavailable. No one from the Caster's branch in Alaska would ever undermine their own Administrator. But then again, this led to another question, which would only lead down a further line of questioning into the larger picture of what all else was going on? No doubt, Gwen would not be giving out information, even if she had any of the faintest of clues as to who or what the man from Devil's Pass was.

She was flying back into murky waters, the thickest of weeds, and the only thing that was certain, was uncertainty. No. That's not true. There was a certainty that she was safe from the rest of the Administration while she was there, and it would be in her keenest of interests to not screwup any part of her objective.

Going there tired would be a colossally poor decision on her part, so the only logical solution was to go to sleep. Resting her redhead on the window, next to a snoring fat man with foul breath, which smelled like rotten fish—not that fresh fish smelled any better.

Approximately eighteen hours later, as far as her watch could tell, she arrived in the dark hours of the night. Early night that is, that wasn't to say there wasn't the possibility of Threckets roaming around in the foggy chilled winter air, coalescing outside and feeding on the poor mundane souls that were the inhabitants of Juneau. She followed everyone out of the pit, grabbing her bag, which was the only thing she brought with her, there was no need to wait for anything else at the terminal.

She smelled the freshly baked and fried food pouring out from the kitchens on either side of her as she walked the brightly lit tiled floor with black marks as if someone shat all over them. She didn't care. She wasn't washing them, stupid fat janitors taking their sweet time, not a care in the world that little rat-sized Threckets come about, poking about in their little heads to gnaw on their brains.

She shook her head, then looked dead ahead. Her eyes gazed this way and that into the blackness of the night through the windows. She made her way down the escalators with lazy people without the need to go anywhere any time fast. People the world would be better off without really. No hurry? No spring in their step? However, they were excellent food for some Threckets out there, and nice distractions for a quick getaway, if need be, even the children, yes, foul little creatures who knew nothing better than their own imagination. Innocent.

If only we were all like little children. If only we kept our innocence. Perhaps the world would be a much simpler, happier place. But here we are, forcing them to adult. Forcing them to grow up in this Hell we created for them, and told them to shoot for the stars, telling them if only they made it would their miserable existences be worth a damn. And when they fail, and they will fail, they'll succumb to despair and their own mental illness, while those that succeed in the farce of a dream, lost everything just to get there, because their naivety grew was so high, they never bothered to count the cost of such a silly dream. In the end, it's all worthless.

Sarah walked down through the rest of the lobby, walking past the threshold of glass doors where the wind whistled through her clothes. It would have swung a lesser woman's arm, but Sarah's grasp was firm, firmer than anyone else's. Even normie men. She exhaled chilled breath.

A black government vehicle turned its lights on, driving toward her. She gazed through the tinted windows, unable to see the driver, or the contents of inside. Her hand gripped an invisible shaft by her side, ready to cause a ruckus should it be one of those pesky Casters looking for her. Just then, did she finally question the validity of Colton's promises, and that she might not be as safe here as she once presumed. Her heart raced.

The car slowed down, and the windows opened. The driver was a woman in a cap, her black hair pulled behind in a bun, and she didn't once take her eyes off the road, a coldness about her. But unlike the stiff coldness of the wind, this was the coldness of a heart; the dear dreaded heart of Alaska was one seemingly without warmth, the same despair held within her presence was the same that plagued her own mind. The back windows opened as the car rolled to a stop, and a woman, vibrant, wearing a black petticoat opened her door, stretching out onto the side, looking at Sarah with a curious eye.

Undoubtedly, this was Ms. Gwen Swan. Lead Caster of the Alaska's branch of America's Administration. Elegant was her face, and her silver hair glimmered in the moonlight. Her face held a sneer that made Sarah's skin crawl, and underneath her skin where she felt like there were rotting worms growing, scouring her insides. Gwen stepped out of the car, slamming the door shut. Sarah saw those pupils investigating her body.

"Y'aren't as tall as I reckoned ye to be," she said, her hand reaching up, caressing her face with the back of her hand, ever so softly, yet, those hands were colder than snow. "Sarah McCurdy, I've heard some good things about you." Her nose crinkled at the touch, as soft as it was, it was unwelcomed, but she had little choice in the matter than to endure this gross invasion of personal space. It was almost like she was being treated like a dog.

The governor took the duffel bag from Sarah's hand and tossed it in the trunk. "Get inside, we've lots to discuss back at my office. Take a look at the lay of the land on your way there."

Sarah nodded, and took a seat, while Gwen sat next to her, paying attention to other things, talking to the driver, or even playing a game on her phone.

Shouldn't be on your phone. Threckets are out at night. You need to be alert.

To say anything about Sarah, anything at all, she was alert and aware as the car started to drive off to an unfamiliar destination. But she was in the military for a decade and a half and moved constantly. So she was used to constant change after all.

The winds outside were whistling, the temperature, while rather cold, was much more due to Alaska's climate, and not due to the mana pockets. Which was unusual; these mana pockets didn't seem to be here in abundance. She didn't sense any in the mountains, the airports, or even the wintery plains.

They drove by some old ports, unloading large drayage shipping containers on a cargo ship, that appeared to be disembarking, heading further up north, if she guessed right. Impossible to tell without the sun to direct the position of the shadows cast on the buildings, and the people underneath those lights, trading paperwork, and signing off on the shipments. However, they must have had something to guide their way, the stars were obscured by the clouds.

But all of this, was what normies would call *normal* human behavior. Nothing related to Threckets, Casters, or the like, keeping them forever sheltered from the lies they were told, and led to believe. This is the kind of thing she wasn't used to.

"So, you notice anything different?" Gwen asked.

"It's safe here," Sarah answered, turning back to the governor.

"In a way yes, but is anywhere safe when trust is always a concern?"

Trust. She suspects something.

"Yes, I always do," Gwen answered.

Sarah's eyes gaped open. Her heart skipped a beat, racing it was as she came to the sudden realization, even her thoughts were no longer hers.

"Oh, don't act surprised, there isn't anything outside the realm of capabilities. Not for me anyways. You can remain silent all you want, but I think it's best that we defuse this little misunderstanding we have with one another," Gwen said, leaning in closer, flicking her finger back and forth. "I know why you're here, and it isn't for your personal protection for the crime you committed against the Administration."

Sarah gawked, turning to the driver.

"Don't be alarmed and bothered. All of Alaska knows,"

"Then why haven't you killed me?" Sarah glared at her. Her eyes scanned the car, now more invested in precisely where she was heading. Administration building, or was she to be disposed of?

"Honestly, even if Colton wanted you dead, it would be a hassle I could do without." She smiled, eyes drooping low, plotting something, but the woman was almost unreadable. She couldn't read her. "So, back to business, you are here to spy on me. More specifically, to find out what information have I been keeping from Colton. Well, you'll get what information I choose to give you, and it will come with a cost. And those costs you will pay up front. Do I make myself clear?"

"Yes, Administrator Swan," Sarah gritted her teeth, feeling like her lungs were going to collapse. She realized how easy one can be an animal, and she was no less. She remembered those nuclear soldiers she led up to die. Was this how they felt in their final moments? Betrayed with nowhere to go, locked in a cage, trapped in a corner, doomed to die, and without a final moment to say their goodbyes.

"You intrigue me, you know, or else I wouldn't have agreed to let Colton send another realm of emissaries here to spy and trap me. The last four did a fantastic job on trying to get to my secrets. They found out, but they were all killed before they could even think of reporting back to Colton, I trust you're smart enough to not make that same mistake." Gwen frowned. "Answer me."

"I will not cross you." She exhaled, her heart racing hastily.

"What you'll notice is there are no Threckets here—not this part of Alaska. The Portal Storms are up in the north, way up in the north, unsettling wouldn't you agree," Gwen said. "This I will give you, there's an army of Threckets amassing at the North Pole. I am doing nothing to them, and they've stayed put. Can you hazard a guess why?"

"Because they have hearts," Sarah said, making it sound like this was a genuine answer, but it wasn't. Of course, it wasn't. They have no hearts, they're mere demonic creatures and manifestations arising from Pandora.

Gwen thought it funny, throwing her head back against the window, grinded her teeth as she laughed, and rubbed the spot where it struck the glass. "Funny, but no. Because it is simply impassable. I can get people there, I can't get people out, so let the Threckets have their fun, and their own little patch of creation, something of which was denied to them."

Sarah relaxed, knowing full well the predicament she was in was paramount to understanding how to deal with it. She admitted she had rarely been in a situation like this before, but as Gwen said, her thoughts weren't her own, and they could be accessed at any such time Gwen saw fit; however, Sarah was nothing if not an admirable liar. She made it leagues this way and that, sending people to their deaths on whims. The lies she played was always the military elite, an officer who was trusted, and one of the few who could actually read a map and lead them in the right direction. Well, if she wasn't hell bent on her own mission, which always resulted in killing others.

She did it before, she can damn well do it again.

CHAPTER 21

NOT ALL BROTHERS

Status Report: Military units were deployed to secure Oregon's borders. Fleets secured, deployed to combat the Chinese fleet. The Airforce pilots sent overhead to keep the airships off the borders. Northern California was bombarded by planes. National Guard and Active Army infantry deployed to push back. Fighting against an impressive display of artillery and air bombs, the front lines were forced to retreat. North California was fortified by Chinese forces on display, importing heavy machinery from their carriers.

Chinese Destroyer ships sailed into Southern California, bombarding San Diego's ports. FOB built and stationed in Los Angeles, filled with Marine and Army Personnel. Fighter pilots discharged to Southern San Diego to assault the destroyers.

Spadero listened to the director of this grand café, or so it said on the banner when he came in. This was a church. Chairs were set in rows, and a number of different people sat among them, all gathered in this room, quietly whispering to one another about their days, or so he guessed, hard to tell with so much chatter, and the director of this event spoke through the microphone. He had some concerns being here of course, being a congressman.

Fortunately, not too many people paid attention to him. Not that he needed the additional publicity. He sipped the coffee in his Styrofoam cup. Of course, tasteless, just like everything else in the world, and without taste, there was no sustenance. The only purpose of drinking coffee was to stay alert. His eyes scanned the room, vigorously looking for this *Ghost*. And yet, here he was, talking like a normal person, standing next to a couple, who, he was certain, were the victims of Culain threatening, or some other bother that prevented them from even coming here to begin with.

He shook his head, thinking just about how this wasn't his job. *Damn Irish bastard, quick on his wits, but hasn't the faintiest clue on how to be tact. Yes, treat this with tact, and all will be fine, and I can get the information I need without rousing too much suspicion. Ghost. Scars on your face.*

Spadero chuckled. Clearly, this Ghost didn't think anything of him being there, and didn't raise suspicion. By the individual accounts given to him by Culain, this Ghost is a Caster. Whether he knew himself to be one or not, or even what a Caster was, well, that's an entirely different matter.

The director ceased talking, and almost immediately, Spadero found the man walking with the rest of the crowd like ocean waves, or specifically of molasses: slow deplorable molasses. He followed him, but at a distance. Laser focused. That was the key. He was so close. And yet, Ghost was a smart man to hide in plain sight, but then, perhaps the poor little dickhead didn't know he was on the Caster's most watched list.

Sakura, against her better judgment, begrudgingly accepted another request for her to come to the café, on Tuesday. There was something that drew her, but she couldn't quite tell what exactly. It certainly wasn't that pissant Ted Anderson. The man—she only ever met him once—was insufferable, and left a detestable taste in her mouth, more bitter than the Saltiest Sailor, home brewed, of course, and something specific to Atlanta. No one else had it.

The night sky lit up, regrettably, unlike Georgia, lights everywhere, and polluted the sky, hiding all the distant stars. The majestic sky was forever out of everyone's reach, and she wondered to herself, if people from Boston knew what laid beyond the pollution of the night.

Sure, they knew of the existence of stars, which might be treated more like a dying fairy tale than anything else.

Of course, coming out of the street at night, she found the disparity to be an annoyance, especially the little group of people. They had worn out cargo pants, holey t-shirts, and backpacks with more to wear down on, and holes in the straps like locusts fed on them like leaves, or termites in wood, now rotting.

And just like she suspected: she remembered none of the details of the Bible Study, but this wasn't the reason she was going. Nor did she remember answering questions, truth be told, all of it went inside one ear and out the other. *How much could one college student handle?* Surely, she wasn't seriously considering new information that wouldn't do her much good in the future, and that's what this was: useless information. The friendships were fun though.

Samantha and Michael were amiable enough, and she couldn't count Lamar Cooper as useless either. The rest of the group came waltzing down the steps, resting and taking a deep breath of that fuel infested air. A hand grabbed her shoulder. "So, are you coming with us tonight?"

"I'm not doing anything, so, sure," Sakura smiled back at Sam who laugh giddily as she attached herself back to Michael, breaking into a conversation that flew over her head, something about finance? Sam clung like an overprotective woman to her boyfriend, declaring, 'He's mine, and no one else's.' Not that it involved her at all. Not in the least.

She noticed Ted, scowling at her with his scarred face, and clearly, her assessment matched up with whatever that man at the shooting range, and Lamar knew about him; he had seen some semblance of Hell, and a certain disdain for people in the military, coming out of the military, or even desiring to join the military. He hated all of them. That was certain, but that prompted a particular question: *why?*

A mystery to be sure, and one that she might not find easily, not without specific details or breadcrumbs to follow, and only with breadcrumbs could someone come close to an answer. The trouble was, nowhere near Ted was there a crumb, or a trail to lead to him, or at least connect anything to his disdain. Nothing at all. Granted, she only knew about him for a short while, and there was nothing particularly useful about him, but there was something that disturbed her.

He seemed to make an active effort to scowl at her, and while he wasn't particularly kind to Lamar, he rarely scowled at him. Sexist maybe. Maybe that's his problem.

As if the stars above sought to make Ted's life a little more miserable, a man in a nice suit, walked in front of Ted, forcing him to break eye contact with her. He spoke to Ted. *Thank God.*

Sakura turned, and a woman with a red head and freckles was chatting away with Samantha. Something finance related, still. Something she didn't have a remote interest in. It didn't make sense to bother one outside the natural cycle of things. Such as using currency to make more currency, which seemed like an oxymoron to her.

Samantha glanced her way. "Come on, you don't need to be by yourself." She ushered her into their little circle, and there was Brian, the most social and likable person of the whole bunch. He was very confident in his demeanor, loud, respectful, but always teetered on the fine line of being too pushy, but how close to the line could he toe without getting into trouble.

"Sakura, this is Erin."

Samantha introduced her to the red-haired woman, who turned with a bright smile on her face, and reached out her hand.

"Erin. Pleasure to meet you. New here?"

"You could say that," she answered.

"Okay, Ted," Erin chuckled. Samantha and Michael didn't seem to find that funny and frowned toward Erin, who's chuckle immediately died. "I'm sorry, that was in poor taste, I shouldn't have said that."

Coddling, again. The man is a jerk. You shouldn't be coddling him!

"Well, come on, what was it that Jennifer always said: 'Very important business at the empire,' or something like that." Michael seemed to want to lighten up the mood to start ushering people up the sidewalk toward the elegantly designed city hall. "Let's go, come around little children."

Sakura shook her head as she followed them up the street. It's where she went last week, but the most notable thing that happened last week was that Ted wasn't there, and she shared her phone number with people she enjoyed talking to. Now, she had no need to share her number, and Ted was there. And then there was this man who took a special interest in him for some reason. In fact, she noticed the man try more than once to get Ted into conversation, and now, there didn't seem to be a place for Ted to deflect to something else.

Ted smiled amiably at this man who had tried numerous times to get him to talk, just walking up from the church and around the corner to their little spot, he said, "And I don't quite understand what that has to do with any part of me, so I implore you, sir, why come to me with this?" Ted asked the man, Spadero. John Spadero, Congressman of Massachusetts. He wondered why the congressman had any interest in him, and of course, all high and mighty, as the higher ups always were, giving orders this way and that. This only led people to their graves, early or well timed, it was always based solely on the circumstances of one's death should they have found anything worth mentioning in their obituaries.

"You were a man of war, were you not?" Spadero replied, seemingly trying to butter him up, as the young men did the older ones. Thinking any of those compliments had any value to anyone other than themselves. *Idiot.* "I'd think a man of your history would have keen insight as we move on toward the future, attempting to avoid further war, the likes of which we've seen on the West Coast already. You'd agree with me, won't you, that further war is better off avoided?"

"I suppose if you want to spend money on saving lives, then sure, spend the money to save lives, but you're only costing people in the future. War is inevitable, and unstoppable. It will happen sooner rather than later, and I think you'll find it is far more costly to avoid war, than to jump head in," Ted answered.

But something tells me, Congressman, that this is not the conversation you mean to have with me. What are you after?

"It was Sergeant, right? Sergeant Ted Anderson of the 75th? Or am I mistaken?" Spadero urged on.

What exactly are you getting at? Don't you dare remind me; I'll make sure you won't be around to get re-elected. "One and the same."

"I read your record. It was a very impressive accolade."

"Please, tell me, what has become of the military, and of myself that my records aren't sealed shut?" *He's dead. What do you know? You dirty little bastard.* "And what business does a congressman have going into my file?"

"Let's call the information I received divinely inspired, shall we?" He sneered.

Ted shook his head. "You're a terrible liar."

"Well, I'm a congressman; I shouldn't be lying at all."

"Well, how's this for divinely inspired. You have had this cozy little experiment for ten years called world peace."

They turned the corner, crossing into the threshold of Teri Nation.

"All thanks to a unit which never existed, and quite frankly came out of nowhere, and it was that unit in particular who ripped the world to shreds, forcing the rest of the great nations to cower, sucking their thumbs like little babies."

"Interesting. I don't remember any of that," Spadero said, following him like a rat scurrying into a little hole right behind him.

Ted was suspicious of this man. This was no coincidence. This man didn't just walk in on a random Tuesday. He came here, looking for something. But what would that be? Ted couldn't help but wonder that this man was up to no good, but what was certain, Spadero was out for something only Ted Anderson would know.

"You wouldn't," he scoffed, sitting at the bar.

Scott, oh Scott, *you're about to see me in one of my moods. Unfortunately, this jackass has my nerves up.* Ted scanned the rest of the bar top, and the crowd blocked his vision of where the foreigners used to be sitting, but regrettably, he didn't see them. *Very curious.* "Anyway, like I said, there are no records of such a unit anymore, it was all erased."

"Let me buy you a drink."

"Hell, no." He snapped. "A gift from a politician is a gift to cast off into the trash, no matter what the intent is. It never leads anywhere good."

"Point taken."

"Scott, Cab please," the bar tender came over abruptly.

"Sure thing."

"I'll just have your house bourbon," Spadero ordered. "On the rocks is fine." He sat.

Ted shook his head as Scott swiftly came by with the drinks. Ted's hand was shaking visibly on the table, heart racing. He stared down at the glass, observing the sweat from his palms dripping from it. *Just like those rich people do. Just like those rich people do. Just like those rich people do. Come on, you can do this. Play the part of a rich man. You've done it before. Don't let this man, whoever he is get under the skin.* But his hand trembled, all the same.

"Yes, I remember reading about such a unit, but their accolades and their existence remains a mystery. Do you care to shed any light about that?" Spadero's eyes fixed upon the trembling hand.

"Look, Spadero, all of that is classified information, even to you. I don't know what clearance you have as a congressman, but I doubt it permits you to go snooping around files of confidential information like that," Ted replied. "Even if I knew why, I couldn't tell you." He took a sip after swirling his glass. *Honestly, I'd like to know the answer to that myself.*

"Oh, Ted. What are you doing all the way over here?" Sam called, cheerily twirling that Cabernet, as only she can.

Thank God! Sam, get me as far away from him as possible. Please!

"Is he being kind to you?" she asked Spadero.

Fantastic.

"Polite and blunt," Spadero chuckled, his hand over his rocks glass, bringing it carefully to his lips. His pupils shifting back and forth scanning the bar.

Hyperalert too, huh? You're disciplined for a bureaucrat.

"So, Ted, how is Jennifer doing?" Sam asked, her hand resting softly on his shoulder. His shoulder jerked ever so slightly, still highly alert with this new *Spadero* right here, interrogating him about information a normal person couldn't be reasonably assured to know.

"She is okay." He smiled at her. *Thank you. Sam.* "She's recovering, resting rather."

"It's been scary," Sam replied.

She's been on and off, some days were much better than others, but sometimes the bad days were really bad. Ted understood what the reality was, and as much as he's faced it before, he didn't want to have to face it again. Not with a woman of which he grew fond of, someone who helped him taste food again. "Yeah." *Again, thank you.*

"Who's this?" Spadero asked.

"Why, none other than our flamboyant biologist, researcher, whatever it is she does," Samantha said, leaning in toward Ted's ear. "Anyway, the reason I came, Spadero, was it?"

"Yes,"

"Apple picking," she replied, pointing at both with fingers, three fingers tucked in, and thumbs resting on the pointing index finger like pistols. "Saturday, noon. Coming?"

"I'll think about it," Ted answered. *Now, Spadero, will you go, or won't you?*

"I'll come. Where?"

Ted looked at him suspiciously, not bothering to hide a frown. This man reminded him of someone cold, and calculating, someone with a lot to gain, but not so much to lose. *Well, Spadero, congratulations. You intrigue me, but don't think I won't kill you if you get too close to the truth. Not that I don't want the truth uncovered of course, but the truth jeopardizes what I have here, and I don't want to lose it. I've already lost everything. Let me have this. Please.*

200

CHAPTER 22

CESSPOOL

President Snells' popularity rating has plummeted to below 10 percent in polls of both conservative and liberal voters.

Opinion: Such a low score reflects the poor handling of the West Coast invasion: the US is clearly losing, losing nearly all the West Coast population, pushing evacuation efforts further into secondary state lines. It is impossible to get the Executive Administration office to do anything of action, despite its efforts to draft.

Chief Commanding Officer Malcolm seems to be the only one remotely concerned and available for questioning.

Still no answers, only more questions. Of course, nothing was ever easy, but this mystery raised way too many questions. At least he knew what the Ghost looked like, physically, his scars made him stick out like a sore thumb. Wounds all over the place. Clearly, this man had seen some semblance of war, but he didn't seem that old and there hadn't been many skirmishes recently with the US forces. At the very least, nothing that would cause a man to look like that, and he didn't seem old enough to be in the armed forces when there was conflict, fifteen to twenty years ago.

The man has a strategic mind, even when presented with external stimulus of which he had no reason to suspect the unexpected, and he wasn't a food. He chooses his words carefully, but what of his friends? Can I use them to get closer to him, to get him to trust me to get him alone? Just for a chat. There are too many additional questions. Spadero had to stop himself, crossing the street. His mind was asking questions. Something it was good at. Many of these questions didn't get him closer to a solution, closer to the problem, or implementing any sort of solution should there be one. He was a tough nut to crack and grabbing hold of him could be like sticking a hand in the open mouth of a crocodile.

He stared up at the blank and empty sky. The lights were on. *Finally, the poor pissant of a congressman can go die in a hole.* He stepped inside the hotel again, walking through the neatly swept lobby, a change from last time. It was storming last time, and the lights were out, and yet, he found a speck of dust, resting on the marble tile. Shaking his head in disappointment, he walked to the elevator, slid through the doors, and then a couple came in behind him.

"Which floor?"

"Fourth," the woman answered.

He pressed the button which lit up before he reached forward for his floor; the tenth. He smiled back, leaning against the metal bar behind him. His ears perked up when they identified him as a congressman. *Great. I wonder what scandal they'll have about me spreading. Someone ends up dead, I get blamed for it? Foul play perhaps? Or Spadero, the great visitor of ladies? No. That title was already taken by John Dunn. No such luck here. Honestly, I wish it was that exciting.*

The doors opened, and he was all alone. Just the way he liked it; silence for his thoughts when he had the energy to meditate on them, but he didn't have a single lick of energy left. All of it, dealing with Culain, his short temper, and the possibility of Blanka's drunk ass waltzing in late at night doing God knows what. For heaven's sake, Ilya and Alexander were the only reasonable ones around, and Ilya just recently returned from a leave of absence for a while, collecting and refining data for their manhunt of this Ghost, along with some personal errand in Russia.

He walked and knocked on the door heavily, and like always, Culain opened the door. Scowling no reason other than to make the

202

world know he's angry. Always angry. Everyone's angry these days. Even himself.

Spadero pushed his way into the hotel room, and the bastard slammed the door shut, locking it behind him. Seeing a spot with his name on it, he jumped over the coffee table into the couch, nearly tipping it over, and crossed his arms. "I hope you don't mind, but I'm staying the night here."

"Don't you have a house?" Culain moved into the kitchen and pulled out two cans of generic beer. He tossed one to Spadero, who caught it firmly with his sweaty palms. The can hissed violently at him as he pulled the ring up, pushing into the tear line.

Spadero sipped it. "Yes, but I had to deal with an annoyance, and I work a stone's throw away. I'll be outta yer potato head in the morning."

Ilya walked in. "You know how to make an entrance, or rather an impolite disturbance. Have some tact, will you?" She didn't scowl at him, she only glanced, and turned away as she went into the kitchen, pulled out some cheese from the drawer, sliced cheddar by the looks of it, and started eating. "Well, what news have you?"

He didn't answer at first, just bit his lip before opening his mouth. "Only more questions, no answers."

"Did you talk to—"

"Irish cunt!" Ilya slammed her fist on the counter. "I'll handle this. You'll only fuck it up," she scowled at Culain. *My God.* Ilya watched him skimp off, shaking his head, and muttering what he only guessed could be Irish insults. "Spadero, tell me, did you talk to him?"

"Yes, I did. A shrewd man, for certain," he said, leaning forward. "Only more questions."

Ilya sat across from him, leaning back in her seat, cozying up in her jacket as if she was freezing. She looked downward to his knees. A wetness seemed to shimmer on her eyeballs, which were redder than usual.

"All right." She bit her lip, crossing her arms over her chest, slouching into the couch. "What questions?"

"All the answers I have are that he is masquerading about as this Ted Anderson, which was a sergeant of the 75th Ranger Regiment before his particular unit merged with Black Eagle. After which, Ted Anderson and his unit went completely off the grid. There are no records. Why aren't there any records? Even he admitted to not knowing why there aren't any records, and I believe he told me the truth in that regard." He took another sip of beer. "Scars stain his face. All over. My guess is shrapnel from explosions, so he's been in war time, which dates his time of service to when Ted Anderson's unit disappeared. But this Ghost doesn't appear very old, I'd guess early twenties at the latest. College aged."

Ilya didn't look up, but she pursed her lips before speaking, "And what are you getting at here?"

He tapped the coffee table repeatedly with a firm middle finger. "I could be off here, but say he's twenty-four. Virtually all conflict would have stopped around nine to eleven years ago, placing him between the ages of thirteen to fifteen at the time. Sergeant Ted Anderson has been dead for about nine years now, hanged in his own apartment. Ruled a suicide. Now, this kid stole this dead man's identity, masquerading as him since then. These assumptions are purely circumstantial. I don't have any hard evidence of this. Whatever training he'd—"

"You're hinging these assumptions based on circumstantial evidence which cannot be verified," she said. "You're taking me down a rabbit hole I have no business being in, Spadero. We need additional details on how we can get him alone."

"I'm getting to that, or rather, the complications of doing just that," he said, his voice growing raspy. "But this man never had a childhood. Likely never knew his parents. And Black Eagle must have stolen him like a thief in the night."

"I fail to see how any of that matters. Get on with it," she said, making eye contact, and tears streamed down her face, as if she suspected this all along.

Spadero remembered Jack, and his family, left dead and absorbed. One of the many acts of violence he conducted to get answers to one problem. There were many problems, and so many innocent bystanders, their blood was on his hands. Add a few more Casters to the mix, and that number rose exponentially. Sometimes children were involved as a last resort, needfully. *We would never needlessly involve children. And this was needless. There's a special place in Hell for you, whoever you are.* "I'm simply saying, if the wrong person knows of his existence, and I assume they do, then we aren't the only person looking for Ghost. I'm getting close with his friends. If need be, I'll use one of them as a hostage."

"Be careful of what you do, Spadero, or else you become the Devil you hate," she said, wiping the tears from her eyes.

He knew it. She knew it. There was something foul, and another hole to dig, just getting the right shovel to dig it was what made it worse, and whatever else is going on in the world. He couldn't be sure it was connected, much like just grabbing at straws and hope an idea sticks long enough to dissect it, and hope the truth makes sense. If it doesn't, just grab another straw; one must find the one that makes sense.

But she was right. He was already in a moral bog. He was at risk, he knew, of digging a hole so deep and dark that he may be swallowed up entirely, and forget why he did the things he did. Already, just to get a grasp of this man's pseudo identity, he killed several different contacts, and half of them, who he didn't kill, went missing after the fact, and their families. No one will ever know why they died, or what tied them to the marsh of the states. Surely, if there be any true patriots among anyone in the states, they'd be disgusted to find their country was nothing more than a toxic cesspool.

"We should get Sander on the phone," John said.

"Yes, if we can." She pulled out her cell phone, dialed it, and threw it on the table.

"Adam here, Ilya, you better have some good news for me," he said over the phone.

"Yes." She smiled. A very fake smile, and it made her sound a little more cheerful. "We have a positive ID, but origin remains unknown. He is going by the name of Ted Anderson, and we think specifically—Ted Anderson of the 75th Ranger Regiment, prior to his unit disappearing off the face of the planet."

"I take it you have yet to acquire him?"

"Correct. But we have been able to plant a congressman right next to him, and his friends, should drastic measures be necessary," she continued.

"And you said there is still no known origin. Did I hear right?"

"Correct. All we have on origin is speculation which won't do us any good. We need Ghost to find his origin, and to tie him to any such activity relating to the Grail, or McCurdy. But, in any case, we can at least get him to clean up his mana messes," Ilya replied. "Which was the reason we were looking for him to begin with. Honestly, Sander, do you really think he's tied to this Devil's Pass man, and McCurdy?"

"No, but I can't let the possibility slide. Too many things happening all at once. Ta ta,"

The phone hung up.

"I don't want to go apple picking," he leaned back into his seat.

"Apple picking?"

"Ghost's friends are going apple picking. Ghost didn't commit to it. He's a shrewd man."

"You mean a shrewd child?" She corrected.

"Yeah."

CHAPTER 23

CONFRONTATION

Status Report: Washington Chinese heavy cavalry, and Northern California Chinese California uproot Oregon's defenses in a pincer attack. With American resistance uprooted and forced to retreat east, Chinese Forces take root into Oregon.

Chinese scouts north of Washington inch forward. The Chinese fleet closes in on Los Angeles, forcing Air Force pilots and personnel to remain stationed at the FOB. The Chinese forces in Southern California inch forward with their heavy cavalry units into Arizona.

Jennifer yawned, waking up from her nap, the moon shining in her room. The covers were nice and cozy, comfortable, but that was all the comfort that was present. She peered out the window, and most of the lights of the city were off. The ones that remained were the streetlights.

The darkness inside her room was comforting, but one thing couldn't be overlooked, she might have her time cut short, but she mustn't let the dreary reality get to her, no. Many times, she read of the cynical passages of Ecclesiastes, and some parts entering into Revelation, and while it talked about thieves coming in at night, Revelation especially, there was a hope of rest, and peace, and painlessness. She spent more time on these passages lately with her diagnosis, and sometimes she felt like it came as a thief in the night with nothing else to do but to cut her time short, and to give her menial tasks she'd rather not be doing. It stole her time from her. She'd much rather spend her time hanging out with her friends, drinking, though, say one thing for leukemia: it didn't stop her from re-reading Jane Austen. The charming writer if ever there was one. Most others were secluded and plagued with naught but simple prose the common person could not understand.

But was that the point for such simple prose? To reduce flowery language and an abundance of adverbs for which Jane Austen was filled with? To make such excellent stories worth knowing in such a simple way, that anyone, if they could read, could read this book? Or series of novels. The biggest crime really, was taking away one's ability to read.

She pulled the blanket off and swung her legs over the side of the bed, her toes gently touching the furry carpet, slowly resting down as the joints in her toes moved in place for easy transition to standing. Her hands rested with the utmost care, on her knees, which, though not inflamed, were stiff, and bending it didn't cause her pain, but it removed a small amount of comfort.

"Move your knee," she spoke to it. "Come on, you can do it. Just move."

It was no small thing, peering out the window. Glass. Easily breakable. If someone was in here with her, they could easily push her out, shattering the glass, screaming out the window, plummeting all the way down until eventually plummeting, striking the ground, shattering her bones, especially as fragile as they were. She was still waiting on a donor for her blood type, the appropriate stem cells for her treatment, but they were in short supply. They always were. *Well, the bleeding would stop.*

She grunted, forcing herself forward. The discomfort entered her knees as she staggered forward, catching herself on her nightstand, standing strong. *I probably shouldn't have done that.* "Oh, well." She stretched her arms and leaned back and forth, loosening the joints of her body till she adjusted her comfort to the discomfort provided to her. She glanced back over to the window, her breath against it, one open hand touching as she looked outside again.

The sky shined all the clearer today, and she was by herself, alone in her apartment. Not that she minded, of course. Sometimes it was good to be in a silent place, away from all distractions. She became accustomed to the silence. She had to. Because that's what Ted needed. He needed someone who he could confide his trust to, portraying it in such a way of a child. He needed these things because he never knew them, and she, and Sam to a degree was able to provide that to him.

Yet so much about him remained a mystery, and though he never said why, she finally picked the pieces together. Quite frankly, it was the reason for him not seeing a therapist. Provided, those were in short supply these days, and new patients were always immediately wait listed for nine to twelve months.

The phone rang.

I like company. Sounds nice.

She turned to her phone, picking it up, not bothering to read which devilish fiend called her at this hour, not bothering to check. "Samantha, dearest."

"Jennifer." Sam squeaked into her ear.

"Yes, Sam, my adorable little carpet," she replied.

"Yes, I am your adorable little carpet," she laughed on the other line. "Speaking of carpets, how do you feel about apple picking this Saturday?"

Honestly, it did sound nice, despite the discomfort she currently found in her kneecaps, which may or may not subside entirely by Saturday. However, there was the risk that it would be enflamed with heightened physical activity, of which apple picking required. But then there was the matter of Ted.

"And Ted? Did you invite him?" she asked.

"Yes, he didn't commit to it yet," Sam replied.

"And Sakura?" She sighed.

"Yes, she's coming," she answered.

Oh, dear. "And Michael's brother?"

"Yes, he's—"

"Samantha Harris," Jennifer screamed over the phone. "I told you, those two can't be within the same vicinity with one another. There's—there's bad blood between them. On the outside, pleasant, for all of us to see, but inside, they hate each other." Jennifer knew Sam was better than this. She felt her own blood boil with her hand gripping the phone tighter at Sam's blatant disregard to what was developing between Ted and Jeff.

"I'm sorry, Jennifer, I forgot," she apologized.

"I'll be there if Ted goes. Wherever Ted is, that is where I'll be," she said. "I'm sorry for snapping, but—"

"I understand," she interrupted. "How is chemo?"

"Hard sometimes," she answered softly. "It still hurts. All this time, waiting for a donor, but every day, some days are harder than others, and there are days that I hardly notice it at all."

"Well, I hope you feel better, get some rest. I'll pray for you,"

"Thanks, Sam," she replied.

The phone went silent.

CHAPTER 24

ENTER SERGEANT EMILY MILLER

Rioters are on capitol Hill.

Picket signs are asking for the removal of President Snells for his inaction of the West Coast, and inability to address the public. The Press Secretary is nowhere to be seen, and the staff remain at the White House. The security is out at force with security fences and riot gear.

Emily Miller walked up to her front porch just as the sun was rising. Her brown hair, her brown fatigues, and her shorts were soaked with her sweat. Why wouldn't they be after running a marathon first thing in the morning? She opened the screen porch door, kicked off her shoes as she went into her kitchen, filling up her bottle with water, and started chugging it.

Her husband just turned on the early morning news. He was exceedingly concerned about the events on the world, but if *you'd heard it once, you've heard it a thousand times, as the saying goes.*

She finished her water, tuning out the horrible news of what she imagined was all but inevitable, and coming to her husband, wrapping her sweaty arms around him as he sat on the couch, her lips kissing his cheek ever softly.

"Babe, it's not worth it to give yourself another stress induced anxiety attack over things you have no control over." She looked at the screen, glancing briefly. An anchorman was reporting with a bulletproof vest, illustrating the decimation of what she guessed was Moscow, blown up Humvees, shattered glass over the place. This channel didn't even have the tact to censor the corpse bent over backward out the shattered remains of the windshield.

You're not the one who must go running into that, I am.

"I know but, our daughter has to live in—"

"There's nothing you can do about it," she said, stretching her neck to rest on his shoulders, feeling his black scruff scratching across her cheek. "Come on, I'm hungry. Make me something to eat."

"Yes, dear," he said.

He moved around the couch and hugged her. "Shower first."

She smiled back at him, hugged him closely, wrapping her arms around his waist, holding her hands tightly.

"Hey, enough of that." His hands tried to pull her grip off him, but she was far stronger than he was. She had to be, with all the equipment she had to carry for her job, which she told him little about. Most of which was classified information anyway.

"I was planning on it," she said.

"Baby, you're sweaty. I just changed this shirt."

She snickered, releasing her grasp and pat his cheek. "Breakfast is the most important meal of the day."

She turned and walked down the hallway.

"Next to lunch and dinner," her husband called.

Opening the door to her room, the early morning sun rays cascaded into her chamber. She walked over to her closet, pulling out a new set of clothes before briskly walking to her bathroom, locking the door, and turning the water on. Undressing, she immediately stepped into the ice-cold water as it slowly warmed up, steaming up the glass walls inside her showering bathtub.

Feeling the hot water cascade over her body, washing herself, her extremities, her hair. Each droplet of water felt like a needle, and she cringed as she brushed her hand through her hair, looking out into the steamy glass walls around her, and muffled sounds penetrated her ears, and slowly, became clearer.

"Sergeant Miller! Get me out!"

Her hand stretched out into the burning Humvee. A soldier, an infantryman stuck, pinned to the ground. Her hand reached his, the warm, thick blood forced her grip to slip. Gunfire raged in the distance, the sand pelting her from the night sky, the whirring of helicopter blades rising above her.

Steps came out from behind the truck. She dropped the man's hand, drew her side arm, aimed to fire. Russian Patches. She fired a shot, and the Russian soldier's head burst like a water balloon. Bone fragments and blood sprayed over the side of the truck.

Another soldier climbed on the truck, aiming a rifle at her. She turned, firing an aimed shot down his throat, and the same, blood sprayed, pushed back. The corpse folded back over the other end of the truck. She heard the body slam onto the ground.

"Sergeant Miller! What the hell are you doing!"

She gasped. Her hand touched the glass. *Oh. It was them or me. That's it.* She shook her head, stepping out of the shower. *Him or me. All for the prize of freedom.*

She dried herself off, dressed herself, and threw her smelly clothes into the hamper. It may be one of the first things Jessica smells, and that was the best sort of love anyone could ask for. Really, she should be honored, taking a dump first thing in the morning, smelling her mother's morning odor. She chuckled at that last bit. *It doesn't smell like blood, so there's that.*

She opened the door, and walked back down the hall, and when she got to Jessica's room, she rested her ear on it. There was no sound, not one. She slowly and sneakily pushed it open, and her daughter, who was just entering high school, was sleeping soundly on this morning, her curly dark hair making a mess over her face.

Can't have that. Not my daughter.

She sat on the bed next to her, and carefully pushed the frazzled hair out of her face, tucking it neatly behind her ear. *Much better. Sweet dreams.*

Standing over the bed, she left. Timidly and sneakily shutting the door behind her, leaving with not a sound.

Briskly walking back down the hall to freshly cooked bacon, eggs, and pancakes, she found the table set for three. Of course, Jessica would be joining shortly after. The large cups filled to the brim with orange juice. But her eyes peered disappointingly at Kevin, who was on the landline.

He covered the mouthpiece and brought it to his shirt. "It's Malcolm again."

"Kevin, if I told you once, I told you a thousand times never entertain calls with him." She firmly struck the hand with her table, the silverware clattering. Her husband jolted and was bringing the phone to his face. "No, you don't."

She sprinted over to him, hopping over the couch, and ripped the receiver from his hand, hanging up the phone. "Don't, talk to him. I mean it."

"What does he want?" he asked.

The phone rang.

"Don't answer it. Let it go to voicemail. He wants me to apply for Black Eagle, that's all, and he won't leave me alone. I swear, I'm getting him processed as processed salted ham."

The phone stopped ringing. She was hoping he would just leave a voicemail for her to ignore. She didn't want to bother with a call from Malcolm. Besides, didn't he have any better things to do than act recruiter?

"There, now I can enjoy my meal." She took her husband's hand. *That son of a bitch.*

Just as they were sitting down, "MOM! MOM! You stank up the toilet!"

"I love you too!" she called, digging into the eggs.

Jessica came scurrying out the hall, sitting at the table, her brown braided hair tucked behind her. She started eating. "Jessica, you going out with your friends later?"

"Yes, we're going to the—"

The phone rang again.

Damnit Malcom.

"Let it ring." Emily spoke softly, and politely as she continued cutting into her pancakes.

The ringing stopped. *Don't call again.*

"So, Jessica, you were saying, dear?" she asked.

"Oh, yes, sorry," she replied. "We're going to the mall later. Jack is picking me up."

"Make sure to stay—"

The phone rang again.

You son of a bitch. You're not gonna stop until I answer the damn phone, are you?

"Babe." She calmly put down her fork. Her rage was getting the better of her, and the last thing she wanted Jessica to hear was her cursing someone out over the phone. Not very respectable, but it was something that needed to be done.

"Hmm?" He asked with his mouth full.

"Can you take Jessica outside for a minute."

"But Mom, I barely touched my food,"

"Outside please," she said, smiling at her precious daughter. *You don't need to hear this.*

"Come on," Kevin put his fork down, and grabbed Jessica's hand, pulling her gently from the table, and walking her outside, closing the door firmly behind them.

Emily wiped her mouth clean, stood, and took herself to the phone, ripping it from the receiver from the base. "What do you want?"

"Well, Emily, as you know we're starting applications again, and we'd like you to—"

"Piss off. I'm not interested," she said.

"You might not be, but war is coming to the East Coast," he said.

"It's America! War is always coming. All because of bureaucrats like yourself who can't get their fingers out of their asses. Stop calling me." She gritted over the phone.

"Pays much better,"

"I don't care if you're offering six figures. You can't buy honor. You can only purchase freedom with blood, and the lives of those willing to put their life on the line."

"And none know that better than Black Eagle."

"No. The difference between you and me, is that I work for freedom, and you work for a goddamned paycheck. I've told you to stop calling me, so stop," she replied.

"Well, I was hoping to not have to resort to this, but your skills are completely invaluable. I don't know how invaluable you think you are, but it is priceless,"

"I'm not interested in anything you have to offer. Your organization is shadier than the fucking Gestapo!" She slammed the phone on the base.

He's a fucking Nazi is what he is. Who would ever think that America, of all places, would become a breeding ground for Nazis?

The phone rang immediately.

She picked up the receiver, hanging up.

It rang again.

She hung up the phone.

And again.

"I told you to—"

"Since you don't want to, I think it would be beneficial for me to send a recruiter over to the high school," he interrupted her.

"You wouldn't dare," her eyes narrowing, teeth gritting, palms sweating.

"I think you and I both know I would,"

216

"If I so much as smell a recruiter walking those halls, I will hunt them down, and hang them upside down from their balls, and watch the crows eat him alive!"

She hung up the receiver and went behind the phone.

And like clockwork, it rang again.

She ripped the mtg cord out, and the ringing stopped.

If you did your homework, you would know, I don't respond to black mail well.

"Come in," she called. Kevin and Jessica walked back in.

They took their seats and resumed eating.

"I'll be over here. I'm a little worked up." Emily turned, taking herself into the living room.

"Mom?" Jessica asked.

"Yes, dear?" Emily sat herself on the couch, leaning back.

"Who was that on the phone?"

"Nobody important. Speaking of," she turned her head to peer over the couch. "If you see someone at school, recruiting for *Black Eagle,* don't talk to them. And you tell me immediately. Do not talk with them unless I am present. Do you understand me?"

"Yes, Mom. I won't talk to them." She continued eating.

Good.

CHAPTER 25

PUPPETS

I was about to cut ties with Black Eagle once and for all. Leave the military behind me. I was about to send my papers in today when I was called into her office to be deployed to Germany. I leapt across Nakamura's desk and broke her neck. I can't tell you enough how satisfying that sound was. My hands are still marked with her nails trying to scratch her way free from my grasp. Killing her was so satisfying. To be rid of her, privately. It's only a matter of time before they find me. I'll be dead before then. Slander me all you want. I don't care anymore.

Malcolm combed his hands through his hair as he looked at his strategy board. His office was small with his large table, holding world maps. He worked with advanced technology and a large grid was in front of him with various elevations. This vertical board showed him where all the planes might by at the present time.

The ships on the horizontal board were all over the place. Ships along the West Coast was in disarray, and from what his intelligence officers were telling him, the US armed forces weren't faring any better with artillery strikes cascading their position. He was standing by, waiting for the funding source from Snells, but there was no such luck.

Not these days. Luck was in short supply. He moved black ships to the board of the map sailing from the Arctic. His ships. Not American. His ships. Operated by Black Eagle alone, and their armed forces were on standby as he commanded. But the funding source was paramount. Without it, he couldn't do anything.

Damn bureaucracy. Snells. This isn't like you.

Truth was, he was hard to get a hold of. He was the president. He should be hard to get ahold of. But to be absent in the state of affairs of war, especially with how poorly the war efforts were going was a travesty. As if just waiting for the Russians to invade the Eastern Shores. That was a certainty. A guess. But he was certain the guess was correct.

Malcolm was tutored by the greatest military mind that he ever had the privilege and dishonor of knowing. *Stay six steps ahead.* Easier said than done, especially when he can't move his pieces across the board without the green light.

He huffed out a sigh before collapsing back into his chair, staring at his ceiling. His hands wove across his chest. Pondering what the next best course of action was. Still, he came up short.

"Flanked by Russia and China. Russia is doing me a grand favor by just staying put, but they won't stay idle forever. Still got that little problem of Ghost being over somewhere in Boston. Clemens called me to confirm that specific information. Only for me to be called by Snells about all reports pertaining to his unit. Around that time, former comrades close enough to our units started disappearing. No explanation. No investigation. Just simply vanished without a trace. Like Ghosts. Higher intelligence officers within the US military might be aware that Ghost is still alive. But why aren't they tracking him? Doesn't make any sense. So then, is someone else looking for Ghost? Who would that be? And what would be the reason for it?"

He kept thinking about all the scenarios, but one thing kept bugging him. More than anything else. Snells was nowhere to be found. Almost dropped off the face of the earth. But then, why hasn't the next in line of the change in command taken the reigns?

Puppet? But then who is pulling all the strings? Assuming there is a puppet master in all of this, why doesn't it allow Snells to make big picture decisions like this? Where is this puppet master? Must be close. The question is how close, and how close am I allowed to get to this puppeteer? Sadly, it is the only thing that makes a fraction of the sense I need it to make. Especially since no one is at all concerned.

If there is some syndicate, it suggests that is who is looking for Ghost. It also stands that the possibility is there, that they are behind the world burning to the ground. It also stands to suggest that Snells is in their pocket and can't do jack about it.

He looked back to his horizontal maps with all the ships. He turned his gaze toward the East Shores.

"As soon as I move my forces from the Arctic into the Pacific, it is guaranteed that Russia will invade on the Eastern Front. I'm not going to be able to coordinate a two front war. But Ghost is in Boston. If he's directly pushed, he will fight. If to protect something. I'm going to have to count on you, Ghost. As much as you're a problem. I'm going to have to use you, for old time's sake."

And there's this problem of this syndicate. I don't know where you are. I don't know how many of you there are. I will uproot you and smoke you out. Once you've been made public, I will hang you. Just as Nakamura would have it.

Well, welcome to World War III.

CHAPTER 26

APPLES

Report from the Front Lines:

Another pincer attack from North and South California closed in on Los Angeles, demolishing the FOB, forcing the last of US forces off the West Coast. Chinese forces push further into the US into Nevada and Idaho. Army and Air National Guard was immediately deployed and holding the front lines into these states, also with the assistance of Army and Air National Guard units from Colorado, Wyoming, New Mexico, Montana and Texas.

Speaker of the House Samuel Monabello has been in contact with the COO of Black Eagle Company. He believes that 'the President and his Vice are not eligible to serve under the current condition.' The nature of his contact with BEC is not confirmed.

The brisk fall air reminded Sakura very much of the nature of life, fleeting and oh so temporary, changing color with age until it withered and finally died. But there was a certain beauty in that, especially out here, with the apples in the trees, low hanging branches for them all. This orchard up north in Andover, a place she never thought she'd find herself, least of all with this small group of Christians of a variety of personalities. Again, no talk of faith here, but perhaps that was intentional.

She was surprised to learn that Jeffrey was Michael's brother and that he showed up, and of all the people here, he was who she could relate to. He appeared not to be a man of faith, but a man of grit, deeply rooted. Not of some far off distant goal that for all she knew, was just a lie, which made certain people feel better, and some worse depending on their own individual walks of life.

She went to pluck an apple from the low hanging branch. It shook, and the red apple was knocked off, falling down onto the ground, rolling to a stop not far from the tree. A red lady, she called it. She bent down, picked it from the ground, wiped it on her shirt and dropped it into her paper bag with all the others, and then there was another one. A large green man she called these, the sour ones were her favorite apples, but she was eager to grab *that* one. It was large, and likely succulent upon sinking her teeth into it. She pushed herself into the trees, the branches rough against her clothes, and the leaves caressing her skin like her mother used to do before she got too old, and the red apples below, bobbed against her for attention. No apple gets left behind.

Her foot pressed against the trunk, and her loose arm wrapped around the tree, firmly grabbing hold of the bark, and lifted herself up to stretch to get that apple.

"Oh, you'll never reach that apple," a voice came from behind her, and a large hand wrapped its grimy unwelcomed hands on her beautiful apple. *Her* beautiful apple.

"Hey." She turned around, tumbling down, smacking her face against the bed of soil. The bitter taste forced her to cough it out. She her face with her sleeve and stood, facing Jeffrey, who wiped the apple clean before offering it to her. "I didn't need your help."

"You are too short for that branch. I don't care how good a climber you are," he chuckled.

She took the apple, inspecting it for malformities. Pleased that there was none, she placed it in with the rest of her apples. "So, uh, when do you go back on duty?"

"I don't actually know," he answered, turning back to the path. "China on the west shore, and Russia threatening us from the East.

They're probably figuring out where to put me before they deploy. So, I was told to stay put, and here I am, staying right where I need to be, until I'm called."

"How exactly did it come to this?" she asked. "Couldn't it have been avoided?"

"'Wars can be prevented just as easily as they are provoked, and we who fail to prevent them must share the guilt of the dead,'" he replied. "Unfortunately, Omar Bradly didn't have mercenaries in mind when he said that. He was a good General; anyone would have been lucky to serve under him. But I guess you must first know what created the peace to begin with, and that was a weapon."

"A weapon?" she turned to him. *One weapon begot world peace? How?*

"Details are classified, but that weapon kept everything at peace, and it wasn't until now that all the major players in the world knew of its decommissioning," he continued. "Now that the threat of using that weapon is null and void, it makes threating nations far easier."

"Why'd they decommission—"

"Classified, and building a weapon like that takes a decade," he interrupted. He looked down to her, "Look, I know you have a need for patriotism, but there isn't any of that in war. Freedom can be bought, but not with anything less than a massacre. I urge you to chase that impossibility, and trust no one else to make the determinations for you. Follow your orders, and place orders when need to. The military is a cesspool, and you'll be asked to do things that disgust you."

She continued to walk with him, clutching her bag close to her chest. Lines get crossed and with a world like this where the actions made are irrevocable, how could she reconcile the horrible things her family did—the horrible things she would do. Where does it get drawn, and how far was too far?

"Where do you draw the line?"

He sighed heavily. "If you want to go home, or if you want to move up in rank, there is no line."

He sped off ahead of her, catching up to Michael and Sam. They were a cute couple. Such a wholesome view should have eased her nerves. But it didn't. Jeffrey filled her with an existential dread, forbearing the future actions which may, inevitably give her nightmares and fill her with regrets, or so she thought. So then, it would take a monster to complete the tasks she has set on her own shoulders, or quite possibly, imposed upon her by her lineage, her proud Japanese American lineage. Could she be that monster?

Jennifer held Ted's warm hand, silently off to the side, with their own collection of apples. Ted was very good at picking apples, getting into places where she couldn't, and wouldn't since she wouldn't tear up her dress; the twigs and thorns might get in the way. Curse her for deciding to do this last minute, but what she did find a certain felicity in, was the fact that Ted continued to smile, and his eyes lit up brightly like a child. A child finally allowed to play, cheeks puffy like a chipmunk with nuts stuffed in its mouth.

Something like this was taken from him, and he never got the chance to have fun, and here he was, climbing trees efficiently. She supposed he had his fair share of tree climbing, marks on his face, but he didn't seem to mind the minor scratches from the branches or thorns on his hand. She wondered if he felt pain. Fearless, he had to be for something like this, and something like this was so casual, so playful considering everything else he was forced to go through. What's one tree to an exploding car?

She noticed his head turned to gaze at a top branch. *Oh no.* He placed his bag on the ground, and she looked up. "Tedward, be careful, that doesn't look too stable!" she said as he scurried up the tree, almost like a squirrel. The thought was cute, until she got a much better look at the top, a cluster of green apples atop the tree, and of course, where all things were considered, it was thin, and easily breakable. "TED! Not those apples!"

But she was much too late. The wind came in, pushing the top of the tree, having the tree wave at her as Ted was reaching for it, and his hand stretched to pull the apples off. The wind whistled as it brushed through the leaves. *Honestly, how is he even going to get back down?*

The top of the tree creaked.

"TED! GET DOWN!" She cried.

Ted slowly picked off the apples, rolling them on his sleeves, and placed them in his pants pocket. He slowly climbed back down, hopping from branch to branch, and came down safely, minus a few bumps and scratches from earlier. She placed her hands all over him.

"Are you okay?"

"Yes," he said, pulling the apples out of his pockets and putting them in the paper bags. "I'm fine. Nothing at all to worry about."

She took a closer look at him. There was one scratch that wasn't there, on his cheek, red and dripping.

"You're bleeding," she said, reaching for her purse to grab a napkin, and spat on it, rubbing his cut clean, and took another look. Ted didn't flinch. As his history with hand trembling became all too constant, his hands stopped whenever she was near. She felt honored that he should trust her, with such frailty, she knew she could never betray his trust in her. This bleeding was natural, she turned away from him briefly, feeling the warm blood in her nose, and wiped it into the napkin, and withdrew it to a waste bag.

She turned her gaze back up to the tree, still swaying in the wind, whistling as it picked up, brushing her hair over her shoulders. She placed her hand on her sun hat to stop it from blowing off. The tree still creaked, but the top remained there, as if it didn't just deal with another man grabbing apples it clearly didn't want pulled.

She sighed, shaking her head. "Well, I suppose we should go meet with the others. With all the apples you got, we can make an apple pie, or maybe a delicious apple crisp." She peered into his bag. "Have you ever had an apple before?"

"No," he answered.

Opportunity knocks for those that open the door. "Well, when we get back and have these apples washed, I'll have you try one of mine."

"Why—"

"Pesticides, germicides, and all matter of other cides to keep the critters and bugs out of these apples," she replied. *He wouldn't have known about this. At least, I don't think he would.*

She heard snapping twigs. She abruptly turned, and that congressman showed up, neatly dressed as if he wasn't important. He came in his own car of course, and she exchanged niceties. He wasn't the regular politician; this she could tell. There was something about the way he carried himself which she found to be suspicious. She caught him following them.

She shrugged the feeling off. Probably just not very good at picking apples.

One as important as John Spadero taking an interest in her dear Tedward. No one but her needed to know Ted's past, and the source of all his despair. In fact, she might even say no one ought to ever know, unless they wanted to violently rip open an old wound, voraciously rubbing salt with lemon juice all over it. Listening to them scream for help in the most eloquent way.

Spadero placed a few green apples in his bag before walking to another tree. The poor man. He didn't know how to pick apples. He always followed behind everyone, getting which ever apples they chose to leave behind, as if to say, 'you forgot some, but I didn't.'

He turned to look at both her and Ted. Smiled to her, and she traded the smile. *Ill placed suspicions. Nothing more. He is harmless. A nice change in pace.*

Upon leaving the orchard, Michael proposed that Sakura should stay a while longer for a little campfire. She didn't have any plans, so why not? A nice cackling fire with the ashes of burning wood assaulting her nostrils with those wonderful smoky scents.

Michael and Jeffrey went off in the brush somewhere to get wood. The clearing was nice, fall autumn leaves decorated the forest floor, the crickets sang, and the owls hooted their lovely songs, and of course, who could forget the stars, and the moon shining up high in the sky.

The lovely forest air was refreshing to her nose, leaning back, and propping herself up with straightened arms. Sam sat down next to her, pulling out some bottled water.

Michael planned this already. What other explanation would there be for coolers, I suppose to keep the apples nice and fresh on the way. She did hear talk of some apple crisp. Oh, what she wouldn't do for some of her mom's home-made apple crisp, with the sweet aromas, the lovely taste sweetened just with the right amount of cinnamon sugar. Nothing too fancy, nothing too bland. Just right.

She took the bottle. "Thank you,"

"No problem," she said. "So, are you having fun?"

"Yes," she replied. "Thank you, for being a friend. And inviting me out like this. I don't really get involved too much at the university."

"Uni life," Sam elbowed her. "I barely remember it."

"Yeah, gotta do it though," Sakura said.

"Do we though? I mean, you're going to be an officer, aren't you? So yeah, you might. I have my BS, and I learned a bit. But do you know how much I use the information I learned there? None." Sam laughed, taking a gulp of her own water, and then tucked her knees to her chest.

Michael and Jeffrey lit the fire, and the logs were burning, red ash floating into the sky, and the smoky scent filled her nose as the smoke rose. Ted and Jennifer's face glowed orange on the other side of the fire.

"Well, I don't actually need a degree to even be hired for my job. You just need to know how to think."

"Doesn't college teach you how to think?"

"Hun, I have met some of the dumbest people who have PHDs, and some of the smartest people never completed high school. All college really does is prove that you know how to think and write, and that's all anyone wants. Officer candidate school is probably the same. Not that I would know of course," Sam argued. "And take Ted, over there."

Sakura scowled and Sam waved her hands down to the ground.

"I know, he's unbearable at times. He is the epitome of what it means to attain success, by American standards. He's rich to the point where he doesn't need a job anymore."

"What did he do, steal from a bank?"

She laughed nervously. "Stockbroker. He did a lot with that job before, then he started doing it all himself, and now he just works from home. Granted, he did put in an unnecessary number of hours. So, if you want success, whatever you do, don't do what he did. It wasn't good for his mental health, although, one could make the argument it was the best thing for his mental health at the time."

"A contradiction if ever there was one,"

Sam threw her head up in laughter. "Humans are funny creatures, aren't we? Say one thing, and upon further reflecting realize the opposite might be true. But I think that you might find he is a valuable source of information—"

"I didn't get that from him," she said, taking a drink.

"Well, he doesn't just talk to anyone either. I'm curious as to how your conversation with him went," Sam asked.

"He said it was all meaningless,"

"You know, we were studying Ecclesiastes when we first met him." She chuckled. Sakura raised her eyebrow, not understanding what was so funny between the words meaningless, and Ecclesiastes. She's never read it, but she had a feeling there was a bit of sarcastic irony there. The fire continued to crackle as Michael moved some wood around with a stick. An orange leaf fell in her hair. She brushed it aside. "So, naturally I'd find that funny." Sam faced the fire, and her lips curled downward to a frown. "The thing is, we weren't designed to take human life. Ted knows that better than anyone. As someone whose job it was to take human life, again and again, and again," she turned and smiled to her, a halfhearted one. "So, forgive him, please. I know he's unbearable, and he has a nasty taste in his mouth for anything related to the military."

Sakura found this oxymoron troublesome, as the man didn't seem to be much older than she was. *Who was he killing? Something isn't right. Okay. Fine, let's have at it a second time.*

Sakura turned the cap on the water bottle, "Thank you for that. I'll try to forgive him." She stood, before walking closer to the flame, the heat caressing her skin. Ted made eye contact with her, and that scarred face and it's deadly scowl turned its hideous gaze toward her. Jennifer smiled, but another halfhearted smile. It appeared that even her presence made her nervous.

"Ted," Sakura began.

"What do you want?" he asked.

"Tedward, please be nice. She doesn't know," Jennifer said, leaning her back into Ted, keeping a careful eye on Sakura.

"It's best she doesn't."

"Look, I don't know why you hate me, I didn't do anything to you."

"You're throwing your life in the trash, is what you're doing," Ted replied. "Look, I don't care what rank you are, what rank you end up being. Become a four-star general or admiral for all I care. You are nothing but a tool and a statistic. Do you know what a statistic is?"

She shook her head, "I bet you're going to tell me." She sighed.

"A statistic is a variable with a numerical value. That numerical value changes. It starts at an infinite value, representing the potential someone has, and over time when their bodies start to decay, or they get their limbs blown off, it depletes. Once that numerical value becomes zero, you're just baggage, the first thing they do is dispose of you in the most efficient and least problematic way possible. I already told you that. It happened to me, it happened to—"

"What about those who came back? They have value. Otherwise, we wouldn't have invested in the funds for the VA." Ted was having that effect on her again, like a pit growing in her stomach, trying to throw itself up. As if those that died didn't have value for simply having the audacity to die for their beloved country.

"Are you ready for something real?" He looked at her, chuckling, as if he knew something of some cruel joke. "The VA gets great pride at 'giving our troops another chance to die for their country.' Your mind blown yet? Not that I care, because I can't even use the VA even if I wanted to. No. You can't ask me why."

He still had that wretched smile on his face. As if he delighted in mocking her, calling her goals stupid, and by way of that, insulting her lineage, and her birth mother specifically. What would she say if she let this slide?

"You came to me twice now, and I said the same thing," Ted continued. "You've met Jeff, an active member of Black Eagle, who undoubtedly told you his way of things, and of course, Lamar Cooper, a discharged gunnery sergeant, which, out of the three, has the most normal experience out of all of us, and didn't bother himself, wisely, with anything classified. I see you've talked to him more than once now, so why come to me? I'm not going to tell you what you want to hear."

She crinkled her nose, exhaling heavily through the cracks of her teeth. She was angry, and it showed, but anger never solved anything, it only added fuel to the fire, so she closed her hands in fists repeatedly opening them up until she calmed down so she could ponder, thinking just that, after all, what did he offer her? Nothing really except the promise of regret. Well, that was his answer anyway.

"Because Sam said I should give you a second chance to—"

"Sakura," Jennifer smiled, and this one seemed genuine. "Ted's experience is...unique. And you don't want to share in his experience, trust me. Samantha doesn't know everything, neither do I, but I don't need to know."

Odd choice of words for someone who's supposed to be a couple.

"You're talking about war time, which, I'm sure you know, you can expect things to go wrong, and you're talking to a man, who, in his entire life. Nothing has ever gone right. He's a flower, with plenty of scars, but it still stands tall."

Sakura shook her head, turning back to Ted. "There's one last thing I'd like to ask you. The other week, I spoke with Lamar who touched on the common bond of having a brotherhood, and which he seemed to share when he met Jeff for the first time. But like me, he told me that you don't share that kind of brotherly bond. Why?"

Ted scoffed. "Doesn't the fact that I don't share that bond tell you anything? Jennifer just told you nothing has ever gone right in my life. *Nothing.*" He snarled at the ground. "Not a single. Damned. Thing." He turned his snarl back at her, smiling with a menacing smile. "Where were my brothers? Where were my sisters when I needed help most? Nowhere to be seen. 'Leave no man behind' was biggest crock of shit I've ever heard."

"Sorry I asked." Sakura turned away, clenching her fists at her side, walking back to the other end of the fire. The man was insufferable. Honestly, what did Jennifer see in a man like that? The man was a dick if ever there was one, who carelessly shits on heroes for fighting for their personal freedom so he can do God knows what behind closed doors. Ted, you got some sketchy things going on in your basement, don't you? Does Jennifer know? Or is she also hiding something neither of you want out?

But that still didn't answer the question about who he was killing. He was killing people, but the answer was just as elusive as his nihilistic nonsense. But the question was an important one. Deductively speaking, he shouldn't have been killing people from overseas with the peace treaties in place. Unless that was part of the initial agreement, or were there other forces at play that remained hidden underneath the veil of world peace, and those forces were the same forces he was fighting, people he was killing? But then, what were these forces? There must be something else going on in the world, otherwise, he would have been fighting overseas, and the last time the US should have been abroad fighting wars was well over a decade ago, which meant that *Ted* was a lot older than he looked.

Sakura glanced over at the congressman, tired as he was, bags underneath his eyes. He sat by himself, and he smiled at her, taking a large bite from his red lady. A sweet apple, crunchy even, but not sour. He gnawed on the skin before he tossed the core into the blazing fire. There was something about him that separated him from everyone else, apart from the fact that he was an important man in

Massachusetts. He was reserved here, but his eyes were ever watchful, scheming by the looks of it.

She took out an apple from her bag, the green one by the looks of it. She looked at it carefully, the stem, elegant, the peel was shimmering with the flames light, and it was still firm. She took the rest of her water and poured it over, using her shirt to dry it off.

Something about an apple. It was so sour when she bit into it, the delightful crunch in her teeth. Part of a peel got stuck, she pulled it out, swallowed it, and slowly sucked some of the apple juice from the exposed flesh from the surface. *Apples.* She took another delicious bite from it. They never fall far from the tree.

CHAPTER 27

DYATLOV'S PASS

President and Vice President's whereabouts are still unknown.

"The USA armed forces are working with Black Eagle Company to secure the West Coast. We assure you, the American people, everything is under control...we strive to take back our borders and remove China from our midst...We will push back the Chinese and send them back home." *Press Secretary Jenna Walters stated, responding to the negative questions regarding the West Coast Conflicts.*

Claire shuddered in her coat and thick pants, waiting for Mikhail to come outside from one of his glory *Atavasta* as it were. Whatever that meant. She waited carefully, her eyes scanning the oncoming cars in this little village, which was secluded from the rest of the world, but not yet isolated. There were some main roads on which postal carriers drove by, braving the harsh Ukrainian blizzard with thick, wet snow coalescing the ground.

She'd been outside this little pub for his *Atavasta* for not more than fifteen minutes, and yet, her entire boot was already covered in snow. She exhaled heavily into her gloves, feeling her warm breath blow back on her face.

The door creaked open, and Mikhail, spoke something in Russian she didn't understand. Must have been a joke, because the people inside the pub, just regular normies most likely, laughed at it. He proceeded to wave as if saying goodbye to an old friend before shutting the door behind him.

"Nice day for a walk, isn't it?" he spoke in his thick accent.

"Of course, and what better way to spend our last days together freezing our tush off, freezing to the bone." She glanced up at the path, a notable elevation.

"You got everything you need? We go on foot from here," he said, hoisting his travel pack over his shoulders.

"Yes, and I could say the same of you. You may be Russian, but you're terribly slow," she said.

"Hey, at least my people win wars," he snorted. "Let's go."

Her journey up the slope began, fighting against the elements, the snow chilling her bones with each step.

After hiking for hours, the sun finally began to set, and she was freezing. Mikhail didn't seem to be near bothered by it, the brute, but he was useful, carrying additional supplies when he didn't need to. Claire was knee high in snow, breathing in mana from the air, melting some of the snow with the additional heat her body produced to making walking a bit easier.

"Hey," Mikhail turned around. "You can't do that here!"

"Why not?"

"Well, you have some jests." He shook his head. "There are still tourists that come this way. It's a pain to try to shoot down a helicopter when all I've got is a spear."

"And what do you propose we do then? I'm not freezing anymore." Claire said as a gust of wind blew snow across her face.

"Look, there's a plateau just up there, it's well off the tourist trail, and we can camp there for the night," he said, leading her. He slowed his steps so she would have steps to walk into, to reduce the lag in her own feet, and thus keep up with him. Mikhail at times was a little much, but he had his uses.

She breathed heavily, frost breath getting in her way from the flash's light, and she saw Mikhail's hand in the snow ahead of him, grabbing hold of an unknown item: a torch maybe? A rock? Perhaps a lever to get out from the elements? That was a little optimistic, she had to admit, but the possibilities were endless.

His foot raised up, and with his other hand, he appeared to be grabbing rocks, or crevices inside the pass itself, climbing up.

Fantastic, my wee little fingers won't freeze off.

She followed him, her hand cold underneath the snow, and colder even with the surface of the rock, clearly iced over. She gripped it firmly and peered down for a crevice to put her feet into another crevice for her to reach. She pulled herself up, grabbing hold of the other slit, and pulled up her feet to grab another spot before leaping upward again, catching up to Mikhail. The muscles in her arms and legs were stiffening like shards of glass, fragile, ready to shatter if she moved anything wrong. She wasn't weak, but as far as Casters were concerned, she wasn't going to the Olympics anytime soon.

Finally, the last of the snow fell from Mikhail's boot onto her face. She shook her head, tossing the snow off. She reached for the ledge, but it was slippery. He reached down, grabbing her wrist firmly with his blue mana veins, lifting her up with ease. "There, hard part is over, now—"

She pushed past him. "You said this was well off the tourist trail, right?"

"Yes," he turned back, a smirk on his lips like he wasn't enjoying himself.

A man in his thirties, all alone with a beautiful damsel in distress. *Yeah, right. Thanks for ruining all the good fairy tales my ancestors wrote.*

"Good. Don't stop me." She shivered, pulling out a knife from her boot. The curvature edge shimmered in her hand with the light. She inhaled the mana from the air, and the moisture of the snow, combined within the hard ore-like mana from the rock. Her mana veins glowed brightly, covering her skin, and penetrated her gloves as they touched the knife, imbuing it with the mana source she created, carefully blending the mixture inside.

She cleared some snow, until the surface of the rock was visible. With a forward motion, she stabbed the rock, penetrating it with ease. Fragments raised up, striking her face, and the wind around her rose from the hole in the ground, blowing the snow away around her. Writing the old runes down, from the language of the ancestors, she wrote: *Snâw Wèohsteall.*

Around the perimeter, bright yellow vein-like lines appeared from the hole, crawling like caterpillars, crafting a box around both her and Mikhail, and rising, creating a golden light fixture and the temperature within this box rose.

"Ah, the little woman does it again, protecting old me from the cold." Mikhail knelt to the ground, pulling out his bedroll, laying it down. He pulled out some small twigs he had hidden, obtained from God only knows where, and setting them up before putting some larger pieces of burnable materials. "Lîgbryne," he said as a spark lit the flame from his lips, and there was a fire. "Now, how about some nice brandy."

"You Russians. All you ever think about is spirits," she said, pulling out some beef jerky, chilled to the touch, but not for much longer as the heat rose to room-temperature

"And you like to stick to your sweet rolls and cheese." He pulled out his metal flask, unscrewed it, brought it to his lips to take a swig.

"It's jerky. *Va te faire foutre.*" She cried out.

"Well," he chuckled again, closing the flask. "Someone's got a mouth. Here."

He threw the flask toward her. She caught it and sealed her container of jerky before throwing it over. She took a swig, and it was bitter as always. Nasty brandy. Not like her fine wine, her favorite, Ca'habielli.

"I suppose you and I never got the chance to discuss in detail what we're doing here," Mikhail said.

"What is there to talk about? We were already told what we need to be doing before assembling a team together." She took another sip, watching Mikhail eat a piece of her salty jerky. The saltiest of jerky. But it didn't seem to bother him much.

"Well, yes, and I suppose we know the why—"

"Do we, Mikhail? Do we know the why? This happened under your nose, somehow flew across radar, heading deeper into the heart of London. Under Adam's nose, all the while, under someone else's directive?" She interrupted him. "You," she snapped her fingers. "Adam," she snapped a second time. "McCurdy, Sarah McCurdy underneath the wing of Colton. America, *Mother* Russia, and London, the heart of our operations, and yet, the most valuable thing in the world disappeared. A mysterious man, possibly two mysterious men, one in America for certain, the other, the last known location is where we're going. Don't you find this to be at least a little odd?"

"Well, distrust is alive and well, I see." He shrugged his shoulders, hand to the side, palm facing the sky while the other one firmly gripped the jerky, almost like his life depended on it. "Look, Mademoiselle, we can spout off distrust with one another all we like, but it won't get us anywhere, and it will make the trip up and down this pass all the more treacherous." His lips curled downward.

"Fine." She spoke softly, eyes facing the rock, and laid down in her bedroll. "How's your family?"

"Very well, very well, thank you," he said, zipping up the jerky and tossing it back. She caught it and placed it in her travel pack. "Children are just about to get mother's first arcane lesson. Teaching them the Anglo-Saxon after all."

"The old language is important," she said, pulling her arms behind her head like a pillow, gazing at the night sky. The clouds were thick.

"And how is your family?"

Her eyes were getting sleepy, but she remembered all the same, her two little children: Juliette and Jean. Young children, taken care of by her husband Hugo. Of course, they'd be about the same age as Mikhail's children, playing with what little time they had left before starting the vigorous training to become a Caster, just like her. They all had to do it. Have fun until eight, and then delve into the pits of training from sunup to sundown, with just enough time for a few hours of sleep before getting to school. Nothing short of straight 20s will suffice for her children. Though, right now, they'd be sleeping. "Nothing beyond the usual. They haven't started learning Anglo-Saxon yet, just French and English. Soon, and very soon, they'll be ready."

Several nights passed just like this one, blizzards one day, and turbulent winds the next, the kind that were so fast, and so brisk, it could rip one's face off. Terribly horrible for one's complexion, especially one so fine as Claire's. She'd have to dress the wounds later, feeling the warmth of her skin receding into her face. Of course, avoiding any possible interested parties, they finally made it to the top of the summit.

She climbed down with Mikhail, taking care with every step along the jagged rocks, and to the smooth surface. There was no dead body here, not where McCurdy said there would be, but she was no new Caster—that much was abundantly clear; McCurdy would have known to erase all evidence of mana residue. *Let's just hope she wasn't too efficient.*

Mikhail walked forward, exhaled, and red mana veins formed over his body, generating heat, melting the snow around his feet.

Claire inhaled mana coming from the rocks, and the generated heat, and she felt the creepy crawly mana veins veiling her eyes. Peering around, a red tint covered her vision, and she saw some traces of blue going into the iron door into the mountain, which was closed. The trace was faint, fading into nothing as she peered into it.

"Mikhail," she pointed at the door. "Right there, that's where she was. We need to get inside. Looks like the Major wasn't overtly thorough."

"Seems that way," he replied, releasing the mana from his veins, fading back into his skin. "I was personally never fond of bunkers, but this place was made a gem for artistic expression."

He walked over to the door, turning the wheel knob, pulling the iron door open. Dust poured out of it, fogging her view as she made the unfortunate error of standing right behind him. She covered her mouth, coughing.

What foul remains lie dormant behind this dreaded door?

Claire turned her eyes toward the pitch blackness of the bunker, iron rust fueled the scent, and of course, a very familiar, and very, unwelcomed stench: blood.

"You smell that?" Claire asked.

"Yes," Mikhail frowned, coughed and covered his mouth. His hand reached for a flashlight. "You remembered to pack one of these, right?"

As if on cue, she pulled one out, and they crossed the streams of light into the abyss.

"Well," he said, eyes narrowing into the deep dark dank of the bunker, "we won't find out one part of this mystery just standing outside, now, will we?"

Claire's heart raced as she stepped a delicate foot inside. Heart pumping inside her chest, and it was places like this, unexplored places with the dark unknowns that she feared the most. She hated not knowing, her teeth clattering against one another. "Let's—"

A screeching door slammed shut in the distance, echoing across the halls like nails against chalkboard. A truly deplorable sound, filled with nothing but the regrettable ear drums which then requested to be ripped out viscerally, never to be of use again.

"Well, something's here." Mikhail sighed and turned off his flashlight. "These probably aren't going to do us much good here."

"Agreed. Let's find what we need." She breathed in the mana from the iron, and the stone in the pass. Her eyes veiled red with it, and she could see clearly, busted doors, creaking cockroaches moving across the halls with nothing to eat: a small trail of blood leading further into the place. "And get out."

Mikhail did much the same—she could tell.

"Agreed but let us take a look at what's on this level first." He reached in the air, and swirls enveloped his hand, and a green spear manifested in it, and he grabbed hold of it like an Amazonian warrior. Truth be told, the Amazonians only learned that from the Casters.

Sighing heavily, her hands up right, she pulled her knife out, just in case. But she was more accustomed to the arcane than most of the other administrators. She just hoped she wouldn't have to prove it today. A terrible business.

She moved into one of the other rooms, climbing over sharpened iron in the crevice. The room around her was filled with dust and other particles but was otherwise undisturbed. She suspected McCurdy never opened the door, but then, there is the possibility this was all an illusion. However, she sensed no trace of that here. She found a desk with a drawer, partially caved in. She pulled it out, and it struck the ground, the noise echoing in the room.

"You know they heard that, right?" Mikhail called from other of the other rooms across the hall.

"Mikhail." She knelt to grab the manilla folders which dropped out. "They've known we were here since we got here. Let's just let them think we don't know that, eh?"

"I found something here. You might want to come look," he said.

She placed the folders into her traveling pack and climbed out to reach him in the other room, almost identical, except a few broken lockers, which seemingly just had some old skeletons with Soviet Union uniforms stuffed in the side violently. "Friends of yours?"

"Ha. No," he chuckled loudly. So obnoxiously loud, that he made it clear they were here by whatever roamed the halls yet, sending the same lie to whoever was stupid enough to believe them, that they didn't know they weren't alone.

He laid out some paperwork. "I've got these files here, now. They were written in Polish, by two different hands, it would seem."

"So, what's it say?" she asked.

"I speak Japanese, English, and Russian. I don't know Polish," he replied.

"What makes you think I know Polish?" She replied.

"So, let's just grab all the files we can, and we'll worry about getting this translated later," he said.

"What we'll do, is find out what's down there," she pointed to the blood stains. "And do what needs to be done and get out. We'll send someone else here to grab everything."

"I can't risk that," he shook his head. "If we miss something, odds are they're going to take the files with them. We need to scour over every little thing while we're here."

She shook her hands. "Gah! You are so thorough."

"No wonder your people haven't won any wars since, uh, well, not in recent memory."

"Shameful." She shook her head as she scoured around for files, which, in all likelihood, had nothing to do with the reason they were here. However, there was something that bothered her immensely, with the certainty that this was Ukrainian territory. These documents should be written in at least Ukrainian, not Polish; in fact, Polish is one language it shouldn't be written in, unless of course Mikhail was lying, but now was not the time for cynicism.

"All right," Mikhail sighed, after bleeding the last of the rooms dry of all files.

"Find anything new?"

"You mean apart from these files being written in every other language when it should be Ukrainian? Or Russian? No. Not at all. I can't read any of this," he said, eyes narrowing down the hall, following the blood.

"No one ever accused you of literacy." She smiled, and turned a death's snarl toward the black abyss, further into the dark, the iron walls coated in dry crimson dust.

"Funny," he said. "We'll get this to Sander, and he'll put together a coalition of linguists to decipher all this nonsense."

"Well, first, we must leave," she said. "Let's be done with it. I want to get out of this bunker."

"Agreed."

The two walked side by side, their steps echoing in the corridor as drops fell—God only knows what was leaking from the bunker's ceiling. The smell didn't get any better, just wafting in. Coming without some kind of hazmat suit was a mistake. Not for the radiation—just to filter out this accursed smell, whatever it was, for it was no longer blood she was smelling, it was something else. She smelled it once before, but she couldn't remember where.

They walked down some steps, grabbing hold of the railing. The steps, were wet, soiled with something, blood perhaps. She was too disgusted to even think of looking down. The noise of the repugnant splashing of her own boots in this foul liquid was becoming squishier, and she only assumed she was stepping in *shit*. Actual shit.

A door was ahead of them, an arch door, and another wheel like crank, and above it, was nothing. There was a grate as if on one side, there was going to be someone kind enough to greet them in and give them the good old welcome of Ukrainian hospitality. But the grate was checkered, and an ominous red light shone from behind it, shining upward.

"You ready for another waft of adventure?" Mikhail asked, grabbing hold of it, and turned the wheel.

She breathed heavily with each turn he made, slowly creaking the locks. She pulled her knife out again, eyes focused, narrowed at whatever was behind this door. This is part of the report that didn't make it in, or perhaps McCurdy just failed to tell them about this in the report. Whatever the reason, they were going to find out, and put a stop to one part of the puzzle, which didn't seem to be doing anything since they only found more questions, and not even a path to an answer yet.

The door creaked slowly open, and there was an altar, candles burning brightly, wicks smoldered, and the tiles around the altar were shattered. Mikhail shook his head as he walked in. "Satanic cultists! Satanic Cultists."

"The worst kind of cultists," she whispered, walking through the threshold.

"There is no worst kind of cultists. All cultists are the worst cultists," Mikhail stood over the candles, "I'm honestly quite disappointed."

"Don't be that way," she said, tracing mana around the room. She found this room itself was like a heart; mana veins were faint, but pulsating, the thrums drumming in her ears. "Something isn't right here." *Something is very, very wrong.*

The door slammed shut behind them.

She gasped, turning around, taking her knife to draw symbols in the air.

The wind swirled around them, freezing the flames of the candles in place, and the room became like an ice prison. Stalactites and stalagmites formed spears from the ceiling and floor respectively. *Damn it. It's so cold.*

Mikhail screamed something in Russian. His spear shattered some of the stalagmites coming for him. He focused his eyes on the door, and his spear lit up, a spire, a purple spire thrust, screeching like a plane, shattering the ice in front of her, blowing the entire wall out. The vibrant action of his spear shook the foundations of the bunker, many bolts coming loose, clinking against the floor they landed upon.

The ice melted, and the temperature rose considerably.

Claire panted, looking at Mikhail, who breathed heavily, sweat coming from his brow.

I see. Immediately bringing out the artillery, huh? She went over to him, letting him rest on her shoulder. She scanned the room again, and the mana veins completely faded.

"Are you—"

There was a large tearing sound behind her. She turned her head around to see a rip in the flesh of creation, protruding against the wall. Of which, there was now a hole, and she beheld bright blue flames in front of an iron furnace. A little creature sprinted out. This looked like a little goblin, a Threcket one with large claws, and did anyone ever tell him? Spiked hair is out of style.

The Threcket bolted past them, stretching an elongated claw. Mikhail thrust his body into Claire's before the claw could reach her, and the nails shredded the flesh in his left arm. Leaving them be on the floor, the Threcket dashed up the stairs, scurrying like the little ugly, wretch it was.

"*Mais quelles conneries,*" she swore.

"Чушь собачья!" he agreed, before turning to the gaping hole in creation. "You go track it down. I'll close this portal."

Mikhail grunted, drawing his own knife, and already, purple mana veins protruded from his epidermis, crawling onto the blade.

Don't need to ask me twice. She inhaled the mana from the air, and her mana veins manifested on her skin, including her legs as she leapt off one foot, tracking down this dreaded Threcket. Clearly, this place only prompted more questions than answers. For a Threcket's heart was in this world, manifested inside Devil's Pass. Such a fitting name for such a dreadful heart.

CHAPTER 28

THREADS OF CREATION UNDONE

Status Report:

Communications are online. Armed Forces, heavy and light infantry and calvaries are deployed to the front line. FOB and Airbases operating at full capacities in Arizona, Nevada, and Idaho. The Chinese forces have come to a halt and the USA are at a standstill.

Black Eagle Company has deployed fleets to the Pacific Coast, sailing in from the Arctic. Fleets have engaged in ship-to-ship combat, while the fighter jets take to the skies in dog fights.

Additional reinforcements expected from China: none.

Claire panted, following this Threcket through the dark, coldness of a Ukrainian winter, following its little footsteps. But when she made it to the base, toward Sverdlovsk, her worst nightmare happened. Their failure here meant a lot of things, and a lot of calls were to be made to cover this up. How the hell was she to explain the disappearance of a large city to the world?

The Threcket blasted through the snow, kicking it up, obscuring her vision, but she could see the larger things at play: the cars squealing, women, children screaming, and men shouting things as they jumped atop their cars, not knowing what this thing was. A natural reaction, really, after all, they never did see anything like it. And such a shame, really, they didn't prepare for this, and now, cars were squealing off, driving away from this base of operations, and they would have to be hunted down, else the Threads of Creation come undone.

"Merde," she swore, pulling her knife, bolting back toward the Threcket, melting the snow around her. She sprinted faster than the truck, trying to escape, but, *"Forðeon!"*

Mana veins seared the truck; glass shattered. Legs and arms of those inside tried to immediately pull themselves out, severed as the truck crunched, gnawing at them inside. She grimaced, the white snow stained with crimson and flesh as the screams from inside the truck died down, but the screams outside only amplified.

The Threcket thrashed a normie, sending the limbs at her. She ducked and wove herself to avoid a direct strike and sprinted forward, warm blood splattering on her face. The Threcket looked terrified of her, as it should be. *"Je vais te défoncer!"*

The Threcket scurried off again, kicking some more snow. As small as this Threcket was, it was far more annoying chasing it down the damn mountain pass to get here, and now, there were places to hide. And so it did, immediately scurrying underneath the foundation of a house. *Damn it. "Nîedðearf!"*

The house in front of her was uprooted, flying upward. The wooden pieces rose, splintering in the air, the wood rotten, blasted apart, the furnishing falling to the ground, and the people still inside, falling out of their house. *Thud.* A body splattered over the ground, bones shattering. The Threcket, in all its cursed demeanor, whimpered like a child.

How dare you! "T'es pas un gamin! Onbryrdan sôll!"

The clouds above dispersed, and the moon glimmered all the clearer. Like a beam from the heavens, it blasted the area right in front of her, melting the snow. She shielded her eyes. More screams followed, piercing her ears. *I'm sorry.*

Crunching metal. Screeching tires. Lots of sunlight. All signs that none of this was going too well. Mikhail panted along the way, just getting down to the base.

She certainly knows how to make an entrance, but it can't be helped.

Shit. He took out his phone and dialed, and the other end was immediately picked up,

"Dimitry, Sverdlovsk, now. Bring all able-bodied Casters."

"What's this about?" He spoke.

"Let's call it, Operation we're gonna kill everyone and cover it up. Send a team to track down some strays heading..." he glanced back at the road. Luck smiled upon him. "...mostly south."

"Got it. Be there in a few hours,"

He hung up the phone.

Shaking his head, his hand reached out, and his spear formed into his hand. His eyes narrowed toward the convoy. The spire around his spear lit up. Hurling the spear, much like a missile that would make Mother Russia proud of her little boy; it threw itself at the convoy. It struck the earth behind it with such velocity, and distorting the mana around creation, which undoubtedly would compromise the way to Pandora significantly, it did its job. The earth shattered, debris shooting ahead, striking, impaling the steal as it popped tires. Squealing, the trucks flipped over, glass shattered as the people inside died, but for good measure, he ran to the massacre.

Dashing through the snow and the debris, he saw men, women, and children here. Only one was barely clinging to life, sitting down, feet sprawled in front of him, hand clutching his chest, back leaning against a flaming truck, without the will to move. He was a beautiful boy. He couldn't have been more than five years of age. Still had his life ahead of him. But this mess, this accursed mess forced his life to be cut short.

"закрой глаза," said Mikhail, summoning another spear in his hand.

The boy obediently closed his eyes. "я напуган," said the boy.

Mikhail looked at him, his hands firmly gripped on his spear, ready to thrust. Of course, he's scared. But Mikhail knew what needed to be done to spare the boy of further pain and fear. "У тебя есть полное право быть, но это не для тебя, а для меня."

The boy panted, closing his eyes, leaning his back against the truck firmly. *I'll try to make this easy for you. I'm sorry. All Hell. I'm sorry.* He thrust the spear again, the boy's heart was thrust outside the back of his chest as the car was pushed back, and the boy just rested there. He didn't make a sound, but his own blood now dripped from the sides of his lips, his life now gone. *And this is how the Administration designed it. A cursed existence to be sure. I'm sorry boy, but Mother Russia cannot save you this time.*

The damned Threcket didn't die, and Mikhail wasn't there yet to help track it down. *Who am I kidding, the poor man is probably out trying to mitigate the mess; however he's going to handle this, a lot more people are going to die.*

She pushed past some more people, her mana veins giving them a slight shock as she brushed up against them, but she didn't care. With the amount of mana being expended here, not only was she abundantly aware she would summon a Threcket, by accident of course. But the people she brushed against would be dead soon after.

The little goblin of a Threcket found its way into a horrible place, a place with children. Ukrainian children. Orphans. Fantastic, as if there wasn't more tragedy in the world.

Sorry your parents died. You'll join them soon. Or perhaps parental irresponsibility created these poor orphans. Who knows? Not her problem, and soon, neither theirs.

She pushed through the wooden doors, thrusting herself against the Threcket, pushing it into a wall. Framed pictures fell down, shattering glass with the collision. She breathed mana from the air, and her left hand emitted a strong blue aura, striking her hand into the ribcage of the Threcket. With a penetrating force, and her hand reached out from inside, grabbing hold of an organ. The screams were enough to make her crazy, piercing at high decibels as its blood poured onto the floor.

She peered forward as she was getting to know this Threcket so intimately. Just like when her husband proposed to her, she had to think about the genetics, make sure the heart was a strong one, and just so, her hand *knew* every part of this Threcket. Children, however horrified, covered their ears, wailing in their own little death throe of an orchestra. Sure, to an untrained ear, it sounded like nothing short of a banshee wailing its last screech.

Finding the heart, a frail little thing, fragile like glass, her hand gripped around it, feeling it's veins and other musculature constructs inside, she inhaled more mana from the air, and her blue mana veins lit her body up like a beacon, burning the external extremities of the Threcket, and ripped its heart out. It wailed on the ground, like a dead fish trying for water, its claws striking every which way.

Only one last thing to do here, make sure this little critter doesn't form his heart again. She crushed the heart with her hand, and with her knife, drew runes in the air. Light shone back at her as she cut the air like flesh.

"Cu'ernavorgen. Cha. Lathukaprath'haken." Purple veins flowed from her body, replacing the blue ones, shining toward the body, restraining the Threcket to the ground. She burned it, turning it to little more than yellow lights, and with those purple veins, like tentacles, they reached for the light, drinking the remains of the Threcket, taking it into her body.

Feeling the toxin fill her, she leaned back against the wall, the children staring back at her. Too so, to move with all that toxin coagulating in her veins. Her purple tentacles grabbed hold of the children, whom wailed as they too were absorbed into her being, and they became like little lights, shining all the clearer, but their clothes remained, and nothing, short of their scent in their wrinkled clothes remained as evidence of their unnecessary existence.

She inhaled and exhaled. Staring in front of her, the fragments of the souls of the children roaming around her, never able to see the world for themselves, but rather, given a hand so cruel only forcing themselves to climb up a social ladder.

"All things considered," Mikhail walked through the door.

Nice of you to finally show up.

"It could be worse," he said.

Don't count your blessings yet.

"Dimitry will be here shortly. Organizing the disappearance of this place and pulling people off the roads. This is one hell of a mess." He opened his flask and offered it to her.

She took it and took one large mouthful of that piss water. It was refreshing, but even urine was tastier than drinking the soul of a Threcket. Lucky those kids were here, or she would have vomited. "I suppose that's some good news, then. Let's take a moment then, and recap what we learned."

"I learned nothing," he chuckled, trying to lighten the mood.

But how can this mood be light? We're going to kill nearly two million people, make it look like nothing happened, and move on. Not to mention it's a great pass, lots of traffic through here. This will undoubtedly raise unwanted questions.

"Yes, let's call Adam up, tell him the two of us went up the pass, found nothing, oh, and by the way, Adam, get this, get this Adam, a major city went missing!"

"Sarcasm doesn't suit you, my friend. I get that enough from Colton." She glared at him.

Colton. That damned American yank can go rot in hell.

"Well," she said. "To condense this report before we get linguistics involved for all the damn unreadable reports, there's a heart in Devil's Pass. Threckets are forming in weakened spots around the world, most notably, Devil's Pass. The existence of reports in Ukraine, in languages in neither Russian nor Ukrainian. What the hell is going on?"

"This may boil to knowing a master code breaker who knows all these languages. You know anyone?" he asked.

"You're talking about fifteen different languages. What you're asking for doesn't exist," she scowled.

"We can always hope, now, can't we?"

CHAPTER 29

NOT RIGHT NOW

Status Report:

US armed forces push back the front line into Washington. Attack Choppers fly into Los Angeles from Delta Force underneath the directive of CCO Malcolm's demands. Delta Force deployed directly into China's FOB in Los Angeles under confusion, disabling communication systems.

Chinese Navy fleet has been sunk. Fighter pilots remaining retreat to carriers to the Southern Pacific. Black Eagle Company's destroyers fire their heavy machinery into the sky, shooting most of the remaining jets before they were out of range. The fleet proceeds to sail south.

Colton stood over his desk, a large map of the United States atop it, some lights shining over all the pieces. Staring down, looking at all the pieces. By himself, as always, gazing over all the different scenarios a situation like this could create. *Snells. You may be stupid, but good job where it's due.*

His finger touched the West Coast, tapping it with his finger. "China's navy is pushing along the West Coast. Granted, I didn't need that, but it does protect McCurdy from prying eyes," he said, turning another index finger to DC "And Russia is moving their fleet to the East Coast. Finally. Thanks Mikhail, I'm gonna need to buy you drinks after this, assuming there's a world where drinks exist after all this is done." He pointed his finger up toward Boston. "And then there's this pesky Ghost here. You should have been killed."

Ping.

Turning his gaze to his computer, a report coming in from the President himself. *Good boy.* He briskly ran to his computer, and opened the email, subject header: Status Report. It was a lengthy report, but no stone was to be left unturned. That was how mistakes were made, and undoubtedly, that's how this Ghost has remained alive all this time.

Concerning the procurement of Task Force Seven:

Stem cells were studied from a group of anonymous donors. Testing these cells and samples, a selection of thirty-two promising couples were located. The sample size exceeded a total of 3,000 couples across all demographics, high socioeconomic status and low, white, Black, Hispanic, Asian, ect. Those thirty-two couples chosen for Task Force Seven gave birth that year.

CIA was charged with creating Task Force Seven, sponsored by Lieutenant General Snells. Addresses of the hospitals where the births would be taking place were immediately placed into the custody of the CIA. All the while, Lieutenant General Snells was given execute authority to create a habitation for such individuals, given temporary family units in an undisclosed location, that location ultimately being Area 51.

Upon the births, CIA operatives were immediately dispatched into the hospitals, taking the selected children out of the units, and bringing them to a CIA undisclosed location, DC underground. Files of the birth were erased from the hospital within that same day, and no notice was ever submitted to the news, apart from thirty-two missing persons reports.

At this time, it is unknown which set of parents belonged to which child. Details of parents are disclosed below:

Colton skimmed the list of parents and siphoned them off to look at later. Eyes scanning the report downward to:

Execution: Area 51

Per your request, Task Force Seven was to be eliminated. They were advised to expect a training exercise, of which, they were given dummy guns and blanks. They were split up into four parties. Party four consisting of Clubs, Spearhead,

Apple, and Mist were immediately dispatched, bodies removed from the scene. No casualties.

Operatives Roach, Ivy, Winters, and Summers were dispatched by the following day, buried themselves in the sand. Casualties: 26,329.

Operatives Metal, Viper, Venom, and Wraith were brought down, buried in an old bunker. The four dropped their weapons, came out willingly, tied to posts before being executed. Casualties: 33,297.

Operatives Ghost, Slithers, Butcher and Ticker.

Butcher was found dead right at the execution site of the previous operatives. Estimated casualties before deceased: 9,000.

Ticker's Body was found well above the skirmish. Body unrecognizable, cause of death, ruled to be blood loss. Body unrecognizable due to radiation poisoning. Estimated casualties: 10,300.

Slithers and Ghost's bodies could not be identified. It is assumed that Slithers died below ground. As evidenced in a report by one Sergeant Jeffrey Clemens of now Black Eagle Company, it is confirmed Ghost was the last one atop Area 51. Bombs dropped by aircraft, leveling the facility before the nuclear meltdown, causing any and all bodies remaining there to be unrecognizable.

Jeffrey Clemens stated in his initial report, Ghost took one final .50 caliber to the chest before the bombs dropped. The meltdown killed a total of 200,000 people, more than half of them were civilians.

This concludes any and all information I have regarding Task Force Seven.

Colton leaned back in his chair. Suppose a Caster could survive all that, he'd be scarred for life, but there's no way one of those couples would have been a Caster. No chance in Hell.

The phone rang.

Damnit Garcia, not now!

He answered it. "I'm busy right now, what do you want?"

"Someone's touchy. So, what are we going to do about McCurdy?" Garcia's flamboyant voice echoed in his ears.

"I told you, right now, I don't know where she is," he lied.

"Yeah, and how are we going to find out, hmm?"

"Let me check the air itineraries and get back to you," he said.

"Why wouldn't you have done that already?"

Because I'm hiding her from you, you dumb shit. "Garcia, in case you haven't noticed, my jurisdiction is about to be assaulted by two fronts."

"That has nothing to do with this,"

Oh, it has everything to do with this. "How about the fact that I'm moving pieces right now to make this more manageable for myself. I haven't had a chance to dissect every last itinerary. I still don't have time for this. Is this all?"

"You need to get on this. You know how important the Grail is."

Oh, I know. I know exactly how important it is. You don't. "Look, give me a week, till I know what's going on with Mikhail and why he sent a Russian mob here, and then I'll give you all the time in the world. I'll fly down and you can throw your disgusting tequila down my throat. How's that sound?"

"Rude."

"Bye!"

He hung up the phone.

He shook his head, biting his lip, eyes narrowed, scrolling back up through the couples, looking over their names, faces and background. The screen was about to make him tear his eyes out of their sockets when he was done with this menial task. With each group of parents, he cross referenced their information with the web, identifying where they gave birth to such individuals, and of course, most of these parents were dead, or incapacitated. No reason why. Unless they all were suicide victims, but he didn't care about that. What they did with their own lives was up to them, and them alone.

But these two in particular caught his eye. In fact, they were screaming at him. Sam and Elena Romanov-McCurdy. *Sarah. How the hell are you involved in this?* He sighed, staring at the computer. Same surname didn't necessarily mean anything, but the possibility was still there that. One suspicion leads to another, and further questions down a line that is so far off from the truth. It was almost like there was another invisible hand working that he didn't see. Such cruelty couldn't be by the hand of God, but perhaps the Devil instead. But why and who? *Well, if nothing else it does confirm my suspicion. Ghost. One cog in a grand machine and we don't even know what it does. You clearly don't, and yet, you're in the center of it all. Britain is especially looking for you. I'm looking for you, and Uncle Sam, the good old Malevolent Uncle is going to have an intriguing interest when they confirm for themselves that you are alive, and this little war from Russia is that catalyst.*

But a nuclear meltdown, and to be at the center of it. Though Mana was, by normies, radioactive, (and caused all sorts of calamities because they failed to fully grasp it's danger in their hands,) was something that Caster's inhaled through their veins to perform all kinds of magic, and of course may open up portals to Pandora. But there were limits to how much one could breathe at any given time. It was not limitless. And to be in the epicenter of one of these is a sure way to blow out all mana veins. It was almost guaranteed. This could even kill a Caster, but could this Ghost be part of McCurdy's line? That would explain some things. He should make a call.

He reached for his phone, dialing it rapidly.

"Yes, Colton?" she asked as if expecting the call. Efficient as ever.

"What do you know about a Sam and Elena Romanov-McCurdy?"

"Why the sudden interest?"

"McCurdy, right now, I don't need you pestering m—"

"Colton, you're on speaker phone, and I want to know. I have no reason to want to know, I just want to know,"

Swan. You silver-haired bitch!

"I should have you know that I am well aware of your ploy against me, Colton, and I don't appreciate it. What's this, two times now?" She cackled on the other end of her phone. His eyes narrowed, gritting his teeth.

"I wonder what Sander might think when you had his pupil the target of political machinations, poorly planned, I might add, killed. I might even add you seem to be losing your grip."

"Get off the phone," Colton demanded.

"No. I'm not going to do that. Now, either you tell me what I want, or you don't get the information you need. You should keep your toys a little closer to you, because I like to play, and I play for keeps. Isn't that right, Sarah?"

"Yes," she said reluctantly.

He hissed over the phone. "Their names popped up in an investigation and I need to know who they are, that's it."

"Now, was that really that hard, Colton. That's all I wanted. Now you can talk to her without my influence. Ta Ta!"

He heard doors slamming in the background. "Take me off speaker!"

"You got it," she sighed. "Who are they? Yes. My uncle and aunt. They've been dead for well over twenty years."

"Okay. Do you feel safe there?" He asked. He may have a need for her to come back to him. Especially when a relative is involved, and it is most definitely a relative. Cousins, it seems like.

"Not safer than any other part of the world. There don't seem to be Threckets here."

"And what of the task I gave you?"

"I'm not permitted to any access of any additional information until such time as Gwen sees fit. No access to facilities. I am really little more than a glorified secretary. I don't need to tell you how hard this is," she answered shrewdly.

Damn you, Gwen.

"Okay, keep me in the know if anything unusual happens, and without Gwen in the room!"

He disconnected his phone from the call.

A moving machine. That's what Colton found himself in the middle of. Just one Administrator trying to navigate so many pieces and more and more pieces just pop up out of nowhere, unplanned. Other administrators are moving their own pieces and he was finding it damn near impossible to predict where all of them were going. And now, Gwen, is by his account acting of her own volition, planning her own plots for what he could only guess.

She's gonna bite me in the ass, isn't she? And she is going to enjoy every minute of it.

He sighed, staring at the safe, and walked over to it. His hand touched it, mana veins, emerald, lighting up his skin as they crawled onto the safe, and into the crevices. The safe's own mana source lit up, red veins to contrast. He squinted as his mana veins wove around the red veins, the light beaming in his face. The veins canceled one another out finally, and he touched the dial to manually unlock the safe, *16, 42, 8.*

The door opened, and purple smoke blew out of it. He focused the mana from the room into his eyes as he saw the artifact, the one holding everything all together, regardless of how hopelessly shattered the world was. He reached into it, pulling the Box out, and bringing it to his table, setting it down.

It was a purple box, bones of various animals, and people, and of course, Threckets, demons of old, a time much simpler than to-day, engraved into the edges. His hand touched the exterior, bone fragments slicing his hand, his warm blood dripped down the sides. He funneled mana from the metal nails in the walls, and silver veins protruded on his hand, and the bones retreated back into the sur-face of the Box. The Box was filled with runes and symbols of the old Anglo-Saxon tongue, interweaving themselves with another lan-guage, unknown to him, but it didn't look like any known human lan-guage he was aware of. It wasn't runed like the Saxons or the Vikings, nor were they filled with symbols or lines like Kanji, or the eastern languages, nor the scribbles of the Middle Eastern Languages, nor Romanized.

And the surface of the Grail, golden metal, where the Anglo-Sax-on runes started, shimmering in the light. Smoke protruded from the bottom of the Grail. He blew into it, waving the smoke away, and at the bottom of the Grail was a hole in the shape of a human heart, but not a regular heart; one of the Old Blood. And deeper into that crevice was a slot. His hand reached inside, the smoke pushing at him. He caressed the edges of the slot, gauging at its length and width. *A sword goes in here, and a heart. First, before anything else, this all needs to be translated, but to get a linguist with this kind of talent is nothing short of impossible.*

CHAPTER 30

ANOTHER TUESDAY

Status Report:

USA heavy calvary rolls into central California into Los Angeles. Chinese forces lose morale, forcing a retreat to the shoreline. Los Angeles was retaken, forcing the Chinese fleet to resort to Artillery strikes on the mainland.

Black Eagle Company deploys heavy infantry and calvary units on the shoreline of Washington. Flanking with the US Armed forces in Northern Idaho, Washington is retaken. Forces mobilize and march Southward to Oregon.

Spadero followed the crowd again in the snow. His hands jittering in his peacoat, following, eyes and ears focused on Ted talking very intently with Jennifer, who, he assumed was his girlfriend with how close they seemed. He didn't see her the previous time he was there, but there were other things he picked up, her overwhelming positivity, and while she was flamboyant, she was not healthy, though, very good at hiding her medical condition from others.

Well, don't offer to buy him a drink. Just ask him questions. What's one question he would know a great deal about? I could ask him about Ted Anderson, but he is Ted Anderson, or masquerading around as him. But that would only blow his cover if he's careful and alienating him is something I'm not trying to do. We need him as willing as possible, but if I can't even get my foot in the door...

He crossed the threshold again into Teri Nation, walking with the smiling faces and the drink trays carried by the waitstaff, professionally dressed like some high-end place. He smiled back, careful to not lose sight of the reason he was here to begin with, Ghost. He was so close, and yet still so very far away.

He followed up some stairs around the back, just like last time, and Scott, that smile on his face hidden behind that thick black beard of his, welcomed them honestly.

"Welcome back." He spoke. Jennifer and Michael hurried to the bar, to their seat. "What are we having today?"

"Oh, you know I'll have the special, whatever that is," Michael said, pulling out his wallet, and grabbed a card. "I'm buying today," he turned. "Ted, what do you want?"

"I'll take whatever you're having," he replied.

Spadero felt more people coming in, rushing past him. He pushed himself to the side as the roar of laughter pierced his ears.

"Whoa," Michael smiled widely, and more genuine than ever. *He's a good person. I thought you were a myth.* "Another special that is."

"Hey, hey, hey," Jennifer said, slamming her palm down on the table. "What am I? A joke to you? Make that three." She held up three fingers to the bar tender.

Michael laughed at that. "You can close me out too."

Lively bunch.

A strong hand reached his shoulder. "You made it again," Sam said to him, with a bright smile, a genuine one, almost as completely genuine as Michael's. *There's something about this crowd. There can't be any good people here, not in this great number in one location. But then there's Ted and myself, and together, we make up for all the hostility that's required to balance that out.*

"Scott, I'll be boring. Just a Cab."

"Boring indeed," Sam called back. "Merlot for me, please and thank you."

"Together or separate."

"Separate," she said.

He disappeared behind the bar, and he pulled out two bottles of red wine and poured them over two glasses. His attention averted to the crowd, around the bar, many smiling faces, and whimsy laughter.

Spadero picked his up promptly just after paying, looking down into the glass, staring at Ted: who seemed to have a good old time with his *concoction of whatever.*

Another man popped up in the bar. Grabbing Michael's shoulder, talking about a good old time playing video games and a first-person shooter. Wasn't sure who he was, but whoever it was clearly made Ted uncomfortable, shifting uncomfortably in his seat, rolling his shoulders forward.

That man, largely built, a large fatigue and some jeans came laughing away when he drank something even more boring than this glass of Cabernet, a damned Boston Lager, is what it was. A boring, bitter, poor person's beer. At least go for something a little more exotic. The man hurried off to the other end of the bar.

He walked closely, noticing a red-haired woman with freckles picking up a conversation with Michael.

"So, about our Christmas party? You in? You all in?" She asked.

He couldn't remember her name.

"Yes," Michael answered. "Secret Santa or Yankee Swap?"

"Secret Santa!"

"Erin, that's a fine idea. Your place in Sudbury? It's big enough," Jennifer asked.

"Yes, that would be fine," she said, sipping on her cider. Not as boring as a Boston Lager. She turned to Spadero. "Hey, new guy, you can come, too. John was it?"

"Yes," he smiled back. He traded phone numbers with her, and she sent him a spreadsheet. It went to a lot of different people, and he could see names of people being claimed anonymously. "Cap?"

"Fifty bucks," Michael said. "That way, we don't end up with another $2,000 bottle of wine."

Everyone but Spadero laughed. *Clearly, an inside joke.*

"December 18th," Erin said, "The address and the time is in there. I'll see you next week!"

He nodded and turned his attention toward Ted. The man of the hour, the man who would have all the answers, or at least more unanswerable questions to be deciphered by no one.

"So, Ted," he said.

"Here we go again," all but Jennifer and Ted went to the other side of the bar, leaving just the three of them.

"You know China nearly massacred the West Coast," he began. "What says an old veteran about what we can do better?"

"I don't care," he replied, frowning into his glass. "Empires Fall and here we are, they're all gone. It might be time for America to set. Rise and fall they say. Doomed to die they say. What point is there, really? Spadero, you're a congressman who has an unhealthy interest in my opinions."

"And yet, you swore to defend the Constitution—"

"'Against all enemies foreign, and domestic,'" he interrupted, turning his head, and sneering. "That's what it says."

Jennifer gazed up at Spadero, a concerned look on her face, eyes watering as if *he* was violently opening a wound.

"Why do I really care? Generals and politicians, not exclusively America, but *especially* America created the rise of the circumstances which led to these wars on our doorsteps. Russian and Chinese navies are floating by, and because of the bureaucratic nature of our government, we didn't mobilize our navy? Why is that? I wonder.

"Let me ask you something, John. You want my opinion, but I'll ask yours on something. If there was a group of people who gave their all for their country, dying in the line of duty, and their bodies recovered, should those bodies have been given a proper military funeral?"

What is he referring to? Task Force Seven? That's a dangerous question, particularly for you. "Yes, without a doubt."

"And if certain individuals were accused of high treason," he peered into his eyes, a scowl of only the ugliest of Threckets. "Should there be a trial before execution?"

"Undoubtedly," he answered.

"And what if I were to tell you that some individuals accused of high treason were executed without a trial? What should happen to the accused?"

"They're dead in this scenario?" He asked. *Clearly, Task Force Seven.*

"Yes, they all are," he snickered. "They all are dead in this fictitious scenario."

"They deserved a trial. They didn't get one, and now they're dead. I think you and I can agree that was a gross miscarriage of due process. But if they're dead, what does us bickering bout it do? What difference does it make?" he asked.

"You're right," he laughed again. "No number of apologies can bring back the dead. Now, what should happen to the system itself that authorized their execution before a trial?"

"The system should be abolished," he replied.

"There, you and I agree on something," he replied, taking another sip. Spadero noticed Ted's hand shaking with the glass, ice berating the edges. "Now, what if I was to tell you that the accused never committed treason?"

"Then the system itself is flawed and should be dismantled. The system is the real traitor here."

"Exactly!" He pointed an excited finger. "The US Army put a lot of resources on thirty-two unique individuals. Sixteen were killed early during the training process. No one notified their families; they received no burials. I watched them cremated. Sixteen other individuals were wasted, all killed by the tragedy that was the nuclear melt-down at Area 51, which, I might add, was no accident.

"They gave their lives, all of them. Not one funeral. Not one family was notified. Not even the general public would ever know of the lives they had, or the hearts they gave. On that day, we remembered the oath, to protect that damned piece of paper that's supposed to mean something. It doesn't, from enemies foreign and domestic, and on that day did I realize the only enemy we ever had was domestic."

He placed the drink on the bar top. Bringing his arms to his chest, bowing his head down so low, and all he did was cackle.

"Tedward," Jennifer turned to him, interlacing her fingers with his, and her free hand on his shoulder. And hanging from her fingers behind him, was one of her napkins, and he saw that the stain, just over the shoulder, was red.

"Do you know what the funniest part about all that is?"

"I can't imagine anyone finding any of this funny," Spadero frowned. *He just accused the government of treason.*

"Those thirty-two people I mentioned, never swore to uphold that oath." He turned his face back to Spadero, tears streaming down his cheeks, teeth gritting. His other hand started shaking, squeezing Jennifer's hand firmly like a stress ball. "And they followed that oath to the letter."

Ted's eyes glazed over, and his gaze averted to looking right past him. A scowl, no. Not a scowl. There isn't a word for the kind of face he made. If Satan stood before him, he would get out of the way. That is the amount of malintent that filled that scowl.

"The only difference between them," he lifted his other hand and pointed across the bar. "And that mother fucker over there, is he took that oath and wiped his ass with it. They obeyed that oath, and they weren't even allowed to take it. Bottom line, any man or woman who wears those patches, wears those tags or flags, is no friend of mine, nor will they ever be. I'd kill all of you if I wasn't trying to be a good little boy."

Damn. The plot thickens. And answers a question.

There was silence all around. The shouting and laughter stopped as the patrons of the bar turned, gazing at the disgruntled veteran at the bar, the one unique to them all, and the one hiding in plain sight.

Spadero managed to lock eyes with him.

Ghost. You and I are seeing the very same thing. "Sorry I asked, Ted. I won't ask again." He turned to walk down the vestibule, out the bar. "Ted, I don't know what happened, but I will find out. I'll see justice for them. Whoever they are."

"How can you when they don't even have names," he scowled.

"Tedward, let's go," Jennifer pulled on his arm.

Sakura watched as Jennifer and Ted exited the bar, following after John. She chewed some gum, watching them go by. She had her Coke in hand. It was the only thing she could drink here that had some flavor to it. She wasn't of the drinking age after all. She turned, wondering exactly what kind of conversation they would have had that prompted Ted to call Jeffrey a "Mother Fucker" all the way from across the bar.

Of course, she still had her own hesitations with Jeffrey Clemens, mainly because he was a mercenary, and she didn't appreciate that. Wasn't an honorable thing to fight and kill for the sake of money. Clearly, more now than ever before, she knew there was bad blood between Ted and him. She walked over to Sam, talking closely with Michael.

"Sam?"

"Yes?" She sipped her wine, winking at her.

"What kind of history does Ted have with Jeffrey?"

"They served together," Michael answered. "Both in the 75th Ranger Regiment. Both secretive and good at keeping secrets,"

"But is that—"

"I watched a video once. I wasn't huge into shows, I still am not," Michael explained, smiling to her. "But this one I found absolutely intriguing, and it gave some excellent insight. Though, as you can rightly tell, Ted is a unique case and the normal rules, even applicable to Veterans' with mental health needs, don't apply to Ted."

"That's a good way to put it," Sam said, her smile fading.

"So, you know something about him that I don't?" Sakura asked.

"Sakura," Sam said. "You just met him."

"That didn't stop either you or Jennifer," Michael laughed softly.

"No, you're right, but then, I saw a veteran on the corner, homeless. I didn't want Ted to end up like him," she replied. "Anyway, I've said this a number of times already, talk to Jennifer."

"Hey!" The little redhead woman came between Michael and Samantha, her arms around their shoulders. "Sakura, right? You want to come to our Christmas party next week?"

"Sure? Where is it?" She nodded.

The redhead smiled brightly. "Sudbury," she released her shoulder grip and shook Sakura's hand. "Erin, nice to meet you. Anyway, let me get your number."

CHAPTER 31

A WORTHY GIFT

Status Report:

Black Eagle Company's fleets engage with forces in Oregon part of the Pacific. Pilots refuel and re-engage in dogfighting over the Pacific.

In a conjoined effort between Air and national guards coming in from Idaho, fueled with the technology of Black Eagle Company, the heavy calvary units roll south, invading the Chinese company in Oregon. In what amounted to not more than a few days, Oregon was completely overrun by USA armed forces and Black Eagle Company.

USA armed forces from Los Angeles, and Arizona roll forward into the southern parts of California, pushing the Chinese Heavy Calvary units out to sea. The Chinese Navy bombards Southern California with Artillery shells.

Ted walked down the streets of Boston. A nice change of scenery to Waltham, always busy, and especially with the sneaking suspicion that he was being watched. John happened out of nowhere, and he only showed up twice to café, which wasn't terribly unusual, but he asked him questions which he found to be an odd icebreaker of all sorts of things, things he wouldn't have any information on.

The snow was slick, his boots slipping this way and that sometimes. He grabbed hold of street signs to avoid slipping in the street.

They didn't salt the streets yet this Saturday morning, or the sidewalk for that matter. Heaven forbid he slipped and crushed his skull into the mailbox. Not that that would kill him of course or cause any serious harm. He'd hate to have to inconvenience the city staff for replacing such an item.

The white clouds were especially thick this morning as he looked up, gazing it just over Summer Street, the large highway leading to south station, a beautiful building if his opinion mattered. It didn't.

The Christmas party was coming up. He knew he was going to pick Jennifer up, some apple pie, her idea, and drive all the way to Sudbury, but something about this overwhelmed him with an aura of unnatural dread, leading him further and further away from the contentment he had grown accustomed to. He saw a large pillar just outside a building, holding another building hovering over it, the shade provided some dry measure from the snow and ice. He leaned up against it, dropping down low, sitting on the ground.

He reached for his back pocket, and pulled out his wallet, opening it and pulled out a picture. A picture that reminded him of the past, which was both a blessing that he still had it, and a curse. Sometimes he wished he would burn it. Hell knows he tried. But he could never bring himself to part from his mistakes, to part from the friends he used to have. Not the nasty friends, wearing masks masquerading around someone one might want to be with for the rest of one's unnaturally short life, but the friends one knew would stick around through thick and thin. They'd still stick around had they been alive, if they weren't unjustly executed for crimes they didn't commit. Ted still didn't know the reason.

Slithers with her beautiful hair hugged him. He sometimes still felt it, a ghost symptom of something he lost. But this time, this time he didn't feel his heart growing heavy. He looked at all sixteen of them. All scarred faces. All dead. No. That wasn't true. He was still alive.

"So," said a familiar voice. He heard the crunching of snow, and someone sitting down next to him. He turned. Slithers. Her hair tied back, and she was in the BDUs. "Ghost, did you finally find the light that flickers?"

"Yes, Slithers," he smiled, leaning back against the pillar, eyes to the sky, watching the snowflakes fall.

"Good," she said, tearing up, leaning her head against his shoulders. "That's good."

Wind blew, and Slithers blew with it, dusting into ice crystals, fading into oblivion with the rest of the snow. His heart grew heavy, feeling a lump inside his chest that she was there one minute, and gone the next. But part of him was able to leave that where it lay, part of him able to move on, and that's the part that mattered.

That part of him that led him to Boston on this particular day was right there with him, urging him not to forget the past, but accept that it couldn't be changed, and he can only move forward to the end of it all. He remembered when Slithers asked him to find the light that flickers, no matter how dim. "Find it," she said. And he found it.

Jennifer.

He stood, rising against the pillar, moving back to Summer Street, walking up to where it turned to Winter, and the hub of Boston started to liven up a bit. People poured back out of the subway stations as if Ted didn't just finally say goodbye to his best friend. But he was asked to find the light, and so he did. It was Jennifer, and she was what drove him off here to begin with. To buy her a present. Nothing too fancy.

He walked down the streets of shops and stores, and he found a jewelry store. He didn't have much experience here, but he could learn. Even the promise ring he gave to Slithers was little more than a bullet and welded metal. A laughable attempt.

He stepped inside. The store was bright, filled with some men looking for a gift for their significant other, and woman who undoubtedly were shopping for the very same thing. He walked on the tiles, searching the store for anything that he could imagine Jennifer would have any interest in. Specifically, something for wearing.

He sighed, looking at some shiny necklaces and then a peculiar feeling came to him. He jumped as an unknown hand touched his shoulder, and he twisted, pushing himself away from her.

"Just here to help," she smiled brightly. Those over abundant fake smiles from overly happy smiles from retail staff, who, one was almost certain were on speed. Or some other drug to keep them happy to deal with all the nonsense.

"Sorry, nobody does that," he panted, heart racing.

"So, how can I help?" She smiled, keeping her distance. In fact, she didn't step forward or backward.

"I don't rightly know," he answered, looking at the shiny necklace again.

"Would you perhaps be looking for..." she said, her eyes shifting toward the item of interest. "A Christmas gift for someone special?"

"Yes," he turned to her, speaking softly, and again, "Yes."

"Tell me about her," she asked. "And I'll find something to suit her fancy."

"She is a kind spirit. Kinder than any I've come across. A faith bearing woman, modest, though, sometimes just a little over the top," he answered.

"Faith bearing? Of what faith?"

"Christian,"

"Protestant or Catholic?"

"Uh," he didn't know the answer to that. "Park Street Church?"

"Protestant it is." She smiled, turning. "Right this way."

So, he followed her. It was the first time, in a very, very long time he came to something new, and yet, he cared about nothing more. This was important to him, he felt it. If nothing else would come of his relationship with Jennifer that would be fine. But he wanted her to know how he felt about her, the flickering light or candle she was to him, but one whose flame must never die out. A flame worth protecting, up to, and at the cost of his own life if necessary.

"Ah, here we are," she said, pointing him to an aisle filled with crosses. Some were extravagant, others were not. Some were simple, just like Jennifer was, as extravagant as she pretended to act sometimes, it was not the norm for the core of who she was.

There was one such cross that caught his eye. It hung lightly on a silver chained necklace. The chains large enough to hold inscriptions, of which, meant nothing to him, but following the cross itself, golden gleaming light shimmering from the chandeliers hanging from the ceilings.

"That's the one," he said.

The retail worker smiled, pulled it off the rack, and packed it in a little box, placing it into a marginally larger gift box so no one would know where it came from, or what was inside, for all the emotions he held inside were meant for no one. None other than her. Slithers already knew what was inside. She didn't need a box. Not where she was.

Taking it outside, he put the box in his coat pocket, and his hand held it so no one would take it from him. If anything ever happened to this, that would be the true tragedy of the spirit of Christmas.

CHAPTER 32

CHRISTMAS PARTY

Status Report:

Black Eagle Company sinks the Oregon Pacific Chinese fleet. The Chinese pilots, low on fuel, fly toward the fleets, shot down by Black Eagle Company's pilots and MG. Some Chinese debris is cast aboard the fleets. The Company's fleet sails southward into California Pacific.

In a pincer attack, Southern California and Oregon Armed Forces with Black Eagle Company flank the remaining infantry and calvary troops in Northern California. The large company came back from the north and moved southward to the southernmost end of California.

Ted pulled up in front of the store. The snowflakes casually floated down, ever so softly, white flakes glimmering the store-light, and Jennifer smiling ear to ear her lips reached, sprinted out from the store, her hand holding a few paper bags, heavy at the bottom. She opened the car, got in her seat, the bags resting on her lap as she pulled the seatbelt over her.

"Hurry. Christmas awaits." She said, clicking in the seatbelt.

"Did you pay?" He asked, putting the car in gear before speeding off.

"Hey, hey, hey!" She turned to him. "We don't talk about that."

"Jennifer," he said.

"Of course, I paid! I'm not a freeloader!" She frowned.

"Sorry, I asked," he laughed.

"Lamar," Sakura called out, honking her horn in her truck. "Come on. My ice cream is melting."

Her car was parked outside a small apartment complex, windows tinted ever so lightly, some cracked windows at the side. The door opened, and there Lamar was, dawdling as he always did. He held some plastic bags. He stepped into the truck, pulled himself in, clasped his seatbelt on.

"What'd ya get?" She asked, peering into the bag. She rolled her eyes.

Potato chips.

"Just chips," he replied.

"Put in the address, will you? I don't want to get lost getting to Sudbury," she said, driving the car into the street as Lamar typed in the address for his phone's GPS.

"Jeffrey." Michael said as he knocked repeatedly against the door. "Come on, we'll be late."

Jeffrey heard the pound on his door. "Coming."

The Christmas party, and of all things, gifts to be exchanged. *I don't want anything from you tonight, Ghost. Keep your gifts to yourself.*

He grabbed his holster, strapped it to his side, pulling out his pistol, the safety on, before placing it in his pocket. Can't be caught dead in this surprise, now, could he? After all, Russians were coming, and they were coming soon. Though he can't imagine having to be the one to use a weapon during a Christmas party, but just in case.

More knocking.

"Come on, Jeff, we're gonna be late." He heard Michael's voice call out from the other side of the door. Michael appeared to be worried about being on time for once. What changed? "The canned bread isn't going to bake itself."

Canned bread. One of the many keepsakes from Mom. You got the recipe?

He shook his head again. He pulled open a drawer inside his room, and grabbed his Kabar knife, sliding it into his boot. *Just in case.*

He rushed back to the door, opening it. "Mom gave you her recipe?"

"No. I borrowed it without permission nor the intent to return it. Yes, she gave it to me, come on."

Samantha was shifting over to the side of the kitchen, scrubbing the plates with her dishcloth. Erin was behind her, setting the table. The table was long enough to fit all of them there. Plates were set down with the silverware besides them, a regular glass for water or a variety of other non-alcoholic beverages. This, Sam knew was mainly for Sakura. The little kiddie of the group with big dreams and aspirations.

"Sam, check on the turkey, please," she said, opening the white door down the cellar, and walked down the creaking steps.

Sam nodded as she went over to the oven, opened it. The heat blasted her face. She took two red oven mitts, pulled it out and set it on the stove top, stabbing it viscerally with the thermometer. She read both thermometers by the thigh bone and the breast, reading one-eighty and one-seventy degrees respectively.

"Erin. It's done. Michael should be here soon." Sam called back.

Erin walked up with several 2-liters. "You didn't bring your carving knife?"

"No, Michael has it. He'll cut it," she replied.

"Sam," she set the drinks on the counter. "You had one job."

There was a knock on the door before she could muster a response.

"Can you get that please?" Erin hurried over into the back of her pantry, rummaging through some things before coming back out with napkins and paper towels.

Sam nodded, pushing the baking sheet to the back of the stove. She wiped her hands before striding briskly down the hall, lightly lit, and the red carpet with yellow engravings framing it. The corner toward the door was a little disheveled. She bent down low.

Another rhythmic knock on the door. Three times.

"In a minute," she called out, bending down to fix the carpet. She patted herself down, smoothing the wrinkles out of her green apron as she reached for the doorknob, turning it.

The door swung open; a cold wind brushed through her. She pulled back, allowing Tim through. "Out of the way," he cried out, holding a large box. Closing the door, she turned back before he ran past her.

"Tim," the tall man wobbled back and forth, the clumsy events coordinator.

"You need a hand?" She asked.

"Yes, please. I thought you'd never ask." He turned, smiling, placing the box on the ground.

"Huh," she put a hand on her hip. "I was trying to be nice. You didn't need to be a jerk about it."

"Oh, Jennifer's not here, so I figured—"

"You don't know that," she quipped, sneering to the side. "Honestly, I'd expect that kind of behavior from her of all people, not you. Do you treat your clients that way?"

"Of course, not." He took his foggy glasses off, cleaned them with a handkerchief.

"Is that Tim?" Erin called.

"Yes, Erin, it is I," he replied, picking his box back up and leading the way for Sam to follow him back into the kitchen.

"You have a carving knife?" Erin brushed her red hair behind her ear with a smile.

You're not being subtle about this are you?

"Nope. Why in the world would I have one of those," he dropped the box again, opening it with such grandiose in a way she would really only expect from Jennifer.

"You miss Jennifer, don't you?" She asked.

He pulled out a Tupperware filled with chopped potatoes marinating in some ingredients he whipped together. "Yeah, what gave me away?" He turned. "Erin, you have a spare pan? I want to put these in the oven."

"Sure, over there," she jerked her head toward her cabinet, wooden with soft engravings. He hurried over, pulled out the pan, and poured all his potatoes into it. Tim refused to make beans, so no one would ever blame him for spilling the beans ever again. Honestly, she couldn't remember if it was his fault or not, it was too long ago and became a recurring joke between her friends and him. Not that it mattered at all.

Another knock at the door.

I swear. This is going to be like that Jackson film and all the dwarves interrupting a peaceful little halfling.

"I'll get it." Sam rolled her eyes, turned around, and scurried back down the hall.

The clamor of pans and activity came from the kitchen, and Erin laughed giddily at her new crush. Sam skipped over the carpet and opened the door to Michael and Jeffrey with their hair covered in snow. She glanced at Jeff, nothing seemed unusual about him, but she didn't realize he was coming. He was holding a large cardboard box.

She turned to Michael. "You bring the carving knife?"

"Yes." He pulled out a little box.

She turned her gaze back over to Jeff. "What's in the box."

"Mom's famous canned bread." He smiled, hand shivering in the cold. "So, can we come in, or do you expect us to freeze our balls off?"

"Well, language like that will get you nowhere," she scowled, turning to Michael. "Seriously, teach him some manners, will you? He may be a decade and a half older than you but that's no excuse to have the mouth of a sailor, now, is there?" She shook her head. "Michael, get in here and get to carving the turkey, please, and take the bread. I'll have a moment with Jeffrey alone."

"Out in the cold?" Jeffrey protested

"Yes, in the cold." She crossed her arms over her chest.

"As you wish," Michael replied, grabbing the box from Jeffrey, and stepping inside, moving along to the kitchen.

Her legs crossed over the ice threshold as Jeffrey frowned, clearly uneasy by this sudden gesture. She wasn't entirely sure if he knew why she was going through such a great length to talk to him, and him alone. But Jeff was the source, unintentionally or not, for Ted's outright hostile behavior. Sure, Ted was the only one of them who swore openly, and rarely. His curses were well meant, and if he decided to curse you out, you best look in the mirror. And Ted, just the other week called Jeff a 'Mother fucker' out in the open, which was unusual, even for him. Sam closed the door behind her, leaning against it.

"If you're going to—"

"Shut it," she said. She peered behind him, the wind howling, snow dusting off the white glistening surface of the ground. Her blood began to chill, and her arms trembled with the cold. She gazed to the left and to the right, and no other lights from cars were coming their way. She was alone with Jeff, but it would not be long before *he* was to be expected. *Need to keep this brief.* "You should know that Ted will be here."

"I was aware of the possibility, but wh—"

"Now, I don't mean to be rude." She began, "but Jennifer and I went through some very dark places. It was like a hole which I barely understand. Now, I do not, and Jennifer does not, nor does anyone want to see Ted like he was when we found him. I don't know what bad blood you two have with each other, but it is clear to me, he isn't fond of you, and because of that, neither am I. I am certain Jennifer feels the same way. So, stay away from him. Do you understand me?"

"I don't think Michael would appreciate you talking to me this way." He stepped forward, his white misty breath in her face.

"I love Michael. And I love Ted. And I love Jennifer. And Ted was in a dark place so deep, we were nearly swallowed up entirely." She stepped forward, standing tall. "If you do anything tonight that forces me to choose Michael over Ted and Jennifer, I will choose them. And you should know that Ted wouldn't appreciate that."

He stepped back, clearly uncomfortable.

"I know you're not afraid of me. Why would you be? But you're afraid of Ted. Now, let's all be civil tonight. And don't touch or even talk to Ted unless he speaks to you. You understand?"

"Loud and clear," he frowned. "May I come in now?"

"Yes." She opened the door for him to briskly stride along as if nothing happened.

Headlights approached from the road. *That was more time consuming than I meant it to be.* She peered over, her hands covering the lights from her eyes as a truck parked in the driveway. The Georgia plate was well visible. The doors opened and shut swiftly as Lamar and Sakura jumped out of it. Lamar slipped on the ice, dropping some bags.

"Ah!"

"Careful!" Sam yelled, running over, exhaling white breath, but Sakura was around the other end of the car first, picking this considerably larger man up with relative ease, or that's how Sakura made it look anyway.

"Samantha, can you grab that?" Sakura pointed to the bags in the snow.

"You okay?" She asked, picking up the paper bags and wiped off the snow.

"Yeah, I'm fine. Just an old war wound, as it were," he replied. "I'm fine actually," he turned to Sakura. "You can let me go, you know."

"Oh, right," she stepped away from him.

"Well then," Samantha smiled. "Welcome again to Sudbury, the home of Erin, or as Ted likes to call her, the Gutenberg Press!"

"What's the Gutenberg Press?" Sakura asked, following behind her.

"It's a joke. Her last name's Gutenberg." She opened the door for them.

"Okay, but what is it?"

"It's the world's first printing press," she answered. "Before then, they just had monks with carpal tunnel rewriting everything on new paper and scrolls. There's your useless lesson for the day!"

Sam led them into the kitchen. Michael was chatting up a storm with Tim, laughing away, carving the turkey; Erin was greeting Sakura and Lamar, simultaneously putting together a few bowls for the potato chips they brought, and Jeffrey was cutting the cans open with a *military knife?* And slicing the canned bread before placing them on a cookie sheet, putting them in the oven underneath the potatoes.

Four knocks on the wood door reached her ears again.

I knew this was coming. Just like that movie.

She ran back to the door down the corridor. She opened the door, and Jennifer and Ted smiled at her.

"Hurry, take this," Jennifer said, giving her some bags. "It's the pie that I totally paid for."

"I'm not entirely sure if she's joking or not," he chuckled.

Samantha hoisted the bags from her, allowing them both to come in. She pointed and waved her hand to both to give her their ears. They leaned forward. *Honestly, I didn't expect Ted to understand that.* "Hey, I was unaware, so don't get mad at me, but Jeffrey is here."

"What?" Jennifer exclaimed softly, peering into the kitchen cautiously, and her smile turned upside down. Her fists were clenched, and when Samantha thought she saw her, gritted her teeth. This was going to be a gritty Christmas party.

Ted immediately retreated his hands into his coat pocket. She knew that gesture all too well. No one else would know, save maybe Jennifer. His wrist trembled in his pocket. With what, she couldn't rightly guess. Anxiety? Fear? Hatred? Truth was, there was so much she didn't know about Jeffrey and Ted together, that it could be anything that would lead to nothing less than a tragedy.

"He came along with Michael, and I literally just found out, so don't get mad," she continued. "Look, I spoke with Jeffrey privately."

"Why would you do that?" Jennifer frowned.

Just like the time from the phone, Jennifer's voice was soft, but harsh, and the sudden reaction to being scolded was not one she was used to. Often, she was the one yelling at truck drivers, not the other way around. But she didn't feel like she understood how to properly read a room anymore, since she got this wrong.

"I told him not to talk to Ted at all unless Ted spoke to him. Now, I've instructed him to stay as far away as possible. Granted, this is a party so that might not at all be doable, but we can try," she looked Ted in the eyes. "Is this okay?"

Jennifer turned to him. "Tedward, it's up to you."

He bowed his head to the ground, panting heavily. Jennifer reached a hand in his pocket, both hands, and wrapped them around his, pulling it out ever so gently. Raising his hand to her chest, softly breathing to match his rhythm. With the little time they had with him, about a year and a half now, perhaps a little longer since she sprung up the courage to force a meeting with him in Teri Nation. It surprised her that Jennifer knew his bodily rhythms. At least as well as she did anyway.

"Ted," Sam said again. "May I touch your shoulder?"

He turned his eyes toward her, not saying a thing, not nodding nor shaking a head. He just stood still as his hands left his pockets. *There's a step. Come on.*

He slowly turned to the door, and Sam touched his shoulder, squeezing it tightly. He didn't jolt, not this time, as if he was at a calm. An unusual calm given the fact that he was about to eat again with an enemy. Though, she was certain with the level of hatred that existed between the two, perhaps it was better not knowing. His free hand reached for the door.

No. Sam thought.

The door was pushed, the lock settling in place as it clicked shut. Ted's palm kept it shut as he reached for the regular lock, turning it. He exhaled one last time, before touching the door with his forehead. "It'll have to be."

So, we can spend Christmas together after all.

"Okay, then that's that," Sam said.

"Ted, are you sure?" Jennifer asked, as if to grant him permission and the agency to leave, to let it be purely his choice, or if evacuation from the premises was a much better idea. She couldn't force him to stay, she wanted him to. Michael never should have brought Jeff here, and it was Sam's fault for not finding the time to tell him.

"Ted, I'm sorry."

He turned, brightly smiling. This was the fakest smile ever.

"It's quite all right," he said.

No. It isn't. But you're forcing yourself to be here now. You don't have to do this.

He looked into her eyes, stepping forward glancing at her as if to say, 'Yes, I do.'

He forced his way past her and passed his way into the kitchen.

The smell of turkey, gravy and fresh baked bread filled her nose, but she looked down, realizing a fatal error. She didn't like this feeling swelling up inside her chest, making it incredibly difficult to breathe.

"Sam." Jennifer grabbed her shoulder.

She felt a strong grip, stronger than any other time Jennifer's grabbed her before. Turning, twisting her feet abruptly to face her. "Look, Jennifer, sorry, I didn't know he was coming. Honest."

Jennifer exhaled a sigh of disappointment. That's what it was, and a sigh of impending dread, as if something absolutely horrible was going to fall upon them this night. Just the sense of dread, and a tragedy. That is exactly what neither of them wanted. "Just, do whatever you can to keep Jeffrey as far away from him as possible."

"I—"

"Can you do that for me? For Ted, I mean?" She stared in her eyes, glazed over, frowning. Her lips curled downward.

"I will do everything I can," she replied.

"Good, now let's go!" She wiped her eyes and returned a smile to her face.

Ted changed something in you. What is it? She turned, taking Jennifer's hand with the bags, smelling of pies, apple and pecan. Her favorite, personally. This was going to be one Christmas she is certain she won't forget, but was this going to be a Christmas she was going to *want* to forget? Truth was, there was only one way to find out, by moving forward, one step at a time. First the left. And then the right. She entered almost unwillingly into the kitchen.

Dinner was already served, and everyone was seated. Jeffrey and Ted were as far away from one another as humanly possible at this table. The turkey was resting in several different carved slices minus the legs, resting on the pan with the steaming carcass plaguing the stovetop.

Wine was poured. Except for Sakura. They gave her grape juice. She didn't mind, or so it seemed anyway, eagerly taking out her cup, ready to be poured into. She glanced over at Jeffrey, sitting next to Michael, and an open seat next to him. Erin was at one head, and on the other end was Jennifer, next to her, seating Ted, to Tim, and Lamar.

"Sam, get over here." Erin ushered her from behind the kitchen counter leading into the dining room, before standing behind her head seat. Sam scurried, pulling off her apron, neatly folding it on the back of her chair. Erin had a nice smile on her face. The freckles made her endearing, like the beautiful host she was, and the role she was to play tonight. This was the first time she arranged everything, and even though it was a group effort, her arrangement for this was flawless. Tim better be careful, if she cared enough, she might come after his job. She chuckled softly at the thought. She liked money too much to take a gross pay cut just for that.

"Thank you all for coming." Erin spoke almost like a politician.

Who was missing? Where's John? Sam's eyes scanned the table to meet those whom Erin was making eye contact with when she noticed an empty chair. "Merry Christmas everyone, and I want to thank Sam especially for cooking the turkey and keeping it fresh since November."

The table applauded. Sam did the Jennifer-like thing to do, and stood, pushing the chair, and bowed to everyone at the table, before promptly sitting again.

"Now, before we get started, I'll pray for our meal, and I'll—"

"Why don't you tell us how this is all going to work before we eat?" Michael interrupted.

"Michael." Jennifer said shouted from across the table. "You mustn't interrupt our host, it's rude."

"Now, now, Jennifer," Erin waved her hands down to the table as if she was pushing on some invisible box. "He has a point. I will pray, we will eat, and then we'll go into my living room. And then we'll exchange gifts. And eat some of the delicious pie Jennifer and Ted brought."

"Your terms are acceptable," Michael put his hands on the placemat.

"Okay, let's bow our heads."

Samantha bowed her head into her hands, listening intently to the words for which Erin prayed to God. Despite all the anxiety this night had come to bring her, she felt within her a spirit of calm as Erin prayed over the meal, thanking God for the food, the blessings, and even something as simple as travel mercies getting here despite the storm outside, heavily laden with snow, obscuring even the finest of eyes.

"Amen," Erin finished.

Just like all the disorganized mess of a family dinner, plates were passed around the table, being served by one another. Forks reaching over the turkey, bread being passed out, brown bread, with melted butter spread all over it, just like she liked her bread, nice, melted butter.

The table talk started as soon as the plates were re-sorted back to their respective owner, taking a part the turkey, and eating, some talking with their mouths open. Oh dear, Jennifer would never let them hear the end of it. Not that Samantha particularly cared, but she knew Jennifer was very concerned with manners, especially with important group intimate events, however much she broke those same etiquette rules from time and time again. Especially the time she made Tim clean up the water he spat all over her floor.

Amid all the felicity of this fine dinner, she did manage to see Ted, snarling from time to time, at both Sakura and Jeff. It was barely noticeable, but she saw it. She had grown to understand why he hated Jeffrey. She didn't one bit understand why he didn't like Sakura at all. Even that time after apple picking around the campfire, she didn't get it. She came from the university, as almost all her friends did, huddled around Park Street Church.

Sakura's family had military roots dating all the way back to the Japanese Concentration Camps during WWII. Certain characteristics defined people with the elongated argument of nature over nurture, and truth be told, nurturing external stimuli had a way of shaping the natural world. These things considered, she was still a nobody. She had no ties to any of them, but perhaps, since it was known of her family's military background was a special reason for him to dislike her. Yet there was one contradiction in all of this. Ted seemed to hate her less than Jeffrey, but almost an unnoticeable amount, and while he hated Lamar, likely for the same reason, his disdain for Lamar was considerably less than either Sakura or Jeffrey. But she couldn't help but wonder if this hatred toward Sakura was justified, she still didn't know enough, but it seemed unfair, whatever the reason.

It was like Ted was Goldilocks, and Sakura, Jeffrey, and Lamar were the three bears. Whatever was within Ted's relationship to these three were the porridge. Only, the bears were at the kitchen table, already returned, and in place of porridge, too hot, too cold, and just right, was steeping right in front of them. One of them was going to serve him part of their porridge tonight, but what was the temperature? *I don't like this bit at all. God, please let nothing happened between either of them tonight. I beg you!*

With her heart rate settling down a bit, the plates and silverware were clattering about on the empty, scraped clean plates, and there was some food on the table. Likely Erin would save that for tomorrow.

"The living room is right there. Christmas carols are playing," Erin said, standing. "I'll be there in a minute; I just need to pack some of this away first."

"I'll help," Tim offered.

"Tim," Sam said as he stood, adjusting his napkin on the table. "Make sure not to spill the beans this time, okay?"

"What beans?" He asked.

"Those beans," Michael cackled.

"Dear, poor Bean. You deserved so much better than Mr. Timothy," Jennifer exclaimed, an authentic smile returned to her face. *Finally.*

The chairs scraped against Erin's beautiful hardwood floors as the rest of them stood, walking into the living room. She heard the clamoring of plates and silverware enter the sink, and the faucet turned on.

She followed the crowd. *Jingle Bells* was playing in the background, and some presents were lying underneath the tree, carefully wrapped, and topped with nametags. The tree was decorated wildly, and Erin spared no expense, wrapped in lots of decorations—some with Santa and his reindeer, angels, other Chrismon's, some snowmen, and of course, tinsel, red, green, and silver lining throughout the tree, and a lot of bright white lights, carefully interwoven in the tree as to not reveal any wires, lighting the tree up like some mystical spectacle for all to see. At the top of the Tree was a brightly lit star, carefully created and crafted to have that crystalline glow.

In the corner of the room, resting underneath a window, decorated with more Christmas lights was a folding table, and a large green bowl and a ladle inside, and some red cups. Erin went hard on the Christmas colors. She walked over, taking a cup, and spooning some eggnog into her cup, sipping the thick beverage which always had its unique flavor. Such a shame it was only around for Christmas, and no other holiday.

If I want eggnog on my birthday, I'm making eggnog!

Jennifer and Ted were walking her way as Michael and Jeffrey were still chatting, this time, building a lovely group of four with Sakura and Lamar. From the many conversations she's had with Michael pertaining to Jeffrey, he wasn't a trusting man, not that this should affect her relationship with him. She reminded herself: Jeffrey isn't who's important, Ted is.

"Ted," she whispered, sipping her nog, and she felt the thick residue on her upper lip, licking it clean. Can't let something like this go to waste. "You okay?"

"Yes," he replied, not letting his façade down. She knew this time, it wasn't for her, or for Jennifer, but for himself, nuzzling back into solitude with people he trusted. She was thankful that she was one of those people. Hard thing, really, trust. It's so easy a thing to come by, to accept, receive and give away, but once someone has sullied that, it becomes a cynical nature, a beast if you will, asking questions as to the motivations for which people place their kindness. But the trust Ted put in them was not of that nature. He questioned it at first over a year and a half ago, but that was then, and this was now.

"Michael," Erin's voice carried over as she wiped her hands dry with a cloth. "You want to be Santa today?"

"Sure thing," he said, walking over to that beautiful pine tree. It looked amazing, and it still smelled of needles. Some people hated the smell, but she loved it. It was a nice reminder of her home up in Vermont filled with so many trees, so many natural scents.

Michael's hand reached underneath the tree for the first gift. "Tim." He said, tossing it as Tim crossed the threshold, and in his Tim-like fashion, fumbled it in his hands as he unwrapped it.

More presents followed. Samantha received a coupon for some coffee from a small coffee shop with some local aromas. Honestly, this was her favorite breakfast place in the morning, slow paced place with fast service, and the food was not processed nor heavily filled with preservatives. As God intended.

"Thank you so much, whoever you are," she smiled.

"Oh, Jennifer, this one's for you."

Michael tossed a small box over to her direction. Jennifer caught it with a grace. She shook the container, and there was a little rattling noise inside. Ted shuddered at that. Clearly it came from him.

Oh God! Jennifer, you didn't break it did you! No! Sam thought.

A knock on the door.

What now? If I hear a knock on that door one more time...

"Must be John. I'll get it," Erin replied, leaving the room.

Jennifer ripped up the paper, and a beautifully crafted box with light silver embroidery around the edges of the box, tied together in a red ribbon. She pulled the ribbon undone, and it floated carefully, gently onto the ground. The gift's container was pulled open.

Jennifer's eyes gleamed with awe. Eyes shimmering with the golden item, carefully interweaving the chains in her fingers, and pulled up a golden cross. She wasted no time putting it on her neck. "Thank you," she said, turning to Ted. "Tedward, this must be you. How can it not. I love it."

"Ted, don't answer that until the end. This isn't how Secret Santa works." Michael pointed at him.

"He's arrived." Erin came in, leading John with a smile on his face.

Samantha peered over to him, who seemed to be eyeing something specific on Jeffrey's side. Samantha peered at the side, and Jeffrey appeared to be reaching for something behind him, as if reaching for something in his back pocket. *Must have forgotten to put a present in the tree.*

Out of the corner of her eye, she saw Ted turning his attention from Jennifer, who in turn followed his gaze, staring right at Sakura. His eyes narrowed, lips frowned, and his fists clenched at his side. "Ted," Sam asked. "What is it?"

"Shit," he replied.

Sam felt something. It was ever so light, almost barely noticeable. It was almost like a small tremor. Her eyes shifted toward the eggnog. Ripples stretching to the edge of the bowl in which it lay. *Oh no!* A whistle, distant, and approaching closer. Closer. Louder. Dropping her cup to cover her ears. The wood in the building cracked, underneath. Fire roared out the kitchen. Her heart pounding. Fast. Flight. Out the window. Glass shattered around her as she tumbled out, rolling into the snow. Splinters shot out from behind her, scratching her face, warm blood dripping down, painting it. She turned.

Erin's house was covered in flames with the roof collapsing. Black smoke sheltered them from the sky, and in the distance, more flames. More whistling. More missiles. The wood on the ground creaked, and she was remiss, to forget her friends inside the house. Ted. By himself, holding up a beam inside a large gash in the wall. Sakura coughed, and Lamar stumbled behind her. Jeff and Michael walked side by side, shielding Erin and Tim. Jennifer, of course, selfless as always, thinking nothing of herself, came out with all their jackets. The beam crumbled, and Ted swiftly jumped behind her, shielding dear Jennifer from the debris.

Calm headed, a frown, eyes angled downward, focused, silent. He snapped his fingers past her. "West! Erin, lead the way!"

"Where to?" She turned her head.

"Anywhere we can get to the sewers."

What?

"I know just the place, but it's far. You think we can make it? It's a five-mile hike."

"We have no choice."

CHAPTER 33

DISASTER

Status Report:

Black Eagle Company's fleet moves south. Pilots refueled and resupplied with bombs and flew ahead. The fleet's large artillery range shot ahead, shooting at the Chinese Naval fleet. The pilots soared through, bombing the waters and the carriers. Distracted, the final Chinese ship was unable to respond before the last ship sank.

The remaining company from the North came in, securing the border, and capturing the last Chinese infantrymen for interrogation.

Samantha panted. Her heart felt like it was going to burst out of her chest. Her palms were sweaty, crusted with coagulated blood pasted on her hands, eyes widened, staring down at the ground, the rubble, rocks overlapped with metal fragments of cars, other debris, glass, shattered as it sprawled over the ground, which was little more than tar of a road, unrecognizable had she even known it. Buildings were nothing but shadows of their former glory, broken into, creaking metal before finally crashing down, sending the dirt and ash her way, fogging the vision of what else lay before her.

Her hands trembled at her side, her ripped pants, and her own blood coursed down in steady streams, just getting out of this nightmare, and walking into another one. Oh, this was a new kind of thrill. She sucked the air through her teeth.

It should be cold in December, and she'd dare say, since she lost track of time, she could very well be in January. *Did that much time really pass?* Yes. It did. There was no denying it. How could she keep track of the time? Surviving day after day, one new Hell after the next, just waiting for God to release her from this. But she was alive. That was an important thing, or so she thought, until Jeffrey and Ted scowled at one another.

The pistol's holster was in view this time, outside Jeffrey's pants, for it appeared, at least to her, he didn't need nor want to conceal it. That was the least of his concerns since he now held a rifle over his shoulder, strapped to his back. Jeffrey's back was against a large slab of concrete. Ted, scowling, but Ted looked unlike himself, grimacing, and in his eyes was rage that he managed to keep hidden, or at least, level. But he made no attempt to hide his ire, face cringing with lines all over, and never mind the blood coalescing on his face.

Ted was coated in it. His hair dripped and crusted, and his face looked painted. His clothes were torn in several different places; the sleeves, the pants, and even the winter boots, shredded. He was armed, but with a rifle of some kind she didn't recognize, a pistol at his opposite side, and a hunting knife by the looks of it, all of which she knew he didn't own. He didn't have it. Clearly picked up from one of the many he killed. Completely discombobulated in her own grief, she didn't recognize it until now. He was wearing a Russian Combat uniform, and everything that came with it.

She now knew, all those words ago when he said to her, "Saul killed his thousands, and David his tens of thousands; I'd be fortunate if my numbers were nearly that low," that this was no exaggeration.

"Sam," Michael put his hand on her shoulder, looking forward, with a blank expression on his face. "Let's turn around, you don't need to see this."

"And what is *this*, Michael?" She turned to him. "I can't. I need to—"

"Is this what you wanted?" Ted shouted at Jeff. "You dumb mother fucker!"

Canine ran in between them. "You two, we don't have time for your pissing contest,"

"No." He pointed at Canine. "No. *You* don't have time. I have all the time in the world. Now get out of my way. Because of him, I now have a bounty on my head the size of the US Treasury. In the middle of this battlefield, I have all the time in the world. It's you who's running out of time, now piss off."

Canine stepped away from the little dispute, retreating to her small unit of eight men. Samantha knew Ted to be vulgar at times of distress and pain, but every expletive was intentional, meaning very well to lay a curse upon Jeffrey.

"Maybe if you didn't—" Jeffrey began, his hand resting at his side, the side with the pistol.

"Didn't what? Didn't what?" Ted interrupted. "If I didn't do anything? Yeah, like that would make a difference." His hands clenched tightly into fists.

Ted. Don't do this. Please.

Samantha turned to Jennifer, who looked on with an irritable expression on her face, also scowling. Of all people, her face was the least scarred, no dirt on it, no blood dripping down it, and even her clothes remained unharmed. These past few weeks were Hell. Must have especially taken a toll on Jennifer, who she left alone to die. But John stayed with her, protecting her. Maybe. Maybe they should have listened to Ted to begin with. *I don't know anymore.*

"I didn't have a choice for what I did. Naka—" Jeff tried to defend himself once more, but Ted wouldn't have it.

"I don't care about her, she's dead. I ensured that." Ted started to choke up. "So, tell me, did you like it? Did you like any of it?"

"No." Jeff's hands reached down, hand around the pistol, swinging it upward.

But Ted was faster. He unfastened his hunting knife, twirling it within his fingers, air whistling. Hurling it through the air, it was like a bullet with dead accuracy, striking Jeff in the arm, and the pistol dropped to the ground. His other arm reached for the knife. Ted bolted, blue veins climbing up his legs, immediately pinning the knife further into his shoulder, twisting it.

"An eye for an eye," Ted said. "When I saw you, in the bathroom, I told you if you did anything that would force me to start over, I'd rip your fucking arms off. Now that you've done just that, I've since changed my mind. I have an objective, and I'm not telling you what it is, but I need you for it. So, when all this is over, I'm just going to break every single bone in your body. All two-hundred and six bones. And I'm going to rip your eyelids off, and then, I'm going to march everyone with the last names Clemens off a fucking cliff, and I'm going to make you watch. Just so you know what you put me through and see what you're missing. Welcome to the thrill of not being able to do a damn thing about it!"

Samantha's jaw opened and her felt skipped a beat. Her heart sank inside her chest, and her hands trembled uncontrollably, her fingers tapping at her side. Slowly, she closed her jaw, and her eyes narrowed down her nose, refocusing her gaze to Jeff. Her heart felt something. At first surprise, and slowly changed to an indescribable hatred.

Jeff wasn't called back to base because they were moving their pieces. Black Eagle stationed him right there, under their noses. She once believed that there was no such thing as bad people. Naïve of her to think so. There were just people who did good things, and people who did bad things, but now, while there may not be such a thing as a good person, she could say now definitively, Jeff was an evil man.

Jeffrey turned his gaze toward Michael. "Do something, Mike. Don't let him do this to me."

CHARACTERS:

Adam Sander: Chief Administrator for the Caster's Administrator.

Alexander: Native to London, a silent type, and a representative of the Caster's Administration.

Alexandra: Malcolm's wife.

Andrea: First Lady and wife to President Snells.

Arjun: Head Caster Administrator of India.

Blanka: An Administrator from the Czech Republic. Enjoys her fine wine and excursions and wants nothing more than to get back home.

Bridgette: A London native, an administrator serving directly underneath Adam.

Butcher: Ted's friend from Task Force Seven.

Claire: Lead Caster Administrator of France.

Colton: Lead Caster administrator from the American Branch.

Culain: From Ireland, this administrator comes directly from Camelot. He's known for his outbursts.

Daiki: Head Caster Administrator of Japan.

Elias: Head Caster Administrator of Germany.

Emily Gutenberg: Erin's mother(currently undergoing cancer treatment).

Emily Miller: A delta force operator.

Erin Gutenberg: A stockbroker in Boston. She is part of how Jennifer puts it, "The dysfunctional family".

Gernardt: General of the Armies

Gwen Swan: Head Caster Administrator of Alaska. She also serves as Governor of that State.

Hector: Head Administrator of everything South of Rio Grande.

Ilya: A Russian representative for the Caster's Administration. She's made her home in Camelot.

Jack: A torture victim.

Jeff Clemens: An officer of Black Eagle Company. Michael Clemens' brother.

Jennifer Miller: A biological researcher in Boston. A close friend to Ted Anderson, and alone knows his secrets

John Spadero: Caster administrator who also serves as Congressman in the state of Massachusetts.

Johnson: Secretary of Defense

Lamar Cooper: A former Marine.

Malcolm: Chief Operational Officer of Black Eagle Company.

Michael Clemens: Business developer consultant. Loves to experiment with his cocktails.

Mikhail: Lead Caster Administrator of Eastern Europe. He has a very playful demeanor.

Obi: Head Caster Administrator of Nigerian.

Oliver: Head Caster Administrator of Australia.

President Snells: President of the United States. To the world, he is considered the single man who brokered World Peace.

Rebecca: Archivist of the libraries inside Camelot.

Roach: Another agent from Task Force Seven

Sakura: An orphan and a college student, looking to serve as an officer of the United States of America.

Samantha Harris: A logistical broker in Boston. Friends with a small group of people, and thoroughly enjoys her Tuesdays,

Sarah McCurdy: Disavowed Caster of the Administration.

Slithers: Ted's deceased beloved from Task Force Seven.

Smith: Admiral of the Navies

Ted Anderson: The man with a past best left buried.

Ticker: Another agent from Task Force Seven.

Tim: An events coordinator. A real silent type.

Wang: Head Caster Administrator of China.

Armanis Ar-feinial, in the gritty pits of despair, he comes from: Bridgeton, Maine, a terribly dreadful place. Currently residing in the Greater Boston Area with his family, he studied Criminal Justice, English, and currently dabbles in a little bit of Finance. His unfaltering passion for writing came from his first exposure from the Lord of the Rings, which he drew inspiration from in his first stories, but alas, as all good things come downward into the grimdark pits, adopting tones from Joe Abercrombie. He loves reading, playing games of all kinds, and he is what you call a practicing writaholic. He is personally known for his witty sarcastic unasked-for remarks.

AUTHOR OF:

The Falling

Secrets of Terra Silenti

The Covenant

The Desecration of the World

The Holy Grail War

The Hedgehog

The Nihilistic Neverending Nightmare

Follow me on Twitter: https://twitter.com/Sarcastic_elf

www.ingramcontent.com/pod-product-compliance
Lightning Source LLC
Chambersburg PA
CBHW021142310726
48971CB00002B/441